WE'RE

WITH

THE BAND

Also by Johanna Flynn

Hidden Pictures
2020 NANCY PEARL AWARD
LITERARY MAINSTREAM FICTION
WITH BOOKCLUB GUIDE

Contributing author, NIWA 2020 Anthology, ESCAPE,
edited by Lee French

WE'RE

WITH

THE BAND

A NOVEL

*With gratitude for the
staff's wonderful care of
Frank + Peggy Brink!*

JOHANNA FLYNN

Palatine Press

Cover design by Amy St. Onge

Cover art by Amy St. Onge, Angel P., Gideon St. Onge & Nika Akin

Johanna Flynn

Visit my website at www.JohannaFlynn.com

Printed in the United States of America

First Printing: September 2021

Palatine Press

ISBN- 978-1-949844-07-8

ISBN eBook- 978-1-949844-08-5

In remembrance of Jim, the drummer who made my heart beat.

BAND OF PIRATES ITINERARY

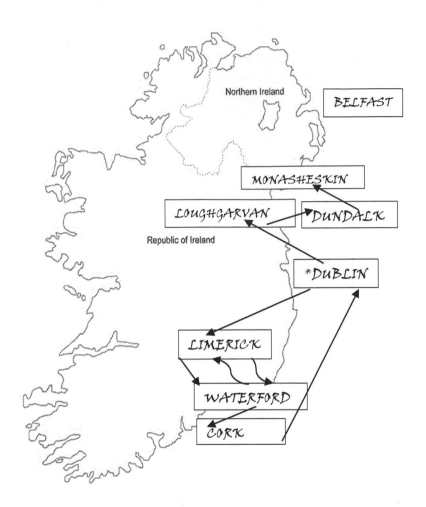

Note to Reader:

If you are not familiar with some of the Irish idioms, terms, and historical information, you can find a glossary at the end of this story.

Chapter One

"Aw shit, Lark, don't tell me you're going to stop." Bev glanced up from her cell phone.

"Well, duh. Wouldn't you want someone to help us if our car broke down?" I slowed my vintage Honda.

"Don't do it. He could be a tweaker or an axe murderer." Bev's thumbs moved spastically on the cell's screen, no doubt looking up serial killers or police homicide reports for the area.

"Right. Oregon's woods are full of them just waiting to jump out and take us hostage."

Cradled in a clump of grass was an ancient, tobacco-colored Westphalia tilted at an angle by the side of the road, emergency flashers blinking, hood propped. In the early September morning, the curtain of fir trees fringed by dense underbrush looked more menacing than the dilapidated vehicle.

My bestie tugged at the bodice laces of her wench costume. "We look like escapees from a Halloween party."

"You look better than I ever did in that." I thought of the times I'd dressed in that costume and anger toward my ex-boyfriend percolated, threatening to snuff out the good mood I was working hard to maintain. "I feel ridiculous, Lark." Bev reached toward the back seat, nabbed her jacket, and inched her arms through the sleeves, zipping up the front.

"You said you'd wear a costume. Dressing up is part of making me feel better."

"Wearing a slutty costume, I can live with. Getting bludgeoned, not so much."

"I'm trying not to think about that asshole. He'll probably be there. Helping this guy is a distraction." Before she could protest more, I eased my Accord onto the shoulder.

A lanky form leaned against the broken-down van, his spine curved like a question mark as his thumb gestured in the direction we were headed and, judging from his attire, the same renaissance faire. A person would have to be a real nut case to wander around in tattered pants and a blousy shirt, although I'd been around a few of them at work in Portland.

"If we look like refugees from Halloween, that guy would've been at the same party, so chill." I switched off the sedan's ignition.

Bev's voice warned, "Here." She shoved a can of pepper spray into my palm as I edged out of the driver's seat.

I clutched the pepper spray as a shiver pinged between my shoulder blades. Would a serial killer dress like a pirate? I approached the guy.

The dude straightened and broke a grin. "You got a cell I can use? Mine died." He was cute. Real cute.

My hand holding the spray snaked behind my back. "Hey, come here often?"

"Only in dire straits."

"You into renn faire too?" The sunbeam he stood in made him look heaven-sent.

"Yeah, I'm with Band of Pirates. Our set starts at two. I gotta call my mates and let them know what happened."

"Am I going to get roaming charges?" I grinned, slipped the pepper spray in my pocket, and pulled out my phone. "What's the number? I'll dial it for you." More than real cute, he was gorgeous…. And early 30s. I listened to the ring, a raucous mixture of grunge, punk, and Celtic

2

followed by, "Leave a message."

Way to go. Now you'll have his number in your contact list.

"Hey, great tunes," I said into the phone. "I'm Lark. Your bandmate is stranded by the side of the road about an hour away. If you want to see him by 2:00 p.m., do exactly as he says." I presented the phone to the guy.

He had this short beard, tinged in ginger, which made me want to taste a bit, so I didn't hear the message he left.

"I hope that's okay that I volunteered you." A hint of dimples creased his cheeks.

"Um, Sure." I'd been thinking that maybe the day wouldn't be such a disaster after all.

"Thanks. Did you say your name is Lark? I'm Jeremy Potts." He handed the phone back with his left hand, extending his right. We did this do-si-do thing. The strong fingers and dry calluses of his grip felt inviting. "I'm trying to place your accent," he said.

"I have an accent? I guess I do. I thought I'd lost it." *Along with a lot of other things*, I thought.

"No, I think you found it. Where are you from?"

"Ireland, but I'm an American citizen too. Why do you ask?"

His smile widened, a gleam of white teeth appearing between his mustache and beard. "No reason." Jeremy spun to walk toward my car, where Bev had planted herself well onto the shoulder a few feet from the trunk of the Honda.

She had a can of pepper spray by her side. In her other hand she hid some bulky metal thing in the skirt to her wench costume. Was she trying to look menacing with a tire jack?

"Awesome that you're willing to give me and my gear a ride to the renn faire." Jeremy flashed a smile that made my knees melt.

Bev studied him. "Not so fast. You failed to consult me about this, Lark. What do you say?" She scrutinized me in case I'd been coerced and we were about to be kidnapped.

"No worries, Bev. He's legit." I nodded, reassuring her.

3

She dropped the tire jack. The pepper spray remained in the folds of her skirt. She once told me that in an attack, catching someone off guard was critical. In that case, the jack would have been the bigger surprise.

"I gotta be at the venue's tavern for our set at two. The van's been acting up." Jeremy nodded toward the dilapidated vehicle. "There's some gear."

I didn't think by "some" he meant a drum set, electric guitar, a mandolin, a keyboard, a washboard, a big cow bell, a little cow bell, a tambourine, a harmonica, and its metal holder.

"I gather you're the roadie?" Bev's face radiated, *Is this fer real?*

"And drummer/percussionist. We're lean and mean." Jeremy had this cute little way of cocking his head.

"We'll make it work, right, Bev?" I lifted the guitar out of the van's back. "Jeremy, this is your lucky day. Bev and I have taken countless road trips together. We are experts on packing. We'll load the drum set in the trunk. The remaining gear will fit on the back seat along with Bev. Cuz of your long legs, you get to ride shotgun, along with the tambourine and cowbells."

We set to work moving the gear in the hot, autumn sunshine. A couple of trips later Bev squished into place. Sweat soaked my scalp under my pirate kerchief. If I took it off, my hair would resemble an Irish Setter with a bad perm. My mood swung from excitement at meeting someone new to anger at my ex-boyfriend, Lance, to embarrassment at my hot and sticky appearance.

"I don't know if your car can handle all this weight. Couldn't we leave some of this stuff behind?" Bev's voice a muffled whine. "If someone crashes into us, I'm toast back here, not to mention Jeremy may as well say goodbye to his head."

I raised my eyes to the rearview mirror to see her face. She pinched her mouth, examining her makeup in her compact, and shoved a strand of dark brown hair back into her pirate kerchief.

Good time to play a guilt card. "These guys have a set to do. They need all this stuff. I'll drive very carefully, and I promise no cutting people off. Being able to help someone else is the best cheer-up present you could give me." I glanced at Jeremy and added. "I just ended a relationship. My bestie, Bev, surprised me with this trip to the renn faire. I'm sorry we have to leave your luggage behind. But no worries. I can bring you back later."

As I pulled away from the shoulder, I glanced over to see our hitch-hiker with the harmonica and holder around his neck. From a distance people would have thought we were giving Bob Dylan—a young, hot Bob Dylan—a ride. The flutter in my stomach reminded me he was just my type.

Blue skies and no sign of rain warmed the day. We traveled for close to an hour, traffic jamming as we neared the renaissance faire. Ahead, planted in a large, sunbaked field were twin squared-off towers flanking the entrance. A large banner swagged overhead, "Welcome to Covington's 2013 Renaissance Faire." The tops of white canvas tents sprouted behind the county fairground's fenced-off area. A thrill scurried up my spine at the sight and the memories of great times, then landed in my jaw that tightened in disgust at what a scumbag Lance had been.

Jeremy said, "Take the next left for the service road."

"Seeing you've never been to one of these, Bev, acts or vendors don't go through the faux castle entrance that customers use. We go through the service entrance, which is majorly cool." I gestured to the twin ruts that comprised the road. "Kind of like the stage door at a theater."

"How do you know about all that?" Jeremy asked.

"I used to have a booth, Hillare, Purveyor of Fine Stuffes. I traveled the Cal circuit for a while."

I drove toward the campsite, tents squatting haphazardly in the field, Jeremy giving directions as he looked for the band's station wagon.

"And you couldn't have put your gear in that?" Bev pointed to a much-loved vehicle blanketed in shade.

"That's where all our camping gear goes." Jeremy stretched his long legs out the car door and stood, the smell of dry grass filling the Honda.

"You've been killer giving up your seat, Bev. And cheering up Lark."

I instantly thought, *Uh, oh. Was he hitting on her? Didn't he understand that a big part of the cheering up meant me hooking up again?*

The other band members rose from the covered eating area and crowded around the car. Jeremy jumped to make introductions. "Matt Brower, keyboard, accordion, and sound engineer. Hugh Arsenal, guitar and mandolin."

Handshakes all around gave that "you belong" feeling like being at a high school reunion.

A dude, about Bev and my age, wearing a black hat with a huge ostrich feather, appeared in the door of an RV parked at the edge of the camp, nudging a set of maple trees on the verge of turning gold.

"That's Rhett Sheehan, lead vocal, harmonica and penny whistle." Jeremy lifted his chin toward the bandmate.

Rhett ambled to my side and took my hand. "Darlin', ah can't thank you enough for your kind assistance." He bent to kiss it, his lips a soft caress over my knuckles. His voice poured pure southern comfort. "If you and this ravishing woman next to you hadn't come to our aid, we would have been in a sorry state."

This guy had presence, legs so long he couldn't sit unless on a bar stool, probably not a foreign place for him to perch. Tanned skin announced he'd spent more than a little time in the Texas sun. Long hair threaded with silver, tied in the requisite ponytail and sunglasses said he knew about stardom. His smile made him chief rooster.

He grasped Bev's hand palm side up and planted a kiss on her wrist. Confusion crossed her face. She frowned as if not sure what to make of the band's leader.

"Great message recording," I said.

"You should hear the ring tone." A woman emerged out of the tent, blond and made up as a gypsy, definitely into her late thirties. She had this accessory aura, more window dressing than a legitimate part of the band. Kind of like Vanna White pointing to letters, only she pointed to

6

Jeremy. "By the way, I'm Candi." She accessorized the drummer.

Bev arched her eyebrows, drawing her mouth down as if to say, *You just made a major fool of yourself, Lark.*

I shrugged. Who knew what would unfold that afternoon?

"Follow the service road to the back of the tavern where we're playing." Jeremy indicated a gate at the top of a slight rise. "Meet us in the parking area."

I looked toward the pub's entrance. From a distance, the sun glinted on the dull metal of a chain mail shirt and helmet that resembled a Campbell's soup can with eye holes.

Lance.

I tugged the handle to the car door and climbed inside. Bev, already in the passenger seat, tapped away on her cell phone. I put the car into gear and would have bet dollars to doughnuts I'd run into that jerk of an ex-boyfriend before the day ended, preferably with me behind the wheel.

Chapter Two

Nothing is sweeter than rolling down the car window to tell the gate attendant, "We're with the band." After the gate opened, we nonchalantly drove behind the tavern to the parking spot. A backstage area, separated by a white canvas wall and curtain, created access to the stage.

The bandmates waiting on the gear from the broken-down van, immediately unloaded the equipment while the bar manager paced. Normally, all this would have occurred by now. But the Westphalia, less than reliable, had forced Jeremy to stay behind for repairs in Salem the night before.

I got busy helping piece together the equipment on the small wooden stage. When Jeremy passed, I pushed my chest a bit forward and down, my pirate vest showing off my cleavage, my eyes shifting to see whether he showed any interest.

Part of the tavern included a stage and entertainment area. Like any renaissance faire attraction, the tavern was rustic, roofless, and skirted with bench seating. Surrounded by a thick wall of hay bales, bouncers stationed themselves at the entrances, some more intent than others in keeping the under-aged out. People jammed the bar, ordering beer or mead. Men I recognized from my own renn faire days leaned on the wooden counter and leered at the serving wenches' requisite cleavage.

The audience packed the benches. Like transports in a Disney time travel movie, a mixture of common folk in the ubiquitous jeans and T-shirts crammed next to a jumble of medieval classes and trades.

Rhett hustled us backstage with the rest of the band, me electric with excitement. I whispered to Bev, "Is this cool or what?"

Her olive complexion had a greenish tinge to it. "Holy shit! We have to go out there? In front of all those people?"

Matt handed her the last of a joint. "Here, this'll help."

She took a long toke, held her breath, a coughing fit turning her green face red. She nodded. "Thanks," she choked out.

The Band of Pirates' entrance couldn't have been finer if they had been at the Rose Garden arena in Portland. Rhett Sheehan, first on, picked up the penny whistle, notes trilling out a jig. He paused, introduced each band member, as they strolled on, picked up their instrument, and joined the intro to their first song. Candi entered last, grabbed her tambourine, and wiggled her hips. And then—this is the best part—the band stopped playing.

Rhett said in his sultry southern accent, "Give it up for our two honorary bandmates, Lark and Bev, who came to our rescue this afternoon."

Out we came. He gallantly escorted us to front row seats, kissed our hands, and bowed, sweeping his huge hat back onto his head. Behind him, Matt, Hugh, and Jeremy, in character, cupped their hands in front of their chests and leered, while Candi scowled and slapped her tambourine. With that, Rhett turned, playing his whistle, and the band continued their first number. I was in heaven. Bev was high. No worries.

The set was a mix, comprised mostly of sea shanties, pirate raids, whoring, and a couple of sweet ballads. I inhaled the smell of beer infused with hay and dust, savoring the crowds, the movement on stage. Watching Jeremy wield his drumsticks, my heart recalled the good memories of traveling in California from renn faire to renn faire. Bev nodded her head rhythmically, her eyes half-closed.

The band ended their set. The next act, a duo carting a dulcimer and lute took the stage. Situations such as this create decision points along the way. We arrived at one of them. Bev and I could leave, go check out the rest of the faire, or stay. A no-brainer.

We cozied up to the band, who huddled in the backstage parking lot among a semi-circle of vehicles, most of which had a lot of miles on their odometers.

Matt reached in his pocket to extract a little wooden pipe carved like a dragon. "We like to be authentic in every detail," he said, stuffing a small bud in the bowl.

At first glance Bev looks like a real prude. But that corporate exterior hides a soul straining to be free. She took the pipe and didn't pull out a wipe to clean off the end before inhaling. Plus, she was already pretty buzzed.

Having set my sights on Jeremy, I didn't want to seem too eager. At my age that comes across as desperate. I sized-up Matt's squared-off jaw, blazing blue eyes, and thick, shoulder-length hair. He reminded me of those men with six packs on the covers of romance novels. Not really my type. I was more into the troubled troubadour. Or God forbid, the gallant knight. But he would do so Jeremy would think I was interested in one of the other band members.

"You're my new best friend." I cozied up to Matt while he reloaded the pipe. "Too bad we couldn't have a bong here."

"Mine's back in the station wagon," he said. "No place here that's safe from getting ripped off. Gypsies lurk around the tavern, right Candi?" Matt grinned.

At the mention of her name, the woman broke off her conversation with Hugh and narrowed her eyes.

Matt's comment intrigued me. I wondered about the backstory. Some whoring that went wrong?

"That why Hugh's guitar and mandolin are hanging from his neck? I can't believe how many times I caught folks pilfering my inventory." I handed the pipe back to Matt.

10

"Inventory? Wait. You sold guitars and mandolins?" Matt was a step too slow to reach the finish line. Gorgeous, but lacking in the brains department.

"When I had my booth, I sold basic attire for those who decided they wanted to get into the spirit of things. I also had a killer collection of pewter dragons, necklaces, and medieval crowns. Stuff like that. What you'd see in a movie: Harry Potter Meets the Tudors."

"Yeah, you can't be too careful. We're headed back to camp in a few. You're welcome to hang out. So you know, if you have allergies, the dust'll wreak havoc. My sinuses are really clogged."

Another decision point arrived. This would have been the time for Bev and me to say our goodbyes, getting lots of "thanks again's", followed by hugs, and we'd be on our way. Tomorrow she'd go back to her corporate IT job, and I'd go back to working at Voodoo Doughnuts in Portland.

I side-eyed Jeremy, bent over the playlist. Having lived the life, I knew relationships could be fleeting, as in one night or a weekend. He may not be that into Candi.

Bev chit-chatted with Hugh.

"Come on, we've been invited to a band party. You're gonna love this." I grabbed Bev's hand, and we followed Hugh.

These guys had been at this for a while, evidenced by the well-organized campsite. The informality said the members had done more than share cups of sugar.

As the afternoon wore on, the party gained momentum. At the far side, Bev and Hugh waved their hands in animated discussion. I sipped a beer and thought about Candi wiggling around onstage banging her tambourine.

"How long have you guys been doing this?" I handed a bottle opener back to Matt.

He flashed a brief smile, underscoring those intoxicating, blue eyes. "Three or four years, but all of us have been into music way back. I compose most of our songs, although we all collaborate. *Brawls in the*

11

Caribbean is our latest CD." He reached into a cardboard box. "Here. Least we could do."

"How come I never heard of you?" I pretended to be won over. "Did you do any of the Cal circuit?"

"We were there." Now, he sounded skeptical. "You must've heard us. We aren't exactly quiet."

"Oh, so that was you guys. Sorry I missed you. You know how busy booths can get," giving me the perfect opportunity for a tour of my renn faire experience, including a quick stop along the way to say I'd broken up a long-term relationship and Bev surprised me with a trip to renn faire to cheer me up.

"You know what would really cheer me up, Matt? If we could be backup singers for one number."

And that's how we ended up on stage with the band.

As the next set began, Rhett strutted to his mic, announced that Band of Pirates' saviors would join them onstage for a number, and escorted us to a mic, placing us on each side of Candi. A cappella, he began "Honky Tonk Women."

We sang the ooh-ooh-ooh parts. Candi clanked the cowbell, trying to hog the mic until I inserted my face next to hers as Bev leaned away, wide-eyed.

We earned a standing ovation! Rhett extended a hand to each of us and escorted us to our seats. Under his breath he said, "Ladies, I'd be most honored if you'd indulge us by appearing at our 9 o'clock set."

"Only if I can have a cowbell," Bev answered.

She lets down her panty hose only on occasion. That evening she'd partied enough that onstage she actually elbowed Candi out of the way. Her ooh-ooh-oohs weren't all that bad either.

Bev and I proved ourselves capable backup singers, so we stayed when the number ended. Because the cowbell became more and more fun, we improvised as the natural next step. How successful we were is hard to say—we were pretty wasted by that point with the booze and recreational stuff we'd smoked.

During the ballads we women didn't sing, a great opportunity to survey the audience. And find Lance leaning against a support pole. Being pissed off at him when he was out of sight was a lot easier than when he was standing right in front of me. I'd forgotten about his delicious, silver hair, wrapped in a strand of leather.

When our eyes met, I almost dropped my cowbell. From my position on the stage, his face drooped like someone had just told him he had a terminal disease. What did that look mean? Maybe remorse at how royally he'd fucked up. I'd find out soon enough.

Besides, my desirability quotient would increase if Jeremy saw me talking to Lance.

All that back-upping made my makeup run. Consequently, when the set ended, the rest of the band went to the edge of the stage to mingle and sell CDs, while I headed to the car to freshen up. Lance would probably saunter up to the stage—he had sauntering down to an art form—and I wanted to be in control.

By the time I rejoined the band, Lance had vanished. On the prowl no doubt. We both knew we'd see each other before the night was over. Living and traveling with him for a year in this kind of community, knowing his habits was second nature to me. Yep, we would see each other.

Bev posed at the edge of the stage, swishing her skirt and flirting. "Do you think they're taking me seriously?" she asked. "I mean I wouldn't want to lead anyone on." Her eyes shone above her sly smile.

"Bev, take a look around. Do you think any of this is real in the end? We're adults playing dress-up. We're pretending."

"Yeah. But I don't want to pretend too much. Have only this much fun." She raised a thumb and forefinger a quarter-inch apart. "I love Elliot, and I'm not going to do anything to ruin that." Several furrows rippled her forehead.

"Easy. You manage the make-believe. Remember when we were little and someone said, 'Let's pretend such and such' and everyone agreed?

Well, you have to be the one to say 'Let's pretend that I'm a pirate cook, and I'm trying to seduce you. But things will never get that far.'"

The furrows disappeared, and she giggled. We sat on the edge of the stage, dangling our legs. A warm, late summer evening awaited.

"I'm sorry I never dropped by to see your booth," Bev said.

"Not your fault. Once Lance asked me to go with him, we were mostly in California anyway."

"I've missed you. Life was pretty boring when you left, girlfriend."

"Mine had more drama than I like. I missed you making me do a reality check. Did I tell you he told me he thought we were great jousting partners?"

Bev raised a perfectly sculpted eyebrow. "Were you?"

"Right. Reality check. My first clue should've been his character's name. Pretty obvious with a name like Lance Allot that he'd be jousting more damsels than me."

"You didn't deserve what he did, Lark."

"You're right. I'm so over him. Pissed more than anything and looking for closure."

"Now what?" Bev dug in her skirt pocket extracting her phone. "I got some great pics today. You'll have to see them when we get back."

"We're on our way to the after party," I said, "so now we hunt down our car in the parking lot."

Chapter Three

As we drove to the party campsite, I steered around faire-goers staggering along the poorly lit road. My headlights reflected the dull flash of chain mail, and from the saunter, I knew it was Lance. I contemplated gunning the engine and bowling him over. But if I did, I wouldn't get the satisfaction of watching him squirm, of him seeing that I had moved on, that I had triumphed. I maneuvered the sedan toward the Band of Pirates' camp and grinned. I couldn't wait. He'd know exactly where to find me.

The band's campsite was pastoral, nestled among a smattering of pine trees towering over a huge white canopy sheltering a picnic table and folding chairs. With the same kind of exuberance as earlier, Jeremy and Hugh moved beer from the station wagon's back to a large cooler. Matt snatched a bag of potato chips off the picnic table, ripped off the top, and sampled a few. He stuck out his tongue in disgust. "Candi, have you checked the freshness date on these? They taste stale."

Glancing at Matt, who continued to extract large unbroken chips, she said, "Then don't eat them." She returned to supervising Rhett as he lit briquettes on a lopsided grill. I had to admit, she had them well trained.

Candi and I had circled each other all afternoon. I now grabbed a beer and went on the offensive.

"Hey, Vanna, what got you interested in the band?"

"Candi."

"Sorry. You remind me of that woman on *Wheel of Fortune*. Anyway, how'd you hook up with Band of Pirates?" What I really meant was how'd she hook up with Jeremy.

"Well," she drew the word out. "There was this party. I hit on Rhett, Hugh hit on me, while Jeremy was with the backup singer at the time. Hugh thought I said I was Irish. Hugh told Rhett—Rhett has this thing about Ireland. So he was all over it and me. I'd been part of this gypsy band, quit, and wanted to get back into performing."

In more ways than one, I thought.

"The next morning, Rhett hired me, and I had a new gig. A couple of weeks later he realized his mistake, that I'm not Irish. By that point, the other backup singer quit. Jeremy and I have been together ever since. Good thing my man thinks women his age are boring and way too into themselves." She lifted her beer, finishing her story with a long swig.

"Wow. That must've been awkward. Hooking up with Jeremy, you know?"

"Not really. Rhett is into the balling thing. He's got this tally going. Wants to beat the record of the entertainer banging the most women. No hard feelings on my part. I was majorly plastered and frankly don't remember. Jeremy and I joke about it. What about you? Most of renn faire knows you dumped some guy. Wicked."

"Which one?" I fluffed my hair. Candi laughed. "I did have a thing with Lance Allot."

She snorted. "Who hasn't?"

"We were together for several months."

Out came the razor blade. "Wow, you must've been pretty special or pretty stupid," Candi said. Ouch.

"Neither. Ask him sometime, but when I'm not around." I gave her a snake-eyed smirk and glided away. While Lance was master of sauntering, I was mistress of gliding. Now would be a good time to chat up Rhett, who was mesmerizing some strumpet.

I'd been aware all afternoon that he ogled me whenever I spoke. As they say, forewarned is forearmed. Only in this case, my arm wasn't what went fore.

"'Scuse me, Rhett dear." My Irish brogue deepened. "Could ye be tel-lin' me where I might be findin' the jacks?"

His head couldn't have snapped my way faster, while his long fingers remained on the thigh of his intended seduction for the evening. His eyes traveled from my face and stopped a little below my shoulders at my boobs. Bingo. My in.

"Well, darlin', you may use the facility in our RV." An early, bus-size RV, the vehicle could have been communal. "I'm fixin' to go there my-self." He fished for a key and rose to escort me.

"Ah, don't be bothering yourself now. I can see meself to the jacks. I promise not to be driving off. But could I trouble you to save a seat for me return?" He nodded. "And to guard me precious stout?" Another nod, a leer forming.

The RV's toilet had little more ambience than the Honey Buckets. At least the bathroom contained toilet paper and a small sink. I don't care how good those sanitizing gels are, I don't feel like I've really cleaned my hands until they've been under hot water with soap. That aside, here was an opportunity to scope out the quarters, check my makeup, and plan the next step.

Dishes crammed the kitchen sink. Not a priority and neither was the couch. However, a queen bed poised, inviting. The main attraction. Did Rhett keep his tally in the bedside table? Okay, I had to check. A stash of condoms, lubricating gel, and tucked way back, a bottle of Viagra. I thought of that TV ad warning the user to go to the ER for an erection lasting more than four hours. From what Candi said, he'd probably see the nonstop boner as a stroke of luck.

Then my fingers felt a book nestled against the far side of the nightstand's drawer. What was he into? Something kinky maybe? Out

17

came *Bogs of Ireland*. Huh? Maybe he got off on mud. He had dog-eared pages. Pictures of bog bodies. Bog bodies? A photograph showed a close-up of a leathery, mummified head with an explanation of the artifact: "Archaeologists believe the remains of Celtic chiefs were from ritual sacrifices to appease their gods".

In ink Rhett had noted numbers separated by slash marks that could have been a date. The caption stated the corpse, called Monaghan Man, was on display in the National Museum in Dublin, Ireland. Hmmm. Maybe he was planning a trip. Or maybe Rhett hid a fetish for leather. I tucked the book back.

As I clambered out of the RV, I pondered what constituted a conquest. Did Lance tally his conquests as well? Was I a vertical tick mark or a diagonal one? Maybe I rated several. But that would mean Lance double-counted. Well, duh I'm worth double-counting.

Not a surprise that Rhett had saved a seat, the strumpet not even a tally mark. He presented me a delightfully cold beer. The man must have a private stash. On came my Irish charm, and not too much later, we were deep in banter. Anyone finding me hot would up my appeal to Jeremy. From the corner of my eye, a blur of grey fox ponytail stirred under the trees. Lance.

"'Scuse me darlin'," I said to dreamy eyed Rhett, his having ascertained my citizenship in the Emerald Isle. "You may be knowing Sir Lance Allot, renowned for his technique at the joust."

Chapter Four

My ex-parrying partner stood at the intersection where the light faded into the night, his face indistinct. Of course, the recreational substances I had consumed may have contributed to his fuzzy appearance. I moved away from Rhett, stepping into the shadows next to my former lover, intending to douse a few anger embers. This confrontation would be private. The expression that he knew what an ass he'd been rapidly crossed his face. Guilt. But I sought remorse.

"Lark," he said. Gone was the bravado.

"Why Lance, you're looking good."

"Yeah, keeps me fit." He gestured the length of his chain mail. "You with him?" He nodded toward Rhett. I gave a slight rise of my shoulders. "When I saw you onstage, I wondered. Hadn't seen you around for a while. I wondered, that's all."

I contemplated how to get this conversation to my advantage. I laughed, a musical kind. Rhett would think Lance had said something amusing. I wiggled my torso, flinging my arm toward the camp.

"Why do you care?" I kept my smile wide and face pleasant, while inside my temper roiled.

"Look, I screwed up. And you matter."

"Is this an apology? Cuz sorry is the operative word here, along with kissing my boot." I extended my toe, my anger flaring.

"Best I can do."

"Well, you do have a sorry ass, in more ways than one."

"You're right. I may have been a fuck-up, but Rhett's in a whole other league."

"Thanks for the news flash."

"He's obsessed with Ireland. I assume he knows you're an Irish citizen. Lark, do you know what you're getting into? Word is he's into some deep shit."

"Not as deep as you are with me."

"No, like international black market deals shit."

"What, you getting bored? I remember when you didn't have time for that kind of rumor crap, cuz you were too busy making your own."

"You trust the wrong people for the wrong reasons, and you trust yourself even less."

"No shit. I trusted you."

"Listen to me, Lark. This is for real."

"What's he doing? Pirating his own CDs?"

Lance shook his head, backing off. "Even though we moved on doesn't mean I don't still love you. Don't get involved. And the rest of the band? Not sure."

At that moment, a nubile, young thing emerged from the dark and attached herself to Lance's side. He must have won the tournament. Not a surprise that he put his arm around this chick. And I mean chick. Had he bothered to check ID? I'd lay money that she wasn't any older than sixteen.

Introductions all around, the kid practically chinning herself on Lance's arm. She had the slightest smell of horse, so she must have been in one of the riding acts. Not a face from a year ago, another indication of her minority status.

"I see you've updated your gear." My glance slithered briefly toward the teen.

20

"Same to you." Never very good at the comeback, he provided another good reason to have dumped him. He couldn't parry worth shit.

"So," I turned my attention to the adolescent. "What high school do you go to?"

She scowled. "As a matter of fact, I've got my AA degree in fashion design."

"No kidding? Did you make your costume?"

Ms. Underage preened. "Yes, I did. I even entered the design in a contest."

"Impressive. How did you do?"

"Crappy. The judges were old." Her eyebrows wormed toward her nose, trying to process where this conversation was going.

"Well, I would have sworn your costume came right off the rack."

"Why, thanks. I think I've got talent too."

Young and dense, I thought. Meanwhile Lance had tightened his grip around her, almost knocking her off her feet. Rhett looked on, oblivious.

"Lance, so good to see you attracting such a young crowd, the next generation of renn fairers."

"Lark, hold on there."

"To what?" As I said, he can't parry worth a shit. He glowered backing a step. "But let's not ruin the evening. I'm sure you must get her home. Her parents must wonder where she is."

"Oh, I have my own apartment," Ms. Underage butted in.

"Then sweetie, you're in for quite an experience." I didn't have anything more to say to Lance. Not really. I turned my back and danced toward the lead singer. "Rhett, I have another stop to make by your man, Jeremy. But I'll be back as soon as soon."

Now to make my move on the drummer. I ambled to the other side of the canopy toward my conquest.

From the time I left Rhett's side to when I stood in front of Jeremy and Candi, something weird happened. I'd taken care of what I'd come to do. Lance faded into the night, no doubt seducing his jailbait. Rhett still sat

21

holding my beer, supposedly thinking of his tally sheet. I'd had fun messing with him, as if I would ever be one of his hash strokes. Jeremy, my mission, swigged his beer at the far side of the canopy. At the edge of the crowd, Bev and one of the horseback riders flirted. She dipped her chin, shimmied her shoulders, then threw back her head and laughed.

What had I said to her earlier that day about this being adult pretend? Yet I had planned to barge forward, seduce Jeremy, and jump his bones. In the morning we'd all go back to the reality of a new day. Bev would have endured a miserable night, probably sleeping in the car, angry and hurt that her best friend used her. Was I willing to throw away a real friendship for a one night hookup?

I'd given up more than my booth when I got out of the renn faire business. I'd given up something else, and what exactly that was puzzled me.

In that short walk to stand before Jeremy and Candi, my plan totally changed. I felt out of it. Cold sober and out of it. The truth was I didn't belong. Bev and I were only honorary members of the band. Kind of like Cinderella, we got to go to the ball and then everything would revert to ordinary once more. Except there was no prince for me, and Bev already had hers with Elliot. In that moment, as if my pirate vest turned into my Voodoo Doughnuts apron, I knew.

"Jeremy," I said. "I promised to give you a ride back to the Westphalia, which by the way, I think is aptly named. Bev and I gotta get back to Portland tonight. Looks like you've got wheels to go get the rest of your stuff."

The decision point arrived. We said good-bye. Thanks all around. Lots of hugs, exchanges of cell numbers. Promises to stay in touch on Facebook. And then we were in the car.

Bev, manic over the day, giggled and clapped her hands. "You were right about managing the make-believe. Did you see the guy dressed as a lord? Talk about hilarious. Like we were in one of those PBS historical dramas, he'd say something in this outrageous accent. And I mean outrageous, not in a good way. Then I'd reply back in just as bad an accent.

22

Can't believe all the beer or how much I smoked. Anyway, he said he thought we sounded brilliant when we sang with the band. That was the word he used. Did you get a look at the horseback rider? God knows where he came from. His voice was like Pee Wee Herman's."

For some minutes her laughter filled the car. "Wish Elliot could've come. But if he had… Thanks so much for insisting we dress up. Didn't you love being an honorary backup singer? And the cowbell. I loved ringing the cowbell. But hey, did you have a good time? I meant this adventure to be about you."

"I had a great time. Got to help someone out. Got to closure with Lance. Got to party and not be so screwed up I won't remember it." In the rearview mirror, the lights from the camp receded then vanished as I rounded a curve, maneuvering the car through the service road ruts.

"Was that guy in the chain mail you were talking to Lance? The Lance?"

"Yep." I navigated the dirt road, lit only by my headlights, and turned onto the main two-lane highway back toward Portland, the oncoming traffic approaching and passing.

"How'd that go? Wish I could have met him. Why didn't you introduce me?" She rolled down the window, trailing her fingers in the night air.

"You were on the other side of the party, and he's not worth introducing to my bestie. I am so over him. He found himself a cheerleader. Weird thing. He said Rhett's into black market shit. What that would be, I haven't a clue. Like I care."

Chapter Five

What's going on, Lark? Here we go all the way to that renn faire and have this awesome adventure. You told me I'd cheered you up." Bev sat opposite at a small table, while I took my lunch break.

"I am cheered up. Notice I stopped eating the Voodoo Doll doughnut? That was a sacrifice. I really liked poking the pretzel into different places and seeing the red filling ooze out. I'm eating Old Dirty Bastard dough-nuts now."

"Yeah, that's what concerns me. I hoped you'd choose one a little less retaliatory or at least not make such a personal statement. Like you know, Mango Tango? Benign," Bev said.

"Right. Like there's anyone I want to dance, tango, or tangle with. You're over-analyzing. I really do like this one. Besides I don't get much say in what they're named." Chocolate cookie crumbles filled my mouth. The switch was a good choice.

"All the same, you seem majorly depressed these days."

"Yeah, I am depressed, but I'm not going to take those drugs. They're not nearly as much fun as the other crazy shit I've done. Just give me some time, Bev."

In the past six months, we'd had this conversation more than once about that feeling I got at the faire. Problem was I didn't know what *that* was. When I had my renn faire booth and traveled with Lance, the fantasy gave me permission to do stuff I wouldn't have dreamed in my alternate life.

Being an honorary member of the band that day sent a clear message. Like a gift when leaving a job. That part of my life had slammed shut.

Bev's face, confused, battled to get her head around what I meant. That night had been an awesome surprise she could tell her friends about, which is what she did. She'd end the story exclaiming, "Being on a stage, let alone singing, had always scared me to death. But in this case, the music was so loud, and we were crazy into it." That did cheer me up, hearing her side.

They say fifty is the new forty. Was I about to experience the new forty or a repeat of the first time around? My fiftieth birthday loomed. No matter what the popular mags say, it's still half a century.

"Look Bev, you're on the way up. VP of IT is in your future. Me? I'm going nowhere. A failed marriage and a failed relationship. No children. A useless college degree in social work. In doughnut circles, working at Voodoo Doughnuts is prestigious, but I don't have dread locks, and the only tattoo I have is of a pelican." I raised my arm and examined the brightly inked creature.

"Then go back into social work. That's got a future. You could come back to Informed Intelligence, Inc." She dabbed the corner of her mouth on a napkin. "Say the word and you're in."

"Because I don't want to work at being social anymore." Bev has been my best friend since I married Joe and moved to this country. But she is so logical, she can be a pain in the ass.

She rolled her eyes to the side as if to say, *I'm not going to dignify that by groaning.*

"I'd always thought I could get serious about my life tomorrow. Well, tomorrow showed up. The depression isn't so much self-pity as self-assessment. Turning fifty is staring me in the face. My options have drastically narrowed."

"Then give the job a chance."

"Right. Aspiring to store manager would make me everyone else's den mother. Besides I'd be a disaster at managing others. I can't even manage myself."

"I think you're running. But are you trying to escape from something or to something?"

"I don't know. Working the counter lets me dodge having to deal with this dead-end feeling. The constant line of customers keeps me focused on the moment. I tell myself I'll take care of it later. After work. After this or that. Except now these thoughts intrude all the time. Pretty bizarre.

"I'm really pissed. Pissed that I'd tried the wife-and-steady-job routine, working at I.I., Inc. Joe looked down the same gun barrel. He ran toward a van and wanted to put in baby seats. I was only willing to settle for a dog. Truth is that while married to Joe, I never felt I belonged. In hindsight, tramping off with Lance was no more than an attempt to cut the ties to the past. In the end, I don't think I belonged in the renn faire life either."

"I'm out of my league here. You should think about seeing a counselor." Bev twirled her hair, a clear signal that my introspection made her uncomfortable.

"And how will I pay for it?" I studied the chocolate stain on my apron, like a Rorschach image that might give me a clue into my subconscious motivations. "I've never been one to run away from things. I want to run toward something else, not away from a dead-end life."

"Why not run to a new career? Get a loan. Go back to school," Bev suggested. "You could become a dental hygienist in a couple of years. All those people buying doughnuts are going to require dental care soon. Not to mention all us Boomers whose mouths hide aging gums and periodontal disease."

For the next week, I went online researching dental hygiene programs. Each time made me sigh, grab a doughnut, then grab floss and my toothbrush. I decided to Skype Mom.

~~~

"Lark, dear. Seeing you does me heart good." Mom's face froze momentarily as the internet caught up with her words. Skype could be patchy, and it always happened when I needed her advice.

"Hi Mom." The sigh travelled all the way to my toes. "How are you doing?"

"Brilliantly. I've launched a new business," she said. "I'm …" Her face moved in slow-mo. "Dublin… corners."

I waited to see if the reception would improve. After several seconds, Mom came back into focus, her mouth matching her words.

"I'd like your opinion. What do you think of me going back to school to become a dental hygienist?"

"Darling girl, whatever for?"

"To have a future."

"A noble profession to be sure, but Lark…" Mom's frown deepened.

"You don't think I'd be any good as a hygienist?"

"I suppose you could make a lash out of it. But sure as I'm your mam, do you not think this is a bit rash? You've not the patience for work that's so detailed and delicate."

"You're right. Also a real conversation is impossible when someone has a mouth full of metal picks and fluoride rinse, but the pay's good. I can set my own hours once I get into a dental practice. Hey, I'll have gorgeous teeth!"

"But how often will you smile when your soul is being stifled?"

"Mom, I'm lost. I'm dead-ended, there's nowhere I can go."

"Come home. You can come home."

"I don't know that I'd fit back in Ireland either."

"How do you know unless you try?"

"Speaking of, what's new?"

Her words staggered, started, and stopped, the service interrupted. She froze, her mouth a corrugated O. I waited for the connection to right itself.

I tried typing, "What did you say?" No response. The PC sighed. I lost her. I echoed the sentiment, feeling as disjointed as Mom looked.

27

Chapter Six

Portland rolled through March, the flowering plum trees bloomed, gardens sprouted small ovals of yellow crocuses, marking the end of a dreary winter. Unwilling to experience a dreary spring and summer stuck in this mental state, I went online, applied for a student loan to pay for a dental hygienist program, and tried to feel excited about school. I would start at summer quarter.

May heralded tourist season. That day a particularly long line looped along the bakery's side. We were hopping. I finished a sale and turned my smile to the next customer, finding myself face-to-face with Rhett. The rest of the Band of Pirates assembled behind him, minus Candi. They were hardly recognizable with their beards and mustaches shaved, one of them being, a totally unrecognizable new guy. What happened to Hugh?

"Wow, Rhett. When did you guys get in town?" The real question? How the hell did they find me?

"We're fixin' to play a gig. Thought I'd look you up, darlin'." Rhett still couldn't get his sight above my neck or below my armpits. In response I crossed my arms in front, placing a doughnut box as a barrier in case he made a sudden grab.

"What can I get for you?" The line swerved out the door and now wrapped the building. Rain sprinkled the parked cars. A bevy of umbrellas shot into the air outside the window.

"A backup singer, darlin'." His commanding voice audible even in the hubbub reminded me of Foghorn Leghorn trying to woo a hen.

"Well darlin', I said flattening my American accent, "I'm not into bands. So I couldn't recommend anyone. I can recommend a box of our Voodoo Dozen, best value and I'll pick good ones."

"Well now, that's mighty generous. We'll take a dozen. Make that two," he said in his best Texas accent. "Far as the singing, that's not what I heard at renn faire. Fact you're damn good. Come right in when you're supposed to and on key."

I made sure to put in a couple of Old Dirty Bastard doughnuts. This guy could use one. "Okay. Two baker's dozen."

Foghorn Leghorn drew out a wallet, extracted a piece of plastic, and attempted to take possession of the boxes.

"It's cash only." I yanked the boxes back, pointing to the notice taped to the counter.

Rhett leafed through his billfold fingering out a hundred-dollar bill cozied next to several companions. In this day and age of plastic? While I counted his change, he put a business card on the counter. "We're playing here tonight." On the back, he scribbled the address, a familiar one. "Come as our guest. Bring that friend of yours. Bev, I believe her name is. Tell 'em you're with the band and they'll let you right through."

"But I'm not with the band." The card on slick, thick stock read Rhett Sheehan, manager, Noted Enterprises, LLC. Really?

"That's the whole point, darlin'. We have a proposal for you. Very least, you'll have a good evening including drinks on us."

During all this I'd totally forgotten the rest of the band, grouped behind Rhett, like a collection of youngsters, excepting the new guy, who ambled around the Pepto Bismol-painted bakery checking out décor you'd associate with Day of the Dead. Matt grinned, and Jeremy did the cute head cocking thing, his hazel eyes searching mine. Really?

I nodded. "I can help the next customer."

29

~~~

The offer intrigued Bev, this being so far out of her every day.

"Look," she said, "you've had the absolute worst winter and spring. You had a great time last fall, right?" I nodded. "Then let's go. We'll have a couple of free drinks. Hear a few great tunes. Aren't you at all curious whether Candi's still in the picture?"

"Not really, although in weird Portland, the band's music probably crosses over pretty well given all the brawling and whoring songs."

That night we arrived at the bar to find a reserved sign on the table, located dead center in the front row. Could they be any more subtle? Was I going to need some Irish courage? As a precaution, I ordered a Jameson's neat and buffalo wings in honor of Rhett.

Flashing a grin of expectation reminiscent of last summer, Bev sipped a Cosmo, dunking celery in the blue cheese dip. My mouth imploded in confusion and anger with the first bite of spicy chicken wing. Going back to school was hard enough—I wasn't that hot about it the first time, and I had felt called to that profession. I'd made my decision, pulled up my big girl panties, and prepared to get real. Now this. I felt like a storm cloud on a sunny day as the band jammed through the first set.

No costumes. Just jeans, tees, and jazz. A whole different act from what they'd been at the renn faire. Rather than the keyboard tethered to a strap around his neck, Matt's fingers flew around a portable. Jeremy still on drums had a looser technique, wielding brushes. Candi's bleached corn yellow hair sported a rainbow of streaks, her voice reminiscent of Fleetwood Mac's Stevie Nicks. No penny whistle for Rhett, who played lead guitar and danced up to Matt as they jammed through a slick improv.

Who was that new guy? The spotlights cast a blue sheen on his black hair. From under his arm he produced a trumpet, the brass gleaming under the lights. In a caress he put the mouthpiece to his lips and puckered, his fingers commanding the valves. Tossing his head back, he let go a riff I didn't know that kind of instrument could produce. My mouth watered, and I tipped my Jameson's, signaled the waitperson, and ordered another.

30

The table jiggled, Bev drumming on the surface in time to the music.

They were smokin'. Was this the same band? When the set ended, the new guy appeared at our table, horn tucked under his arm.

"I'm supposed to escort you backstage," his face indifferent whether we tagged along or not.

"Where's Hugh?" I asked.

"Who knows? I'm told he quit suddenly. I'm Steve Watanabe by the way." He led us to the dressing room, a reluctant errand boy.

"We're musically diverse, great range, wouldn't you say?" Matt slouched on an old sofa as we entered the dressing area.

"Yeah, Steve says Hugh up and left. Pity. We were such buds," I said.

"Our gain darlin'. Steve studied at Julliard. On the road to become a concert pianist, the band bug bit him." Foghorn Leghorn commanded the tiny area from a chair on which he sat backward, legs like grasshopper appendages. "We're fixin' to revamp our pirates act. It's gotta have three backup singers," he said. "Lark, we'll be in sorry straits without you. And of course, Bev, darlin'."

Bev's eyes shone. For someone so savvy in the corporate world, she was naïve. And gullible. She practically melted over the "darlin's" Rhett drawled.

"Besides darlin', the gig is only for three weeks." Rhett's lips curled slightly upward, signaling he knew something enticing.

"That's all you'd have to commit to," Matt cut in.

"I really can't handle it without you two." Candi sounded about as genuine as a hypnotized robot.

"Wanna know where the gig is?" Jeremy reminded me of a kid on his birthday. Bev lapped up his excitement. Were they doing an intervention to deprogram my bestie and me from the evils of the establishment? And Bev, of all people, allowed them to dupe her. She had urged me to go back to school. Try something steady in my life. Good money, better job. Better diet! A stable future loomed a couple of weeks away.

"This is only a proposal meeting. I'm not committing to anything," I said. "When and where is the gig? Las Vegas?"

"End of July and better than Vegas." Rhett was just short of drooling on his pants. "Ireland."

"Ireland?"

"No shit. Ireland." Rhett tipped his head back and opened his arms as if witnessing heaven's gate. What had he been snorting?

"Ireland? I've always wanted to visit the land of a thousand shades of green." Bev's voice floated. "Wait a second. Who's paying for it?" That's the Bev I know and love. At last, some reason and an ally.

"Yeah, who's paying for it?" I asked.

"Comes out of the business, darlin'."

"You see, Rhett has a connection in Texas, who books bands to do relief gigs," Matt said. "We would relieve bands who are working for venues in Ireland while they take a vacation. Apparently, it's a common contractual thing. They are required to get back to the States once in a while. We're also booked at some pubs."

"Great, you're a band aide." I could feel my lip curl.

"Precisely," Steve said. "Except we're the band. You're the aide."

Should I feel insulted at the slam or amused that he could parry? They could see I refused to buy what they had to sell.

"You two as backup singers are critical to our act." Rhett stretched a leg in my direction. "Not to undervalue your knowledge of Ireland, Lark."

Matt said, "How's this? You two join us onstage tonight. See how you like it." His eyebrows shot upwards, blue eyes flashing.

Wow, used car salesman suggesting we take a spin around the block. "You're playing jazz," I said.

"We changed the playlist for this set," Rhett said, "to songs y'all are comfortable with."

"You really planned this, didn't you?" I asked.

"More or less," Matt said. "Does it matter if we did?" The car salesman saying that a crooked frame was hardly noticeable.

"Why, I'd have thought y'all would be flattered," Rhett said. "All the trouble we went to woo you and the lovely Bev."

Surprised that Steve didn't say more throughout the sales pitch, he now spoke up, "You know, they may not want to do this. They have their own lives."

I looked over his way. He leaned against the wall, a bit slump-shouldered, paring his nails as if only eavesdropping on the group discussion. For a brief moment, I had this urge to go over and glide my fingers across his forehead to feel his hair slide away from his face. In my head I screamed, *What are you doing thinking about Steve's hair?*

"What are you afraid of, Lark?" Jeremy asked. He'd pushed a button, the button that hates to leave the gauntlet of a challenge lying in the dirt.

"Why not, Lark? What's the harm?" The Bev I knew and loved evaporated. "Will I get to play the cowbell?"

"Of course, darlin'," Rhett said.

I wanted to bang my forehead on the wall.

"Oh all right," I conceded. "But if you give me any of this honorary crap, I'll walk right off the stage and out that door."

Rhett did the gallant thing again, escorting us to spots on the tavern's stage next to Candi where we ooh-oohed through the next set.

Back in the dressing room I said, "Rhett, you think you can convince me with a cowbell?"

"But wasn't I right 'bout your timing, Lark?" Rhett's eyes were hypnotic, like I was a mouse, and he was a boa constrictor slithering toward lunch. "You're quick on the pick-up. And Bev." He turned to her. "A little practice is all. You'll be right fine." Bev, under Rhett's spell, had no doubt relegated loyal, reliable Elliot to a distant part of her brain.

"Lark, look we need you." As if he had some kind of influence, Jeremy joined the conversation when I might be wavering. Had I been that obvious at the faire?

"Think of the lights, the applause, the rush when we all come together smokin'. You'll be part of it," Matt said. "Of course, those sets when we really suck—"

33

"Which are rare, cuz we spend a lot of time getting to the soul of our identity as a group, the yin-yang of a great band. You can't tell when you're great if you don't blow a set once in a while." Candi glared at Matt as if her soul wanted to slap him.

Throughout all of this, Steve had made only the two comments, one of which didn't seem to have a hidden agenda. My eyes traveled in his direction, searching his vacant expression for whether he wanted us to join or not.

"Steve, you've been awfully quiet tonight," I said. *I sound like I'm facilitating a group in an employee assistance program.*

"I usually am," he said. "You want my opinion, don't you?"

"Why not? Everyone else seems to have one. Jump right in." He sounded so non-committal I wanted to kick his shin just to get a reaction.

"I think you should do what your heart tells you." His sarcasm made me want to take a swing at him.

"Good point," Candi said.

"I believe we may have overwhelmed our dear Lark, this request coming out of the blue, so to speak. Not to forget that she would be our guide in the Emerald Isle. Without her expertise, we would be sorely lost. Darlin', why don't you sleep on it?" The chair squawked as Rhett shoved back and rose. "Give us your answer by tomorrow night. Else we'll look at other opportunities."

The heavy night air sucked us outside, a great relief after that cloying atmosphere courtesy of Foghorn Rhett. Mist clouded the streetlamps, the windshield wipers scrambling. Bev kept up an adrenaline-soaked chatter, which I ignored, aware that she didn't even realize I hadn't said a word since leaving the bar. They—meaning Rhett—wanted a decision by tomorrow. Time pressure, which I could never resist.

Oh, man! How I wanted to get back to the old sod something fierce. I hadn't seen Mom in years. While we get on each other's nerves after any length of time in close proximity—for example, the Emerald Isle—we thrive on Skype, 3,000 miles and an ocean between us. During my bleak life last winter, I would have welcomed her outrageousness, even in the bone chilling cold of Ireland that makes this part of the world seem tropical.

After dropping Bev off, I paced my apartment, as wired as if I'd downed a carafe of super-caffeinated coffee along with a dozen dark chocolate-covered doughnuts. I asked myself, "Like Bev said just now, 'What are you running from?'"

"Nothing. There's nothing here, therefore nothing to run from," I answered.

"Now you're playing semantics games," my alter ego replied like the social worker I'd trained to be. Damn I was good.

"Okay, I'm running from going to dental hygiene school. I'm not sure I'm ready for something that predictable." And there it was. Having spent three quarters of a year letting go of a dead-end life, a fantasy threatened to lure me away: join a band. For real.

~~~

"Well?" Bev asked. "What's your decision?" We sat over lattes the next day before my shift.

"Deciding to delay school is hard enough without you pushing me. I don't know Ireland that well anymore. The Celtic Tiger changed things. Then everything changed again when the tiger went bust." The coffee tasted bitter.

"I don't think Rhett cares. You're the best bet he's got right now."

"What I can't figure out is why the pirate band, when their jazz is way better." I streamed a packet of raw sugar into my drink.

"Because that's what they're getting paid for."

"Don't you find it odd that he's gone to so much effort when we aren't really musicians? I mean, he could have his choice of thousands of legitimate backup singers."

"As I said, I don't think he cares. We aren't bad singers. Candi has the voice to carry us. We're kind of filler. He needs someone who knows Ireland. My guess is he doesn't have much time to put this together. We're convenient." Bev stirred her drink with the wooden stick then licked off the foam.

"Thanks for the support. Getting around Ireland is not that easy. Besides, I found this book on bog bodies in Rhett's nightstand in the RV when I went to use the bathroom the night of the renn faire party. Creeps me out."

Bev's eyebrows shot up. "A what bodies?"

"Bog bodies. Dead Celts who were probably sacrificed to some god, dumped in a bog, and turned to leather. They turn up in Irish peat bogs and are in the museums."

"Majorly gross, but so he's into kinky. Why should you care?"

"Exactly. Candi said he had a tally of all the women he's banged, which got my curiosity up. I snooped. With everything else that happened that night, I guess I forgot to tell you. It didn't seem important."

"If you're not planning to be added to his tally, how's that an issue?" Bev asked.

"Not the tally, the book. The book with the bog body pics." I shivered. "Pretty twisted."

She tilted her head and sighed. "I still don't get why it's an issue."

"What about school? I enrolled in that program, which starts at the end of June." I folded my napkin and began to twist it.

"Then defer until fall quarter. The tour lasts only three weeks at the end of summer, not like you're going to do this for the rest of your life." She checked her makeup in her compact and snapped the lid shut.

"Lance told me to stay away, that Rhett is into major black market deals."

"And Lance is a reliable source how? You're looking for excuses. Do you want to look back and wonder, what if? You're not the only one facing this age cliff. I'd planned to tell you last night. I've gotten the promotion to VP. I'm excited, scared stiff facing a horrendous learning curve before I can get away for a break. But I could negotiate for three weeks off before I start."

"What about Elliot?"

"I think he'd be relieved for me to get it out of my system. All I talked about for months was getting to sing at that faire. I dragged him to *Rocky Horror Picture Show* and *Frozen* sing-alongs. I've got tickets for a *Sound of Music* sing-fest next week. I told Elliot he could dress up as the captain, but I'm not sure he's going to humor me."

"He's not worried about you? Does he even have a clue what this tour is all about?"

"Our relationship is based on deep trust." Bev sounded prissy, righteous.

"Oh, all right. But don't say I didn't warn you when things go sideways."

Chapter Seven

Bev and I arrived for our first rehearsal at an old, brick warehouse tucked alongside one of Portland's overpasses. We circled the building a couple of times before finally spotting the entrance, the only indication of a door being a small window with chicken wire embedded in the glass.

The halls, like a rabbit warren, veered off in odd directions, the walls that dirt brown color that looked like, well, dirt. Bev glued her arms to her sides. She let me know the surroundings grossed her out by the way she kept digging out anti-bacterial wipes from her Luis Vuitton bag, the tooled leather purse probably not a knockoff.

"I think you may have overdressed a bit."

"I thought the rehearsal building would be more like a recording studio, sort of Abbey Road-esque." She tiptoed around the dabs of old gum— and God knows what else—checking the soles of her Prada boots.

She sneezed. I snorted, my sinuses clogging from the dusty air. She proffered a Kleenex, then flipped on a small LED light, which the dun-colored walls absorbed. We continued winding along the narrow, claustrophobic corridors.

I said, "We've been down this hallway already."

"How do you know? They all look the same."

"I recognize the music. Techno. This is crazy." I punched in Jeremy's number, preparing to give a damsel-in-distress line when he answered. We got dumped into voice mail. "He didn't pick up. In all this racket, Jeremy probably can't hear the phone. I guess we keep going until we hear their music."

After another fifteen minutes of wandering the halls, Bev said, "Why don't we flip a coin, choose a room, and see if they could use backup singers? Some of this stuff sounds pretty good."

"I think we finally found everyone." We rounded the corner to see Matt framed in a doorway in the dimly lit hall.

The practice room resembled a 1950s mental asylum, complete with padded walls and minimal space. We were going to get very close in the next few weeks. Music coming from other practice rooms pulsed the floor. So much for soundproofing.

We entered to Rhett snaking an extension cord to the wall socket. Jeremy's thumb and index fingers twiddled the nuts on his snare as he adjusted its angle. Matt checked the legs on his keyboard. Candi concealed herself in the corner, arms submerged in a large bag. Steve's head bent over his guitar, hair falling across his face, ear next to the strings as he tuned it.

I decided I'd rib Steve. Anti-social people are a challenge I can't resist. "What? You didn't bring your trumpet?" I asked. "What a bummer. I was counting on hearing you blow your horn."

"That's not all I'll blow if I blow this. And you care, why?"

"I don't know. Should I?"

"Well, if I were you, I'd take care around some of the bandmates." He directed his gaze at Jeremy.

What was that supposed to mean? A flush of heat whooshed up my body, landing on my face. *Was I that obvious?* My hair stuck to my neck. I scoured my brain. No clever retort seemed forthcoming. He turned back to his guitar. My gut told me to dissipate my embarrassment by chatting up someone else.

I edged over to Candi where Bev scrutinized her while she adjusted a bow on a large bundle of sage.

"What are you doing?" I asked.

"I'm performing a cleansing ceremony to chase off the bad vibes and invite our musical muses in."

"I'd like to do my own cleansing ceremony," Bev murmured under her breath, "with a mop and bleach. Or an exterminator. When I turned on the flashlight in the hall, I swear I saw a humongous rat scurry into the dark corners."

"This is nothing. Wait'll things get really gross."

Beautiful, flute-like singing emanated from Candi as she executed an intricate step and turn, waving the sage.

"Muse of the North, keep watch through the night. Guard our nativity." She wafted the sage in an arc, rising on tiptoe. "Muse of the East, bring rays of light. Like dawn's creativity."

"You're doing that in bare feet?" Bev's face contorted.

"Well of course! I have to connect with the earth."

"That's not all you're connecting with. I saw rat droppings," Bev nodded toward the door.

Candi blanched, ran for her flip flops, and returned, the rubber soles sticking to the grimy concrete.

Curious about her ceremony, I asked, "Why do you do the compass directions?"

"Because these are directional muses. Each has a distinct territory and influence." Candi pirouetted awkwardly on the rubber soles of the flip-flops.

"Then you might want to know that's not east. It's south," Bev pointed to a compass she'd brought up on her cell. Her expression slotted Candi in the same league as fortune-telling eight balls.

"Now I have to start over again." Candi pouted, turning toward her bag. "I hope I didn't piss them off. You have no idea what angry muses are capable of."

"You probably did," Matt called.

Candi pulled a hefty sheaf out of the bag's recesses. "My muses are very sensitive about their territories. But this will calm everything and appease them." She flicked a lighter touching the tips of a bunch of lavender, flames jumping.

A moment later the room reverberated from the keen of a smoke alarm. Actually, the padded walls shuddered as they absorbed the noise. Candi dropped her lavender and stamped out the embers, sparks flying. Steve jolted open the door and fanned the entrance to diffuse the smoke and stop the alarm.

"Candi, didn't it occur to you that we're in a small room with no windows?" Matt hoisted his keyboard and took a step toward the exit, ready to dash.

Jeremy tore off his shirt. Until then, the only six-pack I'd seen was the drummer holding one while extricating a beer. If he worked out at a gym, I'd join immediately. "Are you trying to get us kicked out? Jesus." He flapped the T-shirt, bull-fighting style.

"The contract only said no smoking," she replied. "Our success depends on ritual cleansing."

I peered down the hallway, expecting a horde of panicking musicians heading for the nearest exit or the reverberating stride of the building manager as he came to evict us. But only thumping music emanated from the practice rooms. The hall remained empty. I wondered what would happen in a real fire.

"I'm sure the music muses appreciated your effort."

"Thanks, Lark, I hope they do." Candi's flip flop smeared the herbal sticks into a pulverized mess.

Bev snorted.

"Let's get together, y'all. We've only got a couple of hours," Rhett said.

To imply that the room was big enough for us to get together would indicate the ability to move some distance, rather than we were already in

41

a permanent group hug.

"Hey, this is the non-glamorous part." I raised my voice so everyone could hear. "The part our adoring fans don't see. All the sweat that goes into it."

Jeremy, tightening the wing nut for his upper high-hat cymbal, looked up. I think I scored points on that.

"Like your Zildjains." I pointed at his cymbals.

"Yeah, pretty sweet," Jeremy said. "How do you know about them?"

"I have my ways." I flicked my eyelashes. More points.

Everything tuned and tightened, I expected the guys to sound like the renn faire or that crazy good set in the bar. The Band of Pirates played so tight when I'd been on stage with them. Then I had to recall about how tight I'd been. Either we had a long way to go, or I had been majorly messed up every time we played. Bottom line, we stank in more ways than one.

Mixed with the leftover smell from Candi's earlier burnt offerings, the room quickly became rank, acquiring the kind of odor that reminded me of the days after my divorce where I'd holed up in my dark bedroom, the windows shut tight and the curtains drawn.

Rhett's black tee grew ellipses under his arms. Jeremy's sticks flew out of his hands, rivulets ran from the end of Matt's nose, and sweat soaked Steve's hair. Before long, all the guys had stripped off their shirts. Candi pulled off her top, her breasts bobbing as she continued to beat her tambourine. Not to be outdone, I threw my blouse toward my purse. Thank God I'd put on a relatively new bra that morning. Bev's eyes grew huge. Then Steve broke a string on his bass, bringing everything to a halt.

The lead singer mopped his forehead with his tee. "I'd say we're done for the night. Jeremy, you decide whether to house your drums here until tomorrow. Everyone else, take your equipment. Y'all would be hurtin' if it walked off in the wrong hands. Let's convene here at 6:00 p.m., and Lark, I charge you with procuring a fan."

"Why do I get the honor? Cuz I'm a woman and this is a substitute for making coffee?" His attitude grated my nerves.

"Why Lark, darlin', you are a permanent resident of this city. You will know where the best deals are to be made."

"Not your area of procurement expertise. Is that it?" The thought of his infamous tally popped into my head.

"I'll get the fucking fan." Steve hoisted his guitar and trumpet cases. "Rhett, you need to check your attitude."

Chapter Eight

Later that evening, I lounged on my bed, engrossed in my toes and this killer shade of puce nail polish. The TV distracted me to the point I almost dumped the polish on my bedspread. I grabbed the phone, cradling it in my neck. "Bev, do you have the news on?"

A mass of orange flames cavorted from the roof and windows of an old, brick building. Smoke silhouetted a local reporter, who concluded her piece by stating, "Fortunately the building was vacant, and no injuries occurred."

"Do you believe it? The warehouse! We could've been trapped in that rabbit warren. All that noise, the fire alarm going off, the place a tinder box, Candi with her burning bush, and oh my god!"

"Well, she got one thing right. She probably pissed off the muses," Bev said. "Gotta run. Elliot arrived with a pizza."

The next phone call went to Rhett, who sounded a bit short of breath. No doubt I interrupted his work on his tally. When Candi picked up, she responded stoically, stating she would definitely be more attentive the next time she did a cleansing ceremony, and she hoped she had appeased the muses. Steve's voice was a shrug over the phone, adding at least everyone except Jeremy took their instruments when we left. Matt didn't pick up.

Jeremy, the most upset, lamented his drums were not insured. Me to the rescue, loaning Jeremy my kit—Pearls and Zildjains. As a kid, I embarked on this Karen Carpenter phase. I loved that a woman could play the drums. I loved that she could also sing. The former, I got pretty good at. The latter? I went into social work. Jeremy's voice flooded with gratitude. How could he thank me he asked.

I promised him I'd come up with something.

~~~

I decided to Skype Mom and let her know about my upcoming trip. I hadn't seen her since Joe and I divorced. Remembering the visit was tricky. I had blown all my savings in a funk, drinking more than I should. Blackouts seem to have been part of the itinerary. Counting that as a trip would be lying. I spent my days commuting between the pub and Mom's house. Dublin could have been any city and Ireland any country. If asked, the honest answer would be at least twenty years had passed since I'd trod the roads of the Emerald Isle.

Mom had managed when she divorced Dad and moved back to Galway with me as a young girl. Crazy as I thought she could be, she kept it together, while during my divorce I did not. Maybe surviving divorce requires a bit of lunacy.

Mom's bright face answered the Skype video ring. "My sweet Lark, how grand to see you."

My image froze. Of course, important topics were on my mind. I rang again. "Mom, I'm coming for a visit for three weeks at the end of July. A band hired my bestie, Bev De Trow, and me as backup singers. Mostly cuz I'm Irish, meaning I'm a guide for the gigs. Isn't that wonderful?"

"Sure it's great news. And this time 'round, you're to have a bit of craic. Your last visit broke your oul wan's heart with how shattered you were. Are they not using your gift for drumming?"

"I haven't been behind my drums in years. But I did loan them to the drummer. He lost his in a fire."

"Tis a pity. You have such talent. Wasting you they are. Are you sure this is a good idea? I thought you set your heart on dental hygiene school."

Too much remembering. I changed the subject. "You mentioned you started a business?"

"Brilliant." Her voice splintered into shards. "The busi...ness is brill...i...ant."

The Skype disengagement sounded, Mom's face froze as if I'd taken a bad photo of her, and my own disengagement trundled across my brain. A wispy thought fluttered behind my eyes. Entering a dental hygiene program may not be a stellar choice. Either way—dental hygiene or a band tour—loomed a gut clutching experience. Why was I attempting a backup singing gig other than to see Mom? To delay having to deal with the other. Then the big question overrode my internal fears. Why the hell did Rhett hire Bev and me?

~~~

A friend of Steve's who worked for a janitorial service said we could use the elementary school gym at night.

Band practices were pathetic. Bev and I complained that we weren't picking up the harmonies, Rhett reassuring that we would do right fine after a little more practice. Candi worked overtime to bring us along. The other guys didn't seem all that concerned. Of course, Steve didn't care either way. Matt whined about the acoustics in the gym. Jeremy effused his gratitude to me for loaning my drum kit, but any of my attempts to flirt fell flat.

Then a few days before we were to leave, our numbers stumbled into place. Bev gaped as if she had at last found Mecca. "Do you believe it? I can hear us backup singers, but I also hear my voice. I can hear how I contribute. Do you think this will translate across the Atlantic?"

"I have no idea." To my mind Band of Pirates struck me as mediocre at best.

~~~

Mom's face beamed across the internet in a way that made my heart expand and forget everything but that she loved me. Then I remembered her eccentric behaviors and a thread of anxiety coursed up my spine.

"Lark, my wee dear! You're to be arriving soon?"

"We leave tomorrow. I'll email when I get to Dublin."

"T'will be heaven to wrap my arms around you. But what dire circumstances you're arriving at. Sure, I don't expect the news has reached you. We've had a ghastly thing happen to our renowned relics." Her voice fractured.

"You broke up, Mom. What did you say?"

"Other relics." Her voice's volume picked up and sputtered out again.

"Relics? You mean like Strongbow's tomb in Christ Church? Like vandalizing with gang insignia?"

"Worse. Much worse. A break-in occurred last night at Dublin's National Museum. The thugs stole one of our beloved bog bodies."

My stomach congealed to marble. "Which one?"

"'Twas just on the tip of my finger..."

"Monaghan?"

"Why yes, 'tis the very one. The rotters stole gold jewelry as well."

"What gold jewelry?"

"An ancient torc and earrings."

Mom's face pixilated, and the audio fragmented. Her face froze, wrinkled lips slack, fish-like.

I shook my head at the familiar tones of the dropped session.

That night I dreamt about a bog body in my closet. He burst through the door and hobbled toward my bed, the lower half of his torso missing. From his chest up, he resembled overly tanned leather that had then spent time in a hot oven, his skin shriveled and lined. A gold collar glimmered around his neck while earrings refracted the light. The top of his head sported a knob of hair, the color of Georgia mud, and on his chin was a grizzled, ginger colored goatee. My gut warned me away from looking at his eye sockets. A deep gouge crossed his torso, like a tear in leather. He clasped the Loughnashade Horn against his side, then raised it to his leather lips, issuing forth a mournful bellow.

47

Chapter Nine

When are you gonna see your mom?" Like every other time Bev had asked me that question over the past couple of months, I did this bobblehead thing, accompanied by a big sigh. Only now we were thirty-something thousand feet in the air in a jet bound for the land of a thousand shades of green, the moon a huge spotlight.

"I did see her. Remember? Yesterday on Skype."

"No, I mean see her in person," Bev said.

I cringed and changed the subject. "Remember that book on bog bodies I told you I found in Rhett's nightstand? Thieves broke into Dublin's National Museum and stole a body last week. The one he had highlighted. I had a horrible nightmare last night where a bog body lurked in my closet and busted down the door."

"Just cuz Rhett is kinky or interested in Irish archaeology doesn't mean he's guilty. If that were the case, any professor or antiquarian would be a suspect."

I took a large swig of the scotch and water on my drop-down tray. "And we happen to be going to Ireland."

"So are a lot of people. A plane full. I bet a quarter of them are antiquarians." Bev stirred her drink.

I stretched myself up and around my aisle seat, lifting my chin as if scanning the length of the jet for bog body experts. White heads dotted the rows, like cotton balls against the head rests. Some senior excursion.

"You're dodging the question. When are you going to see your mom? I'd love to meet her."

"I've told you how complicated it is," I replied.

"Like what mother-daughter relationship isn't?"

It's not that I have issues with my mom. In fact, we get along famously, as she would say. How to deal with her eccentricities? How to explain that she's a Looney Toon? Now seventy, she entertained herself by dressing as an Irish peasant woman and begging on Grafton Street, even though she sat on a pot of money most leprechauns would envy. Certifiable or not, Mom and I lived an ocean and continent away from each other. The loss from not feeling her hug over the past few months when I needed her most occupied a big corner of my heart. Nuts or not, she was my mom. The future held a dental hygiene school loan to pay off with little chance to come back anytime soon.

"I'll email her when we land in Dublin." I leaned toward Bev, cupping my hand around my mouth. "What's freaking me out is this bog body thing. Somehow Rhett's involved. Let's keep an eye on him."

"I don't know. That sounds way too woo-woo. But hey, I got your back. You've always had mine." Bev drained her drink, tilted her seat, and closed her eyes.

"We can amuse ourselves by keeping a tally on his conquests. If he says he broke some kind of banging record, we can prove or dispute it." I leaned back in my seat.

I crunched the remaining ice in my cup, sickened that thieves stole symbols of my heritage and my mother country's legacy, perhaps to end up in a private collection where they would fade away from our collective consciousness. As a child growing up in Ireland, I considered myself totally Irish. But I had been Irish American for close to three decades. A bungee cord vaulting across the Atlantic stretched my loyalties and alliances.

Internally I grimaced. In a twisted way, all those Irish Americans sending guns and money overseas made sense. I hadn't considered that kind of loyalty before. For them, loyalty resided in a cause. For me, loyalty resided in symbols of kinship like Monaghan Man, an umbilical cord through time and space. People spend big bucks for black market artifacts. Why wouldn't a narcissistic lead singer steal Ireland's sacred antiquities? Why should Rhett care?

The jet glided through the night. As if I starred in some kind of disaster movie, a venomous snake might emerge from the cargo hold at any second. Only the snake wasn't in the cargo hold. He sat only a few feet away, mesmerizing some hapless flight attendant. In answer, I ordered another scotch.

~~~

Half asleep and hungover are not the way to navigate an airport. We staggered through Dublin International's maze of glass hallways before we found the bank of customs stations. I'd expected the customs agent to be impressed when I announced we were on tour. He stamped my passport in answer and motioned us on.

All our band equipment remained in the States, leaving us little baggage to extract from the carousels. According to Rhett, the expense and risk of damage prohibited bringing our gear. He had rentals lined up in Dublin, so we left everything behind except Candi's tambourine, our cowbells, and Steve's trumpet. Candi insisted she imbued them with only good vibes, critical to a successful tour. Steve stated either he brought his trumpet or count him out. Poor Jeremy, despondent at leaving my kit, had bonded with my drums. It would have been sweeter if he'd bonded with me too. But who's to say what would happen in the next few weeks? Matt stated that he'd yet to rent a keyboard that wasn't totally out of tune.

We stopped to change currency then proceeded through the terminal containing food kiosks and duty-free shops. Rhett's take-charge stride hollered his imagined stardom, with the rest of us relegated to the status of his mere entourage.

After eight hours of recycled plane air and a stagnant airport, a chilly end-of-July morning welcomed us. Having already rained once, the clouds scuttled to congregate for another shower. That day I learned that planning and organization were not Rhett's strong points. In fact, I failed to see the point in a lot of his activities.

Seeing we would pick up our rented equipment the next morning, I suggested taking the bus. Despite my previous life here, Rhett overrode my input and hailed a mini-van cab, public transportation not befitting a musician of his caliber. We peons squished in the back, while he commandeered the front seat next to the cab driver.

"We're fixin' to play at Feeney's Pub tomorrow night. Y'all should come hear us," Rhett said to the driver.

"So you say," the driver's derisive tone barely polite.

I hauled out the brogue. "I was just on thinking that a gentleman such as yourself wouldn't be after going to a wee pub. We're to be playing this Friday week at the Electric Picnic."

"You don't say?" The cabby brightened. "Well now. I'll be telling me niece. She's at University College Dublin doing English literature." His eyes scrutinized me from the rearview mirror. "How long has it been since you're back?"

"A while," I said.

"Welcome home." He'd decided that we were okay. For Americans.

~~~

Rhett had booked us into a hostel close to the O'Connell Bridge. I've always considered myself young at heart and in mind, but I discovered the following morning that after a night in a communal room on a museum quality bunk bed, I am anything but young in body. My back hadn't ached this bad since the last time I slept on the ground, though much of that evening had been on top of Lance. Bev hadn't fared any better. Did she have to be so damn chipper? We'd be adding a regimen of Tylenol to our daily diet.

"Have you seen Jeremy, Candi, and the rest this morning?" Bev stood in front of me in line at a Tesco grocery store with our yogurt purchases.

"They're staggering around the store." I gestured toward Steve with his head in the dairy case, Candi and Jeremy scrutinizing the label on an energy bar. "Matt's probably waiting with Rhett."

Bev grabbed coins from her wallet while I singled out the correct change for her and stepped up. "Any guesses where Rhett went last night after he left the bar with that woman?"

"Who knows? Some poor twit's, I expect." I placed coins on the counter and took my breakfast. "We're not far from Dublin's National Museum. Not far from the break-in. He might have met up with the other thieves. I think the body and jewelry are long gone." I sighed. "I heard back from Mom. She'll catch up with us when we're back in Dublin. She's got business out of town."

"At least you contacted her."

"Yeah, but what would take her out of town when her main activity is dressing in rags and standing on a street corner?"

"What?" Bev frowned in incomprehension.

"She dresses in peasant costumes and begs on Grafton Street."

"Oh, Lark! Is she like homeless or starving?" Bev gasped.

"No, she's a bit of a loon."

"Can't wait to meet her." Bev's grin stretched, her ombre-streaked hair falling across her cheeks. How could she look so great after the kind of night we had?

We ambled out of the small grocery store and around the corner to where Matt sat next to Rhett, who sprawled on a bench. He emanated an ecstatic stupor, no doubt from the realization he was in the Emerald Isle. Or as ecstatic as he could be with an apparent hangover from too many pints the night before and probable lack of sleep.

Bev and I hauled out the tally sheet we'd concocted. We ticked one slash mark and a question mark, but no dots to connect to the missing antiquities.

After breakfast that morning, we headed to check out our first gig in a pub called Feeney's. In the afternoon, we'd pick up our rented equipment for the tour. Rhett, still into his entourage thing, strode along the boulevards, while I trailed along in righteous glee as we roamed up and down streets, lost. My beloved Grafton Street had transformed into a pedestrian-only thoroughfare. Where Irish stores had historically lined the avenue, a McDonald's, a Disney store, and souvenir shops now occupied prime real estate. Mom's dressing up as a beggar wasn't so outrageous after all. I hoped to see her with her shawl and basket posted along the boulevard. My shoulders sagged at her absence. Only a busker played Irish bagpipes while someone juggled tin whistles.

I remained mute, nudging Bev from time to time and smirking. By sheer fortitude, Rhett finally found the pub in a side lane. He elbowed his way to the bar, next to a fellow waiting on a lager while the rest of us milled around the tavern. "We're Band of Pirates. We thought we'd check in and get organized for tonight. Is your owner or manager on the premises?"

The bartender ignored him, finished pulling the draft, placed the pint in front of the customer, and swiped a cloth down the counter. Rhett opened his mouth to speak again.

"Are you now? That be news to me."

Rhett shifted his eyes. "I should clarify that I'm the leader. Our tour coordinator scheduled us to play at this venue this evening."

"To my mind, I don't think a band from the US of A. is playing tonight. Matter of fact, I'm just after looking at my list. The lads playing are an Irish band, Rebels."

Rhett reached in his bag. "My fine owner of this establishment, I have our itinerary right here. Tonight. Feeney's Pub. Confirmed." He placed it on the counter, starting to wind up.

I kept to the back, along with Bev.

"What's this mean? What're we going to do if we don't play tonight?" Bev whispered.

"Get some sleep." I yawned, fatigue hugging my shoulders like an overly affectionate aunt.

"Maybe we're at the wrong Feeney's," Matt suggested. "I don't see a stage here."

"We're not big enough for an American band, is that it?"

Now you've done it. Piss off the owner. That's the way to sort things.

Steve stepped up. "Well, as long as we're getting this straightened out, I'd like a pint." Smart man, Steve. I hadn't guessed his instincts were that refined. Nothing like a pint to smooth the waters.

"You might be right." The owner placed the pint in front of Steve, the creases around his eyes and mouth deepened, the corner of his lips heading up in amusement. "They come and go these pubs. Could be you're at the wrong Feeney's on Dame Street. Then again, you could be here on the wrong day." He disappeared through a door to the back.

We huddled around Rhett. Steve inched away from us along the bar, taking a gulp of his lager. The owners had decorated the pub in an odd mixture of funky kitsch, highlighting the main attraction, a hefty bar banked by stunning mirrors. A sitting area beyond a wall divided the pub, as if this had once been the ladies' side. The establishment had obviously been in business for a while—decades no doubt. Centuries probably.

The owner returned clasping a bound notebook, the kind students in the British Isles use for writing essays. "Well, 'tis easy enough. You're to be playing Friday week." He pointed at an entry.

"Are you sure? My itinerary has us at the University College Dublin." Rhett consulted his schedule.

The owner grunted. "That's the arrangement I made with your man in Texas."

He disappeared again, bringing back a laptop, which he placed on the counter facing himself. "Here's the email confirmation." He turned the screen toward us.

Matt leaned over Rhett's shoulder, pointing at the itinerary. "That says, Sweeney's, not Feeney's. Wonder how many of these are also screwed up," watching his language. Normally, he would have lobbed an *F* bomb.

I would have used the *F* word.

"First day here and already there's a screwup. Move over, Steve." I sidled against him and nodded to the owner for a pint. "Come on, Bev, Candi, Matt, Jeremy. You're gonna need one of these as well."

Chapter Ten

This most certainly is a detour from the itinerary I have. Okay, y'all, we're here next Friday," Rhett said.

"You're to be alternating with local groups. The stage is right behind where you're standing." The pub owner looked straight at Matt.

Jeremy elbowed Matt aside. "My mate didn't mean it."

"We're all pretty knackered from the flight." I took a long haul from my stout.

"From Galway are you?" The manager's round head and grin would be at home on a jack-o'-lantern.

"Via Portland," I said.

"Home of famous lobsters?"

"Sure that's the other Portland," I answered.

"No worries," he said.

Bev licked a bit of foam from her lip, her mouth curling upward as if uncertain about the taste. "Is this Guinness? It's so bitter."

Steve nodded. "Guinness is an acquired taste."

"Perhaps we could trouble you for more pints and a bit of space at that table." Rhett pointed toward the seating area. "I'm fixin' to make a few calls." He replaced his sunglasses with a pair of silver wire rims.

"Sure. Crack on. Is it some black stuff you're after?"

A question mark formed on Rhett's face.

"You can continue with what you're going to do. He asked if you'd like Guinness. By the way, you hired me as your guide, not your translator."

This guy was doing a job creep scam on me. If he could get me to agree to one additional task, he would add more and more.

"Fine. But speaking of duties, while I get our tour in better order, Lark, start earning your keep. Bev, you are to accompany her to pick up our vehicle." He handed me a sticky note where he'd scrawled an address. "I trust you will find this with no difficulty."

"Whoa there, cowboy. You hired me as your guide. Guide does not mean driver." I handed the address back and scooted along the bar, leaving Steve to nurse his pint.

"Why Lark, darlin', it most certainly does." Rhett moved his glasses to the crest of his head.

"In whose drugged-out hallucination?" I drained my pint. To leave any would be bad luck, and so far, our luck didn't look all that good.

"Your drugged-out hallucination must have caused you to forget because I clearly recall our conversation."

I took a gander at the rest of the band to see their reactions. Bland, neutral. Then Jeremy and Candi nodded, followed by Matt.

I turned my gaze to Bev. She shook her head. "Sorry, Lark, I don't remember."

"And if I refuse?"

"You'd let your esteemed bandmates down like that? When we are so newly arrived? You'd be the reason we can't get to our first gig, and because of you, put the contract in breach?"

"I think you should give her ten percent of CD and T-shirt sales as compensation for driving," Bev said.

"That's highway robbery," Rhett said. "Three percent because you have me over a barrel."

"Seven percent. How much will you have to pay to hire another guide?"

"I can fire you."

"What are the odds you'll find a replacement in time to get to the first gig?"

"Rhett, if you fire Lark, you're also firing Bev." Candi's voice crept up an octave. "I can't carry the female vocals by myself."

"I don't know. Maybe Rhett should find someone else." Steve drained the last of his lager and rejoined the group.

I narrowed my eyes and gritted my teeth. "After all the time and effort we've put into this? I put my career plans on hold."

"She could sue you for detrimental reliance," Bev said. "And sue Noted Enterprises, LLC too. She changed her dental hygiene school plans to be a backup singer and guide based on your offer. That's a contract." I threw her a confused look. But if she made my point, I wasn't going to interrupt. "You hired her, and she accepted this job. If you strand her in Ireland, she changed her plans to her detriment. She might not even be able to go to school now."

"You've condemned me to a life selling doughnuts," I added.

"All right, all right, all right. You've made your point. Seven percent and not an iota more." Rhett handed me the sticky again.

I slapped the note back in his palm, connecting with his hand. "We need to shake on this."

The manager had positioned himself behind the bar directly in front of our table, earwigging. Good, a disinterested party to confirm the deal.

"Now that we have that settled, Matt, you are to help get this tour sorted. Candi, Jeremy, and Steve, you are to pick up our rental equipment. Wait at the music store for Lark, Bev, and the transportation. Let's meet back here as our good man behind the counter has been so generous as to allow us to roost." He handed me the sticky.

Bev and I headed toward the back entrance. "God, his handwriting's hardly legible, but I know where this is. At the airport."

Within a few minutes, we emerged from the alleyway behind Feeney's, walked along the south side of the River Liffey, and crossed at the O'Connell Bridge to the bus stop. "This brings back a lot of memories. The biggest one is the narrow streets. I pray driving a van through them won't be a nightmare."

Chapter Eleven

B ang on. I need to copy your driver's license, get your signature, and you'll be on your way." The fellow behind the ABC Rental desk smiled, teeth the color of an unrinsed teacup. A tobacco-stained index finger pointed to the line on the contract.

I scanned the document. "I'd like to take a look at the van and note any damage, to be sure we're on the same page."

"Van?" A bushy eyebrow ascended into frizzy hair that concealed a bad comb-over.

"Then vehicle." I looked toward Bev.

"Suit yourself." He jerked his head to follow him out a back entrance.

We crossed a large tarmac toward a bank of outbuildings, cars visible on lifts. Rental Guy halted before a bus.

"What the fuck! Rhett rented that?"

Bev grabbed my arm as she took in its size. "Have you ever driven one of these?"

"I once drove a nine-passenger van for an employee team outing." I peered through the door. "Someone must have screwed up." Rental Guy's tobacco breath saturated my shoulder. "I don't have a bus driver's license."

"No worries. We're sorted. You've got full coverage on this."

"It's not this tank I'm worried about, it's the poor slobs I'd be hitting."

"'Tis really not all that big. A bit of getting used to is all." Rental Guy patted the side as if he were appraising the flank of a horse.

"Wow. Does it have GPS?" Bev's head swiveled as she inspected the bus's length.

"'Tis the economy model. I am sad to say we are all out of the upgrade at the moment."

"I think that will be the least of my worries." I envisioned the bus toppling over a cliff, trapping all of us inside.

"We can always use my phone for GPS." Bev bent her head to fish the cell from her purse.

"If you're concerned about big, well, that's big." Rental Guy pointed to a tour bus. "Now that luxury coach comes complete with TV, DVD player, AC, and a jacks at the back. But I'm sad to say you can't drive that one. You don't have the proper credentials."

"I don't want to drive that one. I don't want to drive this one!" I banged the side of the bus.

Rental Guy flinched as if I'd hit his prize mare. "Sure you do. It's not that big."

Bev and I strolled around the vehicle.

"The interior is really quite lovely. You'll have twenty-one seats to stretch out in, that's twenty-one reclining seats with three-point seatbelts and AC. You and your mates will be most comfortable."

"Their comfort is not what I'm concerned about. It's mine."

"'Tis not much bigger than a motor home, it is."

"Motor home sounds a lot more doable," Bev said, "but I gotta tell you, I think Rhett's getting the better deal here. We should have held fast for ten percent of the CD and tee sales."

"How long since you've been back?" Rental Guy flashed a toothy grin, pulled out a pack of smokes, and jiggled the pack to offer us one.

We smiled and shook our heads as he teased one out.

"Too long," I answered.

"Well then, welcome home. And what a grand way to reacquaint your-self with the Emerald Isle."

"I can think of better and easier ways to reacquaint myself, and they don't involve driving a tank."

"Why not take a wee spin around the lot? She's a grand touring car she is." He sounded nostalgic as if describing a favored racehorse.

"She's not a car. She's a fucking bus."

"Dear lady, I'm afraid I must ask that you not use that language around her or the customers."

"I am a customer." Had this guy been inhaling too much carbon mon-oxide? My scalp heated as I took deep breaths. I turned to Bev. "Well, Rhett wanted to experience Ireland. It'll be one he'll never forget, assum-ing he lives to remember. Insured for full coverage you say?" Rental Guy nodded. "Then who cares what the outside looks like, cuz it's only gonna get worse."

"Bang on." He dropped the keys into my palm. "You'll have a brilliant time."

Bev and I boarded the bus, whereby she immediately strapped herself in. I turned the ignition, a blast of AC colliding with my sweaty forehead. The knob my hand landed on was for a stick shift.

I rolled down the window. "Hey, you. Rental Guy, this is a stick shift!"

"Bang on, she's a stick shift."

"I want an automatic."

"Have you ever driven anything other than an automatic?" Bev's voice as if she were perched on the edge of a mountain, strapped to a question-able-looking parachute.

"Only a museum quality Beetle, and I was pretty loaded."

Rental Guy responded. "I am sad to say the economy package does not include an automatic—"

"And you are also sad to say that no upgrade is available at the mo-ment." Bev finished for him.

"Fuck you, Rhett!" I banged the steering wheel, setting off a deafening alarm. Rental Guy gestured toward his palm as if holding something, his comment inaudible. We all waited, Rental Guy's mouth slack, my teeth bared as if about to take a chunk of his greedy soul, and Bev, biting her lip as if encountering a sketchy blind date. I punched buttons on the fob at random. Just as quickly, the noise, like a siren at a maximum-security prison, silenced.

"My dear lady, does this mean you do not want the vehicle?" Rental Guy frowned. His comb-over threatened to converge with his chin.

"I don't want this rental. I don't want any rental. I want to survive," I answered, my voice lowered about two octaves. "You got any helmets we can use?"

"It will be extra, and I'm sad to say we're all out at the moment." He stepped back fishing out his pack of cigs. "Take her for a spin around the lot. You'll be amazed at how easy she handles once you get the feel for her."

I released the emergency brake, the bus jumped forward. And stalled. "What kind of crap ride is this?"

Rental Guy approached my window. "She takes a bit of getting used to. She has a few quirks. Go easy on the gas pedal." He backed off, dragging on a smoke as if his day's entertainment consisted of my jaunt around the parking lot.

I began a slow crawl, jerking the gear shift as we circumnavigated the car rental perimeter.

"Now you're getting the hang of it. After a bit more practice, you'll be away to the races." His third cig landed by the others.

"We should have taken one of those when he offered them." Bev's voice trembled.

Five slug-like laps later, I headed toward the exit. "Okay, better get back. I wonder what other damage Rhett has done to the tour? Is your life insurance paid up?"

I flipped the turn signal with my left fingers only to have the wipers screech across the windows. Wrong handle. I took a big breath, turned out

63

of the lot, and lumbered onto the main road. A roundabout appeared. *Mentally think left.*

From the seat behind me, Bev coached. "All right, Lark, you're doing great. I got my GPS up. We're gonna stay on this road for a couple of kilometers, then take a slight turn."

We eased along the road, the bus taking up the lane. I checked the speedometer. We were going twenty kilometers per hour, and I had not shifted out of second gear, the transmission beginning to chug. I slowed. Blaring horns from cars shredded the morning as they passed.

"I think you should go a little faster. Traffic is backing up."

The acrid smell of exhaust fumes filled the bus. Like reading braille, I fingered the door sill for the electric lever, hearing the grind of Bev's window going down.

"Speed up. The light's changing."

I shoved the stick into third gear, pushed on the pedal, the bus taking a moment too long to accelerate. The light flashed red. The bus stalled. Angry drivers streamed into the intersection, honking.

I twisted the key, put the bus into gear, and jumped forward.

"You're doing okay. Keep going." Bev's voice faltered.

"If we don't die before we get to Feeney's, an asshole named Rhett will." The steering wheel jiggled back and forth as I fought to keep the bus in its lane.

I plodded along the four-lane road, gaining confidence, yanking the shift into third.

"You're going to make a slight left ahead. Here," Bev said as a chirpy GPS woman's voice announced the exit from the motorway.

I found myself in the middle lane. "I'm going to take the next left and circle around." I signaled to cross lanes, held my breath, and moved over, receiving a blast from a car in my blind spot.

"Use the horn. Everyone else seems to."

I didn't dare look in the rearview mirror. Bev's face would be sweat-streaked like mine.

We moved into the turn lane and slowed as the light changed to green. I gunned the engine, hearing the tires screech as we rounded the corner, the bus at an awkward angle. The traffic noise faded as we entered a neighborhood of identical houses planted neatly on identically sized lots, a small wooden sign announcing the entrance to Castle Keep. The road narrowed to two unmarked lanes. Parked cars on either side and onto the sidewalk reduced the available tarmac to barely enough space for us to pass.

"Interesting way folks park around here," Bev commented.

"Yeah. I think it's an Irish trait. These houses are all new since the Troubles ended." I didn't dare blink, or I was sure to hit something. "I hope this leads us back to the main road. What's our GPS friend say?"

"She doesn't have an opinion."

We passed a small neighborhood grocery store cozied against a corner. "You think I should park and get directions?" I asked.

"Are you brave enough to stop? The parking area is dinky."

"Too late anyway. What's your GPS say?"

"I lost the connection."

"We'll just have to hope." We passed a church. "And pray." I mentally crossed myself, thinking of St. Jude, the patron saint of lost causes. "The good news is that I'm going the speed limit." The speedometer's needle hovered above five kph, followed by the dispiriting cough of the engine cutting. I twisted the ignition key and pressed the gas. Nothing. On the second try, the bus jumped forward. I slammed the brake, the hood inches from T-boning a parked SUV.

"We're in house hell." I scouted the road for a stop sign that would indicate an intersection to an arterial. The bus toddled forward, the street flowing between rows of houses. The avenue curved like the inside of a nautilus shell. And ended.

"Oh man, Lark, we're in a cul-de-sac."

Lawns and front yard gardens fringed the semicircle. The center was a mandala of pastel chalk from children's games. Snail-paced I crawled

65

forward.

The chirpy GPS announced, "You have arrived at your destination."

"Like hell we have," I muttered.

"Now the GPS decides to work," Bev said. "Once we get out of this cul-de-sac, the main road won't be far."

The long wheelbase meant I had to put the obstinate vehicle in reverse. The gears ground as I backed and wrenched the stick into first gear.

"This thing drives like a truck. Oh yeah, it's not a truck, it's a fucking tank tricked-out to look like a bus."

I tapped the gas. Nothing. I depressed the pedal resulting in a small jolt forward. I pressed harder. The recalcitrant contraption leapt across the sidewalk into a carefully landscaped garden.

"You know, somehow I don't think the owners are looking for a garden ornament in the form of a bus." Bev's voice strained. "This was a beautiful front yard. Until we stopped by."

"You've got a point. They look more like the gazing ball types. Now what?"

"I'll note the address so we can file an accident report. That is if we ever get out of here."

We'd landed before a small maple, sheltering a cement leprechaun. Large rhododendrons flanked us, branches pressing against the windows. The remains of rose bushes lay trampled by the tires. I put the bus in reverse, the tires moved about a foot and then dug in, the engine complaining.

I socked the steering wheel. The horn blasted setting off the alarm, its angry wail bouncing off the houses. Residents should have swarmed into the street at the noise. I grabbed the key out of the ignition, manically punching buttons on the fob.

Then silence suddenly engulfed us like being in a large tuna can or old VW Beetle.

"Everyone must be at work or at school." I scanned the vacant houses with their immaculate front yards, our vehicle partially camouflaged by the huge bushes. "Go to the back and tell me why we're stuck."

Bev's footsteps padded along the aisle. "Looks like the tires are against the curb. You're going to have to rock back and forth."

First gear. Reverse. First gear. Reverse. The front tires dug into the carefully tilled soil.

"Lark, step on it."

I stomped the pedal, the bus flying backwards, rhododendron branches clinging to the windows. We maneuvered in a reverse circle, faced toward the exit to the cul-de-sac, and I shifted into gear, speeding toward an adjoining avenue.

A boy on a low-rider bike crossed in front. "You're gonna run over that kid!" Bev screamed.

I slammed the brakes, the boy skidded onto the lawn, toppling sideways, his face a patchwork of terror and surprise as we passed.

"We could have killed a kid!" The crisis sent my mind scurrying for St. Nicholas, the patron saint of children. Slowly I continued along the avenue. Tears soaked my neck. Bev whimpered, her voice echoing behind me. The bus filled with our high-pitched keening.

"Okay, I got service." Tears lined her voice. "At the next corner, take a right and follow this road."

A stop sign marked the intersection. Ahead a steady stream of traffic whizzed past. We sat for a moment, the bus idling like a rodeo animal waiting to jump into the ring. I checked the rearview mirror. Bev crossed her arms over her chest, clinging to her seatbelt.

"Okay, hang on, I'm grabbing the turn." Tires squealed as I burned rubber, joining the arterial, cutting off a minivan, the blare trailing us down the street. "Sorry, cars, but I'm bigger than you."

We traveled along the N1 and into Dublin. At least we didn't run over anyone or anything, except for clipping the side mirror on a parked car.

"I think this thing's tires haven't been properly filled. It keeps pulling to the right."

We approached the downtown area, my hands clenching the wheel.

"A bus lane. I could give a rat's ass if this is reserved for public transport vehicles. I'm taking it." I checked the rearview mirror to be sure I wasn't cutting off anyone, like a large bus. Terror spread across Bev's pale face.

We crossed the Liffey to the south side of the city, blasting the horn as people crossing against the lights scattered. Bev screamed like someone on a carnival ride or rollercoaster plunging down a steep grade.

"No way I'm going near the music store on Dawson Street. Steve, Jeremy, and Candi will have to figure another way to get the gear to Feeney's." We sat at a long stoplight, me massaging my spasming palms, the bus's idle an irritated grunt.

"Okay, I'll text Steve to let them know."

"St. Patrick's Cathedral has decent parking. We can walk to Feeney's from there." I yanked the wheel to follow the street to the ancient church.

Chapter Twelve

Rhett, you effing snake!" I yelled, slamming the door to Feeney's pub. The band leader shoved his glasses down his nose and looked in my direction. The manager immediately swabbed his cloth along the bar to a place where he could earwig. "A bus! You rented a goddamn bus!"

Bev trailed at my side. I never thought her olive complexion could get that ashen.

"Lark, so good to see you and most especially with much appreciation of your effort to get us our transportation." He smiled as if he hadn't heard me.

Bev swiped a smear of sweat from her usually perfect makeup, wiping her hand on her thigh. "I don't know how she found St. Patrick's Cathedral. The street names change. They're not where you can see them. Never mind that they're all in Gaelic." Her designer hoodie hosted emblems of large, dark circles under the arms.

"I wouldn't worry. As a contingency, I arranged for full coverage." Rhett continued to study the papers on the table next to Matt, who leaned toward a semicircle of empty glasses before him.

"We got lost in a residential area and high-centered in someone's front yard. By the time we could get out, the garden looked like a failed septic tank repair. Thank God Bev got the address. I hope the kid we just missed running over didn't end up in the hospital."

"Driving the bus may be too much for Lark to handle. Or anyone, except a licensed bus driver." Steve stood in the doorway, Candi and Jeremy right behind with the rented band instruments. "Thanks for the text, Bev."

"Got your keyboard, Matt," Jeremy grunted. "You wanted to check it out." Stretcher style, he and Candi lugged a less-than-gently used instrument and placed it in the stage area.

"You obviously have not toured internationally, Steve," Rhett raised his eyes, "or you would know that we do indeed require a bus to carry us and all our gear."

"He's right." Matt unzipped the keyboard case. "But this is a piece of shit. As a former concert pianist, Steve," Matt spat the words, "you should know better."

"It's all they had," Candi said. "By the way, we left the rest at the rental place because the gear was too heavy and bulky to carry on foot." She rummaged in her satchel. "I'll do a blessing chant, so that you get the best notes the keyboard has to offer."

"We can do that later as our imminent departure is of the essence. Where's the bus?" Rhett stacked a pile of papers on the table and shoved them into his portfolio.

"With the tour buses at St. Patrick's Cathedral. The fact that I got into the city minus a major collision is a miracle." I made a mental note to thank St. Christopher.

"Good work, Lark. Y'all will be pleased to know that I spent the afternoon emailing the booking agent in Texas and phoning the venues. Got it all straightened out. Where's Limerick? We're at Sweeney's in Limerick tonight."

I gulped. "Limerick? As in the city of?"

"Yeah. Is it far from here?" Rhett jotted a note on his itinerary, which by now consisted of jumbled arrows, lines crossing out dates, and odd words that must have been his attempt to sound out Irish places. He'd circled and numbered names of cities: Limerick, Waterford, Cork, Dublin, Dundalk, Monasheskin.

"South of here a bit," I said. As in this is a bit of an understatement. Or this is a bit of a jaunt. Or this is a bit crazy.

"Well, the travel guide says everything's about an hour from Dublin. We should make it in plenty of time. You okay driving, Lark?"

"Driving? Are you nuts! Getting to Limerick will take hours, and assuming we don't get majorly lost or in a huge collision in that tank you rented, probably all day." I snatched the guide and threw it in the corner. "Only way we're gonna get to Sweeney's is if I drive us to the airport to catch a flight." *Did I really volunteer to drive?*

"I ordered that bus specially for our tour," Rhett whined, "specifically modified to meet our requirements for comfort and portability of our equipment. We need it."

"No way you can get to Limerick on time in a bus," the bartender called.

Chapter Thirteen

ooks like you got a choice. Cancel tonight or pick up the bus when we're back in Dublin in a few days." The dizzying chill of Bev and my recent ride settled in my stomach. I pushed the thought away that I would soon enough be behind that wheel again.

"Okay then, I say we'd better be on our way. Nice to do business with you, Pat Feeney, my man." Rhett nodded and gestured for us to follow. "We're fixin' to high tail ourselves to the hostel, pick up our luggage, then on to the music store to grab the rest of the equipment. From there, get to the bus. Lark, you take the lead. You know the quickest route."

"See you in a week," Feeney called. I wondered if he made himself a bet on whether that would actually happen.

~~~

We arrived at St. Patrick Cathedral's parking lot in a taxi van and began to load everything onto the rental bus.

"Well, Lark, I suspect this vehicle departed the rental agency premises this morning in a more pristine condition." Rhett's palm traced the scraped sides and tapped along the panel's length.

"Watch it. You think you can do this any better?" I surveyed the buses, lined in perfect parallels to each other—until ours hastily parked at a catawampus angle. Making a quick round and chatting with the tour guides,

I finally located a driver about to return his tour group to Dublin International. When I pointed to our bus and asked if I might follow him, he looked me up and down as if trying to determine if I was for real.

"Looks to me like you're a real chancer, driving that bus. Sure you're to have a special license to even sit behind the wheel. Did you not know that?"

"The rental guy told me my license was okay."

"I'd say he was having a laugh at you. But you're welcome to tag along. Just don't be crashing into me from behind." He tapped the visor of his cap and climbed aboard his tour bus.

Back at our bus, I leaned my back against the steering wheel to face the group, belted in, faces expectant. "We're going to follow a tour group. They're leaving shortly. That'll help us get to Dublin International alive. Also, not a word from any of you so I can concentrate."

My guide in the tour bus pulled out of the slot and honked as he passed. I scrambled to back up and follow. Perpendicular to the main street, he turned. Rather than ride his bumper, I hesitated. Aware of this vehicle's tendency to jump forward, I then eased to the exit onto the main street.

Candi and Bev's screams filled the bus as a woman pushing a pram holding two small kids collided with my front bumper. I added to the shrieks, prayed the brake would prevent a catastrophe, and leaned on the horn.

She gave me the finger, tossed her head, and proceeded along the parking lot entrance.

Not a religious person since reaching adulthood, I astounded myself at how many saints I called on during the next half hour, internally crossing myself at each church we passed. These streets weren't meant for something this big. Ever.

The tour bus in front of me maneuvered seamlessly along the route to the airport. A chorus of voices behind me slid up and down octaves while I slid around the corners in the wake of the tour bus and barely missed a line of parked cars. If an oncoming bus hadn't swerved, we would have been toast.

I stamped the brake and parked in the exact same space I'd vacated earlier that morning. Bev wrenched the door handle, darted down the steps, and ran to the perimeter of the blacktop. She leaned over, shoulders heaving up and down, as if she might vomit.

"You did right fine," Rhett called, descending the steps. "All's it's gonna take is a bit of practice. This precious vehicle will do us well when we return. Lark, take care of the rental business, and I'll go get luggage carts."

"FYI, Rhett, I'm not driving this train wreck of a bus again. I'm not licensed. Either you figure out decent transportation or find someone else to drive." My stomach rose to meet my diaphragm, and I swallowed.

"I'll take your feedback under consideration. Matt, follow me and help. Let's get our gear and hurry or we'll miss our flight. Candi, Steve, Jeremy, y'all unload the bus." Rhett swanned away.

Like a drunkard on a bender, I listed down the steps and heaved onto the front tire. Lifting my head, a handkerchief dangled in front of my nose.

"Here," Steve rubbed my back. "I don't envy you. You did a hell of a job just now."

Accepting the handkerchief, acrid vomit tainting my mouth and stinging my nostrils, I scrubbed at the front of my jacket, then winced, gratitude washing over me. I would have had a tsunami of gratitude if Jeremy had proffered the handkerchief.

"Thanks." He waved his hand to reject my offer to return his hanky. "We'll catch up with you. Bev and I gotta speak to the rental guy about the accidents."

I took Bev's arm. "Are you okay?" She nodded, and we marched into the office. I slammed the keys on the counter.

"Hey, Rental Guy," I shouted banging the little bell.

From a darkened room he emerged. "Back so soon? How'd you get on with that fine touring car?"

"We're bringing the bus back. We have to catch a flight to Limerick.

By the way, seeing *she's* fully covered, you'll have to contact a house in the Castle Keep area on Moat Lane to repair their garden." I wrote the address on the contract. "You may receive a request to reattach the side mirror to a car parked on the side of the road on the N1. Most importantly, check hospitals in case they admitted a kid who narrowly missed getting run over by this crap vehicle."

Rental Guy followed us into the parking lot and gave a low whistle when he saw the rhododendron branches decorating the windows, the large scrape along the side, and the mud-encrusted tires.

"By the way, I met a tour bus driver, who told me I'm not licensed to drive this shit-tub. So bang on."

Chapter Fourteen

We settled into the flight to Shannon airport.

"The good news is the Irish aren't terribly punctual," I said to Bev.

She leaned over. "Did you see what the itinerary looks like?" I shook my head. "What an absolute mess. Something's weird about this tour, where we're supposed to go."

At nine o'clock, we lugged our equipment into the venue. Even by Irish standards, we were late. Needless to say, the owner was perturbed. But we had luck on our side. The first act, a traditional Irish quartet, complete with harpist, played extra-long, followed by dancers who looked like refugees from River Dance. All seemed glad of the potential for extra tips and to sell CDs.

I tightened a screw on the mic stand. "Rhett, did you check out the house?"

Oblivious to his surroundings, he shook his head, then squinted at the room full of white linen tables surrounded by folks whose hair was about the same color. He blanched. "I recognize those heads from our flight from the US," he said.

Steve and Candi emerged from the communal restroom. Bev had remained outside waiting for some non-unisex privacy.

"How tacky." She rolled her eyes, shaking her head.

I grinned. "Welcome to the world of band tours," and dinged my cowbell. "Wonder what he and Candi were up to? A little unisex in the bathroom?"

Jeremy came back from talking up the patrons. "You'll never guess about this group," he said. "They're cemetery owners from the National Association of Cemetery Administrators or NACA." He pointed at the audience seated at large round tables, the linen spotted with wine and dinner droppings.

To me, the acronym resembled a foreign language word for bat guano. "Could be a dying breed," I said. "They all have to be at least 100."

I pictured some hunchback, shovel in hand, digging solitarily in a rectangle of soil, while his master gallivanted through Ireland's megaliths. Maybe these administrators were on a hunt for memorial ideas. Perhaps little megalithic mounds like mini-Newgranges would sprout across the US. Forget mausoleums. Nothing like a cairn that emits light only on the winter solstice.

"They're Americans?" Bev's eyes widened as she surveyed the packed hotel dining room. "That could be us in the not-so-distant future."

"Shut your mouth, girl," I said.

"They're like my grandmother's age." Jeremy craned over my shoulder at the crowd.

"What? Was she ten when she had her kids?" In a dramatic huff, I swung around, only to collide against Steve's chest, my cowbell clattering to the floor.

He shook his head. "Slow down." He placed his hands on my shoulders and turned me. "The mic's over there."

"I know where the mic is." What did he think I was, a recruit from a middle school band?

"Could've fooled me."

The drummer climbed onto his stool. "This is awesome. I found out their motto is 'Can you dig it?'"

I winked at Jeremy, hoping he'd wink back, but he just nodded at Candi, who took her place by the mic next to me, Bev at her heels.

Matt depressed a key on the portable piano, which emitted a moan like an out-of-tune accordion. "This piece of shit is going back."

Steve picked up his guitar. "The audience is not what I expected, but considering some of our gigs back home, at least we get a paycheck."

The pub owner stepped onstage. "And now Band of Pirates just down from Dublin today."

"Isn't that fraud?" Bev mumbled out of the corner of her mouth.

"I dunno. We did come down from Dublin," Candi said.

Rhett began our usual pillaging opener on his pennywhistle. And we began our playlist.

The encore concluded—the crowd loved us—Rhett urged, "Push the CD and T-shirt sales, ya' hear?"

I did the Irish accent thing, so we actually did pretty well. Yay Bev for negotiating the percentage of sales, but in light of the day we'd had, even ten percent wouldn't have been enough.

The last patron departed, the rumble of their tour bus faded into the night. No Rhett in the dining room where the rest of us packed up the band equipment. I hustled through the venue and caught him shepherding a woman out the door.

"Rhett, you didn't tell us where we're crashing tonight. Hostel or hotel?"

"Welcome to the world of touring. I'm afraid you're on your own. Screw up and all with the schedule. You'll do right fine. Limerick is known for its array of accommodations that can fit any budget." Rhett sounded like a sleazy tourist brochure. He draped his arm onto the waist of the barmaid he'd managed to pick up.

"You're leaving us here without a place to crash? What the hell were you doing on the phone all afternoon? Didn't you even think about where we'd stay after the gig tonight?"

He lifted his head, leaning into the woman, and spoke over his shoulder. "Lark, that's where your expertise comes in as our guide. I'm sure you'll quite efficiently lead our compatriots to a restorative place to sleep."

He ambled out the door and into the night down a rain-drenched street through a kaleidoscope of reflected neon lights. By that point, everyone else heard me yelling and gathered.

Bev's look said, *Tally another for him*.

"How did he do that? Hustling that woman. What did he have? Ten minutes while we were setting up?" Steve asked.

"Longer than that. While we were selling tees after the set, he got his own *T*s, not to mention *A*s in the bar," Matt said. "Pretty clever. Wish I'd thought of that, but too late now."

In the next room, a vacuum crooned.

"Where do we go to get paid?" Steve scanned the room, now a bevy of naked table rounds.

"In there." Jeremy jerked his head in the direction of the bar.

I strode to the lounge. "Well, then let's get our pay and get going. We still might be able to get into a hostel. Do you think Sweeney will let us store our gear here for the night?"

The place had a sleepy, whiskey smell that meant everyone had tucked in for the evening. Everyone but us.

"Jameson neat." I tapped the bar to signal the bartender.

"We've already had last call." An elderly gentleman wiped the counter, the mirror behind him a play of glass curves and light.

"Fair enough," I said. "Do we talk to you about our pay?"

"That would be our man Sweeney." He eyed me, his disapproval of a woman dealing with money matters, let alone money matters in a lounge, evident in the squint of his eyes.

"Could you be getting your man Sweeney?" I asked. He ignored me, instead shooting an answer to Matt, who leaned on the cleaned surface.

"I'll see what I can do."

"Thanks, man," Matt said. "In the meantime, would you mind pulling me a pint?" He had apparently not heard about last call.

The fellow, probably in his late sixties, perhaps even older, bent, fetched a mug, and shoved it under the tap. "This is between you and me."

"Much appreciated. Could you draw one for each of my mates here? They've worked awfully hard tonight."

The man slid each of us a pint. Not my choice, but anything looked good. My back ached from the wild mouse ride on the bus, and my body couldn't decide whether it was exhausted or still on US west coast time.

We'd drained half our pints when their man Sweeney ambled in, his face carrying the remnants of too much frowning and brow furrowing for one day.

"Did your band leader not tell you? That is your pay." He gestured to our half empty glasses.

"A pint apiece. That's all we're getting? After all that?" Candi banged her mug on the counter.

Sweeney ignored her, speaking to Matt, whose glass sat empty, a rim of foam around the lip. "You were late. You made a hames of my evening. I had to pay the other acts to play longer. Did you not read the contract? By rights, you should get nothing. But I'm a generous man, so there's your pay."

"Not mine." Steve gestured to the full pint before him. "I'm allergic to alcohol."

"No, he's not," Bev whispered.

"Shhhh," Candi elbowed her. "He's negotiating."

"So's three-quarters of Ireland and that's not stopping 'em. Drink up, we need to close now. So you know I'm not a complete gouger, you can store your gear in the back room." Sweeney waved toward the door. He obviously had said as much as he intended, striding off and making a show of dimming the lights.

Five minutes later we stood outside in the rain, huddled under the venue's overhang. Candi yelled into her cell, ripping into Rhett's voice mail and demanding he find us a place to crash. Did she have a clue about

80

roaming charges?

The bartender locked the pub's door and paused. "Do you not have lodging for the night?"

Candi shook her head.

"You'll have trouble at this hour. You might have been able to get in at the hostel, but they're closed up tighter than a bodhran by now. It's bucketing down. Don't tell me you didn't make arrangements beforehand?"

"We came straight from the airport." Matt's lips were a tight line across his face. "Thanks to Rhett's poor planning."

"All right then. You can stay here tonight, but you're to be up and ready to leave first thing. If my son catches a whiff that you were here...." He led us to the dining room. "You can use the dirty linen for bedding."

Steve and Matt staked out territory in each corner at the far end of the dining room, the former constructing some kind of bed using several chairs with padding from folded tablecloths. Matt settled atop one of the table rounds.

Jeremy and Candi grabbed another corner, the drummer gallantly piling tablecloths and encircling the space with chairs for privacy.

"Looks like chivalry isn't completely dead," I mumbled, remembering how Lance made such a show of spreading his cloak on the grass. Bev didn't answer. I figured she'd fallen asleep. From across the way, a wuffle noise started up as Candi snored.

~~~

The smell of whiskey-infused carpet and Bev tugging on my sleeve snagged me from that odd place between dreaming and consciousness. "You gotta see this," she whispered.

Steve had wedged himself between the group of chairs, the linen like a collapsed hammock. Matt had surrendered his position on the table and curled up on the carpet, swaddled in the cloths. Jeremy and Candi spooned across the room.

"I didn't want to say anything when the others were around." She

81

gestured with her chin toward the storage area where we'd left our gear. "This is pretty weird. Tell me what you think."

I sprang to my feet following her to the closet. She cracked the door, slipped through, and flicked on the light. Checking the room and behind me, she tugged Rhett's portfolio case from a shelf and popped the latch. She teased out a sheet of paper

"That's the set list. What's so weird about that? Did Rhett switch around the song order again?"

"Remember when Rhett disappeared while we sold the CDs and tees? We thought he was seducing some woman. I followed him. He did a lot more. He was studying the papers he had on the table at Feeney's. After everyone fell asleep last night, I snuck in here." She fished out pictures and showed me one of a smashed body, the color and shape of tanned leather. "Take a look. This is way twisted. And creepy."

"That's a photo of a bog body. Like I found in the book in Rhett's bed-side table that night at renn faire."

"That's a bog body?"

"Yeah, those are the ones I was talking about awhile back. We should check them out at the National Museum in Dublin. Looks like a peat combine chopped that one in half before the poor driver saw it. Sucks to be him. Or the family who bought the peat with the other half for that matter."

"I am totally grossed out." Bev shivered. "What about this?" She rifled further into the portfolio.

At first glance, the sheet was another one of Rhett's schedules, a tangle of illegible arrows and squiggles.

"Whoa! Let me see that." I snatched the paper out of Bev's hands. "That's not our itinerary. It's a map of some kind." The markings pointed at odd-shaped, concentric circles and lines. "Those numbers and slash marks could be a date. That's when we're playing the Bog Snorkeling Festival at Monasheskin."

"What are you two doing up so early and in here?" Steve's form

82

blocked the doorway.

I stepped in front of Bev, shielding her while she snuck back the picture and map.

"With the screw-up yesterday, I'm checking our itinerary to be sure we can get there on time." Sweat sprang into my scalp and underarms, leaving me acutely aware that I needed a shower.

"Well, you better put them back. Rhett finds out you've been messing in his backpack, you're worse than toast."

Chapter Fifteen

We sat in chairs like listless marionettes, while Candi scrolled through her phone looking for any message from Rhett. The tinkle of a bell followed by a door being closed announced the bartender in the entryway.

"My wife made you soda bread." He waved a bag. "Follow me." He rustled in the kitchen, producing mugs of tea, cream, and sugar, then set to work frying eggs.

"Chef keeps a tight watch on this. He won't miss the tea, and the eggs are easily explained. But you must be quick. If my son catches us, he'll have me head." Sweeney the Elder placed a plate with eggs and a stack of plates on the aluminum kitchen counter.

Matt wiped breadcrumbs off his chin. "So, the manager we talked to last night is your son?"

"He is indeed."

"Sucks to be you." Candi shoved a forkful of eggs in her mouth. "These are delicious."

"He's not such a bad lad." Sweeney the Elder scrubbed the scrambled eggs pan and hung it in the rack. "Tends to eat the head off when he's knackered."

Jeremy pulled a face.

"He doesn't deal well with stress," I translated.

We ate, exchanging small talk until the front entrance bell rang and Rhett, bless his randy heart, stepped into the kitchen.

"I've rented a van." He snagged a piece of soda bread.

We ignored him. He looked too well-rested, his hair still a tad wet, which meant he'd also scored a shower.

Bellies full, we loaded our equipment into the van, Sweeney having followed us to the curb. I realized that my life in the US had narrowed my ability to feel gratitude along with the sensitivity to appreciate small niceties. Candi impulsively twisted and hugged the elder Sweeney, his eyes exclaiming at the familiarity. But when she backed away, his broad smile said that taking care of us had been worth the risk.

"Lark, darlin', you will take the co-pilot seat for this leg of the journey. I'm fixin' to experience all of Ireland's charm, including its infamous highways and byways." Rhett in the driver's seat adjusted his rearview mirror.

I climbed into the seat, hoping for a little respite. However, that morning I learned co-pilot meant co-vigilant. He did all right on the motorway, except for navigating the roundabouts. Then he took the wrong exit, and we rambled along narrow roads, lost.

"Do you want me to take over?" I sucked the blood where I'd bitten into my lower lip at his sudden braking. *Did I really volunteer to drive again?*

"I'm doing right fine." He crept along a tertiary lane, jammed between two hedgerows that blocked any view of the surrounding countryside, his knuckles white from his shrinking vehicular confidence.

After a few more kilometers, he twisted his head in my direction. "Lark, we require your navigational abilities. Time to step up to the plate, or rather the driver's seat. This handles like a damn bus."

"As if you'd know," I shot back.

He scouted for a spot to pull over. And then a real bus hurtled around the bend, headed directly at us. Rhett bellowed, cranking the wheel. The tires screeched, we screeched, and the van screeched to a halt, teetering on the edge of a ditch. I watched in terror as the tour driver averted the head-on collision, the passengers' faces too close and mirroring our panicked expressions.

The bus disappeared around a curve.

Heavy panting from the back seats matched the van's idling engine. The smell of soap mixed with sweat drifted toward me from the driver's seat. Rhett unclipped his seatbelt. "Lark, I do believe we've had enough excitement for one morning. That tour bus driver should be reported for reckless endangerment. I surrender the wheel to you."

I pried my fingers loose from the door handle as Rhett exited, the rush of cool air causing the windows to fog. "You'd best get your body to the shoulder. Another vehicle comes 'round that corner, we'll be scraping you off the asphalt." I scooted into the driver's seat, while he fought his way around the hood to the passenger side.

"You know, when I commented that all roads lead to where you're going, I didn't mean for you to prove it." I snapped the seatbelt. "I'd forgotten how claustrophobic these roads are."

"I still don't see the point of renting that damn bus at the Dublin Airport." Steve's breath was like a warm breeze in my hair as he leaned forward.

"Let's have this conversation again after we've spent a few days crammed in this thing, like a tin full of gulf shrimp." Rhett elbowed his way into the third row, the click of his seatbelt unmistakable.

"Agreed. Let's also have that conversation about who's going to drive that bus in Dublin. Remember, Lark isn't licensed." Steve's seatbelt clicked into place, and if possible, even louder. Were they having a clicking contest?

We shuffled passengers, Jeremy now in the navigator's seat.

I put the van in gear, thrilled at the prospect of spending a morning with the drummer. "Now that Rhett has experienced Ireland's highways and byways, we can get back to the motorway."

"Did you get any sleep?" Jeremy reached in his jacket pocket. "Candi forgot her nasal strips. If we end up sleeping like that again, you might want to get these." He opened his palm revealing a pair of earplugs. *Would it make any difference to our sleeping arrangements if he knew I didn't snore?*

"Bev, what's your GPS friend say?" I accelerated along the country road.

"Follow this road to a roundabout that'll take you to the highway." She yawned.

My co-pilot leaned his head against the passenger window, shoulders rising and falling rhythmically, my one-on-one with Jeremy lost to his nap.

"Hey guys." The rearview mirror revealed comatose faces. "We have at least a three-hour drive ahead of us. I could really use some noise from you all to keep me awake."

Nothing other than wuffling from the back two rows of seats. I punched the radio button, and out came a chatty voice speaking Gaelic. That would keep me focused, trying to translate what little I remembered from my compulsory Irish classes. Pieces of words fell into slots in my brain. A break-in at the National Museum in Dublin. A body. Then a word I couldn't remember. Dirt? Peat? Gardai– police. Important? Sacred? Professionals. Thieves. That got my full attention. So much for Irish. I twiddled the dial to find an English-speaking station.

A cultured Irish voice announced, "And now the news. Gardai continue to gather evidence in the Kingship and Sacrifice Gallery in Dublin's National Museum, where recently one of the rare bog body antiquities was stolen. James Cahill, the security guard on duty, was found unconscious near the display case that had enclosed the relic. Gardai would only comment that they are following all leads, stating the break-in appeared well-planned. A priceless gold torc and earrings are also missing."

I stifled a gasp, recalling my Skype with Mom and my nightmare the evening before leaving the US. Too strange that Rhett stashed that picture and map. What could he have to do with this horrible crime?

"Hey, let's get some tunes going or we'll all find ourselves in a ditch. How can you stand that boring stuff?" Jeremy jolted awake and twirled the dial until out poured the raucous voices of Flogging Molly. "That'll keep you awake."

"Hey, I was listening to the news." Rhett sat upright, eyes reflected in the mirror and riveted to the front.

"Right on man, no harm." Jeremy twisted the radio dials until a news station once again filled the van. A chill crawled between my shoulder blades, fingering the nape of my neck.

"Expect showers off and on throughout the day. And that concludes the morning news."

"Never mind," Rhett leaned his head against the window.

~~~

Our next gig was on the same order as the previous one: Pandering to tourists. Harps and sentimental songs served with the complimentary pint of Guinness at Sweeney's in Limerick was one thing, but this was in a whole different league. Located on the outskirts of Waterford, this venue resembled a theme park featuring a Cistercian monastery, based on a very, very loose interpretation of history. The grounds hosted a round tower, a crumbling castle, and a couple of beehive huts thrown in for effect. To what effect was hard to say. Tacky, maybe? The base of the tower contained a kiosk loaded with the usual paraphernalia: a huge selection of souvenir Viking helmets, faux gold collars, Book of Kells posters, Guinness tankards, and monk dolls.

"You must be the Band of Pirates." A petite woman emerged from the bowels of a large, oval-shaped building that looked like a Roman had taken a wrong turn somewhere. "I'm Nikki." She dressed in couture trousers and a sweater, her blue-black hair cut in a perfect bob. A slash of eyeliner fringed her almond eyes, and I was immediately jealous of her perfect ivory skin. She spoke in a soft Dublin brogue, and something else as well. Her manner indicated she'd attended one of the best schools in

Ireland.

"Bet she didn't get that from the kiosk." Bev nodded at the exquisite gold necklace and earrings. Her left hand's ring finger flashed a huge diamond.

"The business must be doing well," I said.

Nikki reached out to shake Rhett's hand, which he lifted to his lips. As he released it, a fleeting expression of disgust crossed her features before they arranged themselves into a flawless mask.

"I bet she thinks St. Patrick missed one of the snakes when he drove them out," I whispered to Bev.

When Nikki came to Steve, he hesitated a moment to process the outstretched hand and extend his. Then a surprising thing happened. She clasped his fingers a fraction longer than the others.

"Hmm. Wonder how this is going to play out," Bev murmured.

"Discreetly is my guess." I gave a sideways smile as we took up the tail end, proceeding into the banquet hall.

Nikki turned to us as if addressing a tourist group. "Please follow me. I will give you a quick tour regarding this evening's performance." She pivoted to enter the building without looking to see whether we would follow.

The venue consisted of a huge arena rimmed by a table, so that the customers faced toward the center as if dining at a banquet.

"To be sure you're used to this kind of…event." Nikki gestured to the hall. "Frustrating it is when we book a group who can't get into the spirit of our entertainment." Her expression flickered.

She led the way toward a ladder and descended to the middle of the concrete arena, the slight smell of chlorine emanating from the walls. Standing in the pit, she looked even more petite. She gestured for us to join her.

"You've heard about popular culture? Well, this is tourist culture at its best. Our guests line the oval." She pointed above to the wooden band with table settings surrounding the arena. "We fill the area where you are

89

standing with water. Your boat will come along these tracks." Nikki's arm arced indicating two doors at opposite ends in the side of the arena, an entrance and an exit. A pair of rails emerged from the set of doors, traveled down the middle, and disappeared through another set of doors.

"We do two feasts a day. You do have your contract with you?"

"I just so happen to have it right here." Rhett angled closer, retrieving his portfolio.

"This is gonna get interesting. Whatcha bet Rhett scores tonight?"

"A Viking helmet," Bev answered. "I'm rooting for Steve."

The guitarist's lean form leaned against the ladder, nodding his head as he checked out the concrete oval. He seemed too decent to pull off the crap Rhett was capable of.

"Our event is a reenactment of famous moments in Irish mythology and history." Nikki straddled the rails, delicately stepping toward the far end of the hall. We all followed in a raggle-taggle line and then climbed a small ladder. Bev elbowed me and pointed to Nikki's shoes, probably in the $1,000 a pair range.

At the far end stood a man in gray-green trousers with Wellies to his knees. At Nikki's nod, he leaned over, making a twisting motion. From the sides, water gushed from a ring of fire hoses.

"You're to be about mid-feast. We've made a slight alteration." Nikki increased her voice to compensate for the water as she distributed the program-menus the guests would receive.

Rhett peered over her shoulder. "We're not on here, darlin'."

A sliver of a grimace pierced her mouth at the endearment. "But sure you are." Nikki pointed about a quarter of the way down. "That's the slight alteration."

"We're booked as Band of Vikings?" Matt's eyebrows met at the bridge of his nose, apparently having trouble getting into the spirit of the venue's entertainment.

"Why yes. The transition is seamless. Vikings. Pirates. Both were into pillaging and looting." Nikki's lips pressed inward, resembling more of a muscle twitch.

"But how are we going to sell our CDs and tees? I know that's in the contract." Matt's square jaw jutted.

"No problem," Rhett said. "'Sides who cares about a slight name change? We're the centerpiece."

"But our songs won't make sense. You know, like the ones about Queen Bess."

"We're cutting your first set to about fifteen minutes. You'll be followed by a barge that transports our Viking re-enactment actors. Then you'll come back again as the Band of Pirates. You can sing it then. If you look closely, you'll see your band's name about two-thirds of the way down in the program." Nikki paused. "You are aware that this part of the island was renowned for its pirate activities? The O'Driscolls ambushed Spanish ships bound for Waterford's port from a fishing village at the tip of County Cork. So yes, your repertoire will work brilliantly."

Her voice, barely above conversational volume, had the measured tone that made it hard to determine how she felt about us. I sensed we'd been put in the "dumb American tourists" category, in company with the majority of her customers.

"Y'all, I have ancestors who were O'Driscolls, meaning one of us is extraordinarily authentic." Rhett winked at her, but Nikki remained impassive.

"Give me a break," I whispered. "He's about as authentic as one of those torcs in the kiosk."

"Or one of those bobble head monks." Bev elbowed me, inclining her head toward Rhett, who nodded and grinned, having rested a hand on Nikki's shoulder. The venue owner stepped sideways and continued down a hallway.

She paused. "Your dressing room is in here. You'll find the costumes for your Band of Vikings number. After that number, you'll have exactly nine minutes to change into your pirate costumes for your second entrance. I expect I have answered any questions you may have." Nikki turned on her exquisite heels, disappearing into the bowels of the arena.

We found ourselves in the dressing room, complete with bathrooms and showers. Showers! Never did hot water washing the previous day's grime down the drain seem so delightful.

We prepared for a dress rehearsal.

The whole thing reeked grade B movie set, especially when we had to put on white robes and armor that looked like rejects from the kiosk. We backup singers wore helmets with blond braids trailing and plastic breastplates, resembling escapees from a Wagner opera.

A stagehand escorted us to a dock behind a huge, faux wooden door, where he had arranged our gear on the stern of the Viking boat. A gigantic sail loomed overhead, occupying any space not taken by us and the equipment. I expected the boat to rock as we stepped on deck, but the concrete floor was solid.

"The boat's stable she is." The stagehand bounced his flattened palm as if he had just calmed a severe storm.

"We're supposed to play on this thing?" Matt asked. "You know if we get splashed, we'll be electrocuted."

"Not to worry. The group you're to be substituting for has done this for years and had nary a shock. The boat glides the length of the arena while you play. When your set is done, she goes through the exit on the other side, while the re-enactment barge comes out."

Jeremy rolled his eyes toward the ceiling. "We're like animatronic Disney characters on one of those rides."

"It's a small world after all." Bev snickered, jabbing an elbow in my ribs.

The stagehand planted himself on the dock, folding his arms. "Come to think of it, there are more of you by three. Close quarters it'll be, but not to worry, the water's only this deep." He clapped his chest at his armpits.

"Y'all, let's do a sound check." Rhett picked up his tin whistle and tweeted the introductory notes of a whoring ballad.

"All our gear's setup wrong." Matt hoisted the electronic piano, the legs dangling like spider appendages. He staggered a few steps then placed the instrument down. "I guess this'll have to do." He twirled the dial and ran his fingers over the keys, low mumbles registering his disgust.

Jeremy clambered onto his stool, lifting the sticks, he executed a drum roll. "And the winner is...."

Steve slung his guitar strap over his shoulder, flipped the switch on the amp, the squawk of feedback blasting across the stern.

Candi, Bev, and I huddled by our mics.

"Y'all, let's run through 'Love of Queen Bess' to warm up," Rhett counted, "One and two and three."

The oversized sail absorbed most of the music. We backup singers couldn't hear the guitars or vocals, only Jeremy's drumming. Rhett scowled as we missed our cue.

"What an acoustic nightmare," Candi said as the last bars faded.

Steve bent over his trumpet case, lifted out his horn, and played "Taps." With a flourish, he replaced the instrument in the velvet-lined box.

"Hey, as long as we sound okay to the audience, I'm chill." I scratched my head under the itchy helmet. "Thank God, the worst part of today is wearing these ridiculous costumes."

Chapter Sixteen

From behind the electronic door, dressed in our Viking costumes, we assumed our places and awaited the intro. The helmet and braids wobbled on my head, the stupid thing threatening to fall in the arena and sink to a watery grave. In the dim light, small circles from Steve's amp illuminated his feet. Jeremy sat to the side of us, making a slight ping from his crash cymbal, as he settled into his seat in the dark.

"Where the hell did these cheapo costumes come from?" Candi retied her robe. "This is the last thing I expected."

Bev scanned the dock and hallway leading to the dressing rooms. "With these helmets we look like a herd of Texas longhorn cattle. Are you sure we're in Ireland?"

"I'm afraid so. Used to be Bunratty Castle was the tourist trap, but it had class."

An automated, baritone voice boomed from the other side of the door, intoning about the mists of history, the wild Irish countryside, invaded by Vikings on voyages of discovery and conquest. Deep bass, lost-in-time music rattled the doors. Then our cue, "Ladies and gentlemen, straight from Limerick, Band of Vikings." The doors retracted revealing a laser show flashing across the top portion of the arena. A mass of screens multi-projected images of green hills, shaggy people in woolen garments, monks, and round towers. Our mechanical ship moved forward into vapor drifting from a machine that pumped moisture across the water. The acoustics sucked up the notes and vocals. We sang in foggy cocoons, our signature pillaging song unrecognizable.

The ship sailed past an oval of faces all be-horned with the same kind of Viking helmet we wore. Mid-feast, faux candles illuminated the audience, creating a Halloween orange glow dispersed by the mist.

Surrounded by the surreal venue, we sang and moved like robots. I wondered about the impact to Ireland during the Celtic Tiger, what was lost, what was gained. Was our tour to play only these tourist traps? Maybe this was the new, real Ireland.

Then someone screamed.

The house lights went on.

The ship stalled.

At first, we didn't know what had happened. Bev, Candi, and I had been doing this side shuffle. The boat must have had weight sensors because Candi must have side-shuffled over the edge, and the boat automatically halted.

A roar erupted from the audience, either due to the sudden dissolution of the fantasy or concern about the bedraggled woman standing in water up to her armpits. The obnoxious, baritone voice reassured the spectators that a slight technical difficulty had occurred and to please remain seated.

There we stood, ordinary musicians and not the terrifying Vikings sailing into Waterford.

Jeremy and Steve reached the side, hauling Candi back on board. With that, the boat continued its journey to the other side of the arena. The lights dimmed while the show picked up again, although the magic had dissipated into the mists of illusion.

Backstage, Nikki arrived with little to say, presenting a face that was even more mask-like. I'm sure she relegated us to an even worse category—"drunk American tourists".

Candi, however, had a whole lot to say. "Something awful happened

95

when we were playing. In the fog, I felt a push, like when you hog the mic, Lark." She yanked off the helmet and threw it on the dock. "Then arms like dead tree limbs grabbed my ankle and dragged me off the boat. I fell onto a gruesome, hideous woman who tried to pull me under. The water smelled and tasted brackish." A stagehand wrapped a towel around her. Candi hugged it closer.

I may be a lot of things, but I'm not a diva. A little competitive maybe when sharing the spotlight, but not a diva. "Are you sure the swirling fog wasn't a part of the show? And I don't hog the mic, Candi."

"No, she had Dracula teeth. When I grabbed Steve and Jeremy's hands, she materialized next to Steve."

I tilled my memory for childhood tales of Irish demons, catching Nikki's eyes. "There's an Irish myth that a Dearg Due is buried under Strongbow's tree in Waterford."

"Except she does her blood-sucking on Samhain, which is a few weeks away." Nikki tucked a strand of hair behind her ear, reassessing her appraisal of us. No longer did we hold the coveted role of drunk Americans. We were now druggy Americans, tripping on a hallucinogen like magic mushrooms.

Jeremy stood behind Candi, rubbing her back. Not exactly like a protective lover. More like a friend at a spiritual retreat. What was that all about? He should be folding her in his arms. Shouldn't she be leaning into him? Hmm, a rift.

"You need to get ready for your next entrance. You've got nine minutes." Nikki consulted her watch, gestured toward the barge approaching on the rail for the Viking battle. "I am confident you won't fall off this time." The small, tight smile flew by so fast, I barely caught it.

We dashed to the dressing room to change into our pirate costumes, while behind us the clank of shields and swords meant the Viking actors were taking their places.

"Bev, you think both Rhett and Steve'll strike out?" My voice a mere mumble as we marched back toward the dock.

96

"Quite possibly," she shrugged, "and I was counting on that Viking helmet I bet you."

"Not one step further until I cleanse that boat!" Candi elbowed past brandishing a sheaf of some kind of herb.

"Where'd that come from?" Bev asked.

"Gathered fresh today when we crashed into that hedge. I've been getting these intuitions. Images. Now I know why." She rushed toward the boat, flicked a lighter, igniting familiar curls of smoke, smelling acrid, like weed and not the good kind.

"As if torching a warehouse wasn't enough," I said.

Candi disappeared toward the bow.

"You be keeping that stuff in the dressing room." The stagehand hoofed toward the backup singer.

"She's doing no harm." Jeremy stepped in front of the man, blocking his way. "Cleansing rituals are part of her religion."

"Religion my arse!" Nikki materialized. "She's a fire hazard. I want that put out now." Definitely not the anally constrained woman of earlier.

Candi tore down the gangplank. She stood on the dock and waved the sheaf, little bits of ash drifting onto her arms. "I think we're safe for now."

"You're sure to be burning the place down. Give me that." Nikki reached toward Candi, her tone stony. The backup singer held her ground, diverting her precious herbs. Almost as it happened, I knew where this would end. Nikki lost her balance, grabbing Candi's wrist, and plunging them both off the dock.

"You be getting on that boat." The stagehand shooed us up the gangplank. In a flurry, we took our places, minus our main backup singer.

"So much for Nikki's Italian shoes." I lifted my cowbell.

Bev groaned. "I would have killed for those."

From beyond the doors, a deep voice announced, "Behold Waterford's history, rife with pirates pillaging goods from Spain."

As the venue's doors opened, two bedraggled women hauled themselves onto the loading dock, while another ship approached from behind, soon to contain sword-wielding pirates.

After our set, Nikki had us quarantined in the dressing room until time for the second feast. Like armed guards, she and the stagehand escorted each of us to our positions on the boat. Rhett tried to make light of it, offering his arm and bowing as he took his place. Candi spent the set confined to the dressing room while the stagehand all but frisked the rest of us at each juncture.

Even crossing the border during the Troubles wasn't this difficult. Without Candi our backup support was thin if non-existent. I don't think any of us really cared. We yearned for the hostel and a decent night's sleep.

The show now over, Candi shoved clothes into a small carry-on. "I'm outta here."

Chapter Seventeen

Nikki planted herself in the doorway to the dressing room, monitoring the stage manager she'd instructed to escort us to our van. She glared at Candi as if daring her to make a run for it. Doberman Pinschers on heavy, metal leads, growling at Nikki's side, would not have looked out of place.

"You're forgetting these." Bev proffered a bouquet of herb-y type plants.

"Keep them. They'll save your lives, although you never did take me seriously." Candi pushed the bunch away and snapped up a shirt. "You have no idea about the evil in this country. But I do. You're in for a shit-load of trouble."

"Suit yourself." Bev shrugged. "Need any help packing?"

"Tell me again. What did you see?" A faint memory niggled at my brain.

"I've been having these nightmares. Awful. Angry dead. We've done something horrible to piss them off, and they are pursuing us with a vengeance."

"Okay, what else?" Recognition percolated, a childhood memory traveling through time and arriving in fragments. Maybe not a Dearg Due.

"I keep dreaming about bodies, holding us down. That's what I saw in the water. That's what hauled me off the boat. Horrific murders happened in the countryside. In my dreams, everything is brown, like a cemetery or place of the dead."

Folk remedies popped into my head. "Got any primroses in that bag of yours? Those plants keep the demons away."

"Afraid not. They're out of season. What about primrose oil?" Candi rooted in her satchel. "Here." She handed me a tiny bottle. "Maybe this'll help."

Bev clenched her jaw and rolled her eyes at me. *Don't tell me you're becoming as loony as her.*

"Not sure whether oil will do the trick. Folks used to plant primroses to keep the evil spirits out of their houses."

As we walked out, Nikki and the manager followed a few paces behind to make sure we would leave. No longer druggy Americans, I'm sure we were now mental asylum escapee Americans. She examined each piece loaded into the van as if we might attempt to steal the cheesy, Viking helmets and breastplates.

Candi heaved her bag next to the rest of our luggage, our gear in the boot, me cuddling the drum kit in the van's third row. The band leader already commandeered the wheel. Matt, as copilot, waited for Jeremy and Steve to emerge from the dressing room. If Rhett wanted to navigate those roads at night, he could knock himself out.

"How's Jeremy feel about you leaving like this?" Bev settled against the window in the middle seat next to Candi.

"Well, we sort of slid into friends with benefits." Candi sighed, closing her eyes.

"Doesn't seem very beneficial if you're not here."

Her face composed, she said, "We decided we'd explored our relationship as much as we could."

"Whatever works," I answered. I should rethink my stance on Jeremy. A concept worth revisiting.

The drummer jumped into the middle row at the last minute next to

Candi. I studied the couple, my radar pinging that more negativity or anger didn't flow between them. If Candi hadn't insisted on getting out of Ireland ASAP, we would have spent the night at a hostel, and then gone to play at a shopping mall opening the next afternoon. Instead, we found ourselves heading northwest toward Limerick—again—to drop her at Shannon Airport for a redeye.

We now faced the prospect of sleeping in the van. Everyone except Steve, who remained behind with Nikki. Wow, she'd even consider him given his present company? Generally hard to read, he totally gave himself away by the way he walked toward this Asian goddess with an Irish accent. He was awestruck. Good for him. For once Rhett would sleep in some back-breaking place like the rest of us.

"Looks like I owe you a Viking helmet." I nudged Bev. "Would you settle for a pint instead?"

The road to Shannon was uncomplicated. Exhausted from all the drama, I grabbed a snooze. Until the van quit moving, and Matt's cheap cologne wafted into my nostrils, dragging me out of unconsciousness like smelling salts. Somewhere along the way, he and Jeremy traded places. Neither a house, building, nor streetlamp illuminated the night.

"Where are we? More importantly, where's the motorway?" I raised my head from against the window. Rhett and Jeremy in the front, bent over the map, their faces the color of custard in the console light.

"I swear, Jeremy, you musta' screwed up. My distinct recollection is you bragging about your lengthy experience as a co-pilot." Rhett studied the map as if he had any inkling of where we were or how to get back on the main road.

"I told you to take the second exit off that roundabout." Jeremy jammed his finger at the paper. His ginger beard reflected copper in the interior's light.

"Jeremy, you are beyond passive-aggressive. Do you think if you got us lost, I wouldn't leave?" Candi asked.

"You think I did this on purpose? All you ever do is jump to conclusions." Jeremy twisted to face her. Fireworks between them. That's more like it.

"You've never believed that I am tuned into the nether world. Well, I am! The universe granted me a rare gift. If you're such a moron...." Candi's voice died, like a candle sputtering out.

Silence, the inside of the van like a tuna can, the lack of noise a black hole.

Then came Jeremy's voice, small and soft. "Candi Cane, I'm sorry, sweetmeat."

"Sweetmeat? Too much info." Matt squirmed. "This is not about your nauseating lovers' quarrel. Where we are now and getting Candi to the airport is critical."

"Thank you, Matt, for putting this back in perspective. Lark, can you take a look-see and figure out where we are?" Rhett passed the map over.

"Did all that fake fog soak into your brain? Like I'm supposed to figure out which particular hedgerows we're stuck between and point to the exact curly line on the map? All these back roads are the same." I tossed the map forward from my place in the third row.

"I commissioned you for an occasion such as this. Your fatigue has obviously affected your sensibilities. Y'all, let's reconnoiter at daybreak. A short way back, we passed a parking lot at a tourist attraction." Rhett switched off the overhead and turned the ignition.

The van pulled into a crescent-shaped area for a crumbling archeological site. I didn't care to read the placard. I wanted to go back to sleep. Bev on the bench seat in the second row leaned her head back and sighed.

Candi squished past Matt and hopped out of the van, then yanked open the front passenger door. "Jeremy Jube-Jube, I'm sorry. I didn't mean to lose my temper."

"Jeremy Jube-Jube? Where do you guys come up with that stuff? Make up someplace else." Matt zipped up his jacket, slumped, and propped his head against the seat.

"Watch it, dude," Jeremy said. "Candi, what say we snag the tarp

102

covering the equipment? We can sleep in that cleared space beyond the rocks. You're probably going to have to catch the next flight anyway. But at least we'll do what we had dreamed of, sleeping under the stars in Ireland."

They tugged off the tarp. The last slam of the boot lid brought quiet along with a bit of room to spread out. Candi and Jeremy's backs disappeared behind the gray standing stones. Matt and Bev shared the second-row bench. Rhett settled in the front passenger seat and flexed his grasshopper legs across the console. I remained curled up in the last row and drifted off, wondering whether the lovers' quarrel and make-up sex would work to my advantage once we dropped Candi Cane at Shannon.

Poor sleep brings the sort of unconsciousness that subsequently ushers in disorientation. At that moment between sleep and recognizing where I was, a scream streaked through the night air, flying nearer. The van rocked violently. The driver's side door burst open, admitting Jeremy and a rush of frigid air. Shoving Rhett to the side, he pawed for the keys in the ignition and started the engine, exhaust clouding the parking lot. Candi wrenched the side door handle, crowding against Matt and Bev. The headlights flashed, aimed at the archeological marker.

"I told you! I told you, and you all wouldn't believe me," Candi shrieked. "They came after us. Ripped the tarp to shreds. Horses. They were on horses. Their faces. Ugly, angry, brown faces. Distorted, smashed, flattened. We're all gonna be killed!"

The van spit gravel. "We gotta get outta here. Ghosts rode up over the rocks and through the stones waving spears, shouting, chasing us." Jeremy careened onto the main road.

The force threw me into the equipment, my shoulder taking the brunt of it. Bev crashed into Matt, who shoved Candi into the well by the door. Rhett landed face-first on the dashboard. We barreled past a sign, *Bruff, a Tidy Town*. Jeremy made any turn that came his way.

After a few freaked-out minutes, I calmed down enough to say, "Uh, Jeremy, why don't you pull over. I'll drive."

Like a fast-rotating wheel that gradually winds to a halt, Jeremy slowed the vehicle.

"A right good idea to drive, Lark. Jeremy, I am sure you are quite capable in other circumstances." Silhouetted against the windshield, Rhett held his head. He would have one hell of a bump.

The first thing I did was locate Bruff on the map. Bev forwarded her cell displaying a page about places of interest. "Do you have any idea where we were?" I squeaked. "Lough Gur's Grange Stone Circle. As a kid, I heard stories about that place. Weird, scary stories."

"I knew it. My instincts are always right." Candi's hysterical sobbing reverberated.

"Could you cry more quietly? I'm trying to listen to the GPS." Bev's voice cut through the wail.

I put the van in gear, headed toward the motorway, and hoped our GPS buddy wouldn't decide to abandon us in the middle of nowhere.

~~~

A mass of idling tour buses crowded the Shannon Airport departure area. I set the emergency brake, the predawn mist commingling with the smell of exhaust.

"I wish I could convince you to get outta here. I tried to stop the evil, but it's too powerful," Candi said.

"Well, you've been the backbone, darlin', but unfortunately this hasty maneuver has breached the contract. You'll be forced to forfeit any pay," Rhett said. "Consequently, I must warn anyone else contemplatin' a quick exit that the same will await her." He twisted his body in the passenger seat to speak directly at me.

The departing backup singer waved a middle finger in response and disappeared through the airport's sliding doors.

"Bev, you are to accompany your BFF as co-pilot, while I rest my head in the second row."

Jeremy, having had to say farewell to his beneficial friend, crawled into the third-row seat next to Matt and the drums.

"Good thing the mall opening we're playing is not far from the Viking venue. We still have to pick up Steve." I glanced out the window at the drizzle streaking the windshield.

"Lark, I suggest you earn your keep and haul ass." Rhett stretched his legs into the well by the door, pulled his hat over his face, and fell asleep.

"Maybe she's fey, Bev," my voice low in case Jeremy was listening.

"At the very least bi-," Bev said. "She and Jeremy were together for quite a while, remember? But why is that a big deal? It's never mattered to you before."

"Not gay. Fey. Candi might have the second sight. Growing up, people still talked about being blessed with the second sight, part of fairies, demons, and all those superstitions. But after the Celtic Tiger, I figured they had all disappeared. I never knew anyone who wasn't Irish to be fey. It doesn't add up."

"She's gone now anyway, so who cares what she is?" Bev mumbled, drifting off. The rearview mirror revealed Jeremy's profile, ginger beard drooping. He would definitely need cheering up.

~~~

"Steve, did you remember to get a warrant for our pay?" Rhett, Matt, and the guitarist rearranged the last of the gear in the van's boot. To say he strutted toward his seat or had that I-had-sex-last-night glow would be an exaggeration. At least he did us the favor of not rubbing it in our faces.

"Nikki considered the contract null after the water incident. Strict language prohibits any act that may dispel the venue's illusion. Also, we violated an endangerment clause when Candi lit her herbs. The whole Viking Enactment operation could be shut down just for that. I tried." Steve's mouth turned into a half-grin.

"I may have done some less-than-admirable things, but I'd never consider pimping my bandmates. I am deeply touched that you would do that on our behalf," Rhett said.

"What a load of bull. You struck out." Matt slammed the boot's lid, then headed toward the driver's seat. No one moved to stop him, so I figured, what the hell. We weren't that far from the mall.

"Like Candi failing to collect her pay makes any difference?" Bev, next to me in the second row, stretched her seatbelt across her chest.

"Kind of dilutes your threat, Rhett, especially cuz you directed your warning at me. You obviously don't know or remember that my mom still lives in the Emerald Isle."

"I am more than well aware of your familial situation." Rhett twisted from the co-pilot seat to face me. "I might add that it's beginning to dawn on me that you manipulated my good intentions. You could quite easily abandon us, which is why I'm letting others take the wheel. In the event that you do leave us up a creek without a paddle, so to speak, at least we will be able to fend for ourselves."

"If that's what you think, knock yourself out." I fished for the belt lock, fingers slipping. Steve's hand materialized and clicked the end in place. The scent of an expensive aftershave tickled my nose.

Matt tentatively moved the van forward, following signs for the motorway. Nothing came from the third row where Jeremy hunched in a fetal position.

Chapter Eighteen

The mall's ghostlike quality exuded businesses in distress, seeming more like a closing. We left the van in the delivery area and entered, passing vacant storefronts, a large pharmacy, and a Tesco grocery store. The place appeared empty, except for a distant babble, like the noise in a swimming pool. An old guy on a motorized wheelchair rolled by us alongside a phalanx of women pushing strollers and pursuing a herd of children. Music, reminding me of the ice cream truck back home, echoed from the far end of a corridor.

We rounded a corner. The noise intensified revealing a large area filled with people. Lots more were arriving. Real Irish! Rhett's face glowed, the expression of a pilgrim who has found the Holy Land, if one considers the Holy Land to consist of a child's carousel and music from the movie, *The Sting*.

Matt designated himself as our de facto business manager, which was fortunate, seeing Rhett proved himself inept. What a fiasco the tour had become with two nights resulting in no pay. Our new business manager disappeared into the crowd, returning a few minutes later.

"Found the mall manager, but you're not going to like this. We've been billed as the Band of Privates. You know, as in tribute to all those fallen." Matt dealt out copies of the handbill. "Someone obviously can't spell."

"Privates?" Jeremy dropped his copy of the flyer, watching it float to the floor.

Bev giggled. "Kind of amazing what a little typo can do. They're plastered all over. I saw them in the shop windows."

"Ironic." Steve folded his into a paper airplane. "I considered joining the Air Force after graduating high school." He launched his paper jet toward the ceiling.

"Well, maybe we're private pirates. Or pirate privates. Either way that makes us mercenaries." I scanned the half-completed food court stalls.

"Now what?" Matt grumbled. "Like any of us should be surprised. What a disaster."

"I suppose we could go on stage nude. But something tells me they're not the type to appreciate the humor," Bev said. "I suggest we stay in our street clothes."

"They're also not the type to appreciate our lyrics." Rhett gestured toward the kids on the mechanized carousel and the crowd of moms rocking strollers.

A rotund fellow sporting a military cut approached. "You don't strike me as the sort to be privates. Afghanistan or Iraq was it?"

"As well as relatives of our beloved fallen heroes," Rhett said.

Matt stepped in front of the band's leader. "Quite a mall you have here. We are delighted to be part of this event."

"Well, we've a number of acts before you. You can set up your instruments on the small stage." He pointed to a back wall. "As a by-the-way, we Irish call this a shopping center."

"One slightly small item." The band leader elbowed Matt away. "We've had a run of bad luck. Our military uniforms were lost by the airlines. Best we can figure is their whereabouts are in Argentina. We're reduced to playing in our street clothes."

Matt gaped at him. Bev gulped. Steve engrossed himself in examining a vacant shop window. Rhett was as ballsy as they come, but this was beyond the Pale. Jeremy didn't respond, remaining a few feet back, intent on scrutinizing a copy of the flyer on the floor.

The shopping center manager nodded. "What can you do? What you lack in the uniform department, I'm sure you'll make up in the patriotic music department."

Once the manager left, Rhett gathered us. "Look at all the little kids in this crowd. Our repertoire is not suited to this kind of occasion, so here's what we all are gonna do. We'll downplay the lyrics. Matt, blast the volume on your keyboard. Steve, use your lead guitar. Lark, Bev, ring them cowbells like your life depended on it. Jeremy, bang those drums in the kind of military beat that would make your mama proud. More swaying, less jumping and screaming. Most critical, slur your words."

Matt shook his head. "No need to remind you of the importance of our cash flow."

~~~

We more than frustrated the shopping center manager's expectations in the music department. No amount of theatrics. No amount of cowbell ringing or slurred words could hide the theme of our set. No way could the Band of Pirates morph into the Band of Privates and provide something on the order of patriotic songs about heroes, battles fought and won, or fought and bravely lost, or even fought.

In the end, Jeremy may have saved us, but not before we made complete asses of ourselves. Apparently, he had not been listening when Rhett urged us to downplay our set. If he'd executed a military beat, we might have faked it. Instead, he played this epic drum solo accompanied by a song that would have made Kurt Cobain proud.

The crowd went from exuberant poppy-waving at our arrival to stony silence where we competed with an infant's echoing squalls and the ice cream truck music. With the exception of oblivious Jeremy, we seemed to hold our breaths in anticipation of what might happen next. Would the unhappy crowd storm the stage?

Then Steve stepped up. With his trumpet.

Blasting out the notes to "In the Mood," riffing on the melody, he

109

proceeded to "It's a Long Way to Tipperary", lowered his horn and continued to tap his foot glancing toward Jeremy, waiting for him and the rest of the band to catch on. The drummer extended his sticks toward the ceiling only to drop them on the cymbals. As if we'd ridden a donkey cart off a cliff into the icy Atlantic, our gig crashed.

The manager waddled across the stage to cut off our set. A no-brainer that we weren't getting paid for this gig either. "Thank you, Band of Privates, for that most interesting tribute to our military. And now let me introduce…."

I jumped off the makeshift stage, determined to sidestep the agreement Mom and I made to see each other when the band got back to Dublin. Crazy as she could be, she occupied amateur status compared to this lunacy. Spying a coffee shop a bit down the way, I ditched the crowd to email her while the band packed up.

The free Wi-Fi crawled, my phone's inbox staggering to open. A banner trailed across the top with a late-breaking story: "Dublin's National Museum Targeted Again. Precious Antiquities Stolen." Too strange, so I tapped a quick email to Mom letting her know I was near Cork, not expecting anything back. My cell dinged, indicating an immediate reply.

My dear Lark, please be careful. We've had another break-in at the National Museum. It's in all the news. I'll see you soon. Love, Your Mam.

How bizarre. Then my heart plunged to my knees. All my life, Mom had the strangest way of communicating at the critical moment when I was in distress. In a land rife with spirits, I assumed that, through the umbilical cord or placenta, a woman received psychic abilities during her pregnancy. The reality was Mom always kept me at the front of her thoughts.

The afternoon took on a hallucinatory quality. No wonder. In four days, we'd slept about five hours. The only meals consumed were breakfast from the elder Sweeney and lunch from Nikki. In four days, we'd careened around the Irish countryside chased by pissed off Celtic ghosts and played to the weirdest audiences I'd ever seen—and that's saying

110

something, being a renn faire survivor. In four days, we'd lost a band member while another unraveled in front of us. I wandered to where the rest of my bandmates finished packing up the equipment.

"I know a tour can be grueling, but this?" Bev mumbled. "I've never been so exhausted or hungry."

"I'd sleep on that bench by the yogurt stand if only the parents and kids would leave, and that damn music would stop." My body felt as if it had been dragged through a bush backwards.

Jeremy sat cross-legged on the makeshift stage, staring at the ceiling and rocking slightly. He unwound himself, got up, and headed toward a doorway, the international sign for the restroom on top. I followed, confounded that he wasn't behaving according to plan—that is, replacing Candi with me—and afraid we may soon be visiting him in the psych ward of the local hospital. He hadn't engaged with anyone since she flipped us off at Shannon Airport.

Surveying the long, empty hallway, I gambled and, on impulse, pushed on the door to the men's. The smell of urinal air purifier overpowered my nostrils. I wondered if I should close my eyes in case I stumbled on a row of men in the midst of pissing contests.

The restroom housed a row of urinals preceding four stalls, the farthest being for handicapped use. I can never figure out why the disabled stall occupies such an inconvenient spot.

A gag reflex at the smell crowded my throat along with relief that Jeremy was the sole occupant. He leaned over the sink, the tap running. When he stood, water dripped from his beard, and he drew his palms down his wet cheeks as if attempting to wipe off his anguish. He turned a pained face toward me. His first step sent my radar into orbit. My stomach flipped like a sudden descent on a rollercoaster, and I knew what was coming next. In a single motion, he clasped his arms around me, burying his face in my shoulder, his beard soft and soggy in my neck. His hands ran down my back and grabbed my butt, my pelvis connecting with his. A tingle wrapped my shoulders, trickling down my spine to my stomach. I gasped, his lips traveling across my chin to my mouth. *This is really happening* streamed through my brain before my consciousness went to a place that focused only on the feel of his tongue meeting mine, his teeth tugging at my lower lip, and our bodies crab-walking to that inconveniently located disabled stall.

Jeremy twisted the hooks on my bra, and my boobs sprang free announcing, "Here they are for our mutual pleasure." His hands raced down my waist, fingers, like reading braille, undoing my belt, the button and fly to my jeans. My fingers reacted on his belt, button, and fly. My attention dropped to the pelvic region, the slight scratching of his pubic hair against mine, his penis searching between my legs, making me ache for what would come next. And then a little light in the back of my brain blinked urgently.

"Do you have a condom?"

"Oh shit! No." As if we hit the pause button on a DVD, we froze, balancing against the metal wall. "But I know where I can find one. Wait here." His briefs and pants still around his ankles, he toddled past the other stalls to a machine at the far end. Those damn disabled stalls! See what I mean about them being so inconvenient?

The clank of a dial rotating followed the clipped sound of coins falling through a slot.

Followed by the inward huff of the exit door.

"I see your willy's at attention," a gruff voice said. "Don't know how he can salute after the show you put on." Footsteps entered the stall next to mine, the bolt in the stall's lock engaging. A moment later, the exit door to the men's room closed, followed by a grunt in the neighboring stall.

Then all was silent.

Jeremy had abandoned me in that stinky place. The flip flops in my stomach turned from here-it-comes to run-for-your-life. I crouched in the corner by the toilet, where my neighbor wouldn't see my feet should he decide to look under the barricade.

I waited, the smell from a skirt of pee at the foot of the toilet wafting around the enclosure. My lower back ached, the cold from the tile spreading up my legs.

The toilet flushed in the adjoining stall. The door creaked open. The sound of water running drifted toward my hiding place and the ca-chunk of someone cranking out a paper towel.

"You can come out now," the voice called before I heard the whoosh of the door closing.

I buttoned my blouse, surveyed my clothes to be sure no tell-tale clues existed, then bolted to the exit. Shoving against the metal door, I felt a hard resistance and a loud growl on the other side. Springing out of the men's can put me chest-to-chest against Steve.

"What the hell?" He cradled his nose.

"You're going into the wrong jacks," I said.

"Unless I'm mistaken, the sign for women doesn't look like this." He pointed to the international symbol for men's restrooms.

I tilted my head at the sign. "No wonder the jacks had a urinal. My bad," and raced toward the food court.

~~~

"Where have you been?" Bev asked when I arrived back at the stage area. Standing in a semi-circle next to Matt and Jeremy, she folded her arms across her chest.

"In the ladies. I fell asleep leaning against the baby changing table in the disabled stall."

"But I checked," she began. I elbowed her side. "Everyone but that one."

Steve rounded the corner from the restrooms and snorted. "She went into the wrong can." He ambled to Rhett.

"Don't tell me you fell asleep in a urinal?" Bev's face recoiled as if she had landed hip-deep in a sewer.

"I'll tell you later," I whispered and glanced over to a young woman talking with Rhett and Steve, her fingers waving like starfishes. We moved closer to join them.

"What was that all about?" the woman asked. "I mean, don't get me wrong, the drum solo and Jeremy's song were brilliant, but your new stuff's nothing like your Facebook page."

"Sorry," I interjected. "You've heard of us?"

"Why, you're savage," she replied. "I met this girl online, totally into renaissance faires. She put me onto you. I'm Lindsey by the way."

"Lark," I responded. "So…."

"The stuff you put up online is absolute class." She clapped. "In fairness, what you played this afternoon? Utter shite. Also, are you the Band of Pirates or the Band of Privates?"

"Band of Pirates," Matt said. "Some idiot made a typo."

"Is this the kind of stuff you normally play?" The young woman, black-haired Irish, licked her lips, her complexion the kind seen only in magazines where an expert had applied an airbrush.

"No, we're better known back in the US for our jazz. But we're versatile." Matt flashed a grin, his eyes traveled her torso.

"Glad you asked, darlin'." Rhett ran his fingers down Lindsey's arm, rested them on the small of her back, and steered her away from Matt. The lead singer definitely outmanned the keyboardist. After all, he'd had more practice.

"This was not our regular set. Why, this was not our regular crowd." Rhett poured on the Texas charm. I made a mental note to remind Bev to get out the tally sheet.

"Thank God," she said, "cuz your stuff online is deadly."

"Yeah, we saw the typo and realized the manager held other performance expectations," Rhett continued. "We had to wing it, our improvising not to our usual high standard."

By now the shopping center area that had been our stage was vacant, save a scattering of parents on benches while their children rode mechanized hippos and a giraffe to the ice cream truck music.

Bev and I joined Rhett and Matt, who huddled next to Lindsey and Steve. Jeremy leaned against a wall and had resumed his vacuous stare. I

114

scanned the group for odd expressions. Nothing.

"Brilliant," the young woman said. "You can follow me. Now if you get lost...."

"Which he will," I said under my breath.

"Then plug this address into your GPS." She scribbled on a scrap of a shopping bag.

"I'm afraid, darlin', we don't have the luxury of that device on this tour. We have this device." Rhett pointed at me.

"We can use my cell's GPS." Bev shoved the phone in his face.

"Then here's my number just in case." Lindsey added to her scribbled directions. "Okay, let's head out."

The guys and Bev had stacked all our gear on a large trolley. We followed Lindsey to the parking lot, most of the cars now squatting at the other end of the shopping center.

"So who is this Lindsey person?" I asked.

"Lark, darlin,' please don't distract me while I'm fixin' to drive." Rhett grunted as he climbed into the driver's seat and buckled his seatbelt. "Read out her directions, call out Bev's cell instructions, and do your job navigatin'." He waved for me to join him in the front passenger seat.

"We're playing a hen party. While you were sleeping in the restroom, Lindsey hired us for tonight," Steve's sarcasm not escaping me. "She's the maid of honor." He forwarded a crude map scrawled on the back of a shopping bag.

"Hen party?" This was a new one to me.

"Think Bachelorette Party," Bev explained.

"Best part is we're getting paid," Matt added. "Lindsey gave us a down payment of 300 Euros, with the balance after the event. Need I add that only because of Steve's quick thinking did we get anything for that gig? Thanks, Jeremy, for the fuck-up."

The drummer slouched in the third row, staring at the back of the second-row bench seat, having not made eye contact since the men's room.

Jeremy's disassociation was alarming. Maybe a few words of support from me would help snap him out of it. "Fuck-up? Thanks to Jeremy, we now have this great gig and probably more money than we would have earned from that ghost town of a shopping center, even if we'd played marches that West Point cadettes would envy."

The recent aerobic activity in the disabled stall intruded on reading Lindsey's directions. I considered what the encounter meant. I've been around long enough to know garden variety lust. Deflating as that realization was, Jeremy's reaction confirmed it. Then I thought, *I'm getting too old for this. My back hurts. I don't have the balance I once did.*

I twisted to survey the second row where Steve, Bev, and Matt sat. When Bev saw me, she held up a newspaper. The front-page headline read, "Police Frustrated Over Disappearance of Bog Body, Gold, and Precious Relics." When I turned back, Rhett's cold eyes reflected in the rearview mirror. Directed at Bev.

Chapter Nineteen

The van resisted Rhett's struggle to shift gears. He began a slow crawl around the parking lot, picking up speed. He swerved to the right, the bumper of a new, customized vehicle contacting our right panel.

"Watch out for that BMW. Stay left. Stay left." My voice climbed an octave. "Steer more toward the center of the row."

"I noted the license plate on my cell, so we can file a report when we turn in the van," Bev called.

"Much appreciated, darlin', but that won't be necessary. We barely touched it."

Matt craned his neck back, shaking his head. "You dented it. The owner's going to be majorly pissed."

"I assume you got full coverage on this." I massaged my scalp, trying to decipher a maze of arrows, the directions to Lindsey's house. "Bev, we're going to rely on your GPS."

"Lark, your job is to read the map our fine benefactor drew for us. I've got this under control." He took his foot off the gas and coasted toward a dip in the pavement, indicating the exit to the main road.

"Turn right. You realize you'll have to speed up a bit—"

"That is if you're keen on making this Hen Do before next year," Bev finished for me.

Cars whizzed in both directions, while Rhett sat at the intersection, his head rotating, his knuckles the same white as our near-miss with the bus in the hedgerow. I prayed we wouldn't be T-boned.

"Rhett! Stop! It's Candi!" Jeremy bellowed from his perch in the third-row seat.

All of us lurched forward as Rhett stomped the brakes, my mouth colliding with the dashboard.

"Dammit Rhett! You didn't have to stop so suddenly!" Blood mixed with my saliva, the flesh under my upper lip swelling.

Jeremy vaulted across the seat back, threw open the side door, and jumped onto the pavement.

"Candi Cane, you came back. You didn't leave me after all." His arms enveloped her in a flash. He stripped off his hoodie and wrapped it around her.

A line of cars began to form behind the van.

Déjà vu. Like her dunk in the Viking pool, her hair clung against her head with the exception that her clothes adhered to her frame coated with a slick of mud, scratches crisscrossing her cheeks.

Rhett lowered his window. "I knew you would have a change of heart because your loyalties run deep. Welcome back, prodigal singer. Y'all, now that our troupe is once again reunited, we will proceed to this next engagement."

"Wait! You are not driving one foot more until I protect this van." Candi waved a bunch of broken stems topped by crushed flowers. "Wicked forces this way come. Jeremy Jube-Jube, I couldn't abandon you to the clutches of those demons."

A car horn blasted, drivers leaning out their windows at the holdup.

"Move over and make room," Jeremy said helping Candi onto the bench seat next to Bev, his face lined with concern as he scrambled next to her. The van rocked as Matt and Steve climbed into the third row.

"I can protect you." Candi shivered. "I realized I might not catch the Band of Pirates for the mall opening, but I could try."

"Actually, Privates," Matt said.

"Huh?" Candi swiped a strand of matted hair behind her ear.

"Long story. Go on." My lip throbbed, my mouth tasting like I hadn't flossed in weeks. My insides throbbed seeing Jeremy's feelings for his beneficial friend.

"I hitched a ride at the airport," Candi said. "My ride dropped me part-way next to a field surrounded by a circle of Hawthorne bushes. This little creek flowed through, and the muses directed me to gather these." She held up the weeds. "The fellow, who gave me a lift, said that fairies will protect us and that they like shiny things, especially new coins. I hurled a new euro into the circle and to be sure, one more."

"It'll cost more than a couple of new coins if we don't get moving," Matt said. "We have a gig."

"You're blocking the exit." The driver behind us called, his head craned out his window as he beeped his horn for emphasis. Reflected in the side view mirror were cars and trucks lined up, a cacophony of horns rippling across the parking lot.

"Uh Rhett, are you planning to drive anytime soon?" I asked.

He pressed the gas pedal with no response. He cranked the key in the ignition, the engine complaining. I rolled down the window and motioned the vehicles around us.

"Hey, get your arse out of the way," the driver behind yelled, honked, and thrust a middle finger.

"I suggest, Candi, that you do your voodoo while we're making our way to the gig." Rhett stomped on the gas, but the van remained motion-less. The car honked again.

"You killed the engine." I pointed at the little red icons arranged across the driver's dashboard. "For Christ's sake, Rhett, can't you even find your way out of a parking lot? Let me drive."

I climbed across his lap. Anyone watching would have thought I was mounting him. He shimmied into the passenger seat, while I restarted the van. I burned rubber merging into traffic.

119

"We must have a safe place at all costs, and the van is the safest. Besides herbs, I've got the water I consecrated from the fairy ring's creek." Candi hurled pond scum around the van, rivulets running down the windows.

A dank smell drifted from the bench seat as a splash of cold water landed at the nape of my neck. I'd be wearing a clammy shirt for the rest of the afternoon.

"That water is extremely powerful, so I rinsed out my hand sanitizer and filled it." She held up the small plastic bottle and flung the rest of its contents.

"Ow, my eyes. The water still has hand sanitizer." Matt flinched.

"I'm cool with this as long as you dispense with the burning bush stuff. This is a no smoking van." Bev mopped her ear.

"Give her a break. We need her," Jeremy said.

I stretched my neck, meeting Bev's eyes in the mirror. One great thing about her is I don't have to do much more than that for her to be right on the same page. I would have felt even weirder had that fellow not interrupted Jeremy and me. Yeah, he had that cute little beard and ginger hair, but he was also this melancholy troubadour, my weakness. What was I thinking? I'd been down that roadway too often not to know where these relationships led: having to constantly cheer up a morose male. Besides, Candi adored him.

We arrived at a location outside of Cork, a gated community of ostentatious mansions. So that's where the Celtic Tiger had been hiding! Mom would have shaken her head at the sight. Our lives had been much more modest. We had lived in a stucco house in a row of small, shoulder-to-shoulder, stucco houses, the front yards, aprons sporting flowers and vegetables.

I halted our van in a circular drive before the front door of a huge concrete and steel mansion. "No Georgian elements here. This is pure twenty-first century minimalism. Excessive minimalism, I think."

Bev commented, "That's an oxymoron."

"Well, it's rather moronic to have all this stuff." I pointed to a long, low building with numerous raised garage doors revealing high-end autos, including a DeLorean.

A handyman and groundskeeper opened the boot as soon as we parked. Once they loaded our gear onto a large, garden cart, hauled by a large, garden tractor, they led the way to a large, garden tent in the middle of a large expanse of manicured lawn, where someone had sculpted the bushes.

"I'd say Edward Scissorhands paid a visit." Bev gestured toward the topiaries.

"Aren't those killer?" The maid of honor materialized behind us. "I have a friend who works for this company that provides movie set props. You know *Game of Thrones*?"

"Lindsey, did you grow up in this area?" I asked. Her accent seemed a bit off.

"Kind of. I was born in Canada. Dad moved us here when I was little. He's the Canadian marketing guy for Irish dairy exports to Canada." She turned her attention to Rhett.

"This is indeed a notable estate, darlin'." He made an expansive gesture, wafting the vanilla smell of his couture cologne.

"Bev, did you dig out the tally sheet?" I whispered.

She patted her pocket. "I'm way ahead of you."

"I've set everything up for your stay in the guest house." Lindsey's stiletto heels sinking into the rich soil, she tramped toward a low, stone structure that had once been a barn, the building out of keeping with the rest of the place.

"My raven-haired beauty, after you," Rhett said, ducking under the low door frame behind her.

"Usually, this is a holiday let. You're to make yourselves at home. Bedrooms are off to the right," Lindsey met Rhett's eyes, lowered her lids, and flicked her tongue across her lips.

"Notice where her priorities are?" I nudged Bev.

Jeremy and Candi ambled in last, fingers entwined like a couple of kids in middle school.

"Here's what you're to be doing this evening." Lindsey pulled a sheet of paper out of her purse and studied a schedule. "Our gardener will help you set up in the tent. The catering staff will be arriving in the next few minutes. The Hen Do begins at nine. Be ready to play when I give the signal. I'll lead Moira, the bride-to-be, who will be blindfolded. You're to play a set. Afterward, we hens will go clubbing."

She produced a bag containing T-shirts emblazoned with a flashing pink arrow pointing down, illuminating the slogan, *See what you're missing?* "These are for the guys. Catch." She tossed one at Rhett, who held the swag to his chest. No mistaking where the arrow was pointing.

"I want you three to wear these willy boppers." She fished out headbands, distributing them to Bev, Candi, and me. Crowning the band were a penis and a ball on either side supported by springs.

"At least they're not the cheesy Viking helmets." I wiggled the headgear, the balls dancing and bumping the penis.

The soon-to-be VP of IT turned the headband over, running her finger along the red glitter penis and balls. She giggled and unlocked her cell. "Lark, get a pic I can send to Elliot, so he knows how much I miss him."

"Wow, the color on this is intense. I'm not sure I can wear it without a major muse revolt." Candi held hers at arms' length. "Lark, would you trade your white one for my red one?"

"Not virginal, is that it?"

We made the switch.

"You know, a bridal blessing guarantees joy and good luck to the bride." Candi moved her head in a small circle, her wrists rotating as if casting a spell.

I bounced the headband's antennae springs on my head. "You don't think these would do the trick?"

"This is all fun, but I can enhance the bride's hen party ritual to resonate spiritually," Candi said. "Hen parties have their roots in paganism."

122

"Yeah, I noticed," and I nodded toward the band leader.

Rhett strutted the living room's perimeter in his new T-shirt.

"Of course, these are fertility symbols." Candi wiggled her willy bopper. "Odd. Where are the female symbols?"

"I don't think procreating is the point of this event. Or even potentially procreating." Bev slid her eyes toward the lead singer.

"Ladies, ladies, while I find your cogitating amusing, I suggest you follow your other bandmates and get settled. I want y'all back in ten, dressed and ready to run a sound check." Rhett scooped his palms in a shooing motion.

Did he really do that? As if we were chicks or hens in his barnyard?

~~~

We entered the tent, decorated in a mass of hot pink and penises. Everywhere. Willy candles lit each table. Balloons, penis-shaped of course, saluted the ceiling.

"You won't believe what they're serving." Bev took her place next to me at the mic. "Oysters on the half-shell."

A bevy of squealing women filled the tent, all rushing toward the stage as soon as they saw us. Lindsey led Moira, the bride-to-be, who carried a penis wand and wore an eye mask with a giant dong protruding from between the eyes.

At the signal, we began a whoring song while Lindsey removed Moira's mask. The women went nuts, throwing confetti and squirting silly string from phalluses.

On one of the table rounds, a crowd of shot glasses was arrayed, encircling bottles of tequila in the center ringed by salt and limes in crystal dishes. Each hen grabbed a shot in each fist and in unison tossed them down.

As we prepared for our next song, hens presented us each with a shot glass filled with tequila.

"Ta da! Female fertility symbol." I toasted Candi and downed the shot.

"The only thing missing here is ground up rhino horn," Bev said.

123

"I think that's for men and in a different country." I tapped my cowbell ready for the next number.

Mid-song feedback made Steve's guitar squawk. He moved to confront the amp and fine tune the knobs.

Lindsey called, "Okay hens, let's play Truth or Dare!" She spread a deck of cards on the table nearest to the stage. Moira snatched a card followed by her flock of friends. She turned it over, a hoot of delight erupting.

The hens forgot about Candi, Bev, and me or maybe we were superfluous—after all we lacked the critical junk.

"Do they even care about hearing us?" Candi asked. "I feel like a lounge lizard."

"We might be lounge lizards, but they aren't." Bev nodded toward Steve, two women sandwiching him and rhythmically rubbing against his thighs.

Moira sprayed a coconut mixture from a penis water pistol into Matt's mouth. Lindsey rushed to Rhett and planted a wet kiss on him, knocking his sunglasses sideways, his pirate hat trampled as he staggered backward under the impact. The bride-to-be pranced over to the drummer, her face gleaming, whereby Candi jammed her tambourine into the bride's stomach.

"The bride really could use a white aura, wedding chant," Candi said.

"She could use a little restraint," Bev tipped another shot of tequila.

"I bet the dare is for her to hit on the guys. Wait for it. And there she goes."

Seconds later, the bride wrapped her arms around Rhett, nibbling his ear. She turned, ran toward Steve, snuggled, and purred, "Play the Queen Bess song."

"Sure." Steve back-stepped to his place by the mic, fingering the opening riff.

She waved her willy wand, the stage a mass of young women, jumping and raising arms, the smell of expensive perfumes comingling.

Steve's guttural baritone belted:

There was a fair maid
I caught in a raid
Of booty and loot for Queen Bess.
She was 'trothed to a man
In old Ireland,
And I freed her for good old Queen Bess.
"Please show some restraint,"
She said with a faint.
"I'm a virgin like your patron, Queen Bess."
So quickly I led
The fair maid to bed
All in the name of Queen Bess.
Said she, "Here's my flower
Be gone in an hour
You're my lover, tho' you love Queen Bess."
Said I, "Here's my heart
To keep tho' we part,
But my honor I give to Queen Bess."
All for the cause of Queen Bess.

Finally! The kind of mayhem we had expected from this tour. Candi danced off, banging her tambourine, joining Jeremy, his drumsticks a blur of motion. Two other hens joined Bev and me, waving a liter of rum. At the edge of the stage, Lindsey shook a green bottle, uncorked the top, and directed the spray toward the crowd of musicians and hens.

We slid into our medley of cover songs. In all my fifty years, few times had been this awesome. And never in a shower of champagne.

From the corner of my eye, a fellow in a chauffeur's uniform emerged from the entrance, the driver for their clubbing. He pranced to the music, pausing before our stage. Lindsey and Moira danced over to him.

125

Chauffeur gyrated, his arms and hands locked behind his head. He tossed his hat, unbuttoned his jacket, and flung the clothing on a table. All the while, he continued to pump his pelvis. The two women flanked him, hips swaying. In a single movement he grabbed his groin and yanked off his pants. Down to a sequin-covered jockstrap, Chauffeur wiggled through the crowd of other women, where they pawed at him, tucking euro notes in his strap.

The maid of honor and bride-to-be motioned to the hens, who lined up in a twenty-first century version of a conga line weaving toward the exit.

We found ourselves deserted mid-song. Only the caterers remained.

"Y'all, let's finish the set," Rhett called raising a rum bottle in a toast.

Chapter Twenty

Bev and I lounged on top of a table round surrounded by willy candles burned to gutters of molten wax. Our equipment was packed and ready to load in the morning. Caterers ringed the tent as if on guard for the moment they'd be able to complete clearing the evening. Lindsey had given instructions for them to wait until we were done partying. Only Bev and I continued the festivities. After the evening, seeing pink and red ever again would be too soon.

"Good thing," she belched, "it didn't go any further." She lifted her shot glass, and we clinked.

"Damn right. I'm done with troubled troubadours."

She poured us another shot.

"Here's to no more troubled troubadours." I chugged the shot and slammed it on the table.

"What's Irish for cheers again?"

"Sláinte. It's pronounced slawn-che."

"Slawn-shhhhh." Bev tipped the tiny glass. "Love that you don't sound drunk even when you are."

A cackle flowed out of my throat turning to waves of sob after sob. "You're so lucky to have Elliot in your life."

Bev's arm reached across my shoulders. "I know." She leaned her head into my neck. "You'll find someone, someone who deserves you."

I collapsed onto my back, warm tears trickling into my ears. Earlier we'd cut the weights off the willy balloons, giggling as they rose, penises poking the tent's ceiling. "God, I'm getting old."

"Me too."

"Don't know what I'd do without you." Drifting off to sleep, I found a position that eluded the whirlies.

Warm pressure and a tug on my sneaker caused me to open my eyes to a pair of jean-clad thighs and a belt buckle poking over the edge of the table. Bev and I sat up.

"Don't you think you'd be more comfortable in a bed?" Steve bent and jiggled my foot.

"With you?"

"I think you've had enough excitement for one night."

"You're right. I've had enough of one knight."

Steve frowned, then chuckled. "Yeah, I heard."

"Are you troubled?" Bev demanded.

"Can't be bothered with it. Too much energy. More that I like trouble." Steve said. "Can I trouble you two to clear out? The caterers need to clean up and get out of here."

"Hey, you can parry worth a shit," I snorted, falling backwards.

"Okay you two. Time for bed."

"Yeah?" I lay watching the rotation of willy balloons.

"Then no trouble for us to head out." Bev reached out her arms, and Steve lifted her off the table, placing her on her feet.

"Oh shit. The willies are whirling." With a grunt I hoisted myself up, narrowed my eyes, giving Steve what I thought was a piercing look. "I have to ask you a personal question."

"Yeah?"

"You're always so cool and with it. Do you ever get the willies?" I reached over, high-fived Bev, and collapsed back onto the table, giggling.

"After tonight, I'll think of you two whenever it happens." Steve lifted my elbow. "Up you get, Lark."

I raised myself on my knees, stretching my arms. "Help me down."

Steve paused a beat, long enough for me to wonder what his retort would be. "Just this once."

His arms reached around my waist, lifted me as my chest met his. I closed my eyes, too drunk to keep my head up, my nose nuzzling his neck, his hair smelling earthy. My toes eased onto the floor and then my heels, my knees a bit wobbly. Supporting us on each side he said, "You ladies do remember how to get back to where we're staying, right?"

~~~

A flow of nausea trickled up my throat, dragging me to semi-consciousness. Did I blackout last night? My chilly foot rested on the stone floor of the guest house living room, another indication of the previous evening. If I lay very, very still on the fold-out couch, the urge to vomit would pass. Not a total blackout, snippets of the gig flicked behind my eyelids.

Footsteps padded across the carpet, and I chanced slitting my eyes to peer through mascara-caked eyelashes. A silk bathrobe topped Rhett's hairy legs and knobby knees. He settled in an easy chair across the living room. He fired up his laptop, reflecting in his glasses what looked like a street map for a town or city. On the floor lay a newspaper he'd probably pilfered from the front stoop of the mansion. A stack of brochures rested on the end table by his chair.

In the morning sun and from this distance, his bifocals emphasized his lined, craggy features, canyons of flesh surrounding his eyes. *Wonder if he's feeling the same sort of slowdown as me?*

Bev lay motionless next to me, bits of silly string decorated her hair. On my side, my foot still firmly planted on the floor, the acrid smell of stomach contents laced with booze permeated the air around my nostrils. A garbage can nestled nearby. My mouth felt fuzzy, making me long for the minty taste of toothpaste and mouthwash.

Rhett could have been any guy on vacation, making plans for the day, what sights to see, a wife in the kitchen making breakfast. Instead, he was spearheading a plot to pillage museums and sell the booty.

Still, his age reminded me of mine. If I had had to make a choice between the craziness of last night or the comfort of a good sleep and warm bed, I'd be hard pressed. Whatever the choice, it would have been without the hangover.

Rhett had not noticed me. Queasiness in my stomach raised a red flag to prevent an oncoming barf. Queasiness also warned me he was up to something none of us was supposed to know about.

Rhett snapped the lid to the laptop closed at the sound of footsteps. "Well darlin', you're up early."

A pair of toenails with a fresh pedi then dangled from the chair's arm.

"What a night! Brilliant." Lindsey's voice. "Here's the rest and worth every euro to see Moira's face. Is she up yet?"

"Not as of yet, darlin'. To accommodate such a beautiful, charming woman as Moira was an honor and a privilege." I lowered my eyelids a moment later when another set of perfect pedis arrived.

"Jaysus, Mary, and Joseph," Moira's voice murmured. "Does anyone else know?"

"No. You don't remember, do you?"

"Only bits."

"You were plastered. The chauffeur dropped everyone else at home. Just you and I from the hens came here. Matt's still asleep."

"Absolutely craic. Can you believe it? Band of Pirates. Deadly. So no worries?"

"Well, you wanted the ultimate hen party." Lindsey and Moira's voices retreated toward the bedroom area.

I exhaled deeply, rolling over as if still asleep.

"I know you're awake, Lark," Rhett said.

"What time is it?" I pretended to sound woozy.

"Later than you think." His voice smooth, like Southern Comfort on the rocks.

130

I swallowed to squelch the bout of nausea spreading toward my diaphragm. Each twinge of my gut reminded me of the advisability of a supine position.

He rose and ambled to the kitchen.

Moira entered the room, bride crown over her arm, sash dangling from her shoulder. "A thousand thanks to you," she called.

"We'll stay in touch, darlin'," Rhett waved. "My best to the groom."

She blushed, a nervous giggle erupting, trotted through the room, and hurried out the door.

A few minutes later, Steve emerged, followed by Matt looking smug, then Candi with Jeremy in tow. Bev and I restored the hide-a-bed.

"Candi," I said, "Moira could use one of your cleansing ceremonies."

"She's up for the white aura wedding ritual? She wasn't up for it last night."

"She was up for something else."

"What was that all about?" Bev asked.

"You're asking?" The bride-to-be's figure disappearing behind the Edward Scissorhands topiaries made me grimace.

Candi, silent for a moment, commented, "She's a tough case, but not impossible. Do you have anything of hers I could use?"

"Moira said she remembers only bits of last night. Probably for the best. Maybe a ceremony to keep memories repressed?"

"Excellent suggestion. I would hate to be the cause of marital dissatisfaction." The lead singer crossed to the easy chair with a mug of coffee, picked up his laptop, and placed it in his suitcase.

"I'll see what I can do," she said. Was she taking this seriously?

~~~

"I sure hope this is going to be an ordinary gig." Bev lounged in the van's navigator seat while I drove. Rhett sprawled across the third row, as much as anyone could with his bandy legs. Matt, Steve, Candi, and Jeremy jammed shoulder-to-shoulder across the middle row.

"Ordinary is nonexistent on this tour," Steve said.

"But I expect we'll be in a regular pub in Cork." Jeremy stretched his arm across the back of the seat to modify his cramped position by the window.

"I think I'm going to use the forgetfulness spell on Moira, overlay the faithfulness chant, and end with the blue smoke ceremony to chase away any lingering bad vibes. But this is the best I can do." She paged through a small book.

"That's sweet of you. But I think she's had enough of our services." I head-checked, changing lanes. Everyone laughed except Steve, who shook his head.

Wow, a person with principles and ethics.

"I have to say I thought my service was extraordinary," Matt said.

"Are we in a pissing contest?" Rhett's head leaned over Matt's shoulder. "If so, I can confirm that without a doubt, I can out-piss you anywhere, anytime." He pulled his jacket up to his ears and retreated to a prone position.

The motorway led into Cork and close to our destination, Condron's. Driving in Cork is like most places in Ireland. Terrible. Parking in Cork is like most places in Ireland. Terrible.

~~~

Our setup completed, we ordered pints, jubilant from the previous evening's success. Rhett announced we had reservations at the hostel. "While not as luxurious as our previous venue, I expect the accommodation will surpass sleeping in the dining room of a tourist trap."

"Like you have that experience to compare," Matt said.

Showtime. I thought the previous night had been awesome. We were more than smokin'. The sound balanced. We gypsy backup singers synced seamlessly with the guys. For the first time I understood why the band had hired Candi. When you got past all the New Age stuff, she rocked. Then again, maybe she'd used a few of those weeds on us in a cleansing ceremony.

"To cleanse our black hearts," Bev replied when I told her later.

Our set ended, we mingled with the crowd. Bev at the bar swished her skirt, looking like she was doing some pretending. Steve straddled a stool next to Matt, their heads bobbing in animated motion toward a couple of patrons. Candi clustered with a group of women, swiveling her head, no doubt hunting for Jeremy. Her eyes lit up when she spotted him. In earnest conversation with two fellows, the drummer examined and tapped a bodhran. Rhett's absence wasn't news. He'd probably already scored. Absorbing the scene bathed me in contentment. We'd accomplished something, made people happy.

A guy with black hair and eyes the color of mist on the mountains bought me pints. I acquired my first groupie.

Chapter Twenty-One

In a post-coital haze, amplified by the ego boost of the previous evening, I'd had my own cleansing ceremony in a killer shower. Two great showers in two days. It's the little things in life that matter. Did I mention the bed? I'd found a coffee shop not far from the hostel, nabbed an outdoor table, and left a message for the others to join me.

"Jeremy's missing! He didn't show up at the hostel last night." Candi, holding a coffee cup, joined our outside table, her voice close to a wail. "Has anyone seen him? Who saw him last?" Candi's eyes scoured the street.

"Wasn't he with you?" I shrugged. "I left the pub early and—"

"We know where you went." Rhett's legs like logs diverted the stream of pedestrians on the adjoining sidewalk.

Candi waved her arm as if hailing a cab. "Excuse me, but we're talking about Jeremy. He's missing."

"Maybe Matt's seen him. By the way, where is Matt?" Steve asked.

"Mass. He's been going every morning since we got here." Rhett raised his sunglasses and slid his eyes toward me. "Shouldn't that be your destination, Lark?"

Bev sank into a vacant seat. "What? Like your hook-up didn't hook up last night? Of anyone here, you should be camping in a confessional."

"I think I'll post a little notice on our Facebook wall," I said. "Maybe someone's seen Jeremy."

Rhett shifted a leg to let a woman, who was walking a dog, pass. "Let me enlighten you as a result of my vast experience. Do not—and I repeat—do not, write anything specific. You cannot believe the kinds of tribulation that causes."

I lowered my chin and returned his gaze. "Really? I'll take that under consideration."

"Jeremy's gone. He could have been abducted." Candi flung her arms, splashing her coffee across the table.

"And Bev, darlin', I did see that pic you uploaded yesterday. The one with you and the willy boppers. I thought you were sending that to your beloved." Rhett lowered his sunglasses and cocked his head.

"I did send Elliot the pic, but I also thought the publicity would be good for the band." She pulled out her phone.

"That's right. You are about to embark on a career as a VP of IT for a company specializing in cybersecurity and marketing." Rhett raised his sunglasses. "Yes, quite a recommendation of you and your abilities."

"Oh shit, oh shit!" Bev slapped the side of her head. "I'll take it down. Hope the damage isn't too bad." She dug her laptop out of her purse, flipped the lid, and danced her fingers across the keys.

"Are you listening to me? Jeremy is not here!" Candi hovered behind Rhett, shouting in his ear.

"All right, Candi. We hear you, as does every other person in this establishment." Rhett repositioned his legs across the narrow space between the tables. "He'll show up eventually. All his gear's in the van."

A crowd of empty coffee mugs had congregated on the table when Jeremy finally ambled up with the same guys from the previous evening.

"Jeremy, you had me worried to death. I thought you'd been kidnapped or murdered." Candi jumped to hug him. She froze, his sheepish face bearing the break-up look.

Bev and I rose to get another latte. But mostly to give them space.

135

"This is awkward." Bev held the coffee shop's door as two customers sidled past.

"Yeah, not only for them but for us. We had such a hot set last night. Maybe Candi has a heeling spell to keep Jeremy from wandering off."

We stood in line. Bev pointed to the latte containers. "Now I know what they mean by supersize in the States. These are dinky and not cheap." The line inched forward.

"My wee Lark!"

I would recognize that voice anywhere.

"Mom?" I expected her to be dressed in some kind of getup that involved a black shawl and tattered wool skirt. Instead, she had on an expensive suit.

"To think how you've aged. Such grace!"

"Mom, it's only been a few years. By the way, this is Bev."

Bev extended her hand, which Mom grabbed and wrapped arms around her. "My dear girl, welcome to Ireland!"

"Where did you get those shoes?" Of course, Couture Bev would notice those right off.

"This lovely wee shop on St. Patrick's Street. We could go this afternoon."

"Mom, what are you doing here? I thought you were in Dublin." Who was this stunning woman standing before me claiming to be my mother?

"I got your email. Beside myself I was that you were okay. Seeing I had business in Cobh, when I saw on Facebook that you were going to play at Condron's, I decided to come into town. The hostel owners were such dears to tell me where you were off to this morning."

"We're heading to Dublin after we eat. But Mom, you live and work in Dublin."

"Of course, love. The offices are there."

"Offices? When did you need an office?"

"Why, me own business, the one I've been blathering on about. But you must be staying with me. You and your dear friend, Bev. Everything's

136

ready for you. We'll catch up, and I can tell you about such adventures I'm having."

Through all this we'd finally made the counter. Mom flashed a debit card for our drinks, picked out a plateful of pastries, and we made our way out the door to the group.

The Band of Pirates drooped in chairs. Minus Jeremy. Candi, in a heap, rested her head on Rhett's shoulder.

"Mom, this is the Band of Pirates: Rhett, Steve, Matt, and Candi. Where's Jeremy? He's our drummer."

"Pleased I am to meet you," Mom's Irish charm at full wattage.

"I am delighted to make your acquaintance Ms...?" Rhett paused.

"Devlin." Mom extended her hand, which Rhett took, kissed, and closed his other over the top.

My eyes rolled up and over. Couldn't he leave it alone for one minute?

"I pray you are enjoying your tour in the Emerald Isle and that the good people of Cork have embraced you in their hearts." Mom could be as verbose and windy as Rhett. "But I am afraid this dear city had such a terrible night with the break-in at the Butter Museum."

"Butter Museum?" Matt's nostril curled.

"Thanks be to God, no one was at the museum, and no one was hurt. But the thieves got away with a valuable antiquity. Bog butter found in the bogs of Monaghan."

Steve chortled although it sounded more like gagging. "Bog butter. You have to be kidding. Bog butter?"

"Yes, and proud we are to have these fine relics to remind us of our heritage, of the people, who were here before the ancient Egyptians built the pyramids."

"Mom, this is awful. What do you suppose is going on? What with the stolen bog body and all?"

"I can see, dear lady, this is upsetting you." Rhett again took her hand.

"Well, I think they're going to be sold on the black market to some crazy billionaire, with a fetish for leather, gold, and butter." I tossed it out

137

there. Whatever evil Rhett planned, he now knew I knew. Let him mess with my antiquities and see what happens. But he had messed with them, and I hadn't a clue how to stop him.

"It would be a terrible shame to see a dire end befall those relics or for an innocent person to be harmed in returning them to their rightful place." While Rhett appeared to be speaking to Mom, behind those sunglasses, he directed his gaze to Bev and me.

Candi blew her nose, her face puffy and swollen. "I don't like the aura here. Very negative. I feel the restless energy of misplaced things. I've been doing all I can to summon Jeremy back. But I think it's hopeless."

"What do you mean summon Jeremy and hopeless?" Bev asked.

"He's joined a Celtic band. Apparently, he hung out with his new friends all last night," Candi wailed. "He likes the bodhran better than me-e-e. He's been frustrated for months. The Band of Pirates has gone in a direction he feels is not artistically valid. I came back because of him. I risked myself and my muses." Candi's sobs echoed across the street, loud enough that surrounding tables could no longer pretend to ignore us.

"How are we gonna play our gigs without a drummer?" Steve asked.

"My dear young man, you have one of the best drummers around. Why, my daughter can step in with nary a moment's notice."

A bass drum in my stomach went bada boom, as a pair of cymbals crashed in my head. Was she kidding? "Mom, this is not helpful. I haven't played the drums in ages."

"'Tis in your blood. A few minutes is all you need and you're off to the races. My dear Rhett, I assure you she could make the fairies dance and leap." Mom looked at her watch. "Oh dear, I must be off. Lark, give a call, text, or email. I'll be after heading back to Dublin later today. Just let yourself in and bring your other friend, Candi, as well."

Mom left us in various poses of despair.

Rhett said, "Well Lark, darlin'?"

Chapter Twenty-Two

I stared down the expanse of my legs, stretched on Mom's living room couch, gazing out the window that looked toward the back garden, the foliage lush and misty in the rain. A crowd of garden art marched toward the back door. Rather than an assortment of gnomes, frogs, and mirrored balls, Mom had amassed a legion of saints, each with a little path to access them to intercede on any possible emergency.

Lying flat on the sofa made me remember my Nanna. She had lain there, frail and birdlike in the last months of her life.

"My wee Lark," she would say. And then, "Sure as sure I must know you." Until one afternoon, she flew. Mom and I had nursed her to the end, just as Nanna and her brothers and sisters had nursed their mother and father. Just as it had always been. Would I be here to nurse Mom or leaning over a dentist chair? Where would I be when I closed my eyes for the last time? A river of sadness coursed up my legs and torso, pooling along my spine. I regarded the pebble path leading to a statue of St. Jude, patron saint of lost causes, feeling as if he'd been a close companion this whole tour.

From the kitchen floated the drone of a morning TV program and the smell of an Irish breakfast beckoned.

Mom's up early.

"The Gardai are still stumped by the recent burglaries in Dublin's National Museum." The voice wafted atop the aroma, and for a moment, I pictured the bog body, wondering where he might be. Wherever he was, he would not have the advantage of his feet, the trunk below his waist having met a grisly end with the peat-cutting machine. So much for rest-in-peace, more like rest-in-pieces. Some millennia down the road, would my remains be cut from the earth to be greeted with such a gruesome outcome? Makes a good argument for cremation.

Nanna's clan crest featured a pelican plucking its breast, drops of blood falling into the mouths of hatchlings. A symbol of sacrifice. And sacrifice she did to bring up a clutch of children alone after her fisherman husband drowned off the coast of Galway. One by one her brood flew west to the US, my mom included, until Mom's marriage soured, and she left my dad. She returned with me, giving up everything to stay on with Nanna.

I studied the pelican on my forearm, the inked bird's wings spread protecting the nest. Sacrifice was in our blood, but what had I sacrificed for anyone or anything? Nothing. Absolutely nothing.

When Nanna first showed me the crest, I was eighteen and lost as far as my future. The pelican, a bird, meant sacrifice for the higher cause, whether family or principle. That's another reason she called me Lark. She said signs, the winds of opportunity would let me know. After her death, I thought the higher cause meant to sacrifice my love of Ireland and to fly away to Oregon with the American I'd met studying at Trinity College.

Somehow, I don't think the subsequent higher cause meant a gypsy life with a man who couldn't keep his lance in his pants. I wondered whether I'd find it as a dental hygienist, let alone on a three-week romp around Ireland with a mediocre band.

At fifty, opportunities for higher causes were slipping away. Signs. Where were the signs?

The TV newscaster's voice drifted from the kitchen. "Anyone with information leading to the capture of the thieves and return of the museum's

140

artifacts should contact the authorities immediately."

What? Wait! The signs were there all along, beginning with the book on bog bodies I'd found in Rhett's bedside table that night of the renn faire, followed by Bev stumbling onto that strange map he had. I knew what I must do.

When Bev and Candi entered the living room a few minutes later, I was dressed and ready to go.

"Hey, how'd you sleep?" I asked. "Was the guest room comfortable?"

"Great, except for Candi's snoring," Bev said.

"It couldn't be that bad. Jeremy never complained. Of course, he has partial hearing loss. All those years playing drums."

The whistle from the tea kettle called us to the dining room. Bev sat at the table and scooted her chair. "He's not that deaf. He showed us the ear plugs he wears at night."

Mom emerged from the kitchen with a tray bearing plates crammed with eggs, rashers, and the tiny rounds that were blood sausage. "I've been about making a true Irish breakfast." She distributed plates next to the soup bowls filled with oatmeal. Slices of toast kept company in little metal racks.

"Ms. Devlin, how did you come to call Lark, Lark?" Bev asked.

"You must be calling me Deirdre," Mom said. "Lark's Nanna, who used to say she sang like a wee lark, gave her that name."

I splashed some cream onto my oatmeal. "Nanna was also a wee deaf."

"I don't know about that. I think you've got a great voice, especially for harmony," Candi said.

Bev spread butter on a piece of toast. "Deirdre, you mentioned you have offices here in Dublin?"

"Why yes, I do. I am in the tourist trade."

"Mom led the curve as far as the tourist industry. She divorced Dad just before my third birthday. We moved back to Ireland and lived near Galway." I passed Bev the rashers. "Help yourself."

"Tourists expected to be regaled with Irish blarney," she said. "If

141

Jury's and the Gaiety Theatre could entertain tourists in Dublin, I could flourish on the west coast. I discovered an abandoned thatched cottage on the edge of one of the major thoroughfares. Ireland was awash with them before the Celtic Tiger, no thanks to the famine. I converted the derelict property into a small tearoom."

"Nanna, my grandma, dressed in a ragged shawl and skirt, would tell stories, seated before a peat fire. The Irish language was compulsory in school. Like a lot of kids, I thought Gaelic was a wasted effort. For a while, we did this routine where Nanna pretended not to understand English, and I would translate."

"A fellow from the Gaeltacht stopped by," Deirdre said. "We would have been busted for fraud, except I hired a couple of their people to come and teach the customers a bit of Irish."

"What's a Gael Tech?" Bev asked. "It sounds like an Irish IT."

"Well, the Gaeltacht does have to do with communication. They are regions where folks speak mostly Irish. They were set up in the 1920s as part of the Irish Ireland movement to recapture the culture and preserve the language." I pointed to a framed picture on the far wall. "A group of the more radical Gaeltacht residents protested in front of our shop. The incident made the *Irish Times*."

"I expanded by hiring a harpist and one of Lark's pals to play the tin whistle, while she played the bodhran. Local lasses used to come and dance." Deirdre smiled. "I made a good living during the season. Before long, the tearoom became a regular stop for tourists, and we were written up in all the travel guides. A businessman bought me out, so me mam, Lark, and I moved to Dublin."

"I discovered I was pretty good on the drums, bought myself a set, and joined a band. For kicks, Mom would busk on the corner at Grafton Street."

"Busk?" Bev's perfect eyebrows swam toward her nose.

"Perform for coins. Same as back home with those guitar players on street corners."

"Ach, the morning 'tis flying and I must be off. I've a staff meeting." Mom stood to clear the dishes.

"Staff meeting? Why in the world do you need an office and staff?"

"My dear, for me busking business. With the downturn in the economy, more and more people are getting into the tourist trade. For a fee, I provide consultation and market placement."

"Market placement?" Bev's eyes lit up.

"Success in this industry demands a good location. I happen to know the ropes, the people who can be cutting the red tape in getting a license." Mom disappeared through the swinging doors to the kitchen.

"In the US we have a name for that," I called.

"Extortion and mafia," Bev mumbled out of the corner of her mouth.

"No wonder I'm feeling such mixed vibes here," Candi said stacking plates. "My muses are very confused. They're making me giddy."

Mom reappeared to pick up the remaining dishes, and I followed her into the kitchen. She tilted her head and said, "I'm afraid the days of trust and entrepreneurship are being challenged. Without a license, buskers are loiterers. The powers that be have restricted the licenses and locations. The scant, corner real estate means the difference between failure and success."

"Mom, this is outrageous! What were you doing in Cobh?"

"Expanding. I'm after setting up franchises. The recession has been hard on all the major tourist towns. I've people in Limerick and Cork as well. I'd like to get into Galway, but that may be tough. The Gaeltacht has never forgiven me. Would you and the girls like a ride into town? I can give you a lift to Feeney's."

~~~

"Well, I see you finally sorted yourselves out." The manager at Feeney's stood behind his bar, his laptop fired up. "'Tis this evening you're to be playing. That is if you can find the stage."

Rhett removed his sunglasses. "I believe, Pat, my man, we were highly mistaken about the quality of this establishment and of the excellent

143

opportunity to entertain your customers."

Feeney huffed. "We're to be seeing about that."

"Without further procrastination and with your permission, Pat, we will embark on our tasks to assemble our band equipment."

"Knock yourself out." Feeney moved toward the tap spigots. "Full of shite," he mumbled as Rhett disappeared into the alley.

Candi stepped to the bar and ordered a round. "Are you up for a pint? Bev? Lark?"

I nodded, eyeing the space where the drum kit would be.

From the alley entrance, Rhett emerged shouldering cables, like snakes cascading from his neck. "By the way, I got a text this morning. When we depart this city for the rest of the tour, our mode of transportation will be awaiting us at the same rental location near the airport."

"I still don't see the purpose of a big bus." Steve grunted, lugging the amp.

"Because I say so, if no other reason." Rhett turned toward the three of us. "Good morning, ladies. I require your help." He dropped a jumble of cables in the stage area.

I expected to see a bedraggled trio. Instead, Rhett and Steve appeared rested and chipper.

Where's Matt?" I asked.

"Usual place. Mass." Steve stretched to untangle the electrical cords. "Thanks for the mess, Rhett."

In no hurry to move from my stool, I called, "Glad to see you guys got a good night's sleep."

"Our earnings from the hen party, a tip from our lovely hostess, and a thank-you gift of several euros from the bride enabled us to bunk at a more lavish place than our previous evening in Dublin. Ladies, you wait here. I'll be back later this afternoon." Rhett backed toward the entrance. "I'm fixin' to take a look-see at the bus at the airport to make sure it'll be ready for our departure up north," he called, receding into the alleyway again.

My scalp tingled at the insult. I murmured, "What's he saying? A no-brainer he pimped himself. We all saw him the morning after. But how come he treats the guys to a nice hotel?"

Steve swore at the mare's nest of cables. "This one's frayed." He held up a ragged end. "I'm going to exchange it. I'll be back in a little while." The front door to Feeney's slammed.

Candi, Bev, and I hunkered at the bar, pints before us.

"Something doesn't smell right. I don't like the sour odors coming out of Rhett." Candi grabbed a napkin and blotted her mouth.

"Like rancid butter?" Bev asked. I elbowed her, but too late.

"Kind of. What do you mean rancid butter? I saw what you did, Lark."

Nanna was right when she urged me to pay attention to the signs. Maybe Candi wasn't such a ditz after all. I took a swallow from my lager. "Bev's referring to the break-in at the Butter Museum in Cork."

"That must be the yellow ooze I see mixing with his aura. Butter." Candi half-smiled. "We've been unbalanced since we walked off the plane at Dublin International, but my muses refuse to give me a good read. That explains Lough Gur. Those Celts heralded bad omens."

"Actually, bad's already happened." I licked a bit of foam off my lip. "You gotta admit, Bev, Candi is pretty psychic."

"Parlor trick," Bev said.

"Bev—" My voice stern. I checked my anger, tired of her sarcasm.

"Right." Bev's tone implied I'd asked her to dance in her best shoes in cow manure.

"I knew this tour was majorly screwed up. But what's butter got to do with anything?" Candi asked.

I anticipated her producing a bunch of herbs from her satchel. Nothing materialized.

"Bog butter has gone missing from the museum in Cork." When Bev and Candi looked perplexed, I explained, "The Celts buried butter in a bog as an offering to the gods."

"I don't recommend putting it on toast," Bev's face contorted, "unless you happen to have a loaf of bog bread. Marmalade would help as well."

Candi remained silent, her head swiveling, following Bev and me. She drained her pint. "I'm way lost on this."

"Rhett's bog body book," I said.

"Yeah, I know." Candi twisted her head, nodding down. "He keeps it in his nightstand next to a bottle of Viagra. So what?"

Bev took a long haul on her pint. "The book contains a picture of the bog body thieves recently stole from the Dublin National Museum."

"The pic is dog-eared with numbers and slash marks. We've got a good idea he stole the bog body and stashed it. But where?" I scanned the bottles lining the back of the bar as if the unnerving artifact might be crouching. "Don't you get it?" My Nanna was right. Sacrifice for the good of the higher principle resides in my blood, in my lineage. "I've got to stop Rhett, and I need your help."

"Lark, look at me." Bev grabbed my shoulders. "It's just nerves. You haven't played drums in a while. You're gonna do great tonight."

"You know, sometimes intense events create channels for subconscious processing of data we normally disregard," Candi said.

I ignored Candi's woo-woo comment. "Nervous? I don't think so, Bev. I've never been more calm in my life. Once we figure out where Rhett hid the body and artifacts, we'll grab the body and make sure it, the gold jewelry, and the other stuff get back to the museum."

"This is ludicrous. I often think you are impulsive, but this goes beyond impulsive. This is…"

"Ludicrous?" Candi asked.

Bev edged her pint down the bar's smooth surface. "You have flipped out."

"Are you calling me unstable?" I slid my lager after hers, Candi following.

Feeney's manager eyed us, moving in concert as we proceeded, swiping his towel along the counter.

"Do you think a rational human being would concoct such a goofy plan? The right thing to do is notify the police."

146

"Gardai." I corrected her.

Candi bumped me, spilling my pint, as we side-stepped along the length of the bar, Feeney trailing with his cloth.

"Fine, notify the Gardai. Or the museum." Bev reached the end. Feeney busily scrubbed along the already gleaming surface. "But for my part, I don't want to get involved. I want to go back to Elliot in one piece."

"You're going to put your own self-interests above human rights?"

"Human rights? What human rights?"

Candi's fingers rummaged in her satchel. Out came the lavender oil. "I think we should chill." She dabbed oil onto a napkin and wafted it toward us.

"Keep yourself and your whacko voodoo out of this, Candi." Bev stood. "We are talking about a corpse from a culture that has long since become extinct. These are artifacts."

"No, the culture is alive and well. Why, look at Newfoundland. Lots of Celtic stuff in that province." I circled the bottom of my empty pint on the clean bar.

The backup singer's napkin waving resembled a white flag.

"Candi, you're not helping," Bev said. "Why don't you go hang out with your muses?"

"They are not artifacts. The body is not a rock or pottery shard. He belongs in Ireland for future generations to see, marvel at, and learn. Rhett's such a scum bag, I bet he's going to sell the poor sod, along with the artifacts, on the black market. We have a duty."

"Maybe you have a duty, but I'm not going to risk my life and career over some leather, no matter how valuable. I have enough valuable leather of my own. I need some space. I'm going for a walk." Bev pivoted to leave by the alley entrance. "I'll meet you back here tonight."

She pushed past Matt as he staggered through the entrance with the keyboard. "Hey! Watch it. This is heavy, and we're on the hook if we drop this bloody instrument."

The manager positioned himself before us, arms splayed on the bar.

"What's this shite about bog bodies? I'm cutting you off." He gestured to Matt and the small space set aside as a stage. "That's where your equipment goes. And watch that you don't bang me walls."

~~~

Mom had an errand to check on her buskers, and we had a few hours to kill, so Candi and I decided to join her at Bewley's for tea. As we rounded the corner onto Grafton Street, I spied her chatting with three men, who then picked up their instruments and began to play.

Candi gasped. "Jeremy!"

He accompanied the two men with whom he had been in deep conversation that night at Condron's in Cork. From the distance the keen of the tin whistle sliced the air, the rapid notes of a violin chasing the beat of Jeremy's bodhran. They weren't bad. For a moment, the street scene took me back to my adolescence.

Mom turned as we approached. "Lark, darlin', I believe these fellows will be the next Chieftains."

I nodded, distracted by Candi's face, her feet planted in a puddle, eyes fixed on Jeremy. His face bore the same pained expression as when I found him in the men's can, water dripping from his beard. The other two men appeared equally bedraggled. While we scoffed our pints in Feeney's, Dublin had experienced one of its sudden showers. I remembered that feeling of playing on a street corner and getting caught in a downpour.

"I'm wanting to make introductions. I signed these lads when I was in Cork the other day. Did I not tell you that my acts audition as part of getting their assigned busker areas?"

Candi said nothing.

"Wow, Mom you're a regular one-woman *American Idol*." I still couldn't align her new image: chic, sophisticated.

"Ach, the opportunities presented here. All the foot traffic, the prospect of being noticed. Do you know that several of my acts were discovered by scouts working on popular TV shows? Exposure. I provide them with exposure."

"I don't doubt that." Gray cloud islands floated across the sky. Within the hour, these 'lads' would be in for another downpour.

"Girls, where's Bev?" Mom asked.

"Shopping. She's going through Gucci withdrawal."

"Candi, dear, you've said nary a word."

"I'm fine. Probably a little tired from the hectic schedule. My muses keep me up at night." She hardly blinked, her head motionless, still gaping at Jeremy. I had never seen her this forlorn, and like her mirror image, Jeremy gaped back.

"Are you all sorted for this evening?" Mom asked.

"That we are. Rhett's at the airport assuring the bus meets his specifications," I said. "We're to pick the damn thing up when we head out of Dublin for the rest of the tour."

"He says this one is much more luxurious than the cramped one we rented down in Limerick." Candi directed her comment toward Jeremy.

"That means more room for Rhett to spread out and hog the seat." I made a mental note to increase the accidental death on my life insurance policy. "Lucky me gets to drive it. Or not if he rents a tour bus. I'm not legal to drive a tank or anything resembling one."

"To be sure, he ought to be taking better care of his drummer." Mom shook her head.

"He could use a lesson or two from you."

Jeremy kicked at the cement. Would he confess he was the drummer who had ditched Band of Pirates? An awkward silence followed. As the seconds ticked by, I became more and more ticked off at his callow behavior, but decided to keep my mouth shut. After all, one man's search for his Celtic soul was another woman's opportunity to regain hers.

"My dear Candi, you seem to be fading. A pot of tea and fresh scones will perk you up." Mom jerked her head in the direction of Bewley's. "Lads, I think you are well-placed. Ring my cell if anything comes up."

Chapter Twenty-Three

Okay, I admit my debut as a drummer for the band wreaked havoc on my nerves. Feeney's manager put aside his curmudgeon persona and allowed us to do a little warm up in the afternoon.

Matt's response was typically caustic when I insisted on setting the kit up myself. A ritual for me, I arranged the pieces, adjusted the cymbals, and twisted the seat on the stool to the right height. The expressions on Matt's, Rhett's, and Steve's faces meant I would have to earn my place. A glance at Candi's scowl showed her comparing me to Jeremy.

Climbing onto the stool surrounded by the drums and cymbals felt like scaling a fortress. I cringed and wished Mom hadn't volunteered me. And yet, all those evenings in Portland, when I'd beat my anger into exhaustion after the breakup with Joe and then again when Lance betrayed me, somehow prepared me for this moment. Thanks to my crush on Jeremy, I'd been doing more than obsessing about him. I'd also been absorbing the drum scores. Picking up the sticks, I prayed for muscle memory in my wrists and palms. I ran a rim shot followed by an easy four-on-four on the high hat and inserted a simple bass pattern to cover counts one, two, and four.

Rhett marched over to me. "Y'all done farting around, Lark?"

"Did I not tell you, she can make the fairies dance and leap?" Mom's voice preceded her as she entered the stage area.

"Mom," I gulped remembering disastrous drum recitals as a kid. Telling her to leave sat at the front of my brain until I realized I needed her support in the audience. "Thanks for coming."

"Ach, sure I'd rather swim the length of the Liffey than miss your debut."

Rhett smiled through a clenched jaw, his patience tugging the end of a leash. "I'm fixin' to get us a few minutes practice, dear lady. I'd be honored if you took a seat and cheered us on." He turned his back on Mom and approached me. "Lark, can we at last proceed? Y'all, let's warm up with 'Love of Queen Bess'. It's a simple beat, Lark. Try to keep up."

Steve backed toward me fingering the opening chords. "Don't let the bastard get you down." He nodded and began the opening lyrics. Matt joined with his keyboard and then Rhett's pennywhistle.

I took a big breath, thought of the assholes I'd had to deal with over time and let the energy flow down my arms and legs, snatching the beat from the air.

In response to our music floating out the entrances, customers straggled in, ordered pints, and filled the seats.

On edge expecting the worst because Bev hadn't showed, I hoped she'd found some killer shoes. What was I thinking when I snapped at her? She was my best ally.

She ambled through the alley entrance as I double-checked the tom-tom, everyone else in their spots. Polite, warm, she stepped next to Candi, but the woman picking up the cowbell was the VP of IT Bev, the professional Bev.

A tougher crowd than Cork, rows and rows of expectant eyes scrutinized the stage. If they didn't like us, they would not be kind.

I was to lead off. I felt exposed on the stool all by myself. No refuge with Candi and Bev. Matt, stationed to my far right, stabbed at the keyboard, and frowned. Rhett swooped his gigantic ostrich plume hat onto his head. Steve hunched over his guitar, straightened, looked my way, and gave a thumbs up.

I quickly moved my sticks across the floor tom, snare, and crash cymbal and sank into the first number, my focus on nothing but the kit and my sticks. As the rest of the band took up their parts, I felt as if they were my safety net. The rest of the set consisted of what we'd practiced in Portland, but from a new perspective, me rediscovering my own style.

We opened for the Irish band, Rebels, that the manager had mentioned when we arrived on the wrong day. By the time they took the stage, customers packed the place three deep, lined against the bar. Rebels was deadly. Their female drummer, who played a wooden box, intrigued me. Her confidence made me wonder if, in some way, I had paved the way for her, like Karen Carpenter had for me.

Bodies consumed any available space, dancing and singing, glasses raised. Even Bev managed to get beyond her corporate exterior, prancing through the crowd and handing me a pint. "You did it, girl!" she hollered.

I scanned the crowd, pleased, and relieved. No linen, white hair, willy boppers, or kids in strollers. About to cross off Viking helmets, I spied one, no doubt a refugee from the Dublin Viking Tours. I could live with that. In the front row, my groupie from Condron's in Cork beat the air, arms raised, fists clenched. Truth be told, I'd forgotten his name.

Then, as we packed up, he appeared at my side just as Bev and Candi disappeared into the alley, lugging gear.

"Lark, you were hot tonight," Mystery Groupie said.

"I'll take that as a compliment. We were baking onstage." I scoured my brain for a wisp of memory. What was his name? Yep, same killer eyes and black hair. I was fast becoming a proponent of mandatory name-tags at concerts.

"Do you need a hand?" His eyebrows wiggled suggestively. My creep alert went off.

"Thanks anyway, I think we've got it." *He waggled eyebrows at me? Was that supposed to be an attempt at a come-on? How drunk was I when I went off with him?* "I thought you lived in Cork." I zipped the cymbals into their round case.

"I have a gaff there, but your Facebook page announced you'd be here tonight. I got a leg on, and here I am. Let me at least buy you a jar. I think you've earned it." He took a gulp of stout and swayed.

Did he think that earned him anything from me? "I hate to be a party poop, but I'm really beat. Why don't you give me your number, and I'll call you." His chances were about as good as Pat Feeney serving pints to pigs.

"I won't keep you past your bedtime, which I recall isn't for a few hours yet." He leaned on the bar, propped his chin against his palm, his smile toothier than I remembered. *Was that a hickey on his neck?*

"I really can't. Early day tomorrow." I scouted for Bev, hoping she would come through the door. Or maybe Candi forgot a cowbell.

"Are you blowing me off? Do you even remember my name? It's Aengus." His elbow slipped sending him sideways on the bar's surface. *A Groucho Marx look-alike's trying to seduce me.*

"Of course, I remember your name, Aengus."

The man before me rose, recovering from his prat fall. "Then let's get off for a bit of craic. We were deadly before." He grabbed my arm.

I yanked my arm away and glared. "You're obviously plastered. I'm off to me ma's gaff for a good night's sleep, so away with you." All the hairs on my body prickled, my foot itching to connect with his crotch.

"Jaysus! I meant no harm." Aengus backed out the door, his listing form illuminated by the streetlamps.

Body roiling from the adrenalin, I hunched over my kit again to find Steve's lanky form behind me. His hand cupped my elbow. "Where're Bev and Candi? I'll see you to your mom's."

"I don't need you to see me anywhere," I retorted.

"Well, I do," Bev stepped back into the bar, Candi on her heels. "The alley is jammed with drunk college dudes. Even Candi's muses have fled."

~~~

"We've been booked at the Loughgarvan Rhythm and Blues Festival." Rhett's booming voice emanated from my cell the next morning as Mom placed a plate of rashers on the table. "Tim, Rebel's fiddle wizard of extraordinary style, got a phone call from the event's manager. One of the bands from the US got busted smuggling meth and detained. Tim's put us forward."

"Festival?" I asked. My eyes roved the table, landing on Bev, Candi, and Mom's quizzical expressions. "Rhett, I'm putting you on speaker."

"We're going to resurrect our set bringing into service numbers we worked up before coming over. With Jeremy as drummer, they didn't gel." At the mention of his name, pain scooted across Candi's face. "But Lark, you have the magic. You can make our new playlist work. Ms. Devlin, my dear benefactor, could we prevail upon you to find us a practice space?"

Pure Rhett bullshit. I cut my eyes toward Bev and Candi and mouthed, "Benefactor?"

"To be sure, I'll be lending you a room at my office building. Just yesterday, was I not telling Candi and Lark that my buskers audition? Real estate is limited."

"My dear lady, the weight of that responsibility goes back millennia," Rhett said.

"Why don't we pick this up in person? Your benefactor must get her morning going." Mom blushed, girlish.

I met Candi's eyes, and she nodded slightly.

I tapped the phone icon to disconnect. "Mom, that scumbag hit on you."

"I'm not too old to be flattered by attention."

"He hits on everyone, doesn't he, Candi?"

"Lark's right. Deirdre, I suggest you insist he use a condom. I did, and you don't have the advantage of knowing his track record."

"Candi, you're not helping."

"She's got a point," Bev said, "although you might want to check out

154

the tally Lark and I have been keeping. He's trying to set a record for the most women he's bedded." She patted her jeans pocket as if searching for our now dog-eared sheet.

"My dears, I'm not looking for a shag, so let's be getting on with the day. I'm off to me office. Give Rhett and the lads the directions." The swinging door to the kitchen closed behind her.

Chapter Twenty-Four

Razor sharp tension saturated the practice session.

"Lark, execute a lighter touch on the cymbals. Patter them. Are you using brushes? They guide the rest of us, not batter our heads." Rhett's obnoxious self kicked into overdrive.

I held up a brush. "Hey, I was in a jazz band. I know what I'm doing."

Mom emerged from her office, striding toward me, while Rhett attempted to intercept. "My dear lady, I hope our creative efforts to work our way toward a new solidarity have not disturbed you. Artistic types can be so emotional."

She ignored the lead singer. "Lark, I'm just after finding what I've been searching for high and low. Do you remember these? I hope they will bring you success." Mom presented a well-used pair of combination sticks and mallets. "You may be wanting these as well." She produced a pair of nylon brushes, slightly yellowed by age, the tips a bit bent on the edges.

"Your past experience lives in those. Whether you knew it or not, you have your own set of muses." Candi scurried to her backpack.

"Let me guess. Herbs for a welcome home ceremony." Bev pinched her mouth tight as if preventing any other acidic comment from escaping.

She must be feeling out of her league.

Mom placed her hand on Rhett's forearm. "Sure you'd be getting better band unity if you let your dear members work together."

Yay Mom. That put him in his place. For the rest of the morning he retreated, giving us some musical breathing space.

Candi's range was meant for jazz. Working with her became fun, articulating my cymbals like wings under her throaty soprano.

By mid-afternoon, we conquered the easy jazz classics, while a sense of cohesiveness sprouted.

"Y'all, let's try a stab at Dave Brubeck's 'Take Five.'" Rhett handed me the drum music. "Do you think you can keep up? We're playing our own version. Steve's playing horn for the sax part."

"No problem. I cut my teeth on this." I gave a thankful prayer to Cecilia, patron saint of musicians, and Sister Ignatius, who had conducted our jazz band and insisted we learn the classic.

"Be sure to note where Candi comes in with the scat." He hung the bass's strap around his neck. "We use a bass guitar instead of a bass fiddle. Lark, let's see if we can begin together." He still stung from Mom's rebuke.

Rhett's bass, my snare, and my ride cymbal along with Matt's keyboard created a hypnotic rhythm. Candi's seductive voice floated on top. When Steve jumped in with his horn, the song became erotic.

Until Steve and Matt shattered the cool vibe we had going. They were supposed to share or at least collaborate, handing off to each other while I provided the support. Problem was they didn't, instead trampling each other's notes. *Bastards.* I intercepted, hammering the bass drum, broke a drumstick on a cymbal, and toppled off the seat.

"Can I interest you in a pot of tea to wash down some cucumber sandwiches?" Mom appeared in the doorway.

"Y'all, take ten," Rhett said grabbing the reins.

"Candi, what's the deal between Matt and Steve?" was the first thing out of my mouth in the ladies' restroom, the one place we three women could have a conversation. I lowered my jeans to reveal a bruise on my thigh, already turning an ugly shade of purple.

"This used to happen all the time," she said. "I'm surprised it hasn't surfaced before now. Jeremy kept them in check."

"So why now?" Bev's face a serious VP of IT.

"Not sure. I thought they'd worked it out, but this is new. I think some kind of pissing contest is going on." Candi shook out her hair. "They come from different musical backgrounds. Steve trained as a classical pianist. A protégé. His parents pushed him toward the concert stage. He rebelled, took up the guitar and trumpet, and the parents disowned him."

Bev half-closed her eyes as she applied a fresh coat of mascara. "And Matt?"

"He was self-taught on the keyboard as part of a grunge band he and Jeremy formed. They started out in a garage near San Francisco. They'd been best buds since middle school until a rift. Matt wanted to go to seminary, and he thought Jeremy should too. They joined different bands for a while, and then both joined Band of Pirates. I guess they came to an understanding.

"Steve replaced Hugh Arsenal. Matt has a natural gift, especially with composition, which, I think, makes Steve jealous because he doesn't. He and Matt hafta work it out and soon if we're gonna be any good at the jazz festival. Egos. The downside of band life."

"What did Jeremy do to get them in line?" I sopped a paper towel to mop the back of my neck.

"Out-pissed them. You did that just now. You'll have to break a few more drumsticks, but they'll come around. Bev, this is a new kind of gig," Candi said. "How are you doing?"

"Fine. We're a team." Her voice corporate, her way of saying she was uncomfortable or threatened.

"Well, I think we also need to address the other day, when you were so sarcastic about my concern about the stolen antiquities." I picked at the broken drumstick, my thumb rubbing the jagged edge.

"Your default, Lark, is to swing from one thing to another. Take your bog body idea." Bev extracted lipstick from her new purse.

"My Nanna believed that life has higher principles that we must honor."

"But whose higher principles? This is Ireland. Are you really that vested?" Bev turned her back to the mirror, leaning on the sink.

"I'm an Irish citizen."

"I'm getting a feeling of disconnect here." Candi pulled a tube of hand cream from her backpack.

"But you were born in the US. Are you really connected?"

"As my Nanna would say, I'm neither fish nor fowl. I'm trying to figure my way out." I pressed my fingers against my lower eyelids as tears began.

Bev handed me a Kleenex.

"Your future journey, right Lark?" Candi rubbed cream into her palms and fingers.

"Last thing I expected was to play den mother to Rhett, Matt, and Steve. What a hell of a journey. You two have it together. You have lives to go back to when this is over. All I have is a dental hygiene program that I'm settling for." I blew my nose, my face splotchy.

"Bev and I are also on journeys."

"I can't speak for Candi, but I have to settle as well. My journey in Ireland is a reprieve from what's coming up. Long, grueling hours. And as a result of this Irish gig, I'm beginning to wonder if a VP is worth the headache. I gotta have faith the promotion will work out."

"My muses guide my journey. In a way, I'm neither fish nor fowl too. I have one foot planted in the everyday and the other in the supernatural. Like Bev, I have to have faith that something valuable will come out of this."

Bev took the hand cream Candi offered and handed it back. "I think you should focus on a great opportunity to play drums in a band and visit your mom."

"Yeah, Lark, look where the journey has taken you. Let it go and see where you land." Candi capped the hand cream and tossed the tube in her backpack.

"I suggest the journey's taking us back out to rehearsal." Bev shoved her makeup bag in her purse and pressed her butt against the door.

We emerged from the restroom to find Mom had vacated to her office in the complex.

Rhett jammed the mic in the stand. "You jackasses should have worked all this out long ago." His voice projected the deep resonance you hear in loud radio announcers. "We have a gift horse, so to speak. And I don't want to squander it. We've worked too hard as an average band. I say, we have the possibility to be above average, maybe even great. Matt, Steve, don't fuck this up!" Rhett pivoted on his cowboy boots, marched to his spot, and picked up his guitar. "And Lark, darlin', you're doing right fine. I want you to beat some sense into these boys. Now let's get back to work."

Chapter Twenty-Five

O kay, we have four more days before we have to head north for the jazz festival." Candi huddled beside Bev and me outside the Hodges and Figgis bookstore near our rehearsal building.

Bev perused the window displays. "The good news is we have a decent place to sleep at your mom's." She added, "You know, we need to check out Rhett's stuff while we can."

"I thought you didn't want to risk your valuable career for Ireland's valuable leather." I leaned against the store's entrance and pushed.

We milled through the aisles, noses in and out of books.

Bev picked up a coffee table book, thumbing through the pages. "Candi, I've been thinking about what you said. About the journey and seeing where it takes us. I never in a million years thought I'd end up singing backup for a jazz band. I've got you, Lark, to thank. While I don't necessarily agree with you, I've got your back, and I've gotta have faith this is what we're supposed to do."

"Part of that journey means we have four more days to figure out where the bog body, loot, and butter are." Candi's attention riveted to a shelf of occult reference titles.

"Yeah, but how do we snoop without getting caught?" I rambled toward a display of James Joyce's works, lifted a copy of *Ulysses,* and smiled as I recalled the nun who insisted we read the Irish classic. My creep alert went off at the glimpse of a jeans-clad leg and sneaker disappearing behind a stack of travel guides.

"You two forget that I once had a thing with Rhett. What a nightmare." When Bev looked at her quizzically, Candi added, "When I hooked up with him for those couple of weeks, my muses threatened to quit."

"I hear you, girlfriend. Same problem with Lance. Only you had the unfortunate luck to know him too."

"Gotta admit Jeremy was the one good thing in my life," Candi sighed.

We gravitated toward the cashier.

Candi's arms cradled a number of occult books, intricate mandalas sprawled across their covers. "I'll find a chance to sneak out Rhett's stuff. Seeing I know his habits, the risk of getting caught is less. At Deirdre's, we can see if there's any information on where the body and loot are, then I can sneak it back."

"It'll all be in his portfolio. Bev, did you get everything you needed?" We both stood empty-handed while Candi completed her purchase.

"We'd better get to Feeney's and warm up." Bev held the door.

"You know, for such an old grouch, the manager's rather sweet," Candi said exiting behind me.

The bookstore's display window revealed a black-haired figure stopped at the cash register, the back of a pair of jeans resembling the ones I'd seen earlier. I hoped my douchebag alert was wrong. Who was the patron saint protecting individuals from creeps?

~~~

When I'm onstage, the world consists of only what's in my head and the relationship of that to my body, surrounded by a bubble that includes the rest of the band. I'm rarely aware of anything else, whether one person in the audience or thousands.

During a break, I glanced over to the bar to see the fellow I'd picked up in Cork perched on a stool. He wore the same jeans and sneakers as the man I'd seen in Hodges and Figgis. With a big grin on his face, he spread his legs and rested a hand on his thigh. My heart yo-yoed. I gulped.

I'd forgotten his name. Again.

I read that memory gets spotty as you careen toward menopause. Sweat soaked my hair and tee. A hot flash? *I am on a hot stage. His name has nothing to do with the next number we're about to play.*

What a bummer that Aengus—that was his name—stayed the whole evening. Spooked from the bookstore, I made sure to keep a casual eye for my bandmates, my creep alert blaring in my brain.

The set over, patrons trailing out, Bev, Candi, and I joined the fellas at the bar for a pint and then set to work packing up for the night. Matt and Steve dismantled the keyboard, the former muttering, "Piece of shit."

We'd done a good job. The audience liked our songs, Steve and Matt had finally decided to play nice, and I felt confident. Most of all, the seat Aengus had occupied was now empty. He must have gotten my drop-dead message from the night before. Still, my gut kept up a subtle thrum to be vigilant.

"I've got one of my muse wars. I'm going back to your mom's." Candi massaged her temples.

"Me too," Bev said. "Except my muses are nicely tucked in for the night. I'm exhausted, and these boots weren't made for stomping." She held up a brown suede foot with a stiletto heel.

"Feeney says if we hurry, we can catch the last bus," Candi headed toward the door. "Aren't you coming, Lark?"

"It's all good. I'll catch a cab." No surprise to see Rhett's back going out the door with one of the women from the band we opened for. At the bar, Matt and Steve hunched over a round of stout. If it was any other city, I might sidle over to join them again, and then get one of them to walk me to a cab. But Dublin was my city, one where I'd spent many a night partying on the streets until dawn. Dublin wasn't New York or even Portland. I was in the mood for a nostalgic ramble along the canal. I turned back to packing the drum kit.

"To be sure, you must be ready for some black stuff," Aengus reached over my shoulder to pick up a cymbal bag. I jumped and cringed at his voice behind me.

"No worries, Aengus. I've got this." I grabbed the cover before his clammy mitts could take possession.

"How'd you like Hodges and Figgis? I saw you looking at Joyce. I'm just after buying you this." He handed me a brown sack, its shape the outline of a book.

I studied the bag in my palms, chills joining my soaked stage costume. "You got this at Hodges and Figgis," I stated flatly, the memory of his sneaker and jeans disappearing behind a stack of books. The thought landed in my brain that this was no ordinary fan. *Creep alert, creep alert!* My body buzzed.

"Joyce's *Ulysses*." Aengus grinned and waggled his eyebrows. "To be sure you've missed Bloomsday on June 16th, but we could retrace the pilgrimage anyway."

Really? That was sexy? Nauseated fear does not mingle with stout. I stared at him. "I can't accept this," and handed the book back.

"Away with you, you can. A wee book, I'm giving you and a grand night." Aengus grabbed my sleeve and tugged me through the alley door. I dug in my heels, pulling back, but he tugged harder. "Lark, come out with me. We'll be brilliant. More brilliant than Cork."

My feet slipped along the worn cobblestones, my butt heading toward the pavement. A light went on in my brain. I'd dealt with this type more than once before, only this drunk wasn't wearing chain mail or smelling like a horse stall. I let him take me by the hand, walk a couple of steps, and then I twisted, throwing my arm across my shoulder, bending forward. He lost his balance, and I took advantage of the momentum to pitch Aengus over my shoulder, where he landed on his back, sound escaping his lungs like wind knocked out of a set of Irish bagpipes.

"Aengus, my man, I tried to be nice about this. But apparently you are so plastered, you don't hear 'No' and that I mean it. Let me be clear. I am not going on any Bloomsday trek with you tonight or any night. I don't want your book. I hated James Joyce when I had to read him in school. *Ulysses* was one of the stupidest books I ever trudged through."

He sat up, scuttled backward crablike, and glared. "I heard you, I did," he croaked. "You're a right geebag. You let me think we'd have a bit of craic when I didn't have a baldy, you manky bitch."

"Hey, that's enough. You heard her. Get your ass out of here." Steve crowded the doorway. In two strides he grabbed Aengus's shirt and yanked him to his feet.

"You're welcome to her." My ill-chosen groupie sidled around the corner and into the back street.

My eyes bugged and jaw clenched. "Steve, are you stalking me? This is the second time you showed up when I was perfectly able to take care of myself." The stout swirling with the acid in my stomach threatened to escape onto the cobblestones. My diaphragm constricted. I gulped and swallowed.

"Didn't anyone tell you? One of the perks of being a backup singer and guide is having a bodyguard. You get double perks if you happen to also be the drummer. I'm your escort for this evening." His eyes disappeared into his smile as he swiped a chunk of hair off his face. The motion of his hand made me wonder if his fingers were as gentle as in that gesture.

"You know, I can take a cab by myself." My voice wavered. The run-in with Aengus left me skittish that he could possibly be lurking in the alley's shadows.

"I'm on security duty until I get you back to your mom's. Do me the favor and let me get you home safely, so I can get on with my own evening." He placed his hand lightly on the small of my back, and as if we were skating partners, took one of my hands.

Rather than escorting me down the poorly lit lane, Steve led me back inside Feeney's. He paused near Matt, who leaned on the bar, his face hovering over his phone, thumbs moving to text. "I'm going to make sure Lark gets home okay. An asshole's stalking her."

The bandmate quickly pressed a button darkening the screen and looked up, a grin finding a place on his lips, one that said he'd gotten caught doing something secretive. "No accounting for taste, Lark." Matt pocketed his cell. His hands wrapped around a fresh pint.

Steve slapped his back. "You off to mass in the morning?"

"Yeah, I'll be at rehearsal in the afternoon. Rhett got us rooms at the hostel."

"See you later." The guitarist thumped the keyboardist on his shoulder.

"Not if I see you first." Matt lifted the pint glass, the ale golden in the bar lights.

The guitarist escorted me through the bar, the pub now closed. "I'm not a backdoor man." He winked, holding the door to the front entrance, me tottering along, relief for his company settling my stomach. I stared into eyes as dark as the black stuff I'd consumed.

We made our way onto the parkway. The delicious August evening sported warm air riding on a cool undertone that dissipated the choking claustrophobia of the pub.

"What a strange dude," Steve said. "You knew Matt wanted to be a priest?" I nodded. "Can't imagine who would want to make their confession to him."

"Probably a good career move on his part to change professions, but how come you're on his case?"

"Because he's a poser. He's got talent, but that's not why I ride him. He's a fucking poser, and I don't trust him. He's got another agenda I can't quite figure out."

"How come you didn't become a concert pianist?" My question felt as if it had jumped from a tree and landed at our feet.

"Sounds like Candi's been talking."

"She didn't volunteer. I asked."

"I don't like to wear a tux, and the bow tie hurts my Adam's apple." He pointed at his throat.

My social worker instincts kicked in. *Matt's not the only one hiding an agenda.*

"If that's the reason, I'd be pissed too if I were your folks."

He snorted. "That's not the half of it. The government confiscated their business and interred them in a camp during World War II. I always thought they believed they had something to prove. I was their path to vindication."

We ambled along the boulevard, passing couples window-shopping or entwined in dark doorways. I thought of Lance. Did we ever share kisses that were anything more than lust? Before him had been my ex, Joe. A couple leaned into each other as they passed, oblivious to anything else. A sigh arrived from a couple of decades ago, traveling through the years to compare my idealistic youth with where I managed to end up.

"What was that big sigh about?" Steve's voice broke into my thoughts.

"Having a nostalgic moment. My ex and I used to walk this street when we first met. Were you ever married?"

The streetlamp silhouetted the shake of his head. "Did I miss anything?"

"I'm not someone you should ask."

We walked on, shadows and memories trailing behind like gossamer.

Steve grabbed my hand. "Run! I see a cab. Who knows when the next one will come by?" He galloped off, dragging me after him, the other arm raised as the taxi edged to the curbside.

We settled into the back seat, Steve buckling a seatbelt.

"You really didn't need to see me back to my mom's." The dash to the cab left me winded and upset my stomach again.

The cab driver craned his head to view the backseat. "Madam, I'm not to be leaving until you fasten your safety belt."

"My job is to get you home safely." Steve's arm reached across my torso, yanked on the belt, and clicked it in place.

"It's really not necessary." I folded my arms across my chest, to stifle the tingle running from my nipples to my spine and down my back.

"Just following orders, little lady." Steve's lousy cowboy imitation made me laugh.

167

"Under whose directive would that be? And why am I so special?"

"Do you think we can risk losing yet another drummer?"

"No worries. I'm not about to run off. I've already found and lost my inner Celtic self."

"Yeah, you do seem a little lost."

I didn't like where he headed this conversation. "Let's talk again when you've had a turn in the driver's seat. At least I got us to our destinations."

"From Galway are you?" The driver intruded on our conversation, ear-wigging.

"And on to Portland," I said.

"Portland by way of California," Steve added.

"To be sure California is a long way from Portland," he said, "and lobsters."

"Ach, 'tis the other Portland," I chuckled. "Nary a lobster in sight." Steve's face contorted, quizzical. "Happens all the time," I whispered.

The rise and fall of streetlights passing the cab had a hypnotic effect, the fatigue like an unwanted shawl around my shoulders. I sank into the taxi's cushions, feeling contented.

"What do you think of our fair city?" No surprise we had a chatty cab driver.

"The Liffey doesn't smell as bad," I said.

"Have you been seeing many of the sites?"

"Not too many. We've been playing mostly at Feeney's pub," Steve said.

"You must be visiting Dublin's National Museum, one of our pride and joys, although to be sure what a sad thing about our precious artifacts."

Steve's back deepened as he leaned forward, his face in shadow. "You don't say. Artifacts? The museum is top on my list. I'm especially interested in archaeological finds."

What did he know? Did he know about Rhett's portfolio? Was he involved as well? Nothing in his face or tone indicated anything other than idle curiosity.

168

His arm bumped my thigh. "Sorry, Lark." Fingers slid across my knee-cap as his hands animated his words. "What happened?"

The touch sent a spark up my thigh to the base of my back.

"Why sure as I'm driving you, they've been stolen. But that shouldn't stop you from seeing the rest of the museum. Grand it is." He nosed the car into Mom's driveway.

"Hang on. I want to see her safely in, and then I'll need to get back downtown."

"Bang on." The driver parked the cab in neutral, the engine idling as if impatient with sitting still.

Steve's eyebrows shot into his hairline.

"He didn't mean that the way you think." I crawled out of the cab, feeling as if my butt would sink into Mom's small patch of lawn. Steve held my elbow.

"You know, I'm not some old lady you have to assist into the nursing home."

"Yeah, I get it. Just—"

"Following orders," I finished for him. "You're going to way too much effort. I grew up in this city." My indignation flowed over my exhaustion like a cold shower.

"Problem is you have a knack for attracting bad ass dudes. Aengus is not someone you want to hang with."

"I do not attract bad ass dudes!" What did he know about the dudes I attracted?

"Well, let's see. There was that knight wannabe. Then there was that drummer wannabe. And most recently, there is that groupie wannabe."

"And what do you wanna be? My savior?" I tried to sound coy, but instead my mouth spat sarcasm.

"Honey, I think that's what you'd hoped for all along. And believe me, it ain't me."

I drilled my eyes into him, feeling as if he'd cracked my exterior like an egg. Anger coursed in my arm to slap his smug face, but instead my

169

foot jerked out connecting with his shin.

"Ouch! Why the hell did you do that?"

I raised my fist to punch him, but his arms enveloped me, pulling me close to his chest, releasing the residual smell of cologne, tempered by a night on stage under hot lights. In the warmth of his embrace, his breathing rose and fell, rhythmic, calm, his heartbeat, measured, comforting. He rocked back and forth.

His mouth moved in my hair. "You know, I remember being about six and pissed off because I didn't want to practice the piano anymore. I had a teacher who was very patient. I lashed out one day and kicked her. This is what she did. Just held me."

His arms secured me like a blanket as he rocked, my body relaxing into his. His lips came together on my head as if it were a kiss.

The cabby honked his horn, flashed his brights, and yelled out the window. "Hey you two. Do you need to get a room? I got customers to pick up."

Steve twisted his head toward the taxi. "Hold on a minute." His arms tightened as if reluctant to let go. And then he released me.

"Okay, Lark, time to fly home." He stood on the lawn. I could feel his eyes like beacons on my shoulder blades as I bolted toward the house, flung the door wide, the shutters banging as I slammed it.

The lights in the entryway glared, my eyes taking a moment to adjust. From the window, the cab's headlights arced across the lawn and backed away.

Footsteps and the teakettle's whistle drew me to the kitchen. "Mom, what are you doing up?"

"Couldn't sleep. Sure it's that way when I think something must be troubling you. Can I make you some tea? How was your set?"

"Fine. I'm fine. Probably more fatigued than anything. I can't seem to get past the jet lag, even though we've been here more than a week. Tea will keep me up."

"Well, I'll be off to bed now that you're home. I see that nice boy,

170

Steve, saw you to the door. I'm more than delighted he's taking care of you, my dear."

"He's not a boy. He's my age."

"Is he now?"

"And he's not taking care of me," I called to her footsteps on the stairs.

"Is that so?"

Chapter Twenty-Six

I spent the better part of the night staring out the window, the sofa unwilling to give me any comfortable way to sleep, the memory of Steve's chest an imprint on my cheek. His comments left me wide-eyed and tossing, lost in the pre-dawn hours. Where'd he come off? Like he knew what I needed? Like the asshole men who came into my life were my fault? Like he was any different?

I stared at the array of religious figures in the back garden. The fading night revealed their murky outlines. I vowed I would not pray to St. Jude. No matter what Steve thought, I was not lost. I struggled to my feet, folded blankets, and stumbled into the kitchen with strong tea on my mind.

The morning found me at the dining table, a teapot resting by a cup of Earl Gray. Mom left for the office to audition a new busker group, the slam of the front door reminding me that I was fully awake and exhausted.

I stirred my tea, added honey, and stared at the clock's pendulum swimming back and forth. My head contained no brain matter, a vacant shell, unable to process the previous night.

"What the hell happened to you?" Bev appeared in the doorway and squatted by my chair. "You look like shit."

"I feel like shit."

"Did something happen after Candi and I left Feeney's?"

I nodded and scrubbed at my cheek, my face felt numb. "Aengus stalked us at Hodges and Figgis. He tried to drag me off for a bit of craic after the show. I said, 'No,' which he wouldn't take in his hammered state. I ended up tossing him over my shoulder onto the cobblestones."

"Oh my God! I thought he was creepy, but this is serious. Dangerous."

"The worst part is Steve insisted on seeing me back here."

Bev's mouth, nose, and forehead creased in incomprehension.

"He hugged me."

"Wait. Steve hugging you is worse than a serial nut case?"

"He said I attract badass dudes, that I'm lost and looking to be saved. I kicked him in the shins, so he hugged me."

"I am majorly confused. He is right about the badass dudes part, although Joe was okay, you just grew apart."

"I got zero sleep last night, I'm beyond pissed at him. Where does he get off?"

Bev's cheeks puffed and deflated like a balloon as she exhaled. "He might have a point. Why you dropped everything—a good career, living in a totally cool city like Portland, and friends like me—to indulge in some fantasy business, following a guy who is way out of touch with reality—escapes me."

"Wow. Do you think you could be a little less vague?"

Bev was supposed to commiserate.

A clunking noise accompanied Candi's tread on the stairs and into the dining room. "Vague about what?"

"Where to find breakfast makings," Bev said.

"Mom had an early meeting. We're to fend for ourselves."

"I snuck this out while Rhett hustled his conquest last night. I've got to get this back before he notices." She brought her wheeled suitcase into the dining room and unlatched it to reveal Rhett's leather portfolio. With a precision I didn't think she had, she unzipped it and eased out a book.

"That was in his bedside table in the RV," I said. *When I snooped in Rhett's bedside table, Steve had not joined the band yet.* The thought

173

intruded like an unwanted tagalong.

"That's the book you were talking about?" Bev appeared plate of toast in hand and leaned over Candi to inspect some of the pages.

"Better back away. Toast crumbs and butter stains are the last thing we need." She displayed the book page's full-color picture, the visage the shade of old leather.

"Bev found a topographical map when we were in Limerick the morning after we played at Sweeney's. We had only a couple of minutes and barely missed Steve walking in on us. Besides the book, that's what started this whole thing."

"You mean this one?" Candi teased out a piece of paper, careful not to disturb the others. "Here are a couple of other maps." She spread them on the dining room table.

We peered at the circles and squiggles. "Anyone here ever take a class in geography?" Bev asked. We all shook our heads.

"Know where this might be?" Candi pointed to a map.

Bev inched closer and planted her foot on mine. Candi studied the map, her index finger tracing the roads. Bev's eyes slid in my direction. She clenched her jaw, and widened her eyes, the *don't say a word* look. Who to trust? A new age flake or my solid friend. My nod was no more than a flick of my chin.

"Could be anywhere. The country's changed so much since I lived here." I bit my lip. Definitely not a city and more like a small town. Given that no big body of water bordered the area, the place had to be inland. County Meath or Monaghan perhaps.

Candi looked up. "None of this looks familiar?" She gathered the maps, folded them neatly, and slipped them into the portfolio. I shook my head again. "I found this as well in here." Candi extracted a thumb drive. "Rhett might have stored important stuff here. Bev, do you have your laptop handy?"

"I'll get it from upstairs." The soon-to-be VP of IT returned minutes later and fired it up, inserting the thumb drive. A demand for the password lit the screen.

"Are you able to crack this?" Candi asked.

"I'm management, not a techy. You'll have more luck than me."

"Let me think…" Candi clicked away, little dots planting themselves on the screen. The error message for an incorrect password popped up. She strained her head back to examine the ceiling, then tapped the keys. Same error message. More examination of the ceiling accompanied by the crunch of toast. Candi rested her fingers on the keys and typed. "Crap," she said.

"Why not try channeling the muses," Bev said. "You know. A keyboard, a Ouija board. What's the dif?"

"Good idea. Lark, can you kill the dining room lights?" She closed her eyes. Was Candi that dim?

Bev stared, her mouth a small, upturned smirk in her cheek, stating her opinion about all the bullshit. She placed her teacup in its saucer, making a slight clink. "How come all the theatrics? You repeatedly call on them and don't do all this."

Candi, trance-like, stared at the mid-ground, then placed her fingers on the keyboard. She reminded me of a concert pianist, focused and unaware of any audience. Concert pianist reminded me of Steve, so I drop-kicked any thought out of my head about how right he had been.

"Maybe you should light some lavender. Or maybe some chickweed." Bev made a point of bumping her spoon on the sides of the teacup as she stirred in sugar.

Candi typed. I leaned over her shoulder. Nothing.

"Well, I'm disappointed. Your muses feeling a little out of sorts today?" Bev took a loud slurp of tea.

"I thought it was worth a shot." She powered down, removed the thumb drive, and closed the lid.

"Too bad. My corporation could use a person like you to figure out when and how to beat the competition."

"Couldn't work in a place like that. My muses and I have ethics, you know."

"Which doesn't include hacking into an ex-lover's private documents." Bev shook her head. "I was kidding." She butt bumped the kitchen door to ferry her teacup and saucer.

Candi massaged her neck. "I don't know why Bev has such bad energy, and she seems to direct it at me. Anyway, full disclosure, I'm going to do a rebirth chant to lighten up her aura. You should see some positive change in the next day or two."

"What's this about positive change?" Bev emerged from the kitchen.

"Comes from dispelling negative energy. I gotta get this stuff back before Rhett finds it missing and guesses we're on to him. You know, Bev, at least I'm giving it everything I got. I'll see you two at rehearsal."

I followed her to the front door. "Meet Bev and me at Dublin's National Museum. Rhett said we don't have to be at Mom's office until after lunch." I pulled the shutter up and watched her clip along the rain stained sidewalk, Bev's chin resting on my shoulder. "That was intense."

"That was bogus," she said.

"Yeah, as you've said all along, something's way whacko about her."

"She spent a lot of time studying that map. She may not be as harmless as she seems."

Candi's back disappeared around the corner toward the bus stop.

"Hard to say. I'd hoped she might give us intel." I tipped the shutter down.

"Sorry I let slip yesterday about Rhett and all."

"Not to worry. If she's up to something and thinks we trust her, your slip up will work to our advantage. Let's grab a bus." I rummaged in the closet, the small space jammed with coats, many of them new. *Mom's busker business must be profitable that she could buy all these.*

"So why did you invite her to meet us at the museum?" Bev retrieved her leather jacket from the floor.

"That old saying about keeping your friends close and your enemies even closer. Thanks for having my back. I know you didn't sign up for this."

"No one would sign up for this unless under duress. Or if they were scammed. Or they were on the lam." Bev checked her watch. "We better get going."

Clouds tumbled across the horizon, patches of blue like odd-shaped quilt pieces among them. As if a streak of sunshine illuminated my thoughts, I knew Steve was totally off base. I wasn't lost. I wasn't looking to be saved. I was looking to save a bog body!

Chapter Twenty-Seven

W e're good. I got Rhett's stuff back. He's still out with last night's shag," Candi said. From beneath an umbrella, she gestured toward the museum's entrance. "I don't get why we are coming here. The building has an aura like thunderstorms."

"Because I think we should scope out the site of the heist," I said. "Besides, no trip to the Emerald Isle would be complete without a stop here." A smile swam across my face, recalling my student days filled with the hours spent here.

Security officers manned booths with conveyor belts, the x-ray equipment stationed before the entrance's marble colonnades and domed rotunda. We kicked off our shoes. Everything had to be checked in. A guard moved a wand along our bodies before we could advance through the doorway.

Bev and Candi followed me through the rotunda to the exhibits for the Celtic artifacts, many of them gold neck collars or earrings with incised geometric patterns or twisted torcs. Officers flanked any of the display cases still housing gold items that glimmered as if created yesterday rather than millennia ago.

In the far corner, three sentries blocked the huge doorway to one of the galleries. A grate in mid-installation hovered like a half-open mouth, metal bars like teeth.

"That gallery holds Ireland's most precious relics. That must be where the latest heist took place." I pointed toward the gate. "Too bad the museum has to mar this beautiful interior."

We rambled to the entrance to the gallery holding the bog bodies. The museum's enhanced security exceeded anything you'd see at an airport. We again kicked off our shoes while guards scanned us with metal detectors.

We entered the Kingship and Sacrifice exhibit, gawking at the angry space, the bog body's prior resting place. Security officers limited the number of people passing through the room to a trickle. Normally, we would not have had a prayer to get in, except one of the guards busked on his days off, playing Irish bagpipes, and Mom called in some favors.

In the presence of the dead, we shivered at the room's tomb-like quality. Visitors silently toured the exhibit, as if attending a viewing at a funeral home.

"This room is jangling my nerves," Candi said. "I don't think I can stay very long. I feel a lot of pain rushing at me."

"They look so real and yet they don't." Bev tilted her head, reading the placard. "Like latex monsters you see in grade B movies. Only these had been alive."

I stopped by a roped-off section where the bog body used to be. "Candi, what do your muses tell you when you stand here?"

"I feel a strand trailing off into the distance of time and space."

"Can you be a little more explicit? Time and space are pretty big." Bev ambled a few paces to one of the display cases, which held a cauldron, horse bits, and a horse yoke. The latter might easily masquerade as slag back home in Portland. "For instance, how about this time and this space?" I loved how she played this.

"You don't have to always be so sarcastic. I'm trying to help here." Candi leaned toward the empty space. "I'm listening for spectral emanations."

"Can you tease out an emanation that belongs to the present?" I asked.

Her eyes glazed in a trance, only the slight rise and fall of her chest giving any indication that she was any more alive than the leather-like cadavers.

"Wait a second. What are you planning now?" Bev bolted to my side. "Lark—" her tone cautioned.

"No, I'm not thinking what you think I'm thinking. I'm thinking the right thing to do is find out where the body is and notify the Gardai," I whispered, wondering if Candi distrusted Bev and me as much as we distrusted her.

Bev exhaled, her voice low. "Much better idea."

Candi blinked, rejoining us from her La land state. "Finally. That tacky throb in my temple seems to have left."

"Were you able to pick up any leads to where Rhett might be keeping the body?" I asked.

"Where did the muses say the body and butter are?" Bev frowned, reminding me of a TV reporter at a hot crime scene.

"They haven't left the area."

"That's helpful. Could you ask the muses to narrow it down? Are we talking Republic? UK? The island? Technically, they could be in Belfast and have left the area," Bev said.

"To clarify, they aren't detectives or sleuths. They are inspiration." Candi massaged her forehead and teased a Kleenex that smelled like lavender out of her sleeve.

"Well, I'm inspired to approach this more rationally."

"Would you keep your voices down?" I cut my eyes toward the security person strolling in our direction. I took the offensive. "Officer, did the body that was stolen lie here? Such a shame it is."

"'Tis indeed. But you're to be moving along. Others want to see the display as well."

"Of course. Thank you."

"And for taking such good care of these remains," Candi said.

We stopped at the entrance to the galleries displaying Ireland's renowned Christian relics, our final destination. Two uniformed men and one tiny woman stationed themselves at the doorway. The latter reminded me of women I'd known during the Troubles. Of the three, she was the one I'd least like to meet in a dark hedge grove. Behind them a crew in hard hats attached rollup grating across the entrance, the whine of drills echoing across the large space.

"Can't we go in here?" Bev asked.

"The gallery's closed," came the brisk reply from the woman.

"Not even a little peek? I came all the way from Portland, Oregon," Candi said.

"The exhibit is closed for cleaning." A burly guard moved closer. I briefly wondered if he positioned himself to protect us from the woman in case we made a sudden move she didn't like.

"You need an iron floor-to-ceiling gate to wash a few display cases?" Bev asked.

"Move along now." A third guard now occupied any remaining space in the doorway.

We walked to the tearoom, packed with folks, jammed with chatter, and smelling of wet wool. If nothing else, the disappearance of the antiquities had been good for business.

"All right, what did your muses say at the entrance to that grilled-off gallery?" Bev asked. "Did they hint at what was stolen?"

"Disarray lives in that room. I see shattered glass. The muses showed me that more than gold jewelry is missing. Does the room have a big cup, Lark? Also, they revealed an ancient cross and an instrument shaped like a long horn. The horn had a big bell with raised swirls."

"You're talking about the Armagh cup and the Cross of Cong. The horn could be anything." I yawned to hide my gasp at recognizing the description of the Loughnashade Horn, the one in my dream the night before we flew to Dublin.

"Well, they're missing, vanished. My muses showed me holes and

181

broken glass. Chaos in that gallery."

We stood at the cashier to pay for our tea, her narrowed eyes indicating that she'd overheard us.

"Ladies, we should drink up," I said. "I believe we've outstayed our welcome." Two officers approached the counter, sauntering as if on a break, but their eyes traveled with us as we stood by a window, scarfing our snacks, before making our way outside.

Fleeting sunshine poked through clouds that would release another shower before long.

"We better grab lunch before rehearsal this afternoon," I sighed. "If I hear anymore of Rhett's outrageousness, I'll do more than break a few drumsticks."

"I'm gonna beg off. My muses are warring in my head again."

"To normal people, that's a migraine," Bev said.

"This trip has been really hard on them. I'm aching for some place quiet and dark. Except Rhett told me to go out to the rental place at the airport. He wants me to make sure the bus is ready to go. After that, I'm going back to Deirdre's for a little while."

Before either of us answered, she crossed the street and jogged along the avenue, the bell of her umbrella blooming as another onslaught of rain moved through the city.

"Wonder what she's up to?" Bev flipped the hood of her raincoat over her head. "I still don't trust her, and I trust her stupid muses even less."

"For now, we need her. Great job in the museum, girl." I raised my hand in high-five. "I always knew we were psychic."

"As you say, we're twins of different mothers." She slapped back. "Hey, how come Rhett didn't send you to check on the bus?"

We stood at the traffic light while Candi's umbrella receded along the sidewalk.

"I'm wondering the same thing."

Bev gestured her head toward Candi's form rounding the corner. "She's lying."

182

Chapter Twenty-Eight

D amn right she's lying. Let's follow her. I bet you a pint of black stuff that she's got some other agenda." I bounded across the street, a car horn blaring as I dodged through traffic.

I breached the corner to see Candi paused at the intersection waiting for the crossing signal. She hadn't been in Ireland long enough to figure out that you made a dash for it, said a Hail Mary, and prayed the driver did the same. Behind me, Bev made her way along the sidewalk at a jog, grit coating her bare feet, a pair of Gucci's dangling in her hands. Ahead Candi flagged a cab.

"Might I suggest your next hankering for shoes be a pair of Nike's?"

"Very funny. My sneakers are in Portland. This gig did not include track and field." She massaged the ball of her foot. "What made you think she's lying?"

I waved to hail a cab. "Body language. She folded her arms tight across her chest, an unconscious gesture that she didn't want us to know about whatever she's up to at the airport. When I worked as a social worker, that was a dead giveaway."

"The lie has to do with the bus." Bev smiled.

A taxi eased against the curb. We climbed in, me giving directions.

"Maybe she's in on this with Rhett. She didn't seem too intrigued or grossed out about the bog body book." Bev grunted as she slipped on the Guccis.

"She might be. I haven't noticed anything odd about their exchanges. You know, the bus may be why Rhett whined so much when we had to hire that van in Limerick. Why did he rent such a big bus in the first place?" I shuddered at the thought of driving such a tank again.

"The body and loot must have something to do with the bus itself. Do you think that's where he's hiding them?"

"Good question. We should know more when we get to the rental company."

As the cab maneuvered through traffic, I thought back to the days of the Troubles. How the north-south divide existed even here in Dublin, the demarcation being the Liffey. Now the country's capital was just one big city, and the river was just one big river. In the meantime, we'd had the advantage of an influx of people and cultures, like when the Vikings first sailed down that waterway.

We arrived at the entrance to ABC Rental. The sun broke through, and steam rose from a large asphalt lake surrounded by a barbed wire fence, an office building perched in the middle. The wire reminded me of Derry's city center, the blades of metal glinting in the sun. The roar of a jet taking off split the sky, its shadow trailing across the parking lot and caressing the fence.

"We can go from here," I said to the cabby.

Bev and I stepped onto the lot's perimeter. A wide gate pulled back from the business's entrance. "No sign of Candi, but I'm not surprised. I bet she's someplace on the premises."

"We don't know for sure that she came here." Bev balanced on heels that would make a tightrope walker envious.

"Much as I envy your great taste in shoes, I think you should plant yourself on that bench across the street at the airport where the arrivals are. That way you'll have a better view of this place. I'll take a look around. This could morph into a track and field event. If I have to run, I'll meet you at the bench."

We crouched behind a delivery van. Bev nodded and backed, then rose and dashed toward the bench. I headed through the gate at the edge of the premises.

Once inside the enclosure, I chose an elliptical route to the side of the office building, avoided the front entrance, and walked along the sidewalk toward the back. Behind the office, additional parking nosed against a gigantic warehouse-sized building, its doors slid back to reveal several bays, cars, and vans hoisted, the backs of mechanics under the carriages.

Good thing I knew the place, having picked up and deposited the cheesy tour bus a few days earlier. Rental Guy was nowhere in sight, no doubt in the office telling Candi about all the extras they didn't have.

A fellow in stained overalls emerged from beneath one of the bays, a yellow school bus at ceiling level, the underbelly exposed, a metal panel hanging like a dropped jaw. I noted the black hair. Aengus? Too late to hide or avoid him.

"What are you doing here, you manky bitch?" he growled.

"I should ask you the same question. You said you were from Cork. We went to your apartment."

"So? I have a gaff in Cork. I work as a specialty mechanic in both cities. Your bandmate was just after asking about the bus. Said she's the driver. Wouldn't mind driving her myself." Aengus took a step closer.

My arm automatically rose in defense. I cocked my head, narrowed my eyes, daring him. "She's hallucinating. I'm driving the damn thing, and I'm checking out what I'm in for. That doesn't look like the tank I originally drove."

He backed away. "It isn't." He backed a step further, thumping the wrench he carried against his thigh. "Rhett wanted something smaller, easier to handle. Said the driver isn't licensed for a large bus. Guess he meant you, or that other woman."

"Why's the underside of the bus gaping like that?" I stepped forward.

"Making it road worthy. Last minute check. Oil, tires, windshield

185

wiper blades, spark plugs…." He continued to back up.

"You better make sure of it." I retreated, chills like little fingers running across my shoulders. *Don't let him see he's spooking you*, and deliberately slowed my stroll around the corner. His voice on the phone carried across the tarmac, and my name bounced off the building. Out of sight I made a run for the airport. If Aengus was a bad ass dude, I was not inclined to find out.

Leg crossed and massaging her foot, Bev perched on the bench, among travelers and rolling bags.

"I've got good news and bad news." The jog across the street compounded by my heart pounding exchange with Aengus left me winded. "The good news is I didn't get caught by Candi."

"And the bad news?"

"I ran into Aengus coming out of a bay. He said Rhett ordered a smaller bus that handles more easily. He's modifying the undercarriage."

"Like Rhett cares about your driving conditions? Do you think they're in cahoots?"

"I hope we don't find out. Whatever they're up to must have something to do with a panel Aengus is installing. What about you? See anything?"

"I had a good view of the rental place. Candi came out of the office right after you disappeared around back."

"Did she see you?"

"No, a bunch of new arrivals blocked me."

"She lied to Aengus telling him she was the driver. Wonder how she found out about this bus and its modifications?"

"Her psychotic muses?"

"Or psychotic Rhett. We better get back for rehearsal. Let's see if she says anything to him about her errand."

~~~

And that was how the morning went. It only got worse.

We arrived at Mom's office in mid-afternoon.

Candi entered the practice room on our heels. I nudged Bev. No sign at all that Rhett had sent her to the rental company.

"How's your migraine?" Bev raised her chin.

"Melted away." She gave a bright-eyed smile.

Jeremy, glued to the drum stool, tightened bolts on the floor tom. From the corner of my eye, came a nauseating reunion between Jeremy Jube-Jube and Candi Cane.

"Lark, darlin'," Rhett began.

"Where'd he come from?" I pointed at Jeremy. "I thought he'd run off to be a Celtic revivalist."

"He was in the audience last night. Didn't you see him, or were you too busy flirting with that groupie," Rhett said. "Let me be honest—"

"That's a new one on me."

"You are a fine woman possessing skills that would rival any accomplished percussionist. But frankly, you are not cut out to be a jazz drummer. We've spent the better part of a week trying to get you integrated and to no avail."

"Rhett, you flaming weasel! You know damn well I spent most of our practices dealing with Steve and Matt's never-ending feud." Exquisitely aware of Steve only a few feet away, my body froze, the image of recently seeing Aengus urged me to lash out.

"That's a little harsh." Matt twiddled a knob on the keyboard.

"That's because of you, darlin'," Rhett said. "Jeremy had provided a rhythm, an esprit de corps, and a set that we've been playing for ages. We revived it."

"Well, we don't have any more time. We're off to Loughgarvan tomorrow," I countered.

"I think we're ready. The boys and I have been here polishing the set. Candi will be able to step right in."

"Where does that leave Bev and me?"

Matt played an out-of-tune chord. "You could return this keyboard and get me one that isn't such a piece of shit."

"Return it yourself, asshole," I answered. "By the way, I stopped by the rental place to check on the bus. Just because it's smaller, doesn't mean it's not another tank."

Steve lowered his guitar and strolled over. "Driving shouldn't be a problem now. As I said back in Portland, I didn't think this was something you wanted to do. Band politics."

"Lark, I hired you to be our guide and, I might add, you have been exemplary. We accommodated Bev as a courtesy to you."

"You also hired me and Bev as backup singers."

"Your introduction of us to Ireland has been more than invaluable. Now you girls can enjoy some recreation before we head back. I hope your plans will include cheering us on in the audience."

"Did you forget you hired me to drive a damn bus? Who's going to do that? You certainly aren't capable."

"Why Matt or Jeremy. Both of them have demonstrated admirable skill at the wheel and benefited from your excellent instruction. They'll do right fine."

"Suit yourself, but don't count on me to help out if you get in a jam." I spun on my heel and left the room. Internally, I bleated, *Mom!* Even at my age, I could feel like a kid, want my mom to come to my rescue, and want her to fix everything.

~~~

"'Tis probably for the best. That's no life to be living. Roving you'd be. A settled life should be calling you." We slumped in chairs in her office, Mom at her desk, her finger occasionally poking the screen of her tablet.

"I settled, Mom. For twenty-five fucking years." Bev's quick intake of air cautioned me about speaking like that to my mother.

"Sure you're to be upset, but I didn't raise you to have a command of street language."

"Mom, you've heard way worse in your new line of work, which to me isn't exactly settling down."

"We planned on a three-week romp and then back to the real world,"

Bev said.

"And a brilliant plan it was. Now to be following Rhett's suggestion that you enjoy your remaining stay in Ireland is a grand idea. You've done nothing but see the insides of pubs and tourist traps. From what I gather, you've seen little of the real Ireland."

"Real enough for me, Mom. As they say, you can't come home again."

"Bang on. But don't eat the head off me." Deirdre's face tilted again toward the tablet. She frowned scrolling rapidly, then looked up, distracted.

"What's so important that you can't spend a few minutes with your daughter when she's in crisis?" Old fashioned me wanted to scream about her multi-tasking, dividing her attention between me and some screen.

She ignored my question, a tactic she used when I was little and which still infuriated me.

"Speaking of Rhett, where's dear Candi?" Mom frowned at the tablet.

"She didn't get fired. She's a key piece of the band."

"'Tis a loss. She has talent, and I enjoyed her view on the world."

"Of course, you would," I said. *Yeah, a Looney Toon like you.*

"Ach, Jeremy. The man brings prickles to my scalp. He's a cute hoor. I hired that Celtic band because I felt sorry for the lads. But I could have just as soon wanted someone other than your man Jeremy."

"I agree, Deirdre," Bev said. "He's a major creep show. And you already know what I think about Candi."

I raised an eyebrow. *You're saying too much.*

"Though I must admit, a ginger beard could always melt me knees." Mom swiped the screen. "I've found that whatever brought gray hairs also brought the wisdom to look beyond the outer package. Your band—"

"Not my band anymore. Why aren't you kicking those assholes out of here? You give them a place to practice, and this is how they repay you?" I could change the subject as conveniently as Mom.

Bev scooted back her chair. "How about I get us a fresh pot of tea? I'd like to try my hand at brewing it the proper way."

"The secret is to hot the pot with boiling water. And thank you, darlin'. You can bring along a packet of biscuits from the cupboard to keep the pot and cups company." Mom's mouth gelled in a thin, tight line, an expression I'd seen only once or twice in my life, and both were in dire circumstances.

"Word on the street is that the rotters stole much more than the Gardai and museum are saying." Deirdre tapped to turn off the tablet.

"More than the bog body, torc, and earrings?"

She nodded. "Much more precious. Why do you think the galleries were closed off and the remaining priceless pieces removed?"

"Remaining? Precious like what?"

"I have it from that security fella who busks for me. What's dear to our hearts."

"You mean the Armagh Cup and Cross of Cong?" A jolt ran up my forearms as I remembered Candi's musings and my nightmare about the Loughnashade Horn.

"But what's an auld gal like me to know? You two are well to be rid of Rhett and the rest."

"Then why don't you kick them out?"

"They're off to the races tomorrow, so why bother? Ah, Bev, I see you found the biscuits. Would you do the honor of pouring? As I said, 'tis better the tour turned out this way. You'll have a grand time rooting for them at Loughgarvan."

Chapter Twenty-Nine

Thanks to Mom's generosity, I maneuvered a rental car out of the congested capital and north toward Loughgarvan. Driving a decent vehicle on the left-hand side again felt great. "Mom knows more than she's saying."

Bev turned her head toward me and chuckled. "I noticed how she changed the subject. Like mother, like daughter."

"Why did she continue to allow the band a practice space after they kicked us out?"

"Maybe she was being polite."

"I keep worrying she'll stumble into this. If she knows too much or figures out too much, she'll be in real danger." My cheeks felt like they would burst from huffing.

"I think she'll be okay. After all, who'd want to hurt a sweet, little, old lady?"

"Rhett, if he's desperate enough."

"I wish you could have talked her out of coming to the rhythm and blues festival."

"She insisted that the event was a good place to discover talent. So now Mom's a talent scout, God love her. We'll have to keep an eye on her and make sure she gets back home."

"Maybe she'll skip the Monasheskin Bog Snorkeling Festival, seeing you're not part of the band anymore. Speaking of which, don't you think that's a way weird venue to play?" Bev asked.

"I've got to check something out. I'm pulling over." I eased off the gas pedal, steering onto the shoulder, gravel crunching under the tires as we came to a stop. "Can you fish out the map from the glove compartment?"

Bev unfolded a tattered map, spreading it on her lap. "What're we looking for?"

"Similarities." My finger traced the roads. "Gotcha, you son of a bitch."

Bev's eyebrows connected and then arched. "Wait. What?"

"Remember the map Candi brought out of Rhett's portfolio? How she kept examining it? That's the countryside around Monasheskin." I pointed at the small dot that demarked the town. "Now we know why. The town is in the middle of nowhere."

"Rhett's probably going to do the deal at the Bog Snorkeling Festival." Bev patted the paper on her lap.

"I mean, how many people tromp all the way to nowhere for a band concert?"

"People drive all the way to the Gorge in Washington. That's in the middle of nowhere. Remember that little concert at Woodstock?"

"Well, good luck to Rhett getting to Loughgarvan. Or anywhere, let alone out of Dublin. That bus will be hell on wheels to drive." I put the sedan in gear, picked up speed, and merged back onto the motorway. We left the congested area toward the exit to the rhythm and blues festival, the traffic thinning on the M1.

Bev clicked a picture with her cell. "I miss Elliot. This trip feels like we've been gone for years."

"We need to get ahold of Rhett's portfolio again," I said. "Maybe we missed a document with info on where he's handing off the goods."

"We'd get more info from his thumb drive." Bev abruptly pressed her lips together, then turned her head toward the passenger window.

"Bev—" I drew her name out. "You could have broken into that thumb drive. Why didn't you?"

"I have ethics, you know."

"Yeah, but Ireland's national heritage is at stake." I flicked the blinker and shifted lanes to pass.

"I suppose I could hack in."

"You could've hacked into Rhett's account when Candi brought the thumb drive to Mom's. I'm surprised that you didn't."

"Of course, I might have. Eventually. I was conflicted at that point. Besides, Candi's voodoo is entertaining. I wanted to mess with her a bit. We both agree we don't trust her, so why give her any more of an advantage?"

"I guess we lost our chance." We continued north on the motorway for a while in silence until I mused, "I have an idea. We know the band's routine, right?"

"Yeah?" Bev's voice up ticked with hesitation.

I moved into the right passing lane. "What a shame to drive all the way to the festival for nothing."

"You suggesting we heist the thumb drive?" Bev squeaked.

"Why not? The town will be crowded, the pubs'll be packed giving us lots of opportunity to snatch it."

"Download the data while they're playing?"

"And put it back before anyone's the wiser. All we have to do is come up with an excuse to get backstage near Rhett's portfolio."

"We can wish them good luck," we both said. I reached over to high five my bestie.

The GPS betrayed us as we headed farther north, sheer instinct the only reason we headed in the right direction. I knew the moment we left the motorway to catch the road for Loughgarvan, we'd end up lost. I signaled and moved back into the left lane for the next exit to fill the tank and check directions with the cashier.

"Jesus Christ!" Bev screamed. A beady-eyed face covered in black feathers smashed into the passenger windshield. The car tumbled into a ditch, careened to a stop, and tipped sideways in the mud. Bev slammed against the door.

"Are you okay?" I whimpered, leaning sideways, the seatbelt the only constraint preventing from me toppling on top of her.

"Better than the fuckin' bird." Her right hand cupped her elbow. "I'm going to have one hell of a bruise. How about you?"

"Fine." I wiggled my fingers and rotated my head to prove it.

Entrapped in the windshield was a large black bird, broken feathers ruffling in the wind.

I called the rental company, and after the initial contact, we crawled out the driver's side and hiked the rest of the way to a motorway rest stop. We managed to stake out a table and wait. And wait, drinking some awful brew masquerading as tea.

"What's the tow truck guy doing? Hitching here?" Bev bit into a sausage roll.

"Welcome to the real Ireland. It'll happen when it does and be prepared to chat with the guy. For a while. Perhaps for hours. I gotta pee. I thought he'd be here sooner."

I zig-zagged through the racks of souvenirs, dodging a group of tourists entering from a bus. When I threaded my way back, the tow truck guy towered above our table.

He wiped his nose on a greasy sleeve. "You're takin' yer time, are you?" he said.

"Sorry to make you wait. But I do believe we've been cooling our heels for several hours." Bev pointed at her ankles. Her stunning new designer boots were streaked, revealing where she'd made a valiant effort to clean off the mud.

"You'll be coolin' your hind ends for a few more if we don't get a leg on. I'll give you a lift to your car." Tow Truck Guy turned, waddling toward his truck. "Rental company's closing soon."

At the ditch he said, "Well, the car's a hames and the windshield's definitely banjaxed." He nodded toward the dead bird, who stared at us in its dead birdy state, the windshield a mass of cracks that radiated from the glossy, black plumage. "That's a raven, you know."

"Shite." Flashes of my Nanna's stories ran through my head.

"What did he say and why shite?" Bev asked.

"Basically the car's totaled. My Nanna told stories about the god, Lugh, having raven attendants. He was the god of artists. Ravens were messengers from the world of the dead. Their cry foretold someone's imminent death."

Bev hugged her sides. "The only cry I heard was mine when the damn thing dove into the windshield."

"How long since you've been back?" Tow Truck Guy snickered. "Not able to drive on the left anymore is it?"

"Feels like a donkey's age, but I've been driving the motorway for a couple of weeks. Including a bus. This is too weird."

"If the raven is a messenger of death and the messenger croaks, does that mean death isn't imminent?" Bev watched the breeze stir the feathers, casting them along the motorway.

"You're making my head hurt," I said.

Tow Truck Guy guffawed, studied my face. "I'd be extra careful."

"Are acts of gods covered in the insurance?" I asked.

"You're to be reading the fine print, I expect."

We crammed across the front seat of the truck, the sedan a pathetic heap on the bed.

"You can be thankful that you've got full coverage. Although I doubt it'll cover the bad luck flying your way. You must've done something daft to have a raven after you." He took the roundabout exit to go south on the motorway. "We're to be heading to Dundalk, better than a jaunt back to Dublin. The rent-a-car place will give you the replacement, and you can crack on."

Traffic swam around us, and the day began to dim.

Chapter Thirty

How the hell are we going to get to Loughgarvan tonight?" Bev asked once we were again on the motorway.

"We will. It's actually not that far. Look for the exit to the N53." My bottom teeth ground into my top. With all the clenching I'd been doing, how much longer would I have them, let alone the molars? Maybe being a hygienist will have advantages after all.

"Do you think all those ghouls Candi talked about are after us?" Bev, belted next to me, studied the map, the light from her cell illuminating her face. She'd insisted on using her GPS.

"Anymore, I don't know. I always thought the deities, fairies, and demons were nonsense, but Nanna swore they were real. I've never run into anyone not Irish who had the second sight with respect to them. I think we both agree Candi can't be trusted. I hope we haven't given away too much."

"Small comfort," Bev said. "Okay, here's the exit."

After that, only the GPS interrupted the silence. We moved along at a good clip, me following the instructions of the dulcet British GPS voice. The road became narrower and darker, surrendering any resemblance to a major throughway, let alone a highway.

"We're now lost cuz of this stupid GPS," I said.

Bev waved her phone toward a building under a streetlamp. "Hey, a pub!"

Tucked at a crossroads a whitewashed structure that had probably once sported a thatched roof squatted against the trees. I nestled the car next to a small truck. "I could use a pint," I said, and we made our way in.

Constructed of low ceilings edged by a row of seats with tables, the pub typified rural taverns scattered like grains of barley around the island.

"Wonder if any bog bodies ended up in there." We warmed ourselves before a large stone fireplace, where burning peat created a comforting smell like burning leaves.

"Kind of late for cremation, don't you think?" Bev ran a hand over the rounded stones.

Given the small community, we would rate a fair bit of discussion when we left. An old clock chimed the quarter hour before nine. The band would take the stage at midnight, our one chance to get Rhett's thumb drive and download it. I hadn't a clue where we were.

"We'd like a pint. What do you have on tap?" I asked the owner, a sharp-featured man, whose nose pointed down like an arrow. "And can you be telling me if we're on the road to Loughgarvan?"

I laid the map I'd grabbed from the car on a table. In seconds an assortment of men flanked us. A mass of fingers wormed their way along road lines, illustrating a debate about the best route.

"If you go to Rory's Corner and follow the lane, then turn left, you should be in Loughgarvan."

"Eamon, that will get them lost," a fellow with a gummy leer said.

"As if we aren't already," Bev sighed.

"From the States are you?" Eamon asked, taking a swig of his lager. His corrugated face appraised us. He leaned over our shoulders, a smell of rancid ale surrounding him.

"Ah, yeah." Bev brought her elbow closer to her side, hugging her purse.

"Me brother lives in New York City. Have you been to the Big Apple?"

Keep your answers short, my raised eyebrows said.

"Not recently."

"Eamon, what did you say is the fastest way?" My feet mentally tapped. Was giving us straightforward directions that difficult? Was involving a whole community and consensus necessary? "Welcome to Ireland," I said to Bev.

Finally the bar owner stepped over. "Not such a fine evening to be traveling. Could may well be rain." His pudgy fingers tapped the screen on his cell phone.

The golden lager receded in the glass, the few minutes in the pub a refreshing break from the stress of the past couple of days, of the stress since leaving the US. *Welcome home,* I thought, the peat fire warming my shoulders, the smell warming my heart. I'd missed the slower pace of life in Ireland more than I thought.

~~~

Half an hour later, we were cocooned again in the front seat of the rental. "I'll try to pretend that we needed those pints and all those stories about people getting lost." I turned the ignition. "But then again, maybe we did."

We took a gamble and tried the car's GPS coupled with the bar owner's directions. My shoulders hunched over the steering wheel as we crept along, the headlights of the car a giant flashlight illuminating trees whose branches stretched and closed over the night sky.

Bev's cell dropped any signal. The car's system had been giving us directions in German for the past twenty minutes.

"They were kind of sweet, the way they all tried to help. And if you didn't breathe. Does getting a simple answer always take so long?" Bev tapped the face of her cell. "Okay, I got a signal. The road's gonna split. We're gonna take the bend to the right."

The clock in the car added an additional minute to the evening. I shut off my brain from calculating how little time we had to get to Loughgarvan, find the pub, and locate the band. Anxiety pushed me around the curve faster than I could maneuver, giving me a hare's breath's moment to slam the brakes before landing in a large sink hole. We teetered on the edge, the headlights skimming the black water that could have hidden inches or feet.

"Rule of thumb is never drive through standing water on a road," Bev commented. "We passed a dirt lane to a farmhouse not far back." She lifted her cell. "I know, I'll text your mom. She might have some ideas."

While Bev's thumbs clicked cell phone keys, I held my breath, put the car in reverse, and eased away from the black lagoon. We waited, the windows beginning to steam. Then, the ding of the text coming in.

"She says she's not familiar with this part of the county. Our best bet is to get help at the farmhouse. She'll save us seats."

I edged the car farther from the sink hole and twisted the wheel. "Our luck we'll back into a ditch." I nosed toward the rutted road leading to the farmhouse. The residence disappeared behind a bend, the lane a black ribbon flanked by boulders concealed by overgrown gorse, the sky a mass of clouds absorbing any light.

"You're doing great." Bev rolled down the window and leaned her head out. "Move to the right, you're about to…" The sound of dull scraping filled the front seat as a hefty rock carved a dent on the side of the vehicle. "Still full coverage, right?"

The house's lighted parking area came into view.

"Thank God." I navigated a slight hill, set the emergency brake, a warning chiming as I undid my seatbelt, the ding like an alarm clock.

The porch lights flew on when Bev rang the bell. I hoped for the best, that we hadn't dragged the owners from a deep sleep, and if we did, they would take pity on us.

"So you're to be at the festival this night?" A woman with gray hair flecked in ginger said. "The road's been out for a fortnight, I think. No getting through."

"Can you tell us what other road we could take? Our GPS system is malfunctioning," Bev said.

"American are you?" the woman asked.

"We are, but I'm Irish," I answered.

"From around Galway were you?" A balding man, tightening the belt on his bathrobe appeared.

I nodded. "But a few decades ago."

Bev glanced at me, having learned from our last stop.

"T'other route will take you far too long. You'll never make it. But a track crosses my property. You're welcome to it. Bridget, I'll get dressed." The man retreated, and moments later we found ourselves in the kitchen as the woman put a kettle on.

"Liam will just be a minute," she said. "I've made a loaf of soda bread for breakfast that I'll fetch." She disappeared into a pantry.

"And how long is an Irish minute?" Bev whispered.

"Hopefully only a half hour," I murmured back. "Good news is it's late. They'll want to get back to sleep. If it were daylight, we could be here for breakfast and then lunch."

Bridget re-emerged. She placed a plate with slices of soda bread, small jam pots, and butter on the table. "Where are you from in America?"

"Portland, Oregon." Bev spread a dab of jam on a slice.

"I know that lovely city well. We went on holiday there a few years back. So much like Ireland do you not think?"

I gulped. *Please God, don't let them tell us about their trip and show us pictures.* "This soda bread brings back so many memories. It's still warm."

Bridget beamed. "Welcome home."

Liam entered the kitchen. His Wellies were not a good sign. "The clouds will be bucketing down soon, but we'll have you on your way. We just have to move the sheep."

"Sheep?" Bev bleated. "I've never been near a sheep, even at the state fair. I always preferred the midway." She eyed her boots.

"You're in for an adventure," I said. "And I'm not exaggerating."

"Ach, what a tale you'll have to tell about how you herded sheep in

Ireland." Liam zipped his slicker. "But we must be out if you're to be in Loughgarvan to see your band play. Once we get the ewes out of the pasture, you can drive through to the main road."

"When you get to a fork, you will be at the Dublin Road. Take that road, and it will lead you right to the festival." Bridget held the door and waved us on.

The keg light partially illuminated the pasture. Liam whistled, and through the mist, a rangy dog raced toward him. "We'll be much quicker if you follow in the rear on either side of the track, so the sheep can't run back."

Bev and I moved toward the sides sloshing across a pasture and shepherding a bunch of stupid, stubborn sheep. The ground was amuck with manure. Clouds, like gigantic balloons that someone bashed with a stick, unleashed a downpour. The soggy ground filled and oozed mud, Bev and I sinking to our ankles. She stumbled, and I grimaced thinking about her designer boots and the stink in our car.

The dog expertly circled the animals, guiding them through the gate, which Liam then shut.

"Get your car, and you can pick your way along this." The farmer pointed to two ragged ruts that cut across the field. "If you take a run at it, you won't get stuck."

Once back in the car Bev moaned, "My boots, my boots."

A few years may have passed since my last sojourn in Ireland, and a lot may have changed, but getting down a sludge-soaked track without getting stuck had not. The pasture occupied the bottom of a small decline from the farmhouse with a small incline at the far end. I backed within feet of the house to gain traction and gunned the car. With enough speed to get through the morass, the incline would give me traction the rest of the way.

The car tore down the hill, the momentum carrying us into the swampy water. Sludge splattered everywhere, the wipers smearing mud across the windshield. Both of us strained forward as if that would help the sedan.

201

"Come on, you can make it," Bev urged.

We careened along the ruts, the rear fishtailing.

And then stalled.

I shifted into reverse, then into drive, hoping to rock our way out of the bog. The car only settled in further, the quagmire climbing the sides of the tires. The clock blinked angrily, 10:30. I turned off the engine. We had a mere ninety minutes before the band took the stage. And we still didn't know how far away we were or where the venue was. Not to mention our ability to get lost again.

"You stay here. I'm going back to the farmhouse."

"You know, I didn't think a dead raven could be so vindictive." Bev shook her head, raindrops flinging against the windows.

The mud now caressed my shins, the downpour chilling my shoulders, my hair soaked and flattened against my scalp. I goose-stepped across the field to the back door. Liam immediately answered, still in his Wellies and slicker.

"I'll be getting my tractor. We'll have you on your way in no time." At his side marched Bridget, equally attired.

The keg light at the barn door silhouetted the car's lone occupant. I imagined Bev texting Elliot muttering, "Fuck the roaming charges."

The barn smelled like hay, cattle lowing from the stalls. The couple worked efficiently, located a chain, then Liam started the tractor, which growled and sputtered to life. Bridget opened the barn's other door and Liam backed through while she ran ahead, the light creating a long shadow down the hill. I chased after her, marveling at her agility at this hour and at her age. The tractor lumbered past, diverted into the field, overtook the sedan, and positioned itself in front. Rain streamed down Liam's slicker hat, the tractor's headlights illuminating the downpour like a lit waterfall in front of his face. Then as if someone cranked a spigot closed, the deluge stopped. Oblivious to this temperamental weather, Liam worked on, threading a chain around the front bumper.

"Once you get back in, take off the brake with your car in neutral," he instructed.

"I feel like we're in a perverse car wash," Bev said when I crawled behind the wheel, the warmth a wet, flannel hug.

We began to move slowly along the road and then up the incline. At the top, Liam unhooked the chain and approached the window, his breath a yellow steam in the barn's light.

"You're to be following this now to the Dublin Road. Midnight did you say the band will play? You'll make it in good time."

"Liam, here." Bev thrust a piece of paper at him. "When you and Bridget come to Portland on your next visit, I'd love for you to stay with me."

We picked our way along the lane, found the main thoroughfare, and the outskirts of Loughgarvan a slash of lights on the horizon.

"I had begun to think a real Ireland exists merely as a series of tacky venues," Bev said. "Until tonight the only authentic people seemed to be your mom and Sweeney the Elder in Limerick."

I smiled. "The real Ireland is complicated. Any guesses where Rhett and the crew are?"

Chapter Thirty-One

A fellow in the requisite slicker and Wellies motioned with a flashlight to a place in a field, only a little less soggy than the one we'd escaped. Buildings festooned in neon surrounded the square in Loughgarvan, faint music emanating into the evening.

"How about we follow the crowds?" We trotted by cars slotted along the road, one rocking gently. "Must be keeping each other warm." I nodded at the fogged windows.

"Wish Elliot were here to keep me warm." Bev's shoulders sagged. "I look and smell like I've been lounging in manure, so he might not want to."

"Do you really think he's that shallow?"

"No, but I wouldn't want him to see me covered in muddy sheep shit." Bev held the phone outstretched as if it were a divining rod. "Heard from your mom. The band's in that pub on the other side." She gestured toward a small flat-faced building, hardly bigger than a coffee shop. "Well, that answers my question about going back to my VP job in Portland. I'll be working the rest of my life to pay off my credit card and phone bills." Bev tossed the cell in her purse.

"I'll pay you back." I elbowed her. "That's the bus I saw at the airport rental." The vehicle, a school bus, crouched in the shadows against a building. "What convent did they steal that from?"

Bev trotted across the square toward a line at the pub's entrance. "Wonder what else is in that train wreck of a vehicle besides the gear?"

I scouted the buildings and spied Deirdre's silver-gray head in line almost at the door. From here, she could have been any local. How chameleon-like Mom was. She could be anybody she chose. I waved, grabbed Bev's hand, and ran.

"My dear girls, what a sight you are." The flowery smell of Mom's perfume floated toward us. "A lad who's to audition for me is saving seats."

"I can't believe we actually got here." Bev nodded at her boots, now resembling an archeological find in a bog, perhaps attached to the foot of a body.

"It's a raven you were hitting?" Mom reached an arm around Bev's shoulders and gave a hug. "Lark, do you not remember the tale your Nanna told about the raven stalking her as a girl? The bird followed her for days, its cry foretelling Nanna's imminent death. But the dear plugged her ears with wool, so she wouldn't hear the baleful sound. Then in a far field, she built a likeness of herself dressed in some of her clothes."

The line lurched forward.

"She made a scarecrow," Bev laughed.

"'Tis true. The raven roosted on the scarecrow's shoulder. For three days it cried and cawed doom until a fierce storm swept along the field, Lugh coming to claim his messenger. When the sun came out and the clouds skittered away, the scarecrow had disappeared. The raven had vanished."

"I'd totally forgotten that story."

Mom rose slightly on her toes, neck stretched. "No sign of the boys and Candi yet." Mom tapped the face of her watch.

Late. No big deal. Everything ran late in Ireland. Or rather on time, only late if you were American or anal.

"When did you hear from them last? None of them could drive their way out of a paper bag."

"Do you think they got lost like us?" Bev asked.

Mom's phone pinged and she scrolled through a message. "Rhett just texted that they're here. Except for Jeremy."

"Missing in action again?" Bev asked.

"I've a mind he's out for no one but his own good, the cute hoor." Deirdre leaned to see into the pub. "I let the other lads and Candi know that you made it."

The singer's blond head came into sight, threading herself through the door and along the line.

I stepped out of my place to confront her. "Rhett, that asshole, sent you, didn't he?" I said before she could open her mouth.

"Yeah, he's really sorry. Jeremy's gone missing again. Said he had a quick errand to run down the street. Now he's nowhere to be found. Rhett says we can't wait any longer for him to show." Candi spread her hands palms up.

"Well, tell Rhett to go fuck himself."

"Why not let cooler heads prevail here? Think of the people who will be so disappointed if you don't play." Mom extended her arm, gesturing to the tavern.

"Think of the opportunity we're missing." Bev patted my shoulder.

"What opportunity?" A reptile-like look slithered across Candi's features.

She may not be as ditzy as she's been letting on these past months.

"Why, the opportunity for Lark and me to be part of the band again. That's one of the reasons we agreed to come along. As backup." Bev raised her eyebrows, one side of her mouth twitched.

"Oh, yeah right," Candi nodded, eyes roaming the pub. "Let's get backstage and get you onstage. Bev, the dressing area is really crowded. Hardly any room at all. Why don't you keep Deirdre company, and we'll see you after the set?"

"No, we're gonna negotiate. Bev's coming too. Mom, hold our seats.

We may join you soon. And we may be leaving even sooner."

We inched our way through the pub to the back, ostensibly to make a deal with Rhett.

"The thumb drive," I whispered into Bev's shoulder.

"I know. All I need is a moment next to their gear."

The backstage resembled festival seating at a concert—that is, no seating, just shoulder-to-shoulder standing. I scowled at Rhett, propped in a corner, shades on, even in this gloom. Made me wonder what he'd been sniffing, snorting, gulping, or injecting. Matt's nose was in the playlist, while Steve leaned against a wall, eyes closed.

"Lark, darlin', so good of you to rescue us. I am forever in your debt." My expression reflected in his sunglasses was of a woman with murder on her mind.

"Bullshit. When did you ever repay a debt? You must be really thick to even hope I'd step in." I scanned the jumble of equipment belonging to our band as well as the gear belonging to the others scheduled to play. A rat's nest, Rhett's portfolio bag not evident.

"In my humble opinion, I bent over backward to give you every advantage. I would be selling myself, my bandmates—why the whole profession—short if I were to imply we acquire our musical abilities so easily."

"Cut the crap. If that's the case, why this urgent SOS for me to help out?"

"Darlin', you misunderstand me. Why talent such as yours didn't spring up overnight. That much is clear and was made clearer from my association with your mother."

"You're a total eejit." I held back the gag at the mention of him and my mom.

"My dear, I'm not a humble man. That is one of my shortcomings. I'm endeavoring to communicate, why I'm begging you to re-consider and take your rightful place at the drums."

"What about Bev?"

"As you can see, quarters are more than tight back here, being a mere pub establishment. Out there is no roomier." He gestured toward the small stage.

Bev, who positioned herself next to his jacket, cut in. "I'll make my way to Deirdre. I gotta run back to the car for clean clothes. People are looking at me funny, my boots are ruined, and I smell rank."

I pretended to cave. "I'm covered in mud. No way you want me to play like this." I directed my comment to Bev and noticed her hand clamped around something. Keys?

"Candi, darlin', dig out some clean attire for our esteemed drummer." Rhett gestured to the large tub where we kept our stage costumes.

She dug for a few moments. "Here." She tossed a tee, jeans, and sneakers my way.

I quickly stripped down and grinned. Bev vanished. *God, we're a great team.*

"Break a stick. You know that means good luck, but don't do that on purpose." Matt escorted me to the stage where I climbed onto the stool behind the bass and cymbals. At least the kit was assembled. But of course, Matt set it up for Jeremy. How did I ever, ever think the drummer was anything other than a loser? I moved the stool's height down to accommodate my shorter legs, then moved the cymbals a couple of inches for my arm length. Finally, I scooted the stool forward so my feet could reach the bass pedal.

"Glad it's you and not Jeremy. He can't articulate worth a shit." Steve's warm breath caressed my ear.

I looked up, startled, steadying my balance on the stool. Tamping down the nausea pinging in my stomach, the incredible importance of this event sank in. To be able to play at this jazz festival was epic, world class. We rode in on a fluke.

Steve's narrow smile arced toward his eyes, creating closed lids, black slits I wanted to trace with my fingertips.

"Let's show them what you can do." He nodded toward the crowd, turned, and took his place.

I scrunched my eyes encountering the image of Steve and me on Mom's lawn, his arms wrapped around me. I desperately ached for that and at the same time wanted to run to some place safe, some place quiet, away from the noise.

I opened my eyes, sized up the audience, searched for Mom, and spotted her deep in conversation with the fellow next to her, no doubt the potential client. She faced forward, saw me, and gave a big whoop, raising her bony arms. I picked up the sticks and tapped the wooden jam block for a quick sound check.

Steve, center stage, drew his trumpet to his lips. Alone in a halo of white light, the plaintive, opening notes of Chuck Mangione's "Feels So Good" trickled forth.

He seduced the sweet notes out of the bell, delivering my cue, my stomach a flurry of sparklers, like a first date. I ran a rim-shot on the snare and rolled in syncopation with him.

He strolled next to me, fingers caressing the valves. His back to the audience, Steve moved his trumpet in circles, urging me, his eyes locked on mine. We joined in a musical embrace, our rhythms intense, intertwined. With a splash on the crash cymbal, we split, our sounds chasing each other. We ended our duet, me breathless, ecstatic. He nodded, then strolled back to his place, a contented grin coursing up his face.

Half in shadow Rhett jumped in, for once satisfied to support the trumpet's notes while Matt joined on his keyboard, followed a few bars later by Candi singing scat. Steve handed off to Rhett, who handed off to Matt. All the while, I wove different articulations among the others on my bass, floor tam, snare, and cymbals, until the finale's repeated notes, all of us together, my bass drum leading the way.

The crowd went crazy. We paused, and Matt began "Black Magic Woman," Rhett fingering the sublime whine on his guitar.

The band was deadly. We played three encores to standing ovations. The crowd erupted when we concluded with "Take Five."

Fuck you, Rhett! I nailed it.

We collected our gear and hauled it backstage, the next band crowding past to set up. Stunned by the killer set, nerve ends chased each other around my body. My cheeks burned in confusion about the connection with Steve onstage. He brushed my shoulder.

"Great job. We need to play tag again sometime." His eyes read me like a piece of music.

"Tag?" My voice, weak, floated off in the swell of applause for the next act.

"Yep. You're it." His index finger touched the sleeve of my soaked tee sending a shockwave up my arm. He turned, placed his trumpet in its case, and gently latched the cover.

Heat coursed up my face to mingle with the sweat in my hair. Emotions rattled me, as disarrayed as the hubbub in the tavern. Our interplay was nothing more than a musical moment, I told myself. As I stooped to untwist a nut to the floor tom stand, my intuition totally disagreed.

Bev elbowed through the dressing area to where we congregated. "Least I can do is help." Her arms blurred as she packed equipment. "Found Deirdre. Didn't see Jeremy." She bumped the lead singer in the tight quarters of the dressing room. "Sorry, Rhett." The slightest flash of metal between her fingers disappeared into his pocket. She flicked her eyes back and forth.

She didn't get the flash drive.

Candi's lower lip jutted out. "Jeremy should have been onstage tonight. He worked so hard." She tugged a hank of yellow hair that resembled wet corn silk.

"Well, he wasn't. And I was," I said.

We left the pub and approached Mom and Bev, who huddled in the chilly evening by the minibus Aengus had tricked out. As we clustered by the back, Rhett extracted a set of keys from his jacket pocket, trying one after the other until the handle moved. He flung the back door open. His portfolio lay on top of the luggage. I cut my eyes to Bev, who shrugged.

"Wrong keys," she mouthed.

Now what?

Bev hoisted a duffle bag into the back. "You guys set the place on fire, didn't they, Deirdre?"

"Jeremy would have set the place on fire too." Candi planted herself at the group's fringe, tapping her foot, arms folded across her chest.

Mom ignored her. "Steve and Lark, your duet sounded like you'd been playing together for years." She beamed as if about to invite him for dinner.

"Ah shucks." At Steve's bad cowboy accent, I would have kicked him in the shins again. But if I'd done that, he might have hugged me, and I would have melted to a puddle of tears. Thankful that he loaded drums on the other side of Matt, I elbowed the thought away.

Good time to change the subject. "Hey! Where's that train wreck of a bus I had to drive through Dublin?"

Rhett answered, "I reconsidered our travel requirements. The other bus was way more luxurious than we needed."

I examined the screaming yellow vehicle. "What did you do? Steal this from a Catholic school?"

The vehicle suffered from an identity crisis. Originally designed for transporting students, complete with front lever-activated doors, Aengus's haphazard makeover resulted in a passenger seat crammed next to the driver. Three bench seats flanked a short pathway, the last row running across the back, restricting access to the outside trunk.

Rhett patted the roof. "This will serve our purposes right fine." He rearranged his portfolio on top of the gear.

I lifted the cymbal bag, blocking Rhett's and the others' view. "Steve, can you fit this in? I can't reach far enough."

Bev crowded next to me, the movement of her arm bumping my shoulder while she rummaged in Rhett's portfolio. She'd make a great pickpocket if she ever needed a second career.

"Rhett, Lark came to your rescue. I provided you a space to practice so

211

you could be brilliant tonight. Some gratitude is required. I didn't peg you as having such a puny heart." Mom laid a hand on his arm.

"My dear lady..."

"Oh boy, here you go with this lengthy bullshit. Are you ever able to say anything in twenty-five words or less? At the very least you owe my mom a big thank you and a pint for all she's done for you."

"An encyclopedia of multiple volumes could not convey my gratitude for your kindness, generosity, and good will." The lead singer counted the words along his fingers. "Allow me to purchase you a ...," he stopped, pondered a moment, "golden elixir. Twenty-five words and well-crafted I would say."

"Great idea. Let's grab a pint and hear one of the bands," Steve suggested, securing the last of the gear. "You might learn something, Matt."

Aiming at the trumpet player, the keyboardist pointed index and middle fingers, thumb cocked.

"Do I have to break more drumsticks? When are you two going to get over this?" Although their feud pissed me off, I soared from a newfound sense of accomplishment that included keeping them in line.

"Hey!" Bev said, "Lark and I need to move the car closer."

"Want us to order a pint for you?" Steve asked.

"We'll catch up." My jangled emotions had relegated our major mission, the thumb drive, to the rear regions of my brain. I would have treasured a few minutes to sit and digest the last hour, but there wasn't time.

"If you see Jeremy, tell him where we are." Candi's jaw was clenched so tight, it could have been wired shut.

The group commenced a raggle-taggle march toward the pub with the shortest line.

Bev pulled me along the pavement and away from the venues at the pace of a seasoned hiker.

"Well, did you get the flash drive?"

"Bingo!" She held up the small black lozenge.

I jerked my thoughts to our mission. "How do we download his stuff?"

212

"That's what we're going to do now, go back to the car and find some-place with an outlet."

"They're in a line that's moving quickly." I nodded toward the group shuffling forward at the pub's entrance.

"My laptop's in the trunk. We'll grab it, go to a minimart, copy it, and put the thumb drive back in Rhett's bag. Let's hope we get back before they do." She grabbed my hand. "Run."

Chapter Thirty-Two

Bev called, "Hey, do you have an outlet we can use?" The bell jingled as we entered a minimart.

The cashier tethered to earbuds extracted one. "It's against store regulations." He stuck the bud back in, his head bobbing to some tune.

"But who's to know? Here. How about we buy this and give it to you?" Bev held up a large bottle of ale. "You must get a little thirsty."

He grabbed the credit card. "Make that two."

I glanced at my watch. "That line to the pub was moving pretty fast."

Bev plugged in the converter, then attached the cords to the laptop. "Won't take a moment." The screen lit and she inserted Rhett's thumb drive. "Now the fun part."

"I gather hacking doesn't require staring into space in a darkened room the way Candi did."

"Candi is a fake." Bev quickly moved her fingers around the keyboard, paused for a moment her index finger tapping her lips, then typed again. "Right on, I removed the encryption key."

"So is this part of being a VP of IT?"

"I think hacking falls in 'other duties as may be required,' although subject to an ethics clause."

"Does the clause reach across the Atlantic?" I asked.

"Probably not a good thing to bring up. Anyway, if Rhett's ability to protect his data is any indication, this black market thing is way over his head. We're in." The screen blanched as the thumb drive cracked open, a long list of files scrambling down the page.

"Holy shit." The laptop's screen revealed a succession of images. "The scurvy scoundrel saved emails."

"He's covering his ass, I bet." Bev scrolled through the files. Her fingers stretched, highlighting the contents, then dancing a quick couple of taps, she copied and saved the files onto her laptop. She extracted the flash drive, replaced it with one of hers, copied the files and then pulled the flash drive out.

"Good idea to make backup," I said.

"We're chill." She closed the lid.

A belch rose from behind the counter. "T'anks for the ale."

"Okay, let's haul ass." I yanked the door open the bell dinging.

~~~

"Maybe we should have run back." I nosed the car closer to the center of town.

"We just need to get to the bus before they do. How's this for an empty parking spot?" Bev pointed to a space that might accommodate a tricycle.

I cranked the wheel tight and humped the vehicle against the curb, nudging the car behind, the front wheels sticking into the street. "This'll have to do. We can move the car again once we put the thumb drive back. To most folks, the catawampus vehicle won't look out of place."

I scanned the outside of the pub, the line having shrunk, Rhett, Mom, and the others no longer in sight. "No worries. Service is probably glacial."

I followed Bev down an alley toward the bus.

"Any good at picking a lock?" she asked.

"Won't need to." I nodded toward the avenue. Backlit by car headlights, the troop approached, Mom's lilting voice drifting over.

"Distract Rhett, okay?" Bev turned her back, leaning against the

215

minibus doors and hollered, "Jesus, would you hurry up? We're freezing out here."

Rhett inserted the key. "Y'all hold your horses. If you'd deigned to join us, you wouldn't be out in the cold like this."

Bev immediately released the handle to the boot.

"Jeremy ever show?" I eclipsed Rhett's view. "Did you ever properly apologize to my mom? And what about me? I didn't hear anything along those lines."

"I did, but you chose to absent yourself from the festivities. Ask your dear mother." He moved past me, towering over Bev, and his tone took on a blade-like quality. "What the hell are you doing back here?" He snatched his backpack, her hands deep in its interior. "And what all have you got your mitts on?" He grabbed her wrist.

Her fingers clutched the small black lozenge and a bundle of guitar strings. "Putting your stuff back. I spilled your pack looking for my laptop. I forgot it the other day."

"What laptop? I distinctly recall no laptop in this vehicle." Rhett clenched her wrist harder, Bev's face contorting in pain. "I'll ask again. What are you doing in my portfolio backpack?"

"Was that laptop yours?" Steve inserted himself between Bev and me. "I thought so." Steve's hand on the small of my back sent an electric message scurrying up my spine and down to my toes. He reached past to rummage in the boot. "I remember the laptop right here under your backpack, Rhett."

Rhett relaxed his grip, Bev pulling away, coddling her wrist. "Yes, that's where it was. I don't see my laptop. Someone must have stolen it."

I pictured the device containing all the stuff on the thumb drive he'd grabbed from Bev, safely ensconced in our rented sedan.

"Would your muses be any help?" I ducked under Steve's arm to see Candi peering over Matt's shoulder.

She belched, her speech slurring. "I've got them on the hunt for Jeremy. As soon as they get back, I'll put in a call."

216

"Why would anyone steal only a laptop? All the rest of the gear is where we left it." Matt scratched his head.

"Because your band gear is worthless, and my laptop is top of the line." Bev massaged her arm. "The hard drive contains stuff that could compromise the corporation, not to mention my career. With luck the thieves won't be able to hack in."

My confused expression met Steve's vacuous face. *What the fuck?*

I swiveled an irate gaze toward Rhett. "You asshole. That's how you treat my best friend? After what I did for you tonight? Jeremy's probably off trying to recover his true Celtic self. Again. You know he won't show, the flake. Is that your intention? To treat Bev that way? I can easily walk. You'll be stranded."

"Lark, hold yer whist." Mom inserted herself under my arm.

"No, Rhett held my wrist." Bev raised the limp appendage.

"Ah, Bev pet, I'm meaning for her to hold her temper," Deirdre said. "And I mean it. Rhett meant no harm. He apologized for his behavior when we were at the pub. I'm sure he wouldn't mind repeating his lovely words, so you can hear how genuine he was." Mom's stern look dispelled any thought of romantic interest in him. Her demeanor brought back memories of the nuns. That long silence. If Mom had a ruler hidden behind her back to smack Rhett's knuckles, I wouldn't have been surprised. She waited him out.

"Lark, I am most truly appreciative of your gallant effort tonight, stepping in when I had dismissed you in such an ungentlemanly manner. Please accept my sincerest apologies."

"Accepted. What about Bev? Don't you need to say sorry for practically breaking her wrist?"

"Quite right. My apologies to you, Bev. My mistake on your intentions. My sincere condolences on the loss of your valuable computer."

"Laptop," Bev corrected.

He's about as sincere as any good for nothing I've ever met.

"Let's have a group hug," Candi said. "I can feel the bad vibes turning

217

to mist."

"Maybe the smell of garlic could turn to mist as well. What have you all been eating?" I asked.

~~~

We left the group and after a lot of cajoling, accepted that Mom would be okay. She held a reservation at a hotel in Crossmaglen, not far from Loughgarvan. She would see us in Dundalk the next day. I insisted she should go back to Dublin in the morning. She insisted she wanted to hear our dear boys, Bev, and Candi play, and of course, now that I again took the stool to drum for the band, she would rather die than miss any of our performances. My biggest fear was the last part might come true.

The rental car's tepid heater blew rank sheep fumes around the interior. "We need to get someplace warm and find an outlet to plug this into." Bev raised the laptop cord with the converter attached to the end like some kind of crustacean. "Not to forget someplace that has a decent hot shower. My boots are ruined. God knows if I'll ever get the mud out of my clothes. Still, I'm dying to take a quick peek at what was on that thumb drive."

The motor ran, heater on, the panel lights illuminating our faces, making us look about the way we felt—knackered. Bev powered her laptop and selected the files she'd stolen from Rhett.

Someone tapped on the window and my heart double flipped. Through the fogged glass, the streetlamps shone on a shape covered by a yellow slicker. For sure a Garda had come to arrest us for buying the kid ale. I prepared to lie. The electric whine temporarily muffled the voice as the window descended to reveal my mother, her raincoat shiny in the rain.

"I forgot to ask where you girls were staying. Is Candi not with you?"

The light from the laptop extinguished as Bev slapped the lid shut. "She's hanging with the band tonight. We thought we'd push on to Dundalk."

"Brilliant! You found your laptop. But I won't hear of you driving all that way. Nothing will be open at this hour anyway. I've a lovely room. We can arrange for a cot to be brought in."

"Are you sure? At this hour?"

"Let's take her up on her offer. I'm pooped." Bev's face brightened, no doubt imagining the hot shower and electrical outlet.

"We can always make do." Deirdre waved her arm as if magically making it come to pass. "I won't be a minute. I'll get me car, and you can follow."

We waited, the defogger clearing the windows.

"There's something else. Steve."

"All we need is another suspect. Or is it the other thing? You two on stage tonight were unmistakable."

Chapter Thirty-Three

My blurry eyes tried to focus on the note Bev brandished. "Your mom took your advice. She's gone back to Dublin."

"Good. Can I grab a few more minutes?" I would have gladly rolled over and sought that great comatose sleep.

"You'll miss breakfast," she sang, towel drying her hair.

That roused me in a flash, throwing into a laundry bag yesterday's clothes infused with cigarette smoke, beer, and whatever we had tramped through in the rain. I dashed toward a shower. Considering last night, my bestie looked remarkable. No matter how hard I tried, I'd never be able to attain her casual perfection.

"I haven't slept this well since we left Portland. I'll comb through the thumb drive now that we won't be interrupted."

"What did you find?" I emerged a few minutes later, the hot air from the hair dryer tickled my scalp, a delicious feeling compared to my wet and slimy hair the day before.

"You won't believe this." Bev moved the cursor through the text. "The handoff's happening at Monasheskin. The drop occurs after our set ends at the festival."

"Where's the body?"

"Doesn't say."

"What about the other stuff?"

"Doesn't say either. But look at this." Her fingers skipped down the email and stopped.

I peered over her shoulder. "What's Matt got to do with it?" I pointed to a line that said he would help deliver the property. She shrugged and shook her head. "Wow. All that from the thumb drive?"

She paused for a moment. "I'm not proud of it."

"Well, well, well, the goddess of ethics has clay feet."

"I told you. I'm not proud of it." Bev stabbed at the laptop's keys.

I backed off. "Maybe this will make you feel better. I have a horrible hunch about this. Those are national relics. Someone could get hurt, maybe even killed."

My cell chirped to indicate a text message. "Know where Deirdre is?" from Steve.

"Wonder why he's concerned?" I responded that Mom came to her senses and went back to Dublin. The phone rang.

"For how long?" Steve's voice made my stomach plummet to my feet.

"Forever, if she's smart," I said.

"Not funny, Lark. Did she say whether she's coming to Dundalk or Monasheskin?"

I picked up the note to read again. "She has an important meeting in Dublin. She plans to meet us at the Bog Snorkeling Festival."

"Okay. Thanks." The phone went dead.

"That was weird." I wished he would call again and hoped he wouldn't.

Bev squinted at the next email and swore. "Not as weird as this. We were right. Rhett does have the body and the loot." Her fingernail straggled down the laptop's screen. "Not only that, but they've had the stuff since Dublin when Rhett got the bus."

"You mean I drove priceless artifacts around Dublin that first day?"

"Apparently. No wonder Rhett harped about trading in the Limerick rental van once we returned to Dublin. What'll we do?"

"I need to call Mom."

221

"Your mom? She's a sweet, little, old lady. You'll give her a heart attack. This is far too dangerous for her."

"Who else can we trust?"

"I hate to say this, but now that we know Rhett and Matt are the culprits, we should let Candi know what we found." Bev continued to scroll. "The good news is Jeremy's off nurturing his inner Celt, the creep. We need to be outta here." She slapped the lid closed on the laptop.

~~~

For once we easily found the venue, Tober's. I had to laugh at the leaping, orange tiger painted on the building's brick front. I wondered how this symbol was holding up in post-Celtic Tiger Ireland.

Whoever drove had parked the unmistakable minibus at the back where we spotted Candi and Jeremy, their backs curved as they unloaded the drum kit from the boot.

"What the...? Would he make up his mind?"

"So much for trusting Candi." Bev slammed the car door and stalked toward them.

I followed on her heels. "Jeremy, when did you get here?" *Why the fuck did you show up?*

"Am I glad to see you," Candi said. "Any news? Jeremy knows about Rhett."

"You were right. He has the artifacts." Jeremy hefted the drum stands. "Looks like the drop will take place tomorrow night after the gig at Monasheskin."

"We need to call the police or Gardai or whatever," Bev said.

"I am a Garda. Undercover. Candi's been keeping me posted while I coordinate with the other officers. That's why I was a no-show last night."

"Garda?" I felt my brain wrinkle trying to get my head around this. "You knew about this?"

Both Candi and Jeremy nodded.

"The Candi Cane, Jeremy Jube-Jube thing...." Incomprehension rippled across Bev's features.

"We did get carried away." Candi pushed back a loose strand of hair and wrinkled her nose at Jeremy.

"I wouldn't want to be your muses. They must be totally confused," Bev said.

"Pretty good cover, wouldn't you say?" Candi cocked her head and laced fingers with her partner. "I got a degree in musical theater. This isn't much different than being a fairytale character at a theme park. Much more fun to be honest."

"You've been after Rhett all along?" The cables rested on the floor of the bus like a nest of vipers. I took an end and wound.

They bumped hips. "Yep," both said in unison.

"That's a relief. When are the Gardai going to seize the stolen artifacts?" I asked.

"After the gig in Monasheskin. They want to catch Rhett and the others who've been orchestrating this."

"What about Matt?" Bev kicked me in the shin. Hard. *She doesn't trust him.* Mom's voice saying cute hoor rang in my ears.

Jeremy paused a beat. "You know about him too?"

Bev's shoulders rose with a giant inhale. "He's been acting strange."

"Notice how he's on his cell until the minute you see him, then he shuts it? How come he goes to mass every day? I grew up here, the most guilt-ridden Catholic country in the world. Even I don't go to mass every day."

Jeremy nudged Candi. "Okay. Here's the plan. After the gig tomorrow night, we'll secure the bus, while the rest of the Gardai nab everyone."

"Have you heard from your mom?" Steve's head popped up near the bus's engine.

Bev jumped. "Jesus, could you be a little more quiet?"

How much had he overheard? Candi and Jeremy cut their eyes toward me. Candi brushed her index finger across her lips. Bev searched her bag as if looking for something.

"No," I said. "Why don't you call her?"

"Good idea. As soon as I get a moment. Lark, I need you to haul those

223

electrical cords to the stage. Matt's having trouble hooking up the mics."

Glad of the diversion away from Candi and Jeremy, I followed Steve inside. "Okay, where do you want them?" The door closed to semidarkness, the short hallway leading to the pub and stage.

He placed his hands on my shoulders to stop me, his voice low, intimate. "You need to be very, very careful. Bev as well. Candi and Jeremy are not what they seem."

"Nobody is what they seem." My body tightened.

"Just be careful. We're going back to the States in three more days. If something seems strange, let me or your mom know."

"You or Mom? Don't tell me you get off on little old ladies."

In the dim light amusement crinkled his eyes. "She's not as little or old as you think. And no, I prefer middle-aged, smartass women." He leaned toward me, his lips close, brushing my forehead. "Especially if they can play the drums."

I had to restrain the urge to mash my body against his, which competed with the mandate to run screaming into the night. He raised his head, my moment to make a caustic retort cut off.

Light splashed the hall as Candi, Jeremy, and Bev burst through the door, lugging the last of the equipment.

Bev sneezed. "We could really use some of your herbs, Candi. God, this place is musty."

I marched into the pub area to find the band's leader at the bar. "You asshole," I shouted.

Rhett's torso twisted to face me. "What do you need, Lark?"

"What's Jeremy doing here? Last night you said you'd fired him."

"Well, he had an emergency and apologized profusely about leaving us in the lurch. My gratitude to your heroics still stands."

"Again? You flaming piece of shit. You do this in repayment for my coming to your aid?"

"I'm fixin' to resume our schedule. We'll play the sets we worked on so diligently for this tour. You are a backup singer along with Candi and

Bev. That includes resuming your bus driving duties. Matt and Jeremy are abysmal, while Steve suffers from night blindness." Rhett leaned back toward the bar, lifted his pint, and made a comment to his companion.

I stormed out of the pub. My first instinct was to not perform, to let them all hang. Then I realized we'd lose the ability to keep an eye on Rhett and Matt, that anything out of the ordinary would alert them.

The rest of the afternoon was a gong show getting the band's equipment set up. My efforts to pull Bev aside to let her know what Steve said (and did) were met with Candi or Jeremy flanking her. Or they flanked me. Why were they so chummy all of a sudden? Candi insisted on riding along when we returned the rental car, while Jeremy trailed insecurely driving the mini school bus.

Since morning, everything had changed drastically. I strained to be my usual, smart-mouth self. While I'd known about Rhett from the beginning, the difference was Matt.

As we played through our list that night, competing emotions erased my ability to stay focused. The sight of Steve made my body tingle and heat rise up my neck. But the recollection of his comment about me wanting to be rescued doused the feeling like cold rain. Candi elbowed me when I entered a song early. Then I dropped my cowbell.

At the break when the first set ended, Rhett bitched. "Lark, darlin', whether you're suffering momentary loss of focus, menopause, or early dementia, you are to sit out the rest of the evening. If you think you'll be compensated for sitting on your ass, you are highly mistaken. Bev, I don't recall you being joined at the hip with your BFF. You and Candi will continue."

"Like you'd compensate me anyway," I snarked back.

Bev glanced at her hip and then at the band's leader. "Better her hip than yours."

The pub was the smallest we had played, the cigarette smoke overpowering, the heat overbearing. If we all developed lung cancer, this evening would be why. My absence gave everyone else a bit more breathing room, the lack of my ooh-ooh-oohs unnoticeable. I wandered into the parking lot and texted Mom. Again.

I leaned against the bus. All those artifacts were a big heist. Where were they hidden? I tapped the metal flank, walking from the front driver's side toward the back with no idea what to listen for. A change in sound? A change in density?

"Need some help finding something?" The voice came from a corner by the service entrance, the flare of a joint illuminating Matt's nose and lips.

Surprised, I dropped my phone, swooped it up. "Thanks anyway. I'm a bit hammered. Did you ever notice how sturdy buses are?" I held my breath, pounded underneath the window, then listed my way toward him. "By the way, where'd you get the weed?"

The joint's flare bobbed up and down as he talked. "Some dude. Not like the stuff we get back home. Why's it matter?" He offered a hit. When I passed the joint back, he waved his hand for me to keep it. "You ought to be careful. Wouldn't want our navigator to get hurt." Matt's even tone cradled a threat. "Next set is coming up, if you're interested." The door closed behind him.

I scouted the perimeter, took the last toke—his shit making me paranoid—and smeared the roach under my heal. Forget texting. I needed to talk to Mom.

"Can you be calling me back? I'm just in the middle of something," her voice garbled.

"No, Mom, this is urgent. I need help. Bev and I know Rhett and Matt stole the bog body and loot."

As if cloaked in background noise, she whispered, "Trust Steve." The phone went dead. A moment later a flash mob notice for the Bog Snorkeling Festival lit up my cell.

I tried calling back. "Mom!" I paced, circled the bus, tried to reach her. Her number dumped me into voice mail.

While a crowd exited the front of the building, the service entrance door gaped, and Steve emerged.

"Where is everybody?" I asked.

"Receiving their requisite pints."

"I called Mom. She said to trust you."

"You sure?"

"About trusting you? I guess."

Steve leaned down and cupped my face in his hands. "I might have to save you, and I'm not sure I'm up to the task."

"Stop that. Aren't you taking this seriously?" My stomach felt stuffed with nitroglycerin.

"You, yes. The situation, yes. I'm working with your mother, who's working with the Gardai. I know about Jeremy and Candi. They're going to steal the body, artifacts, and gold and sell them on the black market."

"Oh man! Bev and I told them everything. What about Rhett and Matt? Aren't they going to do that too?"

"Rhett and Matt have their own plans. The next twenty-four hours are critical. You and Bev need to play along with Jeremy and Candi."

"Wait. You're going to stop this all by yourself?"

"I got lots of help. You saw the flash mob notification?" I nodded. "Your mom sent that."

"Mom? Her phone went dead, and she's not returning texts or calls. Aren't you going to call the police?"

"Your mom is fine. Trust me."

Was this for real? "Where's Bev?"

We both looked over to see her butt-bump the door, the light putting her in silhouette. "There you are. What a shit show. You didn't miss a thing." She made her way toward us.

"We need to talk," Steve said.

"I did not sign up for sleuthing," she responded when he finished filling her in.

"Think of it more as preventing further damage," he said, "by continuing as if nothing is out of the ordinary."

227

"Nothing's been ordinary since we joined this circus. I thought computer geeks were crazy, but at least they're harmless."

"Gotcha, but you need to play along," he said.

"Meaning, I have to go back to driving the bus and ooh-oohing." The thought lay like a huge megalithic slab on my chest. "But what about Mom?"

"Would you stop? Rhett's going to pick up on that. He already did tonight, the way you screwed up onstage, so he's suspicious. There's a lot about Deirdre you don't know. Why do you think she started her busker business?"

"Cuz she's a bit daft?"

"No, she's been working with the Gardai for a couple of years now protecting Irish antiquities."

"Either way, sting ops with the police or busker cartel, she's still Looney Toons," I said.

"I think she's awesome," Bev sighed. "But how are you connected?"

"I work for a firm specializing in antiquity loss prevention. We've been active in South America capturing looters in the Aztec and Mayan ruins."

"Right. And I work for the Intergalactic Agency on Voodoo Relations," I quipped.

"Why do you think Hugh suddenly left? Thanks to Deirdre, Ireland and the US got wind of the plan. They contacted my firm, and I got planted," Steve said. "Ladies, this will all be over in a couple of days, so let the pro's do their jobs." He jerked his head toward the back door as the light from the pub's hall spilled across the tarmac. "All you have to do is play it cool."

"Lark, Bev, Steve, get over here and help load the gear." Rhett crossed the parking lot, followed by Matt, Jeremy, and Candi. "Lark, your little break is over. I expect you to be in full form tomorrow, including navigating us to Monasheskin in a timely and noteworthy fashion. Understood? Bev, you did fine tonight, made me right proud."

"Well, you made me right pissed off, kicking me out mid-gig," I said, continuing as if nothing was out of the ordinary.

"You better watch your step, else you find yourself sleeping right here," he patted the minibus, "'stead of the hostel. Now get in that driver's seat and escort us to our accommodations for the evening."

Chapter Thirty-Four

What is this place? Goose bumps spring along my arms and crawl up my shoulders. A blinding light follows a metallic kerchunk. I'm seated on a bench on a stage in a tavern, edged by small, round tables, the backdrop an accordion of black curtains.

"Don't you recognize it?" My ex, Joe, stands stage right under a follow-spot. "We spent a lot of time here." He raises a piece of picket fence.

"This is totally unfamiliar."

"Well, I'm waiting. When are you going to begin?" He waves the white painted wood at me.

"Begin what?"

The spotlight blacks out, the fence a ghost in the shadows. "Caring. You only care if it's convenient. Otherwise, you just let things happen. I'm outta here." His voice trails, his footsteps echoing, fading.

Bales of hay sprout, dust motes like clouds on the stage. Dressed in my renn faire wench costume, I'm positioned behind the cash register in my Hillare, Purveyor of Fine Stuffes booth.

"We're waiting, Lark." A spotlight illuminates the dull glint of chain mail.

"Lance, how did you get here?"

"The usual, although my horse broke down."

"It's lame?"

"Afraid so. Speaking of lame, that was your pathetic attempt to become a renn fairer." The knight thrusts his lance at me. *"When are you going to begin?"*

"Never. We're over, done. You didn't do shit for me, so what's your point?"

He thrusts the tip of his lance. *"The point is you don't do shit for anybody. Why should I give a shit about you?"* The faux knight lunges forward. *"That's why you were so lame."*

"I wasn't lame. I put my heart and soul into it."

"Exactly. You put your heart and soul into it, not me."

"You didn't deserve either my heart or my soul."

"Then who does?" The knight thrusts again, his lance tip ripping a small flower-shaped tear in my blouse. *"Figure it out and begin."*

"Begin what?"

"How many times do you have to hear it. Begin to care about someone other than yourself. Even your BFF can't depend on you." His body pixilates, fades.

I'm stationed behind the bakery counter, wearing my apron. The curtains solidify to painted brick inside a Voodoo Doughnuts shop. Stage lights glisten on walls bleeding pink.

Distant clacking grows, rustles beyond the stage curtains, the volume increasing to fill the empty space. A follow spot illuminates skeletons dancing, arms linked to others, faces painted like Day of the Dead. They line up before me. *"We're waiting,"* they chorus.

"For what?" I survey the jagged queue weaving across the stage. Bones rattle like bamboo chimes in the breeze.

"For you to take charge." The skeleton at the counter points behind my back to a stack of doughnut boxes. I grab one and toss it. Then another as the skeletons move by. The stack continues to grow, to topple. I'm panting. *"I can't keep doing this."*

I glance at the pelican on my arm that materializes into the awkward *bird. She takes flight in a slow loop into the rafters. My arm oozes blood and I suck to stench it, my tongue lapping the metallic taste of blood. I spit and a tooth flies onto the table in the front row. Suddenly all my teeth fly out of my mouth.*

"You should have taken better care of them." A woman in scrubs sits at one of the tables.

"I do. I floss and brush every day." My lips have caved in, and drool covers my bib.

"Doesn't look like that to me." She picks up a molar with pliers and drops it in a glass of cola. "They'll disintegrate."

"Wait! I need those teeth." I run to the edge of the stage.

"Well, getting you to begin is like pulling teeth." The voice tinkles like shattered glass.

"I don't want to do that anymore."

"Begin?"

"The dental hygiene program."

"Then I can't help you." She bunches herself up, shrinks, and dives into the glass of cola.

I sit on the stage, my hand covering my mouth. My gums itch as teeth emerge.

"Get out of the spotlight, Lark. You're ruining my view of the audience." Jeremy's voice erupts behind me.

I twist my neck. "Hey, those are my drums," I yell.

"But you don't play well," Jeremy perches on a stool behind my kit, "with others."

"Fuck you, Jeremy," I holler. "I play damn well." I hurl a drumstick like a javelin at him. "Besides I know what you're up to."

"Up to what?" Aengus grabs a mic, marches across the stage, waggling his eyebrows. "You're not up to or for anyone or anything. You led me on when I showed up at your gigs."

"I led you nowhere."

"Because that's where you are, nowhere." Aengus springs to my side.

232

"Hey, I'm busy here." A drumstick rests in my hand. I wave my stick and run toward Jeremy. "God and all the saints help you if you don't get away from my kit," I snarl.

White, padded walls spring from the floor. The practice room at the warehouse. I climb on the stool behind my drums.

I pound the cymbals, the noise rising like a thousand angry bells. "I can play circles around you, Jeremy." My hand comes down hard. I slam the Zildjains, shrieking, "Unlike you, I am reliable."

"Reliance, now that's the heart of it." A familiar voice floats from the wings.

"It's you," I gasp, the shadow among the curtains so familiar.

"No it's not."

"Then who are you?"

"The question is who are you?" The curtains in the wings stir, the bell of the Loughnashade horn edges forward. Steve raises the mouthpiece to his lips. A baleful moan fills the space. "I'm not your savior."

"I know." I walk toward him.

"When are you going to start, Lark?" He places the horn on the ground.

I'm standing so close I can see his chest gently rise and fall. "Start what?" Tears course down my cheeks. "Just tell me what and I'll start." I reach my arms around his neck, my lips searching, meeting his.

He pulls back his head, his eyes holding mine. "If you can't rely on yourself, how can others rely on you?" His index finger strokes the spot on my arm where the pelican used to be. "This is about more than just a dead body."

I woke in the hostel's bunk bed, cold and shivering, my pillow soggy. A nightmare, and I wondered if a real one was just beginning.

Chapter Thirty-Five

I thought you wanted me to plant my ass in the driver's seat," I said to the back of Rhett's head the next morning. The band leader had just informed me he intended to drive. He ground the gears and lurched the bus forward onto the main road.

I found myself seated next to Steve, the vestigial nightmare crouching behind my eyes, combatting with his physical presence. My body jittery, I reflexively tightened my shoulders, pressing my arms against my ribs, afraid I would come apart if we touched. The space between the outside edge of my thigh and the edge of his thigh thrummed. The bus hit a pothole, the struts bumping on the rural road, jostling us, his knee closing the gap. The air between us charged, electric, heated up.

"Don't tell me you're lost again," Jeremy called to the driver from a bench seat.

From her place as navigator, Bev raised her phone in the air. "Nope, I'm reading the map and the GPS on my phone."

"We're fixin' on taking a shortcut." Rhett jiggled the steering wheel to avoid a downed tree branch.

"If you fuck up, I'm not helping you out this time." My diaphragm tightened like I had to squeeze the words out.

The bus jolted again, my knee shifting toward Steve's. Miniscule hairs on my arms quivered, my pelican tattoo felt as if it might rise up and fly away. My concentration fixated on the shrinking space between us, an unbearable chasm. Should I scoot in the opposite direction and increase the gap? With each jolt the trumpet player's leg shifted toward mine. The air, like liquid, became more and more saturated with tension. The back of my eyeballs replaying the nightmare of him with the Loughnashade horn, I dared to glance in his direction, catching the back of his head. My stomach protested, constricting. The bus jostled again.

"Hey up there," Matt called. "Could you be a little less intent on finding every pothole in the country? You're ruining all the work my chiropractor back home has done."

I was terrified of the outcome if Steve moved a hair's breadth closer or if he looked at me. My lungs deflated like two shredded balloons.

His head swiveled. His eyes met mine. Two brown eyes that I wanted to drown in, and it was like nothing I had ever experienced, not with Joe, or Lance, or any lover. He could see my soul.

And then it happened. Steve bent forward. Our shoulders and upper arms collided at his movement.

"You almost put us in a ditch at that last curve," he called. "Someone else needs to take over."

I choked, gasping for air as if about to pass out, as if a nail had punctured my lungs.

"Okay Rhett, head for the nearest ditch. I think Lark's gonna throw up." He put a hand on my shoulder, rested his head next to mine, the warmth permeating my scalp. "Just take easy breaths. In and out." Cool air caressed my forehead as he straightened. "Does anyone have a plastic bag in case she loses it?" He pressed his palm against the middle of my back. "Try leaning forward."

"Isn't that what you do if you're going to faint?" I mumbled from between my knees. The bus halted, tottered, and tipped toward the edge of a ditch.

"Okay, let's get her out."

"Good going, Rhett. I hate to think of riding all the way to Monasheskin with the windows open and the bus full of puke. It's fucking raining out there." Matt crawled out the door and helped Steve ease me onto the shoulder, then backed into a bush as if I had something like the Ebola virus.

We stood in the drizzle, Steve massaging my back. "How are you doing? Do you get carsick?"

I shook my head.

"How about anxiety attacks?" His fingers moved in a circular motion, coaxing me to relax.

"If I do, this is the first one," I wheezed. A shiver ran across my shoulders as I tried to free myself from the nightmare's images.

The silence was eerie, a fine rain coating the air, the bushes, and the three of us balanced on the edge of the ditch.

Steve's face was a mass of crevices filled with concern. His voice low, he murmured, "Just easy breaths. You'll be fine." He stroked and patted my arm where, underneath my jacket, the pelican tattoo seemed to settle.

"Are you doing any better?" Matt's words were clipped. "We can't stand here all day. If we're late to Monasheskin...."

"Put a sock in it, Matt." Bev said. "All you ever do is whine. What can I get you, Lark?" Her eyes were wide, her face fearful as she peered down the bus's steps at me.

She needs to depend on me.

The damp air soothed my lungs, forced them open. Time took on a slow, hypnotic quality, my body relaxing. The rest of the band members seemed frozen, waiting. I took the first real breath in what seemed like hours, exhaled, then nodded.

"I think it must have been the pork pie I ate last night. I'm okay now." I studied my shoes, lifted my foot, and placed it as if on an accelerator.

"You sure?" Steve wrapped his arm around my shoulder, the heat sinking in.

"I was hired to drive, guide, and be a backup singer." I tapped his chest

236

and turned toward the bus. "Get the fuck away from the wheel, Rhett, or we'll all be killed." I heaved myself up the steps. "Bev, would you stay on as navigator?"

"Just don't throw up on the pedals, darlin'." He grunted and moved to an empty bench seat.

"What was going on back there?" she whispered. "You turned as pale as a rag."

"Steve bumped me," was all I could muster. The bus's engine cranked over, and I shifted into gear.

Chapter Thirty-Six

What am I going to do when I get back to the States and can arrive at my destination with no angst?" Bev copiloted as we yet again wandered the countryside looking for a town called Monasheskin. The rest of the band members slept, or wrapped in exhaustion, stared at the passing countryside.

"Listen up, people," I called to the comatose passengers, "I want to reinforce the playlist for tonight. We are a great band that's great at improv. But I need to say one more time, we are not—I repeat—not to play *We're in a Jam James.* We're too close to the border and despite what you have heard about the Troubles being over, in some sectors of this area, they're not."

The low energy level heralded the lull before the storm. Steve's detachment was nothing new, but a couple of supportive comments from him would have helped settle the booming dread in my stomach. Instead, his upper lip ruffled in sleep.

"We all heard you but let me remind you that I am the one making the call on the playlist." Rhett hefted himself from his fetal position on the back bench seat.

We wended our way through the green gumdrop terrain of County Monaghan. Hills ribboned by dark bushes marked property boundaries, narrow roads wove among them, and on the gumdrops black and white cows lolled. Pastoral scenes around every bend.

Monasheskin, more like a large farm than a town, hosted a campground, although I suspected the gumdrops concealed the requisite churches and pubs. We would have driven by the venue if not for the cars parked along the roadside in any available space.

"Wow," Bev said. "How did all these people find this place?"

"With a GPS that actually works. I guess this must be the Bog Snorkeling Festival. Didn't know it was such a big deal. But then again ..." Candi's voice trailed off.

Born a decade late for Woodstock, this is what I imagined the concert would have been like, only flatter with less mud. And quite a bit warmer. After several passes, two dirt tracks appeared, the service road tucked between thick gorse. We nosed down muddy ruts and passed a sign planted in a clump of grass that announced Spa, indicating a round pond filled with water the color of supersaturated iced tea.

"Is this a Celtic thing?" Bev asked. "Who but the Irish would think swimming in watery mulch was fun. And then create a contest."

"The Celts were also in France, which means your people, the De Trows, are perfectly capable of this kind of thing as well," Rhett said.

"Hate to bust your bubble, but we were Dutch."

"No worries. The Celts inhabited the Netherlands too." I scanned the area for a place to park.

The ruts petered out at a field. Cars, SUVs, and vendor trucks jammed the makeshift lot.

I pointed the bus toward the muddy lane and cut the engine. "Well, if we have to haul ass quickly, a relative term in this country, I guess the bus is set to go."

Rhett slowly removed his sunglasses. "What's that supposed to mean?"

"Nothing. Just saying. What should it mean?"

"That's what I'm askin', Lark. You must have had some meaning in

239

mind."

For a good part of the trip, I'd thought of him as a harmless blowhard. Not anymore.

"As I said, nothing. I'm joking. If we tank our set, we might be on the run. You've never been around a majorly pissed-off Irish crowd."

"Why don't we all just chill." Steve ambled toward the door. The rest of us followed, the gray fatigue from the tour showing on all our faces.

The venue consisted of a steep hill plunging to the lip of a water-filled trench, bordered by a metal fence whose purpose ostensibly was to keep people from jumping in while also serving as a hanging rack for bog-soaked wetsuits.

"Is that the bog?" Bev pointed to the trench. "Reminds me of the drainage ditches back home."

"Yep. The contestant has to swim to the end and back. The quickest time wins."

A snorkel attached to a head, garnished with watercress and algae, splashed into view. Flippers churned the muddy water as the swimmer progressed toward an endpoint, flipped, and slogged back. Cheers erupted.

"Must be the favorite," I said.

"How can they tell with all that muck?" Bev hugged her leather jacket closer. "I don't suppose the ditch water is heated."

We climbed to a huge tent at the crest of the hill. The large number of cables slithering from beneath the canvas confirmed that we arrived in the right place. Groups of partygoers on colorful blankets congregated the length of the hill. Food vendors occupied the lip, followed by the barrier to the bog swim lane. A mass of tents decorated the adjoining hill.

We began to haul gear up the steep slope, Matt went to work hooking up the sound system, and Rhett tested the mics.

"Lark, Bev, get over here and help," the lead singer barked.

"He should be elated at the crowds and publicity," I muttered.

"Whatever he's planning, he may not have wanted so many potential witnesses," Bev said.

Outside the tent a fellow in a mud-covered wetsuit blared through a bull horn not to lean on the fence. Cheers from the bottom of the hill meant another race had started.

I raised my voice. "You know, Rhett, this reminds me of the renn faires. All the tents."

"We'll see. Do your job, darlin'." Rhett grunted and taped down one of the cables.

I glanced around the tent. "All right, where's Candi and Steve? Is Jeremy MIA again? How about Matt? One minute he's helping set up, the next he's dumped everything in my lap. This is not part of my job."

"He's over by the bus, talking to the event organizer," Rhett snapped.

"No, he isn't." Bev held up gear from her latest trip.

Rhett looked toward the parking area, a slip of the yellow minibus's roof visible through the trees at the bottom of the hill. With precision, he placed the mic in the stand, and stormed out, his tall form leaping down the slippery lawn toward the bus. "Matt," he yelled.

~~~

How cosmic to report that the Bog Snorkeling Festival was the best night of the whole tour, that the band was smokin', that the crowd went crazy, that in the coming months and years, this night would live in memory from countless retelling over pints. With the exception of the crowd going crazy, which no doubt resulted in the retelling over pints, none of it happened. We acted as if aliens, who had no idea what drums, guitars, and playlists were, inhabited our bodies. To be blunt, we stank. We were proof of the havoc extraneous distractions can wreak.

The only person the least bit relaxed was Steve. Did he understand the seriousness of the situation? At one point, he played this spontaneous guitar riff, the rest of us petering out as we realized he had ignored the playlist. I prayed undercover police lurked in the crowd.

Like mushrooms sprouting after a rain, mass groupings sprawled on blankets, flicked lighters, or waved the flashlight on their cell phones as the sun flirted with the horizon. Or cavorted whether or not music played.

"I don't see Mom," I mumbled between songs.

"Me either," Bev said. "Candi, what do your muses tell you about Deirdre's whereabouts?"

"Nothing," she said.

"Mum's the word?" Bev asked. "You'd think they'd be a bit more help."

"Look, they can't be watching over everyone 24/7." Candi cocked her hip and dropped her cowbell, making a loud clang.

"Maybe she's not coming." My cheeks deflated with one less worry.

Rhett, tuning his guitar for the medley we were about to play, glared at us, then still tuning, strode over. "Would you fucking knock it off back here?" he hissed. He stalked back to the mic.

Steve strummed the chords to *We're in a Jam James*. My jaw fell in a silent scream. He shifted his guitar under his arm and began acapella:

'Twas the Battle of Boyne
Irish patriots did join
To support our good King James the Second.
To defeat Orange Will
Much blood would be spilled
For Ireland's land we reckoned.

He pulled the guitar across his chest, fingered the strings, and continued, building volume, his voice raw, guttural. The rest of us stared in wide-eyed horror. What was he thinking? We'd rehearsed our set, and I had been adamant about not including this song. The final, defiant chords echoed once to be absorbed by the bog water.

God help us. The Irish memory goes back eons. And we are way too close to the border. I held my breath. Utter silence. Black hole silence. From the crowd's fringe, Aengus's form raged up the hill, arm raised. "One Ireland!" He shouted.

242

That song was a match that lit a powder keg going back centuries. The crowd exploded and rushed the stage.

I grabbed Bev's sleeve and tried to locate Steve. "Come on!" I linked her elbow and snaked us through the angry melee. "We need to get to the bus."

Like a tsunami breaking upon the stage, the mob surged forward. The tent collapsed, the metal barricade gates toppled. Splashes and screams echoed against the hills.

We skidded down the grass toward the service area, two bodies swimming against a river of people. Bev and I shouldered our way to a knot of trees, and beyond, the bus was parked in position for a quick exit.

We slowed to a walk and picked our way. The lot's cars, a haphazard line, spaces now vacated. Anyone leaving had departed. Anyone staying engaged in the brawl at the top of the hill.

"What about the rest of the band?" Bev asked. "Did you spot Steve?"

"Didn't see him. Not sure about Jeremy and Candi. What about Rhett and Matt? Did the Gardai nab them?"

"What about Rhett and Matt?" From the shadows came a voice, low, deep, menacing. "And what did you insinuate about the police, darlin'?" Rhett's ghoulish expression muted my thinking. No sarcastic retort sat anywhere near the tip of my tongue.

"Considering what Steve did and how the crowd went insane, you're lucky that anyone is concerned." Bev's fingers clutched mine, both of us quaking. "Remember what Lark said about how the Irish would act if they didn't like our set? The Gardai are your best hope for safety."

"Seeing you are so concerned about my safety, I do believe, Lark, that you will be more than willing to do a little errand."

"Errands are not part of my job."

"If y'all don't, your best friend, as you like to call her, will suffer dire consequences." Rhett pulled a gun from behind his back and trained it on Bev. "Now ladies, I will escort you to the bus."

We marched through the growing gloom, the lights from the venue flickering behind the trees. We breached the service road, the uproar diminishing.

"What about Jeremy, Candi, and Steve?" I eyed the yellow school bus crouched in the dark. "Or Matt?"

"What about them? Are you concerned about their ultimate safety as well?" Rhett motioned his head toward the underbelly of the bus. "To allay your fears, they will be tied up for quite a while given the tenor of the crowd right now. While I did not expect this kind of reception, the animosity of the spectators has given me better coverage. Lark, you are to accommodate me by crawling under the bus. I must retrieve a few items."

"Well, at least I wasn't thrown under." Gravel scraped my scalp as I inched my back beneath the vehicle.

"Are you suggesting a conclusion to this evening's activities? Because it can be arranged." He waved a flashlight in the general area of the bus's underbelly.

"Nah, I'm trying to lighten things up a bit seeing you're about to lighten up this bus." The cold, soggy ground spread damp down my spine and across my shoulders. I reached the bus's midsection. I prayed Steve would come or send help before Rhett got more out of control. "What am I looking for?"

"A metal lump on the undercarriage."

I felt a small button and pushed, but it didn't budge. "Can't find it."

"I don't believe you." Rhett's head eclipsed the flashlight. "A woman of your ability on drums should have no trouble. Put some effort into it."

I groaned, numb fingers rubbing along the underbelly until they felt another bump, like a large, metal cyst. "Found another lump."

"Then try that one. This doesn't require a mechanic, although to install the trap door in the first place required a mechanic wizard."

"Yeah, Aengus."

"Lark, what can I say? He's an excellent mechanic, but to bed him, I'm unable to comment."

The lump depressed under my thumb. "This one gave."

"Okay, come out. Remember, if you don't cooperate, your BFF will experience an unhappy result."

We boarded the bus, Rhett taking the rear. "Ladies, y'all take a seat at the back."

He slid the key in the ignition, the overhead lights flared on. A slight bulge about halfway down the aisle must have risen when I pushed on the undercarriage. Rhett inserted a knife blade under the rubber matting and pried. A piece of the floor popped up.

"So that's why we had to switch vehicles. You needed this one," Bev said.

"Do me the courtesy of keeping your mouth shut, Bev, darlin'."

A moment later, Matt clambered up the steps.

"You're more than tardy. Where have you been?" Rhett growled.

"I ran into Aengus."

"Will he be joining us in this century? We need to conclude our activities, while everyone is distracted."

"Aengus said to go on without him. He's handling the diversion. Steve is a piece of shit, but for once he did something right." Matt slapped his thigh. "Do you believe the brawl going on up there?"

"In that case, here." Rhett handed him the gun. "Keep these ladies in your sights while I get the packages."

"You don't have to be coy. We all know about the bog body. I bet you have the other antiquities and bog butter hidden in the belly as well," I said.

Matt raised the pistol, sighted down his nose, and aimed toward me. "What does it take to get you to shut up?"

I gulped, caught my breath, "I get your point."

Rhett knelt, then lay on his stomach, his legs stretching along the aisle under the pale overhead light. The hole in the floor swallowed his arms. He retrieved an oblong object wrapped in burlap, which he placed on the seat, the butter. Then he dipped his arms, hauling up a substantial leather bag, the clink of metal indicating the gold. Through the narrow opening, he maneuvered an elongated canvas gunnysack, which could have held spears or skis. It contained neither, the shape intimating the rounded bowl and neck of the long Loughnashade Horn. Were the Armagh Cup and the Cross of Cong someplace else? He pressed his torso further, grunted, and lifted, both arms clasping what looked like a leather bag wrapped in a cloak that had been mauled by an otherworldly beast. The pieces of leather that constructed the cloak reminded me of the one in the Dublin museum. Rhett lifted the body and pressed it against his chest, placing one arm under it as if he were carrying a large infant.

"Bev, you are to carefully transport the butter." He pointed to me and indicated the horn. "Lark, you will be responsible for this bag as if your life depends on it because it does. Matt, hold onto this until I fetch you." He tossed the sack containing the torc and earrings to the keyboardist. "Keep the ladies in your gun sight. Okay, out of the bus." Rhett's Foghorn Leghorn voice filled the small clearing as he carefully backed down the steps to the outside, carrying the bog body.

Bev hoisted the bag with the butter. I shouldered the horn's canvas gunnysack like a pair of skis and staggered behind Bev. Matt right behind me took up the rear.

"I will now lead the way to our destination, that pond over there." The band's leader cradled the bundle and we followed.

"He was probably a king, you know," Matt said as we marched the few yards from the bus past the Spa sign at the edge of black water that resembled an open mouth.

"He deserves respect, not to be gawked at," Rhett added. "My granddaddy came from Ireland, worked as a coal miner in West Virginia. He deserved more than he got. More than a mine cave-in and family wondering what his last days were like and no way to grieve." He stopped at the edge of the pond, our backs to the noise at the crest of the hill. "I'm fixin' that this is the spot."

Light played across the darkened water. He towered over the bank, hugging the cloaked body with more tenderness than in any of the months

246

I'd known him.

"Was that a reason to exhume this poor soul out of his resting place? Because our collective memories forgot why the Celts put him there? Because he was a curiosity? What about Kennewick Man disrupted from his slumber on the banks of the Columbia River in Washington State? At least people rallied around him, creating a hailstorm over moving him from his sacred grounds. Who raised a ruckus over this bog fellow?"

"So how does selling him on the black market solve anything?" I asked. "And aren't you forgetting the gold? Not to be a nag."

"Why Lark, how you have misperceived my intentions. The last locale these precious icons need to be is out of this country or in some collector's private vault."

Matt jabbed the gun's nose in my back. "Move next to Rhett." He waved the pistol at Bev. "Stand by Lark and place the bog butter at her feet."

"This is the next small errand you will do this evening. Get in the water and make your way with the bog butter to the far side. You will find a shelf dug into the peat. I'll be right behind, transporting the body. Bev, you are to sit on the bank with the horn until I require it. In case you harbor other ideas about this activity, Lark, Matt has the gun on Bev."

"What about the gold torc and earrings?" I asked. "Aren't you going to put them with the body?"

"In a moment. This is ritual. This is your ancestor as well as mine."

"What about the Loughnashade Horn?"

"Matt will bring that precious relic and the jewelry as the last part of the rite."

"But what about the Cross of Cong and the Armagh Cup?" I asked. "You didn't bring those."

"Why would those be here? They belonged to the early Christian monks, not the Celts. I'm surprised that you don't have a better grasp of Irish history. 'Sides they weren't part of the heist."

I cut a quick glance at Bev.

"You Irish are all demented," she mumbled.

"Sit here." Matt shoved Bev to the edge of the pond.

"You asshole." Bev knelt in the spongy turf.

I slid over the lip and gasped at the icy impact, the black bog water waist high. "Any chance you've got a wet suit I can borrow?"

"Y'all won't be in that long." Rhett followed, twisted to retrieve the body from the bank, and waded to my side."

We sloshed toward the far rim of the pond, my feet swirling the frigid water at each tentative step, my knees aching in the cold.

"Hey, are you done yet?" Matt called.

My teeth chattered, the cold slowing my thinking. How do Bev and I get out of here? Where's Steve? What about Jeremy and Candi? And ….

A pop erupted from Matt's gun. Rhett grabbed his side, the water around him turning a different shade of black, the bog body sinking in the circle of his blood.

I dropped the butter and ducked in the murky mulch, swam along the side, groping the bank to get out of Matt's line of sight. The watercress like a cap, rivulets of sludge coursed down my face when I raised my head for a breath. The saturated peat gave way as I wedged myself against the bank.

Matt's figure skirted the periphery. "Rhett, you fucking idiot. Did you honestly think I would go along with your shit-for-brains plan?" he called. "What good will any of this do in this stinking bog other than stroke your over-inflated ego?" Matt lowered the sacks containing the gold and earrings to rest at his feet.

"We can negotiate. I'm sure we," Rhett gasped, "can come," he grunted, "to some sort of compromise." In the dark, he was a darker figure, bent and slowly sinking toward the water.

"Who's winning now, asshole? Thanks for the chance to bring about the change this country has fought for, for centuries. Like Malachy I, a new king shall be crowned on the Hill of Tara at the Stone of Destiny. Emain Macha's Loughnashade Horn will raise the people to unite the

248

north and south. The new king will create a united Ireland." Matt popped off another shot at Rhett, the bullet slicing through the water.

Bev, a log of muddy designer boots, jeans, and leather jacket rolled into the bushes.

I heaved myself onto the bank, trying to get a glimpse of Bev, then followed suit, rolling away and into the shelter of a hedge and Bev's soggy body. "Thank God, you're okay."

Whether continued rioting or riotous partying, the tumult from the crowd obscured any noise from the pond. The glow of lanterns in the tents silhouetted Matt, and behind him, a wraith-like figure crept like a shadow.

A hand grabbed my arm. "Shhh, don't move." Jeremy's voice. I squirmed my head. Candi's gloved hand blocked half Bev's face.

Across the pond, Matt aimed his gun at Rhett, who had sunk to his knees, the water up to his neck. The third shot misfired as the shadow grabbed Matt's arm and brought it behind his back. Matt spun and locked his free arm under her neck.

"Mom!" I blurted. Jeremy's hand capped my outburst, trapping the fear in my throat.

Chapter Thirty-Seven

Follow me, we've got to get outta here." Jeremy's voice raspy. "We can't help your mom right now. We'll send the Gardai to rescue her."

He dragged me by the arm. Candi and Bev followed.

"Get in the bus," Jeremy said.

"Rhett. Matt shot him. Matt's crazy. He's got Mom hostage."

Jeremy cranked the door closed. "Start this up and drive."

I sank into place behind the steering wheel, mud spreading under my butt. Swiveling my head, I put the bus in gear, gunned the engine up the service road, and turned onto the blacktop.

"Where are the rest of the police?" Bev asked from the back.

"Not here. We have to meet them. We weren't expecting such a large crowd," Candi said.

"What's the crowd got to do with it?" Bev asked.

"If we could have projected a mob, we would have brought backup," Jeremy said.

I bit my tongue. No Gardai waited. The raucous din meant no one heard the gun shots. Rhett would probably bleed out before anyone found him. Matt would get away.

"What about Mom? Where are the police to save her?" I tamped the panic cramping my shoulders.

"She can take care of herself. We have more important things to take care of." I jumped at the sound of Candi's businesslike demeanor.

"What about Rhett?" I asked. "And Matt?"

"You didn't know?" Candi asked. "Deirdre's working with them."

"Them who?" Bev asked. "Your muses? Rhett? Matt?"

"Who do you think? Rhett and Matt."

"Are your muses drunk? Matt took Deirdre hostage." Bev fell silent, no doubt processing this in the dark and recalling the same conversation where Steve warned us.

I took the corners in the hilly area slowly. Lights from houses dotted the banks like giant fireflies.

"Okay." I needed to stall for time so Steve and anyone else could catch up to us. "Where are we going?"

"Belfast," Jeremy said.

"Belfast? That's in Northern Ireland. That doesn't make sense. This is the south."

"It's an international issue. Both the north and south are cooperating in the investigation," he said.

I wanted to scream at him, "Do you think I'm an idiot?" But I remembered Steve's caution and said nothing.

"Wow, do you believe how dark the night is out here in the boonies?" Bev asked. "I hope we don't get lost."

Getting lost is a singular talent we share. I checked the side mirror. Car headlights behind. I kept driving. I took the next turn, creeping along the road, which narrowed to more like a lane than anything built to support through-traffic. The car complied.

"Wrong turn," Jeremy said. "Take this next left."

"How do you know?" Bev asked.

"We've got a decent GPS. The one you get with a rental car is shit," Candi said.

"You need a GPS? I thought you got directions from your muses," Bev

251

said.

"Drive." Jeremy pressed cold metal against my temple.

"What the fuck?" I squealed.

"I guess you aren't really Gardai or police or CIA or even security guards," Bev said.

"No shit," Candi said. "Now move."

The squishy sound of waterlogged boots and breathing alerted me that Candi and Bev took the seats directly behind. I stared at the road, glanced in the side mirror to assure myself the car still followed.

As we passed a corner streetlamp, the rearview mirror reflected Bev's pale face. Candi had a pistol jammed in her shoulder.

"I don't get why these artifacts are such a big deal. Not to forget the bog body." My mind raced trying to figure out what to do.

"It's a big deal to the right people," Candi said.

"Who'd want a piece of leather that's been tanned for a couple of millennia?"

"Collectors. You'd be surprised. Now shut up and go straight through the roundabout," Jeremy emphasized with a slap of the gun barrel against my skull.

"Ow! You do that again, you'll end up in a ditch." I massaged the side of my head and tasted my fingertips for blood. None, but I'd have a hell of a goose egg by tomorrow morning. That is if I were alive to notice.

"How are collectors going to collect the gruesome collectables if they're swimming in a bog pool?" Bev reminded me of a human resources professional interviewing a job applicant.

Candi smirked. "Who said you dumped them in the water?"

"Bev and I saw Rhett lift the loot out of the hatch in this floor."

"Coulda fooled me," Jeremy giggled. "But we sure fooled you and, no doubt, Rhett and Matt.

"A sack full of leather from one of the stockades did the trick," Candi said.

"And the butter? Don't tell me I carried some bogus snack into that

252

sinkhole." I peered into the night. The car still followed.

"You had the real thing. We couldn't find any buyers," Jeremy sighed. "Too bad."

"I suppose Matt was not carrying gold. Let me guess. You substituted some kind of crap."

"Yep," Jeremy chortled. "The real stuff's all still in the floor." He stamped to make his point.

"What I thought was an ancient Celtic horn was—"

"A hunk of Ireland's finest scrap metal," Candi laughed. "I'd love to see the look on Matt's face when he realizes what he's got, but we'll be far away by then."

"Rhett and Matt didn't say anything about the Cross of Cong or the Armagh Cup," Bev said. "Maybe you should ask your muses."

"Don't have to. They're in the cubby hole keeping company with the other stuff. Nice and safe awaiting our distributor. The dudes who made the heist for Rhett and Matt double crossed them, stole the Cross of Cong and Armagh Cup as well. We convinced them they could make a butt load."

We hit a pothole. The gun bumped against my head. "Didn't you hear me earlier? Move that thing or else I'll crash your priceless cargo. Is that what you want?"

Jeremy eased the gun's nozzle to my shoulder. "Take a left here for the motorway. Our contact will meet us in Belfast."

The signs indicated a roundabout. I found myself on an entrance ramp headed north. The car in my rearview mirror followed.

And passed as soon as we merged onto the motorway.

The face wasn't one I recognized. Hopes for rescue fell a notch.

I reconnoitered the options. Guns aimed at Bev and me meant attempting to overpower them would be foolish. Would flashing my lights get anyone's attention other than Jeremy's? Probably not. Crashing the bus might bring help, but we were still too far in the countryside. Better keep it as an option for closer to Belfast.

Oncoming headlights on the other side approached and passed. I wondered about the people behind the wheels of those cars, where they were going, and wished Bev and I were riding with them. We crossed into Northern Ireland. How different the border had been years ago with the military's tanks and barbed wire fences topped by concertina razor wire like guerilla Slinkys. The deaths, the desperation.

"Not to put too big a deal on this, but do you have any pound notes? We are in the UK now."

"Shut up and drive." The gun inched deeper in my shoulder.

"Poor planning was it?" I flinched for a second, expecting him to hit me.

"Great planning until you and your corporate friend screwed it up."

"All of this was a planned show? The Candi Cane and Jeremy Jube-Jube Show?"

"Not all of it. My muses are legit." Candi's voice traveled from the depths of the bus. "I did get cold feet when we were at that Viking venue."

"Was that purposely poor map reading? Or accidentally poor map reading that landed us at Lough Gur?"

Bev added, "Wouldn't matter with Rhett at the wheel, even with good map reading."

"Candi, I need better cooperation. Next smartass comment from either of them, you shoot Bev."

"No need to hurt her. She didn't do anything." Then I realized Jeremy needed me to get them to Belfast. After that point our survival would be a different story.

As we continued to head north, I monitored the fuel level, the needle balancing above empty. "We're low on gas."

"Quiet." Jeremy poked the gun into my waist.

"Just saying."

"Shut up!"

"Look, I want us to get where we're going, wherever that is. If you didn't get anything else from this trip, we are probably going to get lost.

Once we leave the motorway, the possibility of finding a service station at this time of night is nil. But what do I know? Other than I grew up here."

"She's got a point," Candi said.

"Shut the fuck up and keep driving. We're not leaving the motorway yet, and GPS shows lots of service stations."

We drove in silence, the gun's nozzle pressed in my shoulder, Candi doing the same to Bev. Maybe shifting the balance of power would give us some leverage.

"I need to turn on the heat. I'm freezing." I pushed the lever to the hottest setting. The change in temperature swirled around my feet as the warm air inched up my legs. If the bus heated up enough, Jeremy and Candi might become sleepy. We could overpower them and get away.

Fog crept up the windows, the reek of bog oozing through the interior. I flipped on the windshield wipers. Condensation obscured visibility, so I slowed. "Jeremy, the windows are steaming up."

"Then, turn on the AC. Crack a window. Keep driving, don't slow down."

"I need to change into dry clothes. That's why the windows are steaming up."

Bev stared at me in the rearview mirror. Her sincere face belied her eyes shifting toward Candi and then Jeremy. "Speaking of steamy, I gotta hand it to you, Candi. You're so calm. I'm guessing you did a cleansing ceremony on Jeremy. Good job."

"What cleansing ceremony?"

"Whatever you did, I'm impressed. I mean, if Elliot stepped out on me, I'd be ballistic. Although, not literally," she laughed.

"Jeremy, what is she talking about?" Candi's voice grated, saturated with anger.

"Oops. I thought for sure your muses would have told you or maybe he told you."

"Jeremy, you hear me? What is Bev talking about?" The backup singer sounded like a contestant from a reality show, where the partner is exposed as a slime bucket.

"It's nothing."

"Not what I heard from Lark, but I shouldn't be speaking for her. After all, she's right here, and she was right there then."

"She followed me into the can." Jeremy's voice broke.

"What were you doing in the men's can, Lark?"

"Checking on Jeremy. He was a mess."

"No. What were you *doing*?"

"Nothing happened, Candi Cane," he squawked.

"Hey, you dumped him," I said. "I went to see how he was doing."

"And console him." Bev's eyes twinkled.

The tin walls of the bus echoed Candi's banshee screech. "You just couldn't keep your dick in your pants, could you?"

"If I'd known you were coming back, I wouldn't have." I sucked in my cheeks to suppress a giggle. "I have principles, you know, but we dropped you at the airport cuz you were leaving. I figured he was fair game." My bestie and I were on the same page. "I don't see why you had to bring this up now, Bev."

Her mouth twitched. "Well, given we might not see tomorrow, I wanted to die with a clear conscience."

"That's pretty righteous. You're not the one who's gonna be in deep shit." I raised my voice a decibel or two.

Bev's volume climbed an octave. "I've been swallowing the shit that is this tour when I could've been home with Elliot."

My concentration divided among Jeremy and Candi, trying to follow Bev's lead. Oh, and watch the road.

"Nothing happened," Jeremy protested. Headlights from a passing car illuminated his exasperated features.

"You call that nothing?" I wailed. "I thought I meant something to you."

"You see? He's just one more example of your lousy taste in men. Now

256

if you had someone decent in your life, like Elliot—"

"Elliot, Elliot, Elliot," I yelled. "I am so damn sick of hearing about Elliot. Do you think he's been a monk while you galivanted around Ireland?"

"Don't you trash talk Elliot," Bev screamed. Her face and eyes didn't look the least bit angry. I hoped Candi wasn't smart enough to catch on.

"Hey, what do you mean?" Jeremy bellowed. "Nothing happened. I'm a decent guy."

"I trusted you, and you treat me like this? I was chill, didn't let on you broke my heart when Candi came back."

"Jeremy, you asshole! Shut up everyone!"

"You wanted the truth." Bev matched my voice in amplitude. Yep, we were on the same page.

"I said shut up!" Candi's gun went off. The bullet hit the ceiling, ricocheted, and grazed Jeremy's scalp.

"You bitch. You shot me!" He cupped his hair, then examined his fingers.

"Stop the bus. Now!" Candi shrieked.

I pulled to the side of the motorway, shaking. What had happened?

"Nobody say anything." Candi's tone icy. "Lark, turn on the overhead light."

The drummer held the side of his head. "You shot me," he whimpered.

"I'll shoot you even harder if you don't shut up. You can't be trusted. Get out."

"But I'm bleeding," he protested.

"It's not that bad. Get out."

"You can't leave him on the side of the road in the middle of the night. He could get hit by a car." I pretended to choke down a sob, noting other cars passing. The name of the patron saint for rescue totally fled my mind. I should pray to Saint Christopher for a safe journey, although considering Candi's current frame of mind, a quick shout out to Saint Raphael, patron saint of travelers and happy meetings, was warranted as well, especially

257

if we could happily meet the end of this shit show.

"Open the door." Candi circled the gun's nozzle at Bev, me, and the soon-to-be ex-beneficial friend.

I put on the hazard lights, shifted the bus into park, the exhaust illuminated red by the taillights. I yanked the lever, its rusty groan, a complaint. Jeremy lurched down the steps, placed one foot tentatively on the pavement.

"Hurry up, asshole." Candi spat the words. "Someone'll pick you up, especially when they see you're injured." Her ex-lover stood forlornly on the blacktop, his friend with benefits smoky with sarcasm. "Okay, Lark, drive."

I shut the door and moved onto the motorway. Jeremy receded in my rearview, a shirt wrapped around his head. *Good, the odds are more in our favor.*

"I get that you're pissed about Jeremy boinking someone, but don't you think you should at least light herbs to clear out the bad vibes?" A pistol hit Bev's head. "Ow! That hurt!"

"Drive. We've got a ways to go before we get to our buyers. I have the gun on Bev. You try anything…."

"Got it. Please don't hurt my best friend," my voice now a heavy plea. After the noise, the quiet was a relief, but as I drove, the warning light to fill the tank glared at me, the gas gauge flirting with empty. "We're about on fumes. I suggest we take the next stop and fill up. You don't want to get lost in … where did you say we were going?"

"Belfast."

"Right. Belfast." Images from news stories during the Troubles flitted through my mind. "Parts of the city are dangerous at night. We don't want to find them by mistake." I slowed to conserve what little gas we had left.

Rhett would be floating face down in that bog muck, only to be discovered in the morning, bloated, in no better condition than his precious faux bog body. I hoped Steve had managed to rescue Mom, stop Matt, and send someone to save us. A series of everything that could obstruct our rescue crossed my mind. Candi might totally lose it and go on a shoot-ing spree, bullets ricocheting in this tin can called a bus. Without a doubt, our lives were toast once we delivered the loot to the black market buyers. Did Candi honestly believe that three women and a single pistol were any threat? Even if Steve dispatched a rescue party, he wouldn't know where to find us. In the end, the only person I could count on was me. And Bev. We were it.

Candi cut into my morbid ruminations. "Okay, GPS says an all-night service station's two kilometers from here. Take that exit."

Chapter Thirty-Eight

We stood on the cement pad, the neon lights over the gas pumps seeming to enhance how bedraggled we were.

"Go fill the tank. Remember, I've got the gun on Bev."

"I need to get dry clothes." My voice tinny like a two-year-old about to have a temper tantrum. *Good. We'll go from yelling to whining. As far as Candi is concerned this will be the trip from hell.*

"You know, I'm really cold too." Bev complained like a recalcitrant teenager. "My boots are soaked. They're Jimmy Choo's. Do you know how much I spent on them? They're ruined. Look at my jacket. Trashed. That cost me a thousand bucks."

"I could give a shit about your damn clothes and how much they cost. Get a sweatshirt from the boot."

I angled past Candi, only to have her shove a foot into my shin, causing me to stumble. "We're going to do this together," she said.

We goose-stepped to the back of the bus.

I flung the bus's back door open, rummaging. "I have to pee," I whined.

"Me too." Bev at my side ransacked the contents. "Now where did I put my suitcase? Have either of you seen it?"

"Grab anything. Doesn't matter. We're going into the gas station to change. Then we're going to fill the tank. Then we're going to Belfast. Got that?"

"Our stuff should be right here." I heaved gear to the side, backing against Candi.

Bev clutched her stomach. "I got cramps. It's my period, and I don't have any tampons. I'll need to bring my purse to buy some." She shouldered her bag.

"Bullshit. You're too old for that."

I laced my tone with sarcasm. "And you know about peri-menopause how?" That shut her up.

"I got an idea. Let's each fill a sack with clean clothes for us to change into in the bathroom." Bev sounded like a team building expert at a corporate retreat.

We trooped into the minimart, Candi walking in lockstep with Bev, the gun hidden in the folds of her jacket. At the back, a small hallway led to bathrooms.

"Bev, you take the third stall. I'll take the middle one. Lark, you take the first one. No farting around, you hear me?"

"Isn't that something that happens in a place like this?" I locked the stall door, quietly extricated my phone, and texted Steve. *Matt has Mom hostage. Get help. Jeremy shot and kicked off bus. On way to Belfast. Call police.*

"What's taking you so long?" Candi's face appeared over the top of the stall.

"Just zipping my jeans. Jesus, Candi." I bent at the waist, hid my cell behind my thigh. "There's nothing to see here unless you get off on this kind of thing."

"You know, this place could really use some of your herbs, Candi." Bev's head popped above her stall. "It smells like shit in here."

"Did you get a tampon? I've got one in my purse." I stood on the toilet seat. We all looked like gophers emerging from our dens. With one hand I rummaged in my purse and tossed a tampon across the stalls to Bev, hoping to distract Candi while I secreted the cell phone back in the bag. My fingers slipped and with a sickening splash, my cell sank to the bottom of the bowl.

"What was that?" Candi alerted.

"Nothing," I sang.

"Are you one of those people who don't flush?" Candi's head craned as if to look in the toilet bowl.

I gulped —the cell was now nonfunctional anyway— and pulled the lever watching the water swirl around my lifeless phone.

As if sensing the need for distraction, Bev clapped her hands, the sound reverberating like firecrackers around the walls. "It fell in the can. Got another?"

"Sorry, I don't."

"Goddamn it. Here." Candi threw a tampon over the wall. "Now be quick. Lark, get out of that stall. Now!"

I appeared, already grieving my connection with the outside world and the slim hope of rescue. Outside Bev's stall, Candi pointed the pistol at the metal door.

"You know, if you shoot that thing in here, the noise will be like a canon. Not exactly a discreet way to kill someone," I commented.

"Shut up! Shut up!" Candi waved the gun like a baton.

She's losing it. Better back off.

"How're you doing, Bev?" My voice like a sales associate in a lingerie department.

"Okey dokey," Bev sang, thrust back the stall door, and stepped out. "Ta da!"

Candi circled the revolver's nose. "Stop wasting time."

Tank filled, bladders emptied, dry clothes donned, Bev took the bench seat right behind as I scooted into the driver's seat. I thought about my bestie having my back. Our captor perched next to me. I pressed in the clutch, shifted, and accelerated away from the gas pumps.

"He was a lousy fuck anyway, right?" Candi nudged me with her gun.

"I wouldn't know. We got interrupted."

"You mean I shot him for nothing?"

"Kinda looks that way," Bev's voice floated at my shoulder.

"You sneaky bitches. All you've ever done is gang up on me. I never did anything to you."

"Until now," I said.

"Get back on the motorway and head south. We're going to get Jeremy." Candi jammed the revolver in my upper arm.

"Whatever." I felt like a boomerang. "What is it with you and Jeremy poking me in the shoulder with guns?"

"Keep a lookout for him." Candi craned forward.

"Can't. Have to keep my eyes on the road. Driving a monster like this is hard enough."

We passed where we dumped Jeremy and continued. Candi slumped back in her seat and sighed. "Take the next exit. We'll head north again."

"Someone probably picked him up. I bet he's at a hospital," Bev said. "I hope he ditched his gun. He'd be in more trouble than he is already."

"Keep going. We have to get to Belfast ASAP." Candi was silent as if her mind lagged in processing Bev's comment. "What do you mean he doesn't have his gun?"

"Maybe he does, maybe he doesn't. I only saw him tie a T-shirt around his head, probably to stop the bleeding."

"Not my problem. We'll get to Belfast before him. His sense of direction is worse than Rhett's."

I entered the roundabout. *Now the getting lost and BFFs fighting part.*

Bev moved to the bench seat edging the bus's stairwell where I could see her better.

"GPS says take the next exit off this roundabout," Bev said, "and follow the signs for Belfast."

"No, we take the third exit." I kept curving the bus in the roundabout.

"I told you to take that exit. I read the signs." Bev's tone sing-songy.

"You missed the on-ramp north." Exasperation permeated Candi's voice. "Turn around as soon as you can."

"Hey, you try driving this tank."

"I'd do a hell of a lot better job than you. But I'm not getting paid for it." Bev added a holier than thou tone.

"Like I am? You'd probably drive off a cliff."

"Diving off a cliff would at least put us out of our misery," Bev snarled. "How did I ever let you talk me into this shit show in the first place?"

"I didn't talk you into anything," I snapped. "I had resigned myself to going back to school until you got all dreamy-eyed about the adventure."

"I trusted you to be honest about what a disaster this was going to be." Bev's tone glittered with anger.

"I was honest. You chose to ignore me."

"Your superior attitude and righteousness piss me off. If I were home right now, I'd be with Elliot. It's your fault we're in this mess," Bev cried.

"Elliot, Elliot, Elliot," I bellowed.

Candi slammed the revolver's handle on the dash. "I told you to drive back to the motorway," she roared. "If I hear one more word about Elliot…."

"Uh, which way is the motorway?" Bev pointed her fingers in a bunch of directions.

"Hell if I know." I slowed the bus to a crawl, leaning forward to peer into the night.

"Just hurry it up and get us back on the motorway." The metal frame of the dashboard clanged under the assault of Candi's gun handle. "Take the next left."

"Some driver you are. How many times have you managed to get us lost this trip?" Bev's sarcastic nature came to the rescue.

"You get what you pay for." I grinned at the bug-stained windshield. "Goose egg and it ain't gold."

"Just keep going, Lark," Candi said. "We're bound to see signs for Belfast."

Way to go, Bev, we're muddling her thinking.

Within half a kilometer, the streetlamps thinned, the road narrowed to accommodate the dense undergrowth found in deep rural areas.

"Look! A sign for Newry. Is that far away? We could stop at a pub and get directions," Bev called.

"Great. We're headed into the Mourne Mountains." They rose darker than even the sky with no sign of houses. I shuddered at the prospect of a breakdown if we proceeded into the barren countryside. "Candi, what does your GPS say?"

"We're in a gully. No service."

I maneuvered the bus into a rutted lane, the struts bouncing and squeaking. "I bet we'll stumble on a house at the end of this lane. You could drop us off and be on your way."

"What do you think you are, hitchhikers? You're driving this to Belfast. You will turn around. Got it?" Candi rose, supporting herself on the seat backs and retreated next to Bev, the nozzle of the gun poised within inches of my friend's skull. I gulped at the prospect of Candi becoming totally unhinged.

The headlights gleamed across a gated paddock, sheep noses poking through the fence. The lane widened, making room to execute a bootleg. Fortunately, the gas pedal wasn't as touchy as the huge bus I'd driven in Dublin; otherwise, we would have crashed through the fence and the rental company would have been responsible for mutton. Unfortunately, the school bus got stuck anyway.

"Goddamn it, you're doing this on purpose." Candi jumped into the navigator seat again.

"Why the hell would I get us stuck in a sheep pasture? How many times do I have to tell you getting lost is a part of driving in Ireland?"

"I don't care why you stranded us here. Get this crap mobile moving back on the motorway."

Bev's giggle burbled to the front. "Afraid the buyers will think you stood them up? Then what will you do? I don't think you'll get this stuff through customs when we leave in a couple of days."

"Get us out of here, Lark. Get us to Belfast. Then you and Bev can do whatever the fuck you want."

Is she feeling as defeated as she sounds?

The gears in this tub shifted easier than the Dublin tank, so rocking between first and reverse gleaned results. We bounced our way back to the blacktop. The road gradually resumed a decent width, merging into the roundabout and signs for the motorway to Belfast.

No one spoke. Traffic thickened, cars passing us. Others coming to-ward us, high beams on. Exits became more frequent. We weren't far from the city, the density illuminated like a jumble of Christmas lights through the trees.

"Do you know where we're going? I mean, we're heading into a pretty big city."

"Yes, I do know where we're going. Take the exit after this." We looped along a parkway arriving at a T-intersection. "Turn left," Candi said.

And there they were. Samson and Goliath, the double cranes of Har-land and Wolff, the builders of the Titanic. Beyond was the bay. We passed a sign that read Titanic Quarter.

"Are you sure we're not lost again?" I asked.

"We're going to a tourist trap?" Bev said. "I don't get it."

At this hour, not far from dawn, the area was deserted. We approached the huge, stylized hulls of the Titanic exhibit. To the right stood buildings that once housed the Harland and Wolff offices, the White Star Line.

"Turn left here," Candi said.

Chapter Thirty-Nine

Inching forward, I navigated a long driveway or walking path, the tires bobbling on the cobblestone pavement. To my left, a sign on a locked gate read "SS Nomadic Now Open."

"What is that? A duded-up tugboat?" Bev asked.

"The Nomadic ferried people to the Titanic because the ship's size prevented her from coming into the dock. Mom said the public conducted a huge effort in 2006 to get the ship back from France to restore as a museum."

"Jesus! Now you start doing your job when I could give a shit," Candi said. "Stop here."

Ahead, an old brick office building sported a sign to purchase tickets. The River Lagan bordered it to the right. To our left, the S.S. Nomadic flaunted her yellow funnel, decorated in multi-colored flags. The ship roosted in the Hamilton dry dock. She perched on metal pilings in a rectangular hole, lined with steep brick steps descending to tidal water skimmed in algae. Awnings covered gangplanks leading down to the entrance of the vessel.

"Isn't this bus going to attract a lot of attention?" Bev asked.

"As far as anyone passing, they're going to think we're making an early morning delivery. Nothing suspicious about that." Candi swiveled her head, distracted.

Bev's voice contained disbelief. "Right. A school bus making deliveries."

I hoped we had managed to tire Candi out. *Good for Bev continuing to dig at her.*

"We're not going to be here long."

We sat in the fading night while the engine idled, gas fumes wafting through the interior.

"I wanna turn this off for a few minutes or else we're all gonna die of carbon monoxide poisoning." I reached for the ignition.

"Don't even think about it." Candi smacked my knuckles.

"Ouch!" I massaged my hand. "You would've made a great nun. I remember this one nun—"

"Shut the fuck up." Candi raised the gun and slammed the nozzle on the steering wheel.

"If you carry a weapon without the safety on, someone could get hurt," Bev said.

"Yeah, but it won't be me. No more talking. I'm waiting for the buyers." She rose and moved next to Bev. "No need to remind you, Lark, where I have the gun aimed."

Fierce gull cries cut through the sky as they landed on the cobblestones, waddled toward the boat, picking at tourist leavings from the day before. Sunrise would soon lace the clouds migrating across the bay. How much of the emerging day would Bev and I see? My stomach hardened into a granite block of worry about Mom. I scouted the location flanked by dark high-rise buildings, preparing for anything—running, hiding, identifying possible weapons for fighting back.

After a few minutes, Candi said, "Circle around to the other side. They may be waiting."

I reversed the bus, hugged the port side, and skirted the bow. Checking my rearview mirror, I noted that Bev fidgeted with something in her palm.

"You know, Jeremy said the heist would be easy peasy," Candi sighed.

"All we had to do was steal Rhett's loot and meet the buyers here. Then get the hell out. Go to Venezuela or a country where we can't be extradited. We thought Rhett planned to sell the stuff on the black market. We were going to step in after he'd done all the work. Instead, he screws up our plans by trying to re-bury everything in that bog. Who would have predicted that Matt had hooked up with some lunatic fringe wanting to bring back the Celts?" Candi studied the revolver, then leveled it, squinting down the barrel. "The guns were just for show, and now I've shot Jeremy."

"No wonder your muses have been warring. Had you thought to consult them on the probability of success in this kind of venture?"

"Cut the muses crap, Bev. I'm sick to death of you." Her gun barrel tilted down as she stood.

"Well, I'm not amused. I took it all very seriously." Bev's voice muffled as her back bent, her arm moving.

I grabbed the opportunity to divert Candi's attention. "Personally, I think everyone's been watching too many fantasy shows. Hey, is that them?" I pointed to a group of three iron statues.

She twisted her head.

Down came the stacked heel of one of Bev's boots. Candi slumped sideways onto the bench. Bev snatched the gun. Hoisting the window, she tossed it, a blast of salt air coursing into the bus, along with a faint splash as the pistol landed in the River Lagan. She shifted the unconscious singer, sidled past her, and hobbled her way to my side, slipping her foot back into the boot. "Let's get outta here!" Bev sank next to me.

Burning rubber with a museum-quality, tricked-out school bus is nearly impossible. I stomped the gas pedal. It crawled forward. I watched the tachometer to shift again, circle the boat, and head for the straightaway. The gears groaned, and the bus grudgingly picked up speed.

"Come on, bus." Bev pushed her hands against the dashboard as if urging it on.

We bumped along the cobblestones in front of the brick, ticket building. Ahead lay the T-intersection to get back onto the main road. "I wonder where the nearest Gardai...."

The sound of metal hitting metal reverberated. Bullets penetrated the bus's hood and tires, our escape halted. Boiling water geysered from the engine.

I slammed my foot on the gas. Nothing. I shifted into reverse. Nothing. The smell of damp rubber filled the air. Three men approached, one wearing a shirt wrapped around his head.

"Shit, the buyers."

"I don't think so. I recognize Jeremy's T-shirt."

Bev crouched below the windshield. "We gotta hide."

We both dove under the dashboard.

The drummer shoved his gun through the bus door's broken glass. "Get out."

We crept from beneath the dashboard.

"Hey, aren't these the guys you ran off with to embrace your Celtic soul?"

"What of it?" Jeremy adjusted his T-shirt with his free hand. A large red stain blossomed in the fabric.

"I'd say you were embracing your Celtic gold," Bev said.

We hunched forward on our hands and knees.

"Well, this answers Candi's deep question about whether or not you had the gun when she kicked your ass onto the M1." I peered through the shattered glass at the barrel. Two others huddled behind Jeremy. Neither seemed to have a weapon. "You are aware that having a gun will land you in a shitload of trouble. It's against the law. The good news is you didn't shoot anyone as far as I know. Now Candi...."

"You know I voted for having you stay. Did she always have such a temper?" Bev asked.

"Me too." Should I push my luck? Would he have the guts to shoot us? After all, we were bandmates. "I'm a social worker. Counseling could help you two. Stress can really do a number on relationships. Sex and money are the biggies. You two have major biggies going on here. But I also see that you two have been through a lot together."

"Candi says this heist became a little more complicated than you anticipated." Bev's tone conversational, as if discussing a glitch in some new software. Cool as ice in a crisis. No wonder Bev was a VP.

The drummer cocked his head and nodded. "A couple unexpected things came up, yeah, but we got it under control."

"These the buyers?" I lifted my chin toward his companions.

Jeremy gestured the gun at the two standing behind him. "They're the brokers. I phoned them after Candi dumped me by the roadside."

I frowned, nodded, and scrutinized the fellows outside the bus. *Perhaps we could rush and topple them.* They resembled bowling pins the way they were grouped.

"Too bad. You had such potential as buskers. Mom's gonna be really disappointed. She gave you prime real estate. Okay Bev, we better do as he says," I grunted.

Linking arms, me hoping we could outwit Jube-Jube, Bev and I supported each other to standing. Distracted in glancing back at the still unconscious Candi, I leaned on the bus's steering wheel. The horn blared.

"Sorry, sorry. Didn't mean to do that. At least the horn still works." Steam embraced the hood. The vehicle resembled a junk yard occupant. The bus was a hames.

The three Celtic souls were definitely out of their league. Were other nefarious assholes lurking?

Candi moaned, opened her eyes, and sat up. "Where's my gun?" She scanned the seat, then the floor.

"In the water," Bev said.

"What water?"

"Well, most likely the river."

"You knocked me out, you bitch."

"Yeah, the best way to keep you from shooting someone else, for example, Lark or me."

271

"Jeremy Jube-Jube, I didn't know. I'm sorry. I thought you'd betrayed me." Candi called through the window, half-rose, then collapsed massaging her scalp.

"You know, Jeremy, I'm not sure shooting up our ride was such a good idea," I said. "If you wanted to stop us, wouldn't a better strategy have been for you and your buds to take out only a tire or two? Not to mention positioning you for a better getaway. Or that the buyers may have wanted to—" The sudden scowl on his face told me I'd gone too far.

"If you don't stop shooting off your mouth, I'll shoot it shut. Get off the bus."

From the covered gangplank descending to the Nomadic's entrance, more shots rang out, shattering the bus's rear window, piercing the far side.

"What the…?" The drummer backed away, turned, and ran.

"Jeremy, wait. Help me!" Candi's footsteps in the aisle clanked forward.

"You shot me." Voice trailing, he and the two others dashed toward the vicinity of the Titanic exhibit, the unmistakable shape of cloth flapping around his head.

Bev and I scrabbled back under the dashboard, crouched, and hunkered, arms over our heads.

"I smell gas," I whispered and squeezed Bev's hand, cramming closer to her.

Eerie silence encapsulated us, like the sudden change in sound when plunging under water, the steam from the defunct engine drifting past.

The accordion door burst open. A figure leapt up the steps and shoved an angry-looking assault rifle at Bev. "Get out," a gravelly voice said, gloves jerking her to her feet and propelling her onto the cobblestones below.

Camo-covered arms ending in leather-clad hands hoisted me, throwing me onto the street next to Bev, the pavement digging into my knees, my body shivering. We cowered, encircled by half a dozen people all dressed in the uniform of terrorists, camo and black ski masks. These guys were the real deal. I yearned for Jeremy and his mates.

The same leather-clad hands toppled Candi down the bus steps to join us, whereby they wrenched our arms behind our backs. A plastic tie, cinched tight, dug into my wrists. I glanced up to see two red lipstick mouths poking through the opening of the black masks on two faces. The urge to blurt, "Great fashion statement," tickled my lips. I swallowed, my throat dry.

Two women stood over me. We couldn't outrun them. The bus was no good. My brain accelerated into overdrive. "Are you Irish?" I asked. They nodded.

Good. A chance to make allies. Sisterhood.

"Bev and Candi, did you know that Celtic Irish women were fierce fighters?"

"What the hell? Are you a tour guide or something? Hey, Colleen, we trapped a tour guide."

"Do you not think it's fitting one would be lurking, Sinead?"

"What did we tell you two? No names!" The tallest one, the leader stepped forward and straddled the cobblestones. His voice was familiar.

"Who are you guys?" Candi cried.

"The Irish Celtic Liberators," the leader said.

"TICL?" I asked. "Doesn't sound very funny to me." For that I got an AK47 aimed at my head.

"You two, guard the bus. I need to dispose of these people," the leader said, deploying his comrades. He turned in profile, bushy eyebrows protruding from the mask's eyeholes. Aengus. I groaned. I'd made a big mistake in underestimating him, in humiliating him. His manner indicated a personal interest in assuring he dispatched me properly.

"Let's go. Get up, Lark." The assault rifle's nose nuzzled under my elbow urging me to stand. "Do you even know who I am?" Aengus lowered his face to my ear, his breath hoppy, sour with molasses from whatever Irish courage he'd imbibed. "You don't remember me, do you?"

I knew that question was coming.

"I do, Aengus. I do remember you. Did you think I wouldn't? I'm afraid I was majorly plastered when you wanted me to go on that Bloomsday jaunt. Perhaps we can, next time I'm back in Dublin."

"No next time. No second chances." Aengus gestured toward a fellow who emerged from the shadows. "Let's go. Bernard, you take up the rear."

"Just out of curiosity, how did you find us?"

The TICL leader pranced and hooted, his rifle bobbing up and down. "GPS tracker on the underside. They don't call me a mechanic's mechanic for nothing."

Both Bev and Candi tottered to their feet, Colleen and Sinead's rifles in their backs.

"Sorry that Jube-Jube ran away, Candi," Bev said. "Looks like he threw you under the bus, figuratively speaking."

One of the group cut a hole like a giant maw in the fencing. Protected by an overhead awning, we goose-stepped down the gangplank to the entrance. Bernard at the rear, wagged his weapon like a dog anticipating a tasty treat. The door to the SS Nomadic yawned wide, the lock jimmied. No one would hear or see us. No way anyone could rescue us.

We marched through the intricate iron-laced entrance doors and confronted a large plexiglass case housing a huge replica of the tender boat. AK47s butted our backs, directing us around an ornate staircase leading to an upper deck. I scanned the room for possible escape routes. A line of windows swept along each side of the boat, topping wooden benches. Would the panes be tempered glass?

We doglegged toward a long bar. A flash of red metal at the far end intimated a fire extinguisher.

"Down these stairs and speed this up," Aengus growled. "This ain't a tour."

"What do you mean, no tour? I've been dying to see this for donkey's years," Sinead said.

"Me too," Colleen said. "Can't we take a quick roundabout? After all, we're to be the last to see this."

"Dry up, Colleen," Aengus barked.

Bev's sallow face flickered in my peripheral vision, Candi right behind, her eyes wide, cheeks drawn.

"Keep going." Aengus grabbed my bound arms as soon as we reached the bottom of the steps and pushed. I stumbled forward, falling to my knees, now a pulpy mess. "Get up." He kicked my butt, and I collapsed onto my belly. "Get up."

I gagged then vomited, puke soaking my chest, tears stinging my eyes.

The large lower deck displayed memorabilia, knapsacks, and boxes stacked against pictures of soldiers from World War I and World War II when the boat serviced troops as a transport. More wood-slatted bench seats defined the perimeter along with a few tables and rounded club chairs. Would any of this help us?

"I can't get up."

Aengus's hands hiked my bound arms at an odd angle, a flash of pain encircled my shoulder blades. The cessation of thumping boots meant Bev, Candi, and their captors paused behind us. His arms reached under my arm pits, his hands cupping my boobs, and lifted.

"Hey!" I whimpered. "Don't you think you had more fun when we mutually consented?" His erection dug into the small of my back. Was he excited by the memory of our night in Cork or the anticipation of what was to come?

The groupie's jabs made it clear I better move forward. We rounded the stairs and stopped at the engine room where a hole gaped in the ceiling-to-floor fencing that cordoned off the public.

"Aengus, you've got your gold," I said.

"That bog body would get you a lot of good money to fund your movement," Candi shivered at my side. "We've got contacts we're meeting here."

"I'm sure she would be glad to make introductions. Sorry about the bog butter," I added.

"We're sure to miss the butter, but the other artifacts and the body are critical to our rise to power."

"We won't say anything," Bev said. "We promise if you let us go."

"You staying here will be much more effective. A little tit for tat."

"Actually, Aengus, you probably remember my tit isn't little." I looked down. "As for tat, I'm not sure what tat is." I immediately regretted my big mouth.

Aengus slammed his rifle butt against Bev's head, and she crumpled. "Maybe that'll get you to dry up, Lark." Sinead and Bernard hauled her into the cage, her feet dragging along the cement.

"Leave her alone. She's not even Irish. She's Dutch," I cried.

"Get in there." Aengus pointed to the engine room.

A jolt of pain spread across my back as a boot connected with my spine. I found myself sprawled on the other side of the wire fence, the cool floor smacking my chin. I inched my way to sitting, arms still bound. Candi cowered next to me. Bev lay on her side. What had I done to my best friend?

"My great grandfather worked the docks here. They took his life, leaving my great grandmother with seven children to raise. This is a little payback. By the time the demise of the Nomadic gets sorted, we'll be in power. You're a casualty of war." Aengus's voice, harsh, explosive. He gestured toward a small, evil-looking box tucked in the shadows near the boat's old engine.

"What war?" Candi asked.

"The war that's been raging for centuries. We need a true Celtic Ireland once again." Aengus yanked off his ski mask, his eyes crazed.

Are you nuts? I bit my tongue. "You are aware that successive invasions are the hallmark of Ireland's history. What about the Vikings? Or St. Patrick and all those monks and nuns? Not to put too fine a point on the Normans. What about the recent immigrants? Aren't they Irish as well?" *I need to connect.* "So, Aengus, tell me more. After all, I am Irish. Shouldn't I have a stake in this too?"

"We need to get back to the era of the Irish Kings where the political and spiritual power should reside."

"That being?" I asked.

"For a geebag who grew up in Ireland, you're pretty thick," Aengus said. "The Hill of Uisneach and the Hill of Tara, the area around Meath and Westmeath."

"You know, you have a very confused aura," Candi said. "Did you mean for your plan to go like this?"

"Dry up," he gestured toward Bev's prone figure, "or you'll end up like her."

Bev moaned and raised her head, her voice garbled. "Maybe Candi has a point." Blood oozed into her dark hair.

"Auras are very spiritual. They may not like what's going on here." I cut a glance to my bestie, worried she may have a concussion. If we could just get them to agree to let us go.

"Don't muddy the issue. That's been the problem. The issue gets muddied," Sinead said, followed by assent from Colleen.

"Aengus, we need to get a leg on. Sure you didn't say that others were part of this," Bernard jerked his head toward us.

"A little change in plan. These three won't be coming." Aengus nodded at Bev, Candi, and me. "As a bonus, they're to atone for all the harm done to us through the centuries."

"You've been making little changes in the plan so often you're sure to banjax the whole operation." Bernard waved his rifle at us, his heavy northern accent, sharp as slate, barely understandable beneath his mask.

"Had these geebags not put their hind ends in where they didn't belong, we would have finished at Monasheskin and been well on our way to Tara with our treasures for the new Celtic Ireland. Rhett was a bit of craic compared to this lot." Aengus tapped Candi's head with his rifle butt. "Too bad I didn't get to taste this one. Or this one." He pointed at Bev.

Aengus's troops milled in a listless circle around the enclosed engine room.

I eyed the box in the corner, icy fingers at the base of my neck. *Maybe I could get them a little more confused and buy time.* Hopefully help in some form would come.

"Now that you mention it, what about Rhett? I mean, a little misguided, but his heart was in the right place. Did you have to shoot him? You lost an important ally. Isn't he important to your movement?"

"No dealing with Rhett. He had a totally different agenda. He wanted to rebury the body, the gold, and the past. We want to resurrect it."

"From what Lark says, a lot of bad stuff got buried when the Troubles ended," Bev said. "Don't you think the Celts should remain there as well? In the past?"

My gut shook. *Wrong thing to say.* No reasoning with a crazy man. "Is what you mean, Bev, that the Celts need to be in the twenty first century rather than way back in ancient history?"

"Perhaps more inclusive," Candi said. "Like you don't have to be Celtic to be Celtic."

Sinead tapped her watch. "Aengus, we gotta go."

"My man, we go now." Bernard pointed his rifle at the stairs.

Aengus's face tightened. He gestured toward us. "Gag them. I'm tired of their blather."

He approached me the way he might accost a horse he was about to bridle and break. "This is what you get for making a laugh of me."

"I'm not laughing Aengus. I never was."

"Well, I am, you geebag. I'm probably no more memorable than all the others you screw." He snapped and stretched the gag reaching toward my face.

"Not at all, Aengus. You're getting more memorable by the second. I do remember the craic we had, and I don't go around screwing…Aengus," I said, although his name sounded more like uh-nuh, the smell of drying vomit on my shirt wafting to my nostrils. Now I got why it was called a gag. I felt as if I would throw up when he shoved the wad of cloth between my teeth, pushed my tongue down, and slapped electrical tape across my mouth.

"Bang on. I hope that's the last thing you remember as your guts get splattered," he flung open his arm, "and the boat gets blown to bits."

He took a final survey of the room, nodded. He pointed toward the exit and pushed a button on the box stationed near the old engine.

We huddled in the corner, arms bound by plastic ties, while Aengus and his band secured the fence. Their boots, thuds on the wooden floor and stairs, receded toward the upper areas of the ship.

Chapter Forty

Aengus and his troops' bootsteps echoed across the deck above. Overhead the vestibule's heavy doors slammed with finality.

My breathing fast and shallow, I fought to stay calm, to not panic. Bev rocked on the cold cement. Candi squirmed under the bonds and butt-scooted to the heavy metal barricade where the fencing had been cut and reattached, setting Bev and me in motion to follow her lead. With her back to the fencing, Candi shifted up and down vigorously, the metal eating through the plastic bonds, cutting her wrists. Her hands freed, she ripped off the electrical tape and spit out the gag, a red, raw stripe erupting on her cheeks.

"Lark, Bev, move here next to the fence. Hurry!" She wrapped the gag's cloth around her bloody wrists.

We backed into the thick chicken wire where Candi guided the torn metal, cutting through the ties. In a flash, we tore off the gags, ran to the bomb's box, and squatted on our haunches.

"I don't suppose your muses have any remedy for this situation," Bev said.

I stared wide-eyed at the timer Aengus had set in motion, willing it to stop, the LED lights' seconds a blur of fleeing, red digits. "So now what? The bomb goes off in thirty minutes."

"Jeremy said tonight would be a no-brainer." Candi circled the enclosure.

"A no-brainer was to not even think about doing this in the first place," Bev said. "You should have stuck to your muses and herbal remedies."

"I'm counting on my text getting to Steve," I said. "He's our last hope."

"You texted Steve?" Candi asked. "Why?"

"Because he and Mom are trying to stop this craziness."

"Whaaat?"

"What did you text him?" Bev asked.

"That we were on our way to Belfast, to contact the police, to save Mom."

Bev huffed. "Glad you thought of your mom. Not helpful for us."

"Yeah, I know. Then my cell fell in the toilet at the minimart. Maybe he's sending someone."

"Well, I probably wasn't much more help," Bev said. "I hid my cell in my boot, but it fell out when I conked you. Sorry, Candi."

"I would have done the same," she said.

"How about we break down the fence?" I studied the heavy wire enclosure.

"Too strong." Candi rattled the mesh. "They've sealed us in here pretty good."

"We gotta do something. Help!" I rattled the metal support poles. "We're trapped down here!"

"I got an idea." Bev crouched in front of the frantically ticking device. "We could disable the bomb."

"Yeah, right. We'd probably blow ourselves up." Aengus's description of guts sprayed around the engine room played in my head like a gory movie.

"Maybe there's something we can use." Candi sped around the enclosure's perimeter, head down, eyes intent on the floor.

I considered our dwindling options. "Okay, what do we have to lose?"

Bev scrutinized the clock, fingertips brushing the surface. A bead of sweat coursed down her nose and landed on the back of her hand. "This may have a remote. We need to get the cover off."

"I found this in the corner." Candi crouched by Bev and held up a small wedge-shaped piece of scrap metal, her fingers shaking.

Bev inserted a metal edge into the screw head and gently swiveled her wrist. Nothing. She pushed harder. We held our breaths. The LED light flicked, the seconds evaporating. She pushed again.

The screw didn't budge.

"Let me try." I leaned in, wiggled the metal make-shift tool into the bolt, my hands shaking. The screw moved. "Righty tighty, lefty loosie." I twisted. The bolt slowly swiveled upward, my fingers pinching the ends as I extracted it. "Okay, now for the other side."

"Hurry," Candi whispered.

The second screw wound up delicately, revealing threads as it rose. "Okay, the lid's loose."

Bev lifted the covering and peered inside. "I have no idea what these wires are. They look like they're controlled by a remote. I think Aengus can detonate the bomb, so they can get away without being blown to downtown Belfast."

Candi grabbed the metal blade. "Help me pull the fence apart." She darted across the cement floor and wedged the scrap metal between the claws, where Aengus's troops had closed the heavy wire.

Bev and I dashed to her side. The jerry-rigged bandage on her wrist had turned the color of old ketchup.

"We need to keep the metal from gouging our hands." I whipped off my jacket over my down vest and shoved it under the metal prongs as Candi pried them loose. "Okay, Bev, you push the fence while Candi and I pull open the prongs."

Candi and I yanked, our neck muscles stretched taught. Bev threw her weight against the heavy chicken wire. An opening sprouted.

"A few more inches," Candi grunted.

The fence's metal fingers surrendered a gap at the bottom, large enough for us to crawl through. On her belly, Candi wiggled to freedom followed by Bev. Then me. One of the metal fingers halted my exit, sliced through the fabric of my T-shirt, and notched a jagged tear across my back.

"I'm stuck," I called. "Keep going." *That's what I get for having decent-sized boobs.* I backed into the enclosure, tucked my shoulders together, smashed my chest into the cement, and slid through the gap. I stood.

I scrambled up the stairs to the main deck to find Candi and Bev at the entrance.

"We're locked in!" Candi wailed. "We need to bust this down." She pounded the door to the gangplank, which stretched like a dark umbilical cord to the street.

A quick reconnaissance showed plexiglass display cases, benches, and windows admitting pale dawn light.

Bev ran to a chair and tried to lift. "They're all bolted to the floor."

Nothing in the room could be used as a battering ram. What had I seen when Aengus marched us through that we could use to break out?

"Down here." I dashed back down the stairs, Candi and Bev right behind. "The World War I display has stuff we can use."

Candi and Bev hoisted a box. I grabbed a knapsack.

We raced back to the doors. I swung the pack against the barricaded entrance, hitting the accordion grating.

It bounced.

"We need to try a window." In the back of my brain, the LED lights blinked, the seconds scrambling, the minutes diminishing. Would Aengus detonate the device remotely?

Bev and Candi rammed the box at a window, the force sending them sprawling, the box shattering. Candi jumped up and darted back down the stairs.

I hurled the knapsack against the pane. A crack wormed across the glass. "Come on! We can break through."

"Here, use these." Bev kicked off her boots.

"We must be setting off the alarm system," I panted. "But I don't know that any help could get here before the bomb detonates."

Bev and I hammered the heels of her boots against the window. The cracks widened, forming a lacework of splintering glass.

Candi tore back up the stairs with another box and a helmet. "Okay," she wheezed, "let's have another run at the window."

Bev in her stocking feet, hefted the box, backed up, and with a yelp, slipped and fell, plummeting down the stairs.

"Bev!" I screamed.

"I'm okay. Keep smashing the window."

"What else can we use to bust this open?"

The fire extinguisher. I raced to the other end of the bar and hoisted the red canister.

Rushing the window, I hurled the extinguisher, penetrating the glass. The early morning air blasted our faces. Candi hammered the window with the helmet, clearing glass shards.

Bev's head emerged from the stairwell. Supporting herself on the banister, she hopped, one leg bent. She limped toward us, then attempted to stand on both feet. "I think I broke something." Her face crumpled in pain as she collapsed into a lounge chair.

"Can you lean on us? We don't have time to make a splint." I extended an arm and Bev nodded, her blanched face contorted as if she might faint.

Bev's arms draped across our shoulders, we hobbled our way to the broken window.

"Candi, hold onto her, while I figure out how to get her out." I clambered up the bench seat beneath the window and balanced on my stomach in the windowsill, feeling the remaining shards sink into my thighs. An eddy of cold air formed around my head and swam down my back. "We have to jump, but we're two stories up, and we'll land on the brick steps at the bottom of the drydock. Bev won't make it." I pictured us lying in the slimy water like three broken watermelons.

"Take a look at the miniature in the plexiglass case." Candi pointed to the display and then to the elegant staircase leading up. "I bet the stairs go to a promenade deck." She gulped to catch her breath. "We can go up there and climb over the rail onto the entry gangplank's awning. Then scoot to the edge and drop onto the dock."

Bev perched on one foot, her arm around Candi's shoulder.

"Let's do it." I took Bev's other arm. "Okay on three, we step up, and Bev, you hop. One, two, three."

A chorus of grunting echoed in the stairwell with each step. The stairs ended in a T-intersection, wooden doors to the deck on either end.

"Sit tight." I wrapped an arm around her shoulders and hugged. "Candi and I are going to bust down the door."

Bev nodded, her eyes pressed closed, her breathing jagged.

On the small landing we balanced on our butts, feet resting against one of the doors. "Okay, Candi, raise your legs and thrust." I pulled my knees to my chest, stabbing knives of pain in my straining muscles. Two pairs of feet connected against the locked door, the sound like an angry invader.

I rested my hand on my spasming thigh, my fingers coming away sticky with blood, glass slivers burrowed in my skin.

"This must be mahogany. Only way we're gonna get out of here is if the hinges break. Let's try the door jamb." We rammed our feet against the door's frame and were rewarded with a slight creak. "The door's giving. Hang on, Bev. On three."

"Move over," Bev crawled to us. "I still have one good leg." She wedged herself between Candi and me. The three of us thrust forward against the doorframe. With a metallic groan, the hinge surrendered, the door falling outward.

The welcome chill air slapped us in the face. We lay on our sides like toppled dominoes.

"How much time do we have left?" Candi asked.

Bev looked at her watch, shook her head. "I don't know. Aengus could detonate the bomb whenever he wants."

"We're going to carry you stretcher-style. Candi, get her legs. Help me ease her through." I scrambled outside, positioned myself, and wrapped my arms under Bev's armpits and heaved.

Candi raised Bev's feet, her voice strained. "God, you're heavy."

We rotated Bev through the broken entrance and to the bridge deck. We needed to round the corner and move along a corridor to the canvas awning covering the gangplank. Listing toward the railing, I stepped backwards, feeling my way for tripping hazards with each footfall. Beyond the railing, the white canvas awning of the roof over the gangplank loomed by my right shoulder.

Candi, red-faced, panting, froze. "No! No, no, no, no, no. She dropped Bev's legs. "We're not going to make it. I don't want to die here!"

My knees faltered under the sudden shift in weight, my arms stretched, shooting pain clutching my back muscles. The shards in my legs dug in further, blood soaking my jeans.

"Wait!" I pleaded. "We can do this."

Candi slithered over the railing onto the awning. "Sorry, but I can't die here. If we get rescued, I'll be arrested for sure. This is the best I can do. Good luck!"

She sprinted to the end, dropping to the ground. Her footsteps echoed as she raced past the bus carcass toward the Titanic exhibit and the Harland and Wolff office building.

Deep breath. What are the options? Gray sky and darker gray clouds signaled rain later in the morning, early traffic whizzed past the end of the parkway. *We're too far away for any help from there. No one would hear us.*

"Now what?" Bev's head nestled under my chin, her back against my stomach. "We could shelter here. The engine room's at the other end of the boat. I think we're far enough away that we have a chance in the blast."

"I'm going to drag you." I leaned forward to take more of Bev's weight. "Anyone know a good chiropractor?" I scuffed a foot forward, dragging another after it. "We'll be okay, Bev. Hold on."

"We won't get down unless we can go faster. If you support me, I can use my one good leg." She inched herself up my torso to stand, draped an arm across my shoulders, my back taking the brunt of her weight. We hobbled to the gangplank awning where Candi had clambered over the rail.

The roof rose at a slight angle until it stopped at the street above cobblestones worn smooth from years of use. We could crawl up the awning to the edge, but we'd still have to drop a good ten feet. If we missed, we'd go crashing down the set of brick steps to the bottom of the slip, landing in the slime and water. Surviving that would be a miracle. I took a big breath. Now was when I needed St. Jude's help.

"Bev, do you think you can haul yourself over the guard rail and up the awning? You'll have to drop at the end, but I can go first to break your fall."

"Doesn't look like I have much choice. My jeans are ruined anyway. My boots are still in the boat." A gray smile dragged across her face.

"What will you do without your Jimmy Choo's?" I slid over the rail and crouched on the awning.

"I'll deal with it." She stretched her broken leg over the metal bars, yelping in pain, then supported her weight with her arms to straddle the railing. She lowered herself, her good leg following.

I balanced and reached to help her down, my thigh muscles screaming. Her breathing laced with tears, she heaved a last oomph and landed like a newborn delivered from some awful womb, the two of us a tangle on the narrow roofing.

"Not far now." I inched my way toward the dock. *Crawl, just crawl.* "Bev, you can do it. You have to make it. What would Elliot do without you? What would I do?"

"You'd probably get in worse shit than this." Her faint voice trailed behind me.

"Then I'd better get you out of here."

We reached the end of the awning, the drop below treacherous, unforgiving. She inched behind me on her belly, her arms urging her forward, a swimmer on dry land. I sat up, my feet and legs dangling. I studied the pavement below, looking for a way down.

"When do you think the boat'll blow?" Bev's chin rested at my ear, tears soaking into my shoulder.

If we didn't jump now, we'd become part of the Nomadic rubble. I took a deep breath as if I was about to dive into deep, murky water. "Hang on Bev. I'm going to jump. Sit on the edge and then fall on top of me."

Movement at my peripheral vision indicated a figure in black approaching the Nomadic's bow, running toward the entrance.

"Bev, they're back." If I wasn't so scared, I would have sobbed in frustration and regret. "I don't want to die."

"Lie down. Maybe they won't see us."

Bev at my shoulder, her face trembling in my neck, we lay flat like two kids crammed into a twin bed. Her shallow gasping let me know how much pain she must be in. The figure halted at the gangplank.

"I'm sorry Bev," I whispered burying my face against her, bracing for gun fire or fire from the belly of the boat.

A woman's voice. Familiar. Cultured, the accent from an elite Irish school. "We caught Candi about half a kilometer from here."

"Nikki?" I called. What was she doing here? Wasn't she supposed to be overseeing tacky Viking reenactments?

"Yes, we can get you down now."

"Bev's hurt."

"There's a bomb in the engine room set to blow by remote," Bev's voice barely audible as if it had been carried by the wind.

"You're okay. We deactivated it."

From the shadows emerged other black clad figures slipping along the awning and lowering us to the cobblestones, the brick steps a maw that would have swallowed us if Bev and I had jumped. I made a mental note to thank St. Jude.

Police trills echoed off the surrounding buildings, the lights of an ambulance bouncing against the abandoned minibus, its belly gaping like poorly conducted surgery.

"Another SWAT team rounded up The Irish Celtic Liberators. We've got to get you two to a hospital." Even Nikki's SWAT maneuver attire was haute couture. Had Bev checked out her boots yet?

Medics strapped Bev and me to gurneys, then wheeled us to waiting ambulances. Nikki stood between us, supervising the attendants.

"All the artifacts and the bog body were hidden in the floor of the bus. Looks like Aengus and his thugs took them. Well, except for the bog butter, which ended up in the water at Monasheskin. Sorry." I felt like I would puke. "Where's Mom? Matt Brower and this lunatic group took my mother, Deirdre Devlin, hostage. They want to go back to living in mud huts."

"Yes, we know about the artifacts. We caught Aengus and the others in a van entering the motorway a few minutes ago. We've been tracking this group for several years. Steve rescued your mum. We're completing cleanup operations now."

"We're considered cleanup operations? Doesn't seem too optimistic when you think of the bomb in the belly of that boat." Bev winced as a paramedic splinted her leg.

"Nikki, how did you find us?" I asked.

"Steve. You texted him. And he texted me. He, your mum, and I've been working together."

I felt like a pan of soda bread being shoved into an oven, the gurney making its way into the back of the ambulance. Bev in the one parked next to mine was visible through the window where emergency staff raised an IV onto a pole.

I flinched at the sting of the needle the paramedic inserted into a vein, the fluid bag on the IV pole waved slightly.

"What's going into my arm?" Exhaustion slurred my voice.

"Fluids." The paramedic shone a flashlight in my eyes, wrapped a cuff around my arm, and pressed a stethoscope against my wrist to listen for my pulse. I looked into eyes the color of Irish Breakfast tea, thought of Mom, then I thought of Steve.

Nikki smacked the hoods of the ambulances to signal we were ready for the hospital.

Chapter Forty-One

I woke to find Steve asleep in a chair at the foot of my bed, the enclosure hardly bigger than a shower curtain around a bathtub. He jolted awake in crumpled clothes as if he'd spent more than a few hours in that spot.

"You flaming jerk," I croaked. "Where's Mom? How is she?"

"She's fine. She's in the geriatric unit. A bit dehydrated and she suffered a couple of broken ribs. She'll be sore for a while, but she told me the doctor said she'll be in fine fiddle before long." Glancing down as if he'd just discovered them, he held out a bouquet of daisies.

I scowled.

"What? You were expecting roses?" He looked as if he was enjoying his own private joke while he ambled toward the head of the bed.

"What I expected was not getting hijacked by Candi and Jeremy. You left Bev and me in that awful mob to fend for ourselves."

"Hang on there, little lady." That awful cowboy imitation again. Not funny. "You told me on more than one occasion that you were perfectly capable of taking care of yourself."

"Granted. I am. But Aengus. You could've told me he was dangerous."

"I did. I distinctly remember telling you he's a bad ass dude."

"You never mentioned Matt. We could have been shot."

"You sent a text, which I responded to. I saved your mom. Besides, you're too ornery to be shot. And Bev, she's too corporate to get shot."

"Why the hell did you sing the one song that would create that mess? I specifically warned you away from it."

He rose, shuffled to the head of my bed, and held out the daisies in response. Despite myself, I took them.

"Because I needed the distraction." He leaned toward my face, his mouth slack and slightly open.

"Not so fast." I moved my head before he could connect with my lips. I swallowed. "You haven't answered my question. Why did you leave us?"

"I didn't leave you and Bev. We had eyes on you two the whole time. Remember the car that followed you and passed?"

"We almost got blown up."

"I admit we cut your rescue a little close. Nikki's team apprehended Aengus and crew and disabled the bomb. You can imagine the outrage if that precious boat ended up as kindling." Steve smiled again. "You weren't in that much danger. Relatively speaking."

I nodded, moving my lips toward his. He leaned in, me feeling that quick intake of air. His face moved toward me, in slow-mo. I pursed my lips, expecting, thought better of it and clamped them shut. I searched his face. "I think that's what you were hoping for all along," and turned my cheek.

"Good on you, Lark." He planted a kiss on my forehead.

I exhaled. "Where is everybody?"

He laced my fingers. "I extricated Rhett from the bog and handed him over to the Gardai. He's in Dublin facing charges of international espionage. Matt won't be seeing much of the Celtic revival. He, Aengus, and his TICL cronies will experience the hospitality of Maghaberry prison pending trial for treason, stealing national treasures, and attempted murder. Candi Cane, Jeremy Jube-Jube, along with an international ring dealing in stolen artifacts, will stand trial, but it's anybody's guess whether the trial will be in Ireland, Northern Ireland, or the US. I don't think her muses are going to be able to get her out of this one. Gotta get to a debrief." He kissed my forehead again. "I'll be back later. Your mom asks that you stop by her bed this evening." He slipped through the privacy curtains to the outer corridor.

I found myself staring at the ceiling, chin raised. What would my ex, Joe, think if he saw me here? Or Lance? I grinned, especially because Steve could parry worth a shit.

~~~

Mom's lilting voice mingling with her roommate's nasal vowels flowed through the door as I hobbled into her room in the geriatric ward. She had the gift of making fast friends. Or maybe she was scouting for her busking business. Hooked to an IV, pale as a banshee, she appeared fragile under the sheets. But I knew this tough, old bird better.

I closed the privacy curtains.

"Why didn't you tell me you were working alongside Steve?"

She'd always been in my life. As I hugged her, the reality sank in that she may not be around that much longer.

"My wee Lark. You're not to be crying. I'm back safe and sound carrying a great tale to tell."

I drew up a rickety chair that had housed many an occupant. Uncomfortable as the seat felt, I relished that I would be regaled by Mom's adventure.

"Ach, Steve and I agreed I should send a flash mob message so that the bog snorkeling event would be crowded. I knew what he planned with the song. We hoped the confusion would disrupt the handoff of the artifacts.

"Your oul wan has been at too many gatherings during the years not to be knowing the outcome. Now before I go any farther, I want you to hold your whist. Your man, Steve, specifically said for me not to come to Monasheskin."

"He's not my man, Mom."

"Jaysus, Mary, and Joseph, it's a figure of speech. The dear boy made

293

me swear I'd stay in Dublin because of the danger. I'll be making my confession to the Father as soon as he makes his rounds today. I ignored Steve, I did, because I was worried beyond sick about you and Bev. I came anyway to warn you. I made my way to Monasheskin, but I arrived too late to catch you before the set started. So I stayed at the outskirts of the crowd."

"What happened to you and Steve when the riot broke out? What a madhouse!" I scooted the chair closer.

"To be sure I spotted you and Bev heading to the bus. Rhett hid in the shadows, Matt not far behind. The flood of people screaming and shouting swept Steve away. Candi and Jeremy skulked their way among the bushes surrounding the spa. I kept a gander on the bus."

"But Mom, how did you learn to disarm someone? I saw you come up behind Matt."

"Did you not know that all those years in Galway, I was to protect you? Remember, I was just after seeing the arms and money pouring out of America."

"Don't tell me you're a member of some fringe group!"

"To be involved with any of that would be inviting the devil to me own wake. You don't think I had many a good reason for me leaving your da? 'Twas his joining the Real IRA in Boston that put the nails in the coffin of our marriage. I'd no patience for him sending money for a cause that brought such heartache. The Loyalists were no better. Our dear land has seen too much bloodshed and ill will throughout the centuries."

My dinner, which threatened to spew across my hospital gown, settled and decided to stay in my stomach. "I had no idea. Well good, you haven't gotten caught up in some kind of radical craziness."

"Because of all the unrest in Ireland after I left your da, I decided to learn self-defense. Then we moved to Dublin, you met and married Joe. Of course, you must be remembering that I used to dress up and entertain the tourists on Grafton Street."

"By begging. Honestly, Mom, did you ever consider that you were reinforcing foreign stereotypes of us?"

"'Twas no harm in it. But to be getting back to my tale, I became bored. I made a grand living—"

"Which you didn't need."

"I made a comfortable living until one day a Garda stopped me on the street. That's how I began me franchise business."

"You're saying you're an arm of the Gardai?"

"Now that you put it that way, I suppose I am. They trained me. My job is to keep an ear out for suspicious activity."

"That's why the security officer at the Dublin museum busks on his days off. I suppose that's why you positioned a terrible trio like Jeremy and his cronies on Grafton Street."

"My darling girl, I'm protecting our countries, both the republic and the north. We've lost too much over the years."

"Steve mentioned he got involved when the US learned black market dealers planned a heist."

"Yes, we got wind of Rhett first. We discovered Jeremy and Candi's scheme once we inserted Steve into the band. Aengus, Matt, and his ilk were the real surprise. And the real danger."

"Finish your tale, oul wan." Typical of Irish storytellers, Mom wound along roads of thought and whimsy. My body relaxed into the uncomfortable chair. I leaned my chin on her hand.

"Let's see. There I was among all these scoundrels, flummoxed on what I should do. You, Bev, Rhett, and Matt disappeared onto the bus. Turns out, Steve had his hands full with Aengus and his lads, who were waiting on Matt to secure the artifacts.

"I'm standing in the shadows with nothing but me two arms, two legs, a black belt in karate, seeing you and Bev were in dire straits. Presently, you came out of the bus carrying quite a load and made your way to that mud hole. Then you climbed into those waters. Matt's gun glinted ever so faintly in the night, followed by a flash when he shot Rhett. I tried to bring Matt down, but the rotter grabbed me.

"He threw a bag over me head, and we drove for a long distance where he put me in a mausoleum. I could hear the rustle of rats in the rafters. Seeing a dark and gloomy future I was."

The thought of her in that awful place sent me grabbing a garbage can and depositing my meal. *To hell with hospital protocol.* I climbed into Mom's bed. She wrapped an arm around me, much as she did when I was little and I'd had a bad dream. Only this was her nightmare she described.

"The Gardai had installed GPS trackers in my shoes, but I didn't know if anyone would be able to pick up the signals. Donkey's years passed before anyone arrived. Grateful I was to see your man, Steve."

"He's not—"

"Sure are you?" Mom arched an eyebrow and kissed my cheek. I smiled, gazing into eyes that had loved me for as long as I could remember.

~~~

When I arrived in Bev's room, she said, "You missed Elliot." She regarded the flimsy fabric of her hospital gown, her lip curling. "I'm so embarrassed," she said. "This cast is really ugly," she lifted a leg, "and I have no makeup on."

"Maybe you can get a designer cast. Does Jimmy Choo do them?" I asked. "How'd Elliot get here so quickly?"

"I called him when we were at the gas station, ostensibly getting into dry clothes. Remember how I said I had my period? He picked up the call, but he couldn't hang up because I didn't disconnect."

"Sucks to be you, Bev. Your phone bill is going to be worse than the national debt."

She nodded and sighed. "He grabbed one of his colleague's phones. Ended up contacting the American embassy in Belfast, then the Belfast police, then the Gardai in Dublin. He took the next flight, and here he is." Bev gestured to Elliot, who moved the privacy curtain aside as if he'd materialized via a magic portal.

"I brought you a get well gift." A new pair of boots hung from his

296

fingers. Bev met his eyes in a way that let me know everything else around her evaporated. Maybe someday I'd look at someone like that.

~~~

At Belfast International, Bev and I held out our boarding passes to enter a jet bound for JFK airport.

"On the plus side, Steve is miles ahead of the losers who have populated your life in the past," Bev commented.

"Yeah, maybe. We're staying in touch, but I'm giving it a rest," I replied. "He's off to London for another case. Something about the Victoria and Albert Museum." The window seat looked inviting. A whiskey or two would keep me company back to the US.

The plane flew over the last of Ireland, the saw-toothed land passed below and disappeared into misty clouds. The first order of business on returning to Portland was to withdraw from the dental hygiene program and quit my job at Voodoo Doughnuts.

Teaching drum lessons seemed like a noble cause. Mom's busking business in Ireland beckoned. She would need the help. Who knew? A woman in her eighth decade has to slow down sometime.

GLOSSARY

OF

IRISH TERMS AND IDIOMS

Bang on: Right; correct

Banjaxed: Broken

Black stuff: Guinness

Bodhran: Celtic drum

Bog Body: Bog bodies are mummified remains found in peat bogs in Ireland as well as other countries. Archaeologists have a number of theories why they are there. One theory is that they were ritual sacrifices of kings. https://en.wikipedia.org/wiki/Old_Croghan_Man

Bucketing down: Raining hard

Celtic Tiger: Refers to the rapid economic growth helped by foreign direct investment. Beginning in the mid-1990s and lasting until around 2007, the Republic of Ireland went from one of the poorest European countries to one of the wealthiest. The term comes from the similarity to Hong Kong, Singapore, South Korea, and Taiwan (four Asian tigers), who also experienced periods of rapid growth. Growth declined in Ireland, and by September 2008, Ireland became the first European country to enter the recession. https://en.wikipedia.org/wiki/Celtic_Tiger

Chancer: Someone who takes a risk or pretends to be someone they're not

Craic: (pronounced crack) Fun

Cute hoor: Individual who gets things to go for their own advantage

Da: Dad

Deadly: Great, fantastic

Donkey's years: A long, long time

Dry Up: Shut up

Earwig: Eavesdrop

Eat the head off: Be verbally angry, aggressive

Eejit: Idiot

Feck/Feckin': Polite term for fuck

HIDDEN PICTURES

Gaff: Home
Garda/Gardai: Irish police officer/officers
Geebag: Unpleasant woman; a shrew
Hames: Complete mess
Haven't got a baldy: Haven't got a chance
Hold your whist: Be quiet; wait a minute
Jacks: Restroom
Jaysus: Jesus
Knackered: Very tired
Make a lash out of it: Give it a try
Manky: Disgusting; filthy
Newgrange: Located in County Meath, Newgrange is a prehistoric monument. Built about 5,000 years ago, it is older than the pyramids and Stonehenge. The entrance lines up with sunrise on the Winter Solstice.
Oul Wan: Mom
Shite: Shit
Sláinte: (pronounced slawn-che): Cheers
The Pale: Dublin; beyond the Pale is outside of Dublin
Thick: Stupid
The Troubles: Historical events of a political, religious, economic, and nationalistic issues drove the conflict. Violence broke out in the late 1960s over whether Northern Ireland should remain as part of the UK, a position that the Unionists (who were mostly Protestant) supported. The Irish Nationalists (who were mostly Catholic) advocated for the Northern Ireland counties to become part of a united Ireland. Conflict occurred primarily in the Northern Ireland counties, with guerrilla warfare in areas of the southern counties close to the UK- Republic of Ireland border. In 1998, the Good Friday Agreement was signed to bring an end to the open conflicts. Source: https://en.wikipedia.org/wiki/The_Troubles.
Willy: Penis

ACKNOWLEDGEMENTS

First and foremost, in memoriam, I want to thank Johanna Rosenberry Lane for consulting on international band tours. Unlike the characters in this novel, she was the real deal, an extraordinary guitarist. I think she would have gotten a hoot out of the final product. Thank you, Alan Shue, Vanessa Palensky, Tiffany Grassman, Marlee Riggin, and Lindsey Pierce of Olympia Writers Group for their good humor and support for the early pages when I didn't know what this story was. Stephanie Hakala provided patience and great input when We're with the Band was in its first draft stage and was a hames. Nancy Johns translated boat architectural plans for me, so that the climax made sense. Jonah O'Brien's expertise in IT was invaluable at critical late stages of the manuscript. Tracy Perkins's content editing and moral support gave this novel legs and kept it from wandering off in the wrong direction. Connie Jasperson contributed critical beta reading and editing at a time when I had my doubts about it as a project. Ellen King Rice's input saved the novel from a fate worse than death, boring opening chapters. Mimi Nickerson, thank you for your support, kind heart, and late beta reading. Heidi Schubert, I am so grateful for your expert eyes, finding all those little holes in the story. Irene Luvaul went above and beyond in copy editing. You are awesome. The Tuesday Morning Rebel Writers held my hand and put up with my whining. Thank you, Lee French, Connie Jasperson, Ellen King Rice, Melissa Carpenter, and Heather Kitzman. Thank you Amy St. Onge, Angel P., Gideon St. Onge & Nika Akin for the beautiful cover design. You captured the essence. Thank you Liz Osborne, my dear friend for so many years and for your support at Palatine Press.

Jim, you were along for the gig, from concept, to attending a bog snorkeling championship in Ireland, to drafts and rewrites. Your expert advice on drum techniques and equipment made the novel what it is, not to forget your teaching me how to play "Wipe Out". This one's for you.

Here's an excerpt from

HIDDEN PICTURES

2020 NANCY PEARL AWARD WINNER,

LITERARY MAINSTREAM FICTION

PROLOGUE
1987

Watching his employees go had been an act of surrender. His new rival had snapped them up, and he knew he could not run the family business alone. He stood before the entrance to his store, Carlson's Hardware, and thought how insignificant all those times had seemed, when he or his father or grandfather had paused in that spot in the bright morning sun. How insignificant inserting the brass key and turning his wrist had been, feeling the deadbolt slide, shoving the door open and stepping inside.

He knew of only two momentous occasions. The first was the day in 1892 when his grandfather had inserted the key for the first time. Old photos and newspaper articles in the museum depicted him in a morning coat and top hat before a crowd of Forester residents, a fledgling community that was just minutes by train to Chicago.

This was the second momentous occasion.

He wondered what kind of boss he had been. A fair one, he hoped. He wondered what kind of boss they reported to now. He'd soon find out. As some kind of cosmic booby prize, Superior Hardware had hired him as well, his role to convert Forester do–it–yourselfers to their loyal customers. He was thankful the cosmos had at least spared his wife and mother from witnessing this.

Dressed in stained overalls, Gordon walked to the heart of the store, the fluorescent lights dim in the unheated space. Discarded placards bellowed "Going Out of Business" and "Everything Must Go."

He skimmed his palm across the dusty surface of an empty display case. Above him, a rusted hairline fracture snaked across the painted tin ceiling, the result of a broken pipe he'd fixed a few years back.

Gordon turned his back on the bare interior, made his way outside, and shut the door. He twisted his wrist to lock the store and removed the key. Carlson's Hardware was officially closed.

The limestone building now belonged to the bank. In a few minutes, he would hand the keys to the property manager. The substantial key ring that held them had worn a number of holes in his pockets over the years and, most assuredly, those of his father and grandfather.

His house key had occupied a place on that ring for so long, removing it was tough. Gordon knew that when he returned home, inserting the lone key in the lock and twisting his wrist would not be insignificant.

CHAPTER 1
BREAKFAST, 1996

O livia Dimato, get in the car this minute." Patricia Wrenowski's voice ricocheted off the houses lining the street.

The girl ignored the vehicle and kept walking, focused on her pink and gray Moon Boots, focused on getting to the school bus stop. Recalling the day before—her former friend, Brian, doubled over, his face contorted in pain—she attempted to increase the distance between herself and the van, the path slippery in the late winter slush.

The outraged driver yelled, "Olivia!"

She looked for refuge at the house on her right. Lace curtains in the windows hung motionless, dark. Nobody home, so she set her sights on another, her boots lifting and falling, lifting and falling. Olivia didn't dare check where Patricia was, but she could hear the slursh of chemically induced road muck.

"Stop right there," Patricia's voice barked.

Now desperate, she reached the driveway at the side of Gordon Carlson's house. She barely knew him, but her parents said he was an eccentric, sweet old man.

"Olivia!" Patricia shouted. "I told you to get in the car, and I mean it."

She made a choice, turned her back to the van, raced along the front walk, shot up Gordon's steps, and fell onto the veranda, the wood hard against her belly.

"Do you hear me, Olivia? Come here! I want to talk to you!" Patricia pulled into Gordon's driveway.

The girl scrambled across the porch. Ringing the bell and pounding the door with her mittened hand, she prayed for Gordon to please be awake and answer.

Olivia whipped around and saw Brian's profile in the front passenger seat. Her clenched mitten raised to pound again, she swiveled back, her fist connecting with the soft pile of a frayed bathrobe.

"You won't get away with this. Your mother will hear from me, so don't think this is the end of it!" Patricia gunned the engine in reverse, backed out of the driveway, knocked over a garbage can, and sped away.

"I'm sorry," Olivia stuttered. A tall man with stubble on his chin filled the doorway. She took in his quizzical stare. "I didn't know what else to do. She was chasing me."

"All right, then come in. I was about to make some breakfast." His tone was hesitant, edged with irritation.

"Oh. Well. Okay, sure." She would now miss the bus, but she was more afraid of that lunatic woman and her bullying son. She stepped into the foyer, dripping gritty slush onto a worn area rug, while Gordon shambled toward the kitchen.

Around her the piles of boots and shoes huddled by the coat tree, smothered by a mound of jackets, hats, and scarves. To her right, piles of paper, books, and magazines staggered up the stairs. Olivia wrinkled her nose, removed her backpack, coat and boots, making her own pile, her neon hat and scarf on top like a dollop of raspberry sherbet.

She followed the sound of kitchen cupboards being opened and shut, passed closed pocket doors, and stopped in the kitchen's entrance, the faint odor of cabbage and garlic still circling from the previous evening. Like all the Victorian houses in Forester, the kitchen was small by modern standards, similar to hers, except for missing the rich cherry cabinets and granite countertops.

Along the wall, a brown stove kept company with a matching fridge, minus the door handle. The cupboards had been painted many times, but not recently, spatters of caramelized grease filling the cracked surfaces

307

like some old masterpiece in the Art Institute. This was a house no one ever visited.

Gordon pried the fridge door open with the tips of his fingers. "You live across from Patricia, right?" He pulled out a quart of milk, set it on the counter, and fished out an egg carton. "That her son in the car?"

Olivia nodded.

"Hell of a way to start the day, being chased by a banshee. What got her hair in a frazzle?" He used the finger-prying technique to open a drawer and select a fork.

"Not sure." She watched him work, curious about this man no one ever saw.

"Must've been something. She runs this block with a whip," he said, breaking eggs into a bowl.

"Yeah. Guess so." Her lungs burned from running.

Gordon seemed more interested in the eggs than her. He added milk and began beating. "You know her boy, right? What's his name?"

"Brian Wrenowski."

"Have a seat." He handed her plates and jerked his head toward a built-in breakfast nook.

Olivia sidled toward it and slid onto a bench. The cold linoleum seeped through her socks, and she shivered, longing for her coat.

"We're both freshmen at Forester High." She thought of her mother's admonitions to be polite and not just answer in monosyllables.

"That so? My mom taught Patricia at Oak Elementary. As a girl, she was very quiet. Hard to believe, isn't it?" Gordon pulled a skillet from the drain board and moved toward the gas stove. "Somewhere along the line, she changed."

Olivia swung her feet under the table, still indecisive about leaving or staying. The crisis was over, so she could go. But her mom's rules about being polite told her it would be rude. The smell of bacon wafted her way. Before she could make up her mind, Gordon placed an oven mitt on the table and balanced the skillet on it.

"Why was she yelling at you? Help yourself." He eased onto the bench across from her.

She busied herself with spooning eggs onto her plate. Patricia was right to be angry. Yeah, but Brian was such a jerk. As she thought about what had happened, it just slipped out. "I kicked Brian."

"Kicked him." Gordon nodded. "He probably deserved it."

"Not according to his mom." Maybe this old man would take her side. For sure, Mom and Dad wouldn't. She took a taste. "That's why she was chasing me."

"And according to you?" Gordon's lips closed over a forkful of eggs.

Olivia took a breath. "He won't leave me alone cuz I won a computer programming contest, and he thought he should have. First, it was teasing, calling me names. Mom said to ignore it. I did. He started giving me a bad time in the cafeteria at lunch. I still ignored him. Then he got caught throwing spit wads at me and had detention."

"He got what he deserved." Gordon rose, grabbed two glasses, and put them on the table. "So why did you kick him?"

He turned his back to her and reached in the fridge.

"Because he trashed my locker. I saw my Boyz II Men poster sticking out of his backpack, so I know it was him that did it." Gordon splashed some orange juice in each glass.

"He called me a 'ho.' So I kicked him."

Olivia took a gulp of orange juice. It tasted fizzy, old. She swallowed. "In the balls. Patricia got there just after I did it." She watched Gordon chewing a slice of bacon, waiting for a reaction.

"Want some toast?"

"No, thank you." She wanted salt and pepper, but this man had given her refuge, so she thought better of asking. She didn't want that either. She wanted to kick Brian again, maybe harder. She swung her legs at the sudden thought.

"I'm not ignoring you, Olivia. I'm thinking about it, giving it careful consideration." The furrows between his eyebrows deepened.

309

Okay, here it comes, she thought. *The lecture. You should have just ignored him. Eventually, Brian will go away. Now all you've hurt is yourself.*

Outrage at having to deal with yet another righteous adult hardened around her chest, along with an awful tension in her shoulders that told her she should not have lashed out so violently.

"He called you a 'hoe,' and that was it. That was what did it. You hauled off and kicked him." Gordon wiped his mouth with a napkin.

"Yeah," she said.

"I may be a little behind the times here. But a hoe is what I use in my garden."

"No, not that," Olivia said. "You know, a 'ho'." Her voice dropped. "A whore."

"Tell me about the poster."

"You never heard of Boyz II Men?"

"Probably. But this was your poster," Gordon said.

"I'd taped it inside my locker door. He took it."

"You liked this poster. It was your property."

"Yeah." she said.

"He must have figured out your combination to get in. He must have been watching to know when you wouldn't be around."

Olivia quit kicking her feet, sat very still, concentrating on her hands folded on the table. She nodded.

"He broke into your locker, took something you like. Something that means a lot to you."

"It's the raddest concert I ever went to. I'd wanted to see them like, forever. My dad took me. He said, 'Do you think you should get a poster for your locker?' I stood in line for hours. Everyone was soooo jealous."

"And on top of it, Brian calls you a 'ho'? I'd be pretty insulted too."

"It's worse than that. He ripped it!"

Olivia met his eyes, which were looking straight at her, not at something else, but at her, like she was important to him.

"Did you get it back?" Gordon asked.

She shook her head.

"Do you know what happened to it?"

She shrugged, her words riding out as she exhaled. "I think the principal's got it. It's trashed anyway."

"So what are you going to do now?" Gordon gathered plates and utensils, ferrying them to the sink.

"Don't know. Guess I'll go home. Cuz of this stupid stranger danger, I can't walk to school and I've missed the bus. Mom says I have to be dying before she'll call me in sick. I'll probably get grounded too."

"Stranger danger?"

"Yeah, it's all over the radio."

She walked to the door, balancing on the rug as she pulled clothing from her pile, her jacket cool with a wet slick from her slide across the porch, her mittens soggy clumps around her fingers. As she slung the backpack over her shoulder, she stepped outside, feeling as indecisive as the overcast sky.

Above were the gray, tumbled clouds of late winter, bringing a light stirring that promised spring, but Olivia knew it was a lie. The arctic weather would continue for more weeks than she had patience.

Footprints marched in the other direction, and she could see the slushy swooshes where she had slipped and caught her balance, reminding her of the fear she felt when she made them, not only of Patricia but also that no one was on her side. She blinked. That weird old man had actually listened to her.

Once inside her own house, she scuffled to the fridge, where on the door was a magnet stating *Holy Cow, are you eating again?* A cartoon cow, black and white, with the saying in little kid letters was her dad's idea of a joke. Mom had objected sparking an argument. Olivia had insisted it remain on the fridge. She could tell when her mom was pissed off at her dad because her mom kept glancing at it.

She shoved around the fridge's contents and grabbed a carton of milk.

Just as she reached for a glass, the phone rang. She froze, perked her ears. Patricia had said it wasn't the end of it. For sure the woman had called the police. At the third ring, she backed toward the vestibule door, her glass of milk sloshing, and held her breath. With the fourth ring, the answering machine clicked while the message played, then another click followed by a beep.

"Hello, Mrs. Dimato. This is Forester High School. Could you please call the office as soon as you receive this message? I'll also try you at your work number. Your daughter did not arrive at school today and we want to be sure she's safe. Thank you." Beep.

Punching buttons, she soon had her mother's extension and prepared to confess.

"This is Donna."

"Mom?"

"Olivia? Where are you?"

"Home."

"Are you okay?"

"Yeah, I missed the bus."

"Missed the bus? How did that happen? Wasn't Patricia going to give you a ride?"

"No. She chased me in the van, and I missed the bus. I went to Gordon Carlson's house."

"Chased you in the van? Why on earth would she do that? I hope you did not disturb that sweet man."

"She's mad at me and she was yelling at me to get in the van. And no, I didn't bother Gordon. He invited me in for breakfast."

"What is going on, Olivia? This is not like you. I just got off the phone with the school. Mr. Perry wants to see us tomorrow afternoon. Do you know what it's about?"

"Yeah."

"And…?"

"And I kicked Brian in the balls."

"Testicles."

"Whatever." Olivia could feel tears crowding the back of her throat. "Mom, he stole my poster and ripped it."

"Well, that explains why you didn't get a ride from Patricia. At least you made a good decision to not walk to school by yourself. That rapist has us all rattled." Her mother paused. "I can't call you in sick. You know my rule." Another pause. "We'll talk when I get home tonight. But I'm very disappointed in you."

"Yeah, whatever." Olivia said.

She could hear her mother thinking out loud. "When I get home, I want to see that you have called your friends and gotten your assignments. You can show me that you have started your homework. Pull out the hamburger in the freezer. We'll have spaghetti for dinner. You can start on a salad before I get in."

"Yeah right. Whatever."

"Olivia. I can't talk right now. But we have a lot to cover, one of which is your tone with me. I'm not the bad guy here. I love you, sweetie."

The girl's stomach lurched, contemplating the meeting with Mr. Perry. Just like she thought. No help from her mom. But what about her dad? He got her the poster. He knew how rad it was. He would set them straight. After all, he was the village president. Except he wouldn't be able to set them straight. He was in New York.

About the Author

Johanna Flynn's debut novel, *Hidden Pictures*, won the 2020 Nancy Pearl Book Award for Best Contemporary Fiction. She is a contributing author in the NIWA 2020 Anthology, *Escape*. Her third novel, *Hemp*, will launch in 2023. She lives in Western Washington. Johanna can be found at www.johannaflynn.com. She is available to meet with book clubs and reading groups and would love to hear from readers.

Made in the USA
Middletown, DE
11 March 2022